Windswept Way

Center Point
Large Print

Also by Irene Hannon and available from Center Point Large Print:

Pelican Point
Hidden Peril
Driftwood Bay
Dark Ambitions
Starfish Pier
Point of Danger
Blackberry Beach
Labyrinth of Lies
Body of Evidence
Sea Glass Cottage

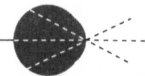

Windswept Way

A Hope Harbor Novel

Irene Hannon

CENTER POINT LARGE PRINT
THORNDIKE, MAINE

This Center Point Large Print edition
is published in the year 2023 by arrangement with
Revell, a division of Baker Publishing Group.

The text of this Large Print edition is unabridged.
In other aspects, this book may vary
from the original edition.
Printed in the United States of America
on permanent paper sourced using
environmentally responsible foresting methods.
Set in 16-point Times New Roman type.

ISBN: 978-1-63808-718-2

The Library of Congress has cataloged this record
under Library of Congress Control Number: 2023930215

In loving memory of my parents,
James and Dorothy Hannon.

Though you are both gone now,
your legacy of love lives on in my heart—
timeless and treasured.

Until we meet again.

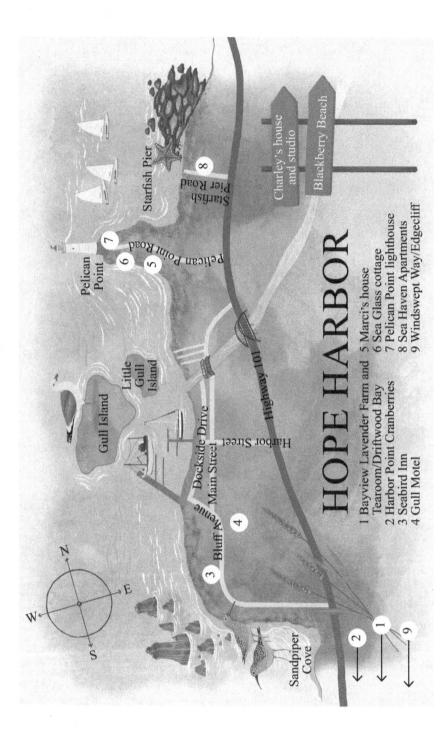

HOPE HARBOR

1 Bayview Lavender Farm and
  Tearoom/Driftwood Bay
2 Harbor Point Cranberries
3 Seabird Inn
4 Gull Motel
5 Marci's house
6 Sea Glass cottage
7 Pelican Point lighthouse
8 Sea Haven Apartments
9 Windswept Way/Edgecliff

Gull Island

Little Gull Island

Pelican Point

Starfish Pier

Starfish Pier Road

Pelican Point Road

Dockside Drive

Main Street

Bluff Avenue

Harbor Street

Highway 101

Charley's house and studio

Blackberry Beach

Sandpiper Cove

N
W — E
S

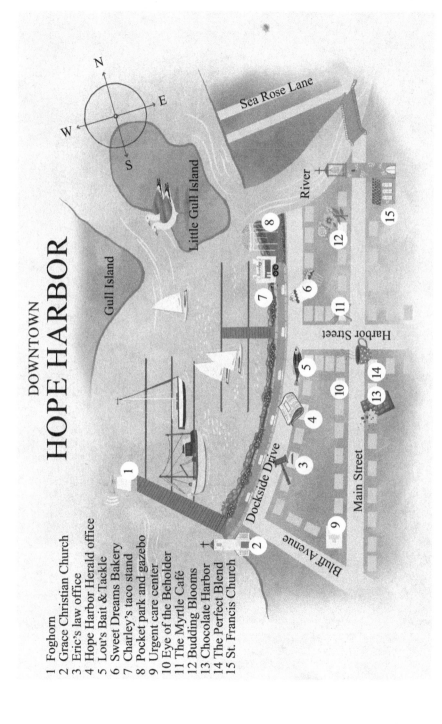

DOWNTOWN
HOPE HARBOR

N
E
W
S

Gull Island

Little Gull Island

Sea Rose Lane

River

Harbor Street

Dockside Drive

Bluff Avenue

Main Street

1 Foghorn
2 Grace Christian Church
3 Eric's law office
4 Hope Harbor Herald office
5 Lou's Bait & Tackle
6 Sweet Dreams Bakery
7 Charley's taco stand
8 Pocket park and gazebo
9 Urgent care center
10 Eye of the Beholder
11 The Myrtle Café
12 Budding Blooms
13 Chocolate Harbor
14 The Perfect Blend
15 St. Francis Church

Windswept Way

1

Maybe buying a haunted house wasn't her best idea.

Stomach churning, Ashley Scott braked as Windswept Way dead-ended at two open but imposing iron gates bookended by a tall, overgrown hedge. Surveyed the large, faded "Private Property—Keep Out" and "Trespassers Will Be Prosecuted" signs posted at the entrance. Read the word carved into the weathered stone block on the left.

Edgecliff.

Also known as Fitzgerald's Folly, according to local lore. A place with a storied past filled with triumph and tragedy. Where nocturnal sightings of a woman in white and ethereal music seeping from the house fed the rumors that the estate was haunted.

Ashley massaged her forehead and blew out a breath.

No wonder her mother thought she'd gone off the deep end.

But after forking out the money for a cross-country trek to Hope Harbor, Oregon, it would be even crazier to turn tail and run without keeping the appointment she'd made last week with the owner.

Besides, after all the times she and her father

had driven by these then-closed gates during summer vacations and speculated about what lay on the other side, she owed it to both of them to check the place out.

Especially since the money that might or might not be used to buy a stake in Edgecliff had come from the inheritance Dad had left her.

Tightening her grip on the wheel of the rental car, Ashley transferred her foot to the gas pedal and—

Sweet mercy!

Gasping, she mashed the brake to the floor again as a tall, muscular man emerged from behind the hedge, brandishing a chain saw and wearing a black, Covid-style mask that covered his nose and the bottom half of his face. The brim of a baseball cap pulled low over his forehead shadowed the rest of his features.

Ashley groped for the auto lock button and secured the doors as he stopped in the center of the driveway, blocking the entrance.

Now what?

Before she could decide, he began walking toward her.

Pulse skyrocketing, she raised her window. Scanned both sides of the shoulderless narrow lane.

No room for a U-turn.

All she could do was put the car in reverse and back away.

Fast.

As she fumbled with the gears, the man picked up his pace, heading straight for the hood.

Heart galloping, she tried to engage the left side of her brain.

Did she have a weapon?

No. Not unless a nail file or three-inch dress-shoe heel counted. But both were in her luggage in the trunk anyway. And her key-chain pepper gel was languishing in a bin of confiscated items at the airport back in Tennessee.

Ruing the day she'd decided to embark on this uncharacteristic adventure, she tried to coax the unfamiliar gearshift into reverse with one hand and lifted the other to the horn, prepared to press and hold on the off chance someone would—

All at once, the intimidating stranger veered toward the passenger side of the car, brushed past the door, and strode away.

What?

For a long moment . . . or two . . . or three . . . Ashley remained frozen in place.

Only after the thundering in her chest subsided did she peek in the rearview mirror.

The guy had vanished.

Meaning he hadn't had any nefarious intent after all.

Sagging in her seat, she lowered her forehead to the steering wheel and faced the truth.

She'd overreacted. Big time. Jumped to the wrong conclusion, thanks to every nerve-racking headline she'd ever read about lone women in isolated places meeting untimely and gruesome ends.

No wonder Jason had preferred someone who was more daring and exciting and bold.

Maybe she ought to eat the cost of this trip, can her half-baked idea, and slink home. Like she'd done the day their so-called relationship had crashed and burned.

As all the emotions she'd felt in those first devastating moments—hurt, resentment, anger, shock—swept over her again, Ashley clamped her lips together and straightened up.

No.

She was not going to run at the first little glitch. She would see this through, even if the trip ended up being a bust.

Easing back on the brake, she continued through the gates and into a tunnel of dense foliage that put the brambles and thorns Sleeping Beauty's prince had battled to shame.

Thank goodness a passageway had been cleared for vehicles.

But if the rest of the grounds were as overgrown as this, and if maintenance on the house had also been allowed to slide, she was out of here. She may have let herself get carried away with the fanciful notion of owning a piece of a historic property, but she wasn't about to get lured into a bank-account breaker.

Blue sky appeared around a bend at the end of the tunnel, and she pressed harder on the accelerator. The house should be—

Whoa!

Ashley jammed on her brakes yet again as she exited the warren of tangled greenery. Stared at the house, situated across a wide expanse of lawn dotted with stately evergreens and deciduous trees and backed by the deep blue June sky.

Double whoa.

The pictures supplied by the owner hadn't lied. Nor had they done this place justice.

Edgecliff wasn't crumbling. Or overgrown with vegetation. Or missing any vital parts.

It was beautiful. Stunning. Exactly what a classic 1910 Queen Anne Victorian-style house should be.

And the setting?

Breathtaking.

Surrounded on three sides by the sea, the house had a commanding view from its perch on the ten-acre promontory it had claimed as its own long ago.

Easing back in her seat, Ashley studied the details of the ornate three-story home. The wide wraparound front porch, with a rounded, domed-roof extension on the right and decorative railings, posts, and spindles. The asymmetry of the façade, with a section bumped out beside the front door. An octagonal turret on the left, its roof steeply pitched. A multitude of windows, all different shapes and sizes.

The brick exterior also gave it a sense of permanence and stability often lacking in shingled Queen Anne houses—but unusual for this part of the country, particularly in that era.

Even more unusual given that a lumber baron had built it.

But perhaps the solid construction was why it had held up despite its exposure to the Oregon coast's notorious fall and winter storms, when powerful winds and the raging waters of the Pacific put on quite a show.

Or so she'd read while researching the location.

If this trip panned out, however, she'd find out firsthand what—

Her phone began to vibrate, and she picked it up off the seat beside her. Skimmed the screen. Grimaced.

She did *not* need any more negativity undermining her confidence. Especially on the heels of her unsettling encounter at the gate.

However, if she didn't answer, her mother would keep calling until she picked up.

Bracing, she pressed talk and put the cell to her ear. "Hi, Mom."

"Have you arrived?"

"You know I did. I called you from the airport

16

in North Bend, after I picked up my rental car."
Ashley squinted into the distance as one side of
the house's double front door opened partway.

"I mean are you at the house? Have you seen it
yet?"

"I just pulled through the gates."

"And?"

"It's amazing. From a distance, anyway."

"Oh, Ashley. It's too soon to make that call."
Dismay, along with more than a hint of exasper-
ation, flattened her mother's inflection. "You're
so like your father. You know how he got carried
away whenever a new project lit a fire in him—
and how he often ended up getting burned. You'll
find a structural engineer to go over the place
before you commit to anything, right?"

"Yes. That's the plan. But the house is brick."

"It's also more than a hundred years old."

"I know. That's part of the charm."

"Charm can be a money suck. For all you know,
the foundation is crumbling and termites have
turned the support beams into Swiss cheese."

Now those were cheery thoughts.

"I promise not to leap without doing my homework, Mom."

"You've already leapt. Traveling 2,500 miles
tells me you're serious about this. What if it's a
scam?"

"How can it be a scam? I'm the one who
initiated contact, remember? And I already

told you I talked to the references the owner provided. If you can't trust a minister, a police chief, and the director of a reputable charitable organization, who can you trust?"

"Are you certain no red flags came up in those conversations?"

"Not a one." Unless you counted the fact that while all the references had said the reclusive owner was generous and law-abiding, they'd admitted they didn't personally know her very well.

A sigh came over the line. "The background check I ordered didn't find anything negative either—other than a scandal in which she apparently played no role . . . and which you neglected to mention."

Ashley blinked. "You ran a background check on her?"

"SOP in the business world. Please tell me you knew about the scandal."

"Yes, I did. But that was eight years ago, and all my research indicated she was an innocent party." And an injured party.

Bad as her own experience with Jason had been, having a husband indicted and sent to prison for a Madoff-like con would be far worse.

"I'm relieved you were at least aware of it. Listen, are you certain you don't want me to fly up there? You're only a few hundred miles north of San Francisco, and two heads are better than one if big money is at stake. I could block a day out of my schedule."

The door of the house opened a few more inches, but whoever was behind it remained inside. "I appreciate the offer, Mom, but I'm thirty-two. I can handle this. Listen, I think the owner's spotted me. She's probably wondering why I stopped halfway down the drive. I should go."

A beat ticked by.

"You think I'm meddling, don't you?"

"I don't know if I'd call it meddling." But it was clear her mother wasn't confident in her daughter's business acumen or common sense. "And I appreciate your concern."

"You know I want what's best for you, don't you?"

"Yeah. I know."

And she did. Even if their ideas on that score seldom overlapped.

If Mom had had her druthers, her sole offspring would have followed her into a high-profile career in Silicon Valley or become an attorney or engineer or doctor.

She certainly wouldn't have followed her heart, as her anthropology professor father had done, and picked a major as impractical as historic preservation and architectural history. Nor would she have considered a low-paying position as an assistant curator and events

19

director at an antebellum mansion in Tennessee a dream job.

One that had, alas, gone up in smoke.

Literally.

But the experience? Priceless.

And if she had it to do all over again, she wouldn't change a—

". . . what I say, you always go your own way. Like your father did."

Whoops. Better tune back in to the conversation.

"Dad did okay."

"Depends how you define okay."

That was true. And her parents' definitions had been miles apart. No wonder they'd split when she was ten. Yet while it was true that Dad had never had a high-end condo or traveled first class to Europe or become a corporate executive like Mom had, he'd loved what he'd done. And the tidy sum she'd inherited after he'd died last year proved he'd had more money sense than Mom had ever given him credit for.

However, debating philosophy and priorities wasn't on her agenda today.

"I agree that okay has different meanings for different people." The door to the house closed. "I have to go, Mom. I'll give you a full report later."

"I'll be waiting to hear. Remember to be

businesslike and sensible. Put away your rose-colored glasses and don't let romantic fantasies about historic seaside estates muddle your thinking."

Ashley stifled a snort.

No problem on the romantic fantasies score. Not after Jason, thank you very much. Going forward, her head, not her heart, would prevail— with houses and with men.

"Got it. Talk to you soon."

She ended the call, set the cell on the passenger seat, and pressed on the accelerator again.

Gravel crunching beneath her tires, she traversed the extended drive that ended in a loop in front of the house. From there, a long stone walkway led to five wide brick steps that ascended to a hydrangea-rimmed porch, where a lone fern hung between the posts supporting the roof. Like the ones in the old photo she'd found. Except back then, there'd been a fern between every post. There had also been a lush garden on either side of the walkway that had long since succumbed to weeds.

Still, while the grounds displayed little of their former glory, even at this closer range the structure showed no obvious signs of decay.

Ashley set the brake, picked up her purse and the notebook containing the multitude of questions she'd jotted down, and slid from behind the wheel. Time to see whether her long trek was the beginning of a new journey or an expensive, waste-of-time detour.

Purse slung over her shoulder, she walked down the path toward the steps that were flanked by empty stone flower urns. Ascended to the porch and moved toward the impressive carved double door, which featured textured, opaque glass overlaid with filigreed ironwork on the top half and was crowned by an elliptical stained-glass transom.

Man.

They didn't make entryways like this anymore.

As she leaned toward the bell, one of the doors opened a few inches. But the figure on the other side remained hidden.

Ashley's hand froze.

Not the warmest welcome—but in keeping with a woman who had no social media presence, communicated by email rather than phone, and was known as a recluse.

"I thought perhaps you'd changed your mind and were going to turn around and drive away."

The voice that came from the shadows sounded rusty.

Also consistent with a woman who kept to herself.

"My mother called as I pulled in. She, uh, wanted to be sure I'd arrived safely."

"I expect she also offered a few words of

advice. Mothers are like that. Come in. You must be tired after your long trip."

The door opened wider, and Ashley got her first look at the mistress of Edgecliff.

Rose Fitzgerald Warner—or Rose Fitzgerald, as she now preferred to be called—was tall and slender, her silver hair secured in a soft French twist. She wore modest makeup on a face that had remarkably few wrinkles for an eighty-year-old. Nor did her keen blue eyes hint at eight decades of living.

Her attire, however? Different story. The long black skirt, white lace blouse with high neck and leg-of-mutton sleeves, and cinched waist were turn-of-the-century.

The last century.

A red alert began to beep in Ashley's mind.

What rational person would wear hundred-year-old clothes?

The woman's lips quirked, as if she'd heard the unspoken question. "I thought, with your background, you'd appreciate the vintage attire."

"Oh, I do. The outfit is, uh, lovely."

"In case you're concerned, I don't dress like this every day. I exhumed this ensemble from a trunk in the attic to add ambiance to our meeting. Please come in. The drawing room is on your left." She moved aside and motioned that direction.

After a brief hesitation, Ashley crossed the

threshold. The woman might be eccentric, but she was well-spoken and seemed lucid. Her emails had been articulate. She came with solid references.

There was no reason to be concerned.

None at all.

Reining in her overactive imagination, Ashley stopped in the middle of the foyer and gave it a slow perusal.

On one wall, a fireplace with an elaborate carved mantel dominated. A double stairway with ornate spindles hugged the walls on each side as it wound to a landing that was backed by another large stained-glass window overlooking the foyer. The light from the late-afternoon sun spilled through, creating a mosaic of colors on the parquet floor and brightening the space despite the dark wood wainscoting. All of the furnishings were period.

It was like stepping back in time.

Exactly what she'd hoped to find.

"Impressive, isn't it?"

At Rose's question, she angled sideways to find the older woman watching her.

"Very."

"As a child, I loved to sit in here in the afternoon whenever we visited. Delicious aromas would waft from the kitchen, and I'd watch the kaleidoscope of colors on the floor. It always felt safe and peaceful . . . and permanent." Her melancholy smile faded. "But of course, nothing is." She swept a hand toward the drawing room through a broad opening that could no doubt be closed off with pocket doors. "Shall we have tea and a chat? Or are you having second thoughts?"

Third thoughts would be more accurate. But admitting that could kill this deal—assuming she decided to go through with it after additional due diligence. Rose wasn't likely to sign on the dotted line with a stranger who was less than enthusiastic or committed about the plans they'd discussed.

"More like taking everything in and keeping an open mind."

"Always wise in a new situation." Rose closed the front door. "Have a seat. I'll retrieve the tea and join you in a minute." With that, she disappeared through the archway between the twin staircases.

For a full thirty seconds, Ashley remained where she was, breathing in air redolent of history and opportunity.

It was possible, of course, that this trip would end up being a waste of time and money.

But maybe . . . just maybe . . . it would be a once-in-a-lifetime chance to leave her own past behind and forge a new path in a town with the promising name of Hope Harbor.

2

Why was a drop-dead gorgeous woman visiting Edgecliff?

Jonathan Gray stowed the chain saw in his equipment shed as the question that had looped through his mind during the entire quarter mile walk back to his place echoed yet again.

A question that refused to be silenced, despite his concerted attempts to muzzle it.

Muttering a few choice words, he yanked off his mask.

Who cared if Rose Fitzgerald had a pretty visitor or why she was there? As long as he got paid for keeping the canopy of foliage at the entrance to Edgecliff clear and the lawn cut, the goings-on there were no concern of his.

Still . . .

Very few visitors came to call at the remote estate, aside from UPS drivers and the regulars who delivered groceries or did maintenance or had other business to attend to. Near as he could tell from traffic patterns, social guests were nonexistent.

So maybe the woman with the wavy, light brown hair and big eyes had business to conduct at Edgecliff.

Somehow that didn't feel right. But why else would she—

A welcoming yip sounded outside, and he exited the shed, shoving his mask in his pocket as thirty-five pounds of enthusiastic border collie barreled toward him.

He crossed the lawn to meet the joyful ball of fur, dropping to one knee to accept an affectionate nuzzle. "Hey, Daisy. Did you miss me?"

A slurp on the cheek provided his answer.

Scratching behind her ears, he shifted toward his logoed pickup truck as it swung into the driveway.

Huh.

Kyle was back early.

Was that a good sign or a bad one?

Hard to know when you employed ex-cons.

But in the eighteen months Kyle had worked for him, the man had been a model employee. As had the other two crew members who'd been vetted and recommended by the husband of Hope Harbor's police chief—an ex-con turned successful businessman. Endorsements didn't come with a better pedigree than that.

After giving Daisy one more pat, Jon stood and walked over as the man climbed down from the cab.

"You finished early." He stopped next to the truck, and Daisy plopped onto her haunches beside him.

"Pulling out the old landscaping didn't take as long as we expected. Half the bushes had root rot. The design you created looks great, by the way. The owner loved it. Wish I had your knack for layout. Then I could use a pen instead of a shovel." He grinned. "Not that you don't do your share of heavy lifting."

"Like on tomorrow's job. That will require all hands on deck. But after working on bids and designs all day, I'll be glad to trade in my laptop for a shovel. Thanks for covering for me on the site today and picking up the last load of mulch."

"No problem. I told the guys to be there at seven thirty sharp. We should get an early start."

"I agree." Jon motioned to the man's older-model Nissan, parked off to the side. "Go on home to that new wife of yours. I bet she'll be glad to have you for an extra hour today."

"That's my plan. I already talked to her." Kyle slid his fingers into his back pockets. Transferred his weight from one foot to the other. "Listen . . . you want to have dinner with us? Sarah's roasting a chicken, and she said she'd bake cookies if you came."

Jon throttled a groan. Kyle's offer was kind, as the previous ones had been.

But pity never sat well, no matter how good the intentions.

He reached down and stroked Daisy's head as he framed his response. "I appreciate the invitation, but I'm covered for dinner. Besides, I'm sure your bride would rather have you to herself."

"It was her idea this time." Twin creases appeared on the man's forehead. "Can I tell you something?"

Uh-oh.

That question always led to an uncomfortable exchange.

Jon kept his tone neutral. "Am I going to like it?"

"Probably not. But someone needs to say it."

"Don't put your job in jeopardy." The implied threat in his response ought to put a stop to this conversation.

Except it didn't.

Kyle squared his shoulders. "I'll take the risk— because I owe you. You took a chance on me when most people wouldn't. On the other guys too. We felt like outcasts until you came along, and that's a lonely place to be. I'm guessing you know about loneliness. But the thing is, you don't have to stay in that place. I bet if you gave people in town a chance like you gave us a chance, they'd welcome you into the community. Once they got to know you, saw what's in your heart, nothing else would matter."

If only that were true.

Stomach clenching, Jon fisted his hands at his sides.

While Kyle's take was plausible in theory, real life didn't always play out that way. Not in his experience, anyway. If the woman who'd professed to love him hadn't been able to get past his issues, how could he expect any more of strangers?

"For the record, I'm not lonely. I have Daisy." He gave the pooch a pat.

"A dog doesn't take the place of people."

"Don't tell that to this one. She'd be insulted."

Kyle studied him. "You've been here two years, right?"

"Yes."

"Have you made one friend?"

"I used to think you were one."

"Still am, I hope." Kyle fingered his keys. Sighed. "Sorry if I overstepped. Since I met Sarah, I've been thinking about you all alone out here with that crazy old lady as your nearest neighbor. You deserve more than that."

"I'm fine, Kyle. Don't worry about me. Enjoy your dinner with Sarah and give her my regards."

After a brief hesitation, his foreman shrugged. "You're the boss. But dinner is a standing invitation if you ever get tired of being a hermit."

"I'm not a hermit. I interact with clients."

"After putting on your protective armor. And I'm not just talking about the sunglasses, ball cap, and scarf."

"Go home, Kyle."

"Fine. I'm outta here. See you tomorrow."

The man struck off for his car, slid behind the wheel, and drove down the gravel drive. Once on Windswept Way, the Nissan disappeared behind the dense hedge of vegetation that bordered the road. Total silence descended.

A silence Jon had always welcomed on his isolated rental property.

He filled his lungs with the fresh, salt-tanged air as Daisy chased after a squirrel with a happy yip, his pup the picture of utter contentment.

That made one of them.

Huffing out a breath, he furrowed his brow.

Where had that sudden, depressing, and unwanted discontent come from? He had a good life. A beautiful place to live, a lucrative and fulfilling landscape design business, a loyal dog who loved him for all the right reasons and was a faithful friend. What more could he ask?

An image of the woman with brown hair flashed across his mind, and he scowled.

That was nuts. He'd seen her for all of . . . what? Fifteen seconds? And only through a windshield, for crying out loud.

He ought to forget about her.

But perhaps the difficulty he was having erasing her from his mind validated Kyle's observation that he needed more than canine companionship in his life.

He wiped a hand down his face. Exhaled.

May as well admit the truth.

He *was* lonely. And more than a tad envious that Kyle had a loving wife waiting for him at the end of the day. An option that wasn't open to him, as his experience with Melinda had proven.

Gut twisting, he whistled for Daisy, who did a one-eighty and hurtled back toward him.

He needed to tamp down this rare case of self-pity and melancholy and get on with his life, as he'd been doing every day since his world imploded five years ago.

And do his best to stop letting images of a beautiful face, or questions about why such a woman would be visiting Edgecliff, disrupt the placid and carefully constructed life he'd created on the fringes of Hope Harbor.

"Now that we've had our tea and a chat, I expect you have any number of questions for me." Rose patted her mouth with a linen napkin, set it beside the plate that held the crumbs from her scone, and leaned back in the upholstered armchair with tufted back and curved, carved legs.

Ashley set aside her delicate antique cup, flipped open her notebook, and switched into business mode. "Yes, I do."

"I'll answer as many as I can, but first I have a confession to make. I had my attorney run a background and credit check on you."

O-kay.

Not what she'd expected from an eighty-year-old, vintage-clothes-wearing recluse who appeared to have few dealings with the outside world.

"I, uh, take it I passed."

"Yes, or you wouldn't be here." The woman linked her fingers in her lap. "I hope you understand why I was wary about an unsolicited inquiry such as yours, intriguing as it was. Especially in today's world, where scams are quite common." A hint of pain flickered in her eyes.

She had to be thinking about the one her husband had used to bilk people of their life savings.

"I do understand. And to tell you the truth, writing that letter was out of character for me. But sometimes you have to take a leap of faith."

"Indeed, you do. The very reason I agreed to the interview you read in the *Herald*, which was out of character for *me*. But the editor was both persistent and charming, and of course any story about the lumber industry in Oregon wouldn't be complete without paying tribute to my father and grandfather. Who better to do that, and to ensure the story was accurate, than me?"

"I agree. Primary sources are always the most reliable."

"Spoken like the historian you are. One with impressive credentials. I also read a few of your well-researched articles. They were impressive too."

A rush of pleasure warmed her. "I enjoy what I do. For me, research is a joy, not a chore."

"I assume you delved into my family history too."

Whoops.

She'd walked straight into that one.

"Um . . . to some degree."

"Give me the highlights of what you found, and I'll fill in the gaps."

Ashley smoothed out a wrinkle in her slacks. How much should she share? Too little, and it would appear she hadn't done her homework. Too much, and Rose could think she'd been overzealous about digging for dirt.

It might be prudent to skirt around the more sensitive details.

"Your grandfather, Patrick, made his fortune in the lumber industry. He built this house in 1910."

"Yes. As a wedding present for his bride."

"Why brick instead of wood?" None of her research had uncovered that nugget.

Rose's lips twitched. "Because he could. Building it out of lumber wouldn't have cost him a cent. Brick, on the other hand, was money out of pocket and therefore more impressive. Since he came from nothing, the outward trappings of success were important to him. That's also why he often threw lavish parties here until my grandmother died, three years before I was born."

Sensitive detail number one.

According to historical accounts, the woman hadn't just died. She'd been swept off the cliff by a high wind during a storm.

"I did read an account of that tragedy." To pretend she didn't know how the woman had perished would be disingenuous.

"I assumed you had. My grandfather always warned her not to venture too close to the cliff, but she was a bit of a daredevil. He deeded the house to my father as a wedding present in 1942 and never returned."

"Did you come here often?"

"Yes." Rose stood and walked over to the mantel, stopping beside a faded, framed photo of a couple and a young girl. Ran a finger down the edge of the tarnished silver frame. "This was our weekend and holiday retreat."

"And your parents moved here permanently after your father sold the lumber business in 1985."

"Correct. A few years later, my mother began showing signs of dementia. Eventually she started wandering the grounds in her nightgown. I imagine that's what gave rise to the haunted rumors. And then history repeated itself." Rose's demeanor remained placid, but sadness darkened her irises as she turned back toward the room. "I expect you know that too."

"A few of the details. It happened twenty years ago, I believe."

"Yes. My father kept close watch over my mother, but one foggy night she escaped from the house, wandered too close to the cliffs, and fell off." Rose swallowed and rested a hand on the back of the chair beside her, a match for the one she'd claimed earlier. "My father was devastated. Consumed with grief and guilt. After the funeral, he shut the gates and withdrew from the world. I joined him here after my own tragedy and cared for him until he died last year."

There was no dancing around her reference to the scandal.

"I read about your husband's conviction. I'm sorry."

Rose's expression remained impassive, but pain shimmered in her eyes. "Finding out he'd bilked people of their nest eggs, robbed them of their security, was shattering. We'd grown apart over the years, but I still couldn't believe he would do such a terrible thing." Rose slowly returned to her chair and sat. "After it all came to light, I was tainted by association. Once he was convicted, our so-called friends deserted me and our son."

Ashley stared at her.

Son?

Rose had a child?

Why hadn't her diligent research uncovered that fact?

"You didn't know about Mark." Rose's comment was more statement than question.

"No."

"Not surprising." A shadow passed over her features, and for the first time she appeared closer to her age. "Mark was a late-in-life child. He also had Down syndrome, which was an embarrassment to my husband. After the scandal, I set divorce proceedings in motion, moved across the state, and retook my maiden name. I also changed Mark's last name and tried to shield him from the mess. But all the disruption was too much for him. He became depressed, and within a year he . . . he took his own life." Her voice choked, and she tugged a tissue from her sleeve. Dabbed at the corners of her lashes. "That was when I came back here. Seven years ago now."

Ashley took a deep breath as she digested Rose's story.

The Fitzgeralds and Edgecliff had known far more than their share of tragedy. More than even her diligent research had revealed.

And that raised a very important question.

Did she really want to be part of a place that was plagued by misfortune?

"We're not cursed, you know." Rose locked onto her gaze, as if she'd read her mind. "Nor is this place haunted, despite the rumors."

Warmth spilled onto Ashley's cheeks. "I don't believe in curses or hauntings."

37

"I'm happy to hear that." Rose wadded the tissue in her fingers and leaned forward, her posture intent. "Edgecliff has seen sadness, but it was built in love. For a bride. There was also much happiness here. I have many wonderful memories of this place. I'd like for love and joy, not tragedy and grief, to be its legacy. That's why your note seemed providential. I was struck by how you picked up on my passing comment in the article, about wishing to preserve the history in this house and bring the place alive again. It made me think you could be the person to help write its next chapter."

She'd thought so too. But all at once, it felt like a tall order.

"I don't know about next chapters, but I do have a few ideas that could help accomplish your goal."

"And I like all of the ones you've shared." Rose leaned back. "I knew from the credit check and the bank statement you provided that you had the financial wherewithal to enter into an agreement, and your correspondence certainly brimmed with enthusiasm, but words and numbers on paper don't provide a total picture. That's why I asked you to come out here. Tell me again about your vision for Edgecliff."

Ashley glanced at the page of questions she'd prepared for this meeting.

Looked like they'd have to wait while she

rehashed the ideas she'd laid out in her proposal.

She closed the notebook and folded her hands on top. "Most of the concepts aren't original. I adapted many of them from my experience at my previous job. Since the property where I worked wasn't as well preserved as yours or furnished with original pieces, there was less emphasis on historical interpretation there. It was primarily an events venue. Edgecliff has much more to offer."

As Ashley gave voice to her ideas—tours of the house, programs featuring speakers knowledge-able about the era's architecture and customs and clothing and food and landscaping, hands-on educational opportunities for school groups in addition to the use of the house and grounds for weddings and other gatherings—the sense of excitement she'd experienced as she'd put her plan together again bubbled to the surface.

If the animation on Rose's face as she finished was any indication, her passion was contagious.

The woman's next comment confirmed that.

"All of those sound wonderful." Rose's lips curved up. "As my father used to say in happier days, there's nothing like a new project to stir the blood. I believe he would approve of this one. It has tremendous possibilities."

"I agree. The property in Tennessee was very successful, and it didn't have nearly as much to offer as Edgecliff. The setting here will be a bride magnet." Ashley paused, tempering her enthusiasm, because there were some caveats.

Rose tipped her head. "I sense a *but* there."

Age hadn't dimmed the woman's acuity.

"Beautiful as the house and property are, changes would be necessary to accommodate special events. Like putting quite a few pieces of the furniture into storage to make room for crowds and updating the kitchen for commercial use. From what I could tell as I drove in, the grounds could also use attention."

"I'm open to all of that. The grounds in particular. They're a shadow of what they used to be. I remember when they were glorious. My mother loved planning the gardens each spring, drawing elaborate diagrams for each one. I have all of those, along with various journals and ledgers that may prove useful to you."

"I'd love to see everything. Your mother's diagrams could be very helpful during the restoration."

"So you're still interested in exploring the possibility of a partnership?"

Ashley hesitated, but only for a moment. While the news about Rose's son was a surprise, nothing else she'd heard or seen today—other than that masked man at the entrance—raised serious concerns.

"Yes."

"Excellent." Rose picked up a folder from the table beside her. "I think we've talked enough for today, and I'm in need of a nap. We can meet again Thursday afternoon. That will give you a few days to get the lay of the land, see the town, arrange for any inspections you may want to have done. You're staying until Friday, correct?"

"Yes."

"Then here's what I propose. Wander through the house at your leisure, beginning today if you like. My bedroom is on the second floor, first door on the right. Other than that, the place is yours to explore. Take a walk around the grounds. You'll see where the gardens used to be, and the remains of the gazebo. And read through this." She held out the folder.

"What is it?" Ashley took the file.

"The draft of an agreement I had my attorney prepare. I included his contact information if you'd like to see maintenance records on the house or have any questions of that sort. I'd suggest you also have an attorney review this document. I've put the name of one in Hope Harbor inside the file if you care to consult him. He was recommended to me by the pastor at Grace Christian Church. I'm sure this man can also refer you to other local firms you may wish to contact for additional advice." She stood.

Ashley rose more slowly.

Their teatime chat was over, and she hadn't asked one of the questions on her list.

Her mother would have a fit.

But tomorrow, as Scarlett O'Hara had always said, was another day.

For now, a walk-through of the house and grounds would give her a ton of firsthand information.

Ashley followed Rose to the foyer. "Thank you for the tea."

"It was a pleasure to put my baking skills to use for someone besides myself." Rose pulled a key from her pocket. "Please lock the door as you leave. Few people venture to the end of Windswept Way, but it never hurts to be careful. Occasionally strangers or curiosity seekers do wander out here."

Speaking of strangers . . .

"As a matter of fact, there was a man at the entrance when I arrived." Maybe Rose could shed a ray of light on his presence. "He, uh, had a chain saw."

The older woman gave a dismissive wave. "I expect it was someone from the firm my attorney hired to keep the entrance passable and mow the grass. He could have been clearing up downed limbs from the storm we had a few days ago. I imagine he's gone by now. You shouldn't run into anyone else as you wander about. I enjoyed our chat today." She extended her hand.

"I did too." Ashley gripped the woman's delicate fingers and received a strong squeeze in return before her potential business partner turned and slowly ascended the grand staircase.

Leaving her alone to explore this amazing place.

A wave of excitement swept over her, and it didn't abate for the next two hours as she poked through all the rooms, peeked under the dustcovers shrouding the furniture on the second and third floors, ogled the large library and lavish ballroom, and wandered the grounds while staying far back from the cliff edge.

As the sun began to dip over the sea, she ended her tour on the large stone terrace at the back of the house, sitting on the edge of the low wall that surrounded it.

Everything was as she'd hoped it would be. Period furnishings, essentially intact except in the somewhat updated kitchen. Expansive grounds that would be an ideal backdrop for weddings once the gardens were restored. No obvious signs of decay in the house itself. A caretaker's cottage and carriage house—the future residences for her and Rose, should they end up agreeing on terms—that appeared to be in excellent condition, even though they were locked.

It was perfect.

A lone pelican soared across the sky over the sea, its wings gilded by the setting sun, and Ashley inhaled the fresh, briny air. Already this felt like home.

Yes, she had much work to do. There were

experts to consult, bids to solicit for the work required, legal reviews to arrange. Any of those could produce deal-breaking information, and she'd be unbiased and objective as she considered the data.

But every instinct in her body said this was where she was meant to be. That in bringing to fruition Rose's dream to infuse Edgecliff with joy and life, she'd find her own destiny.

No doubt her mother would chide her for such quixotic thinking. Exhort her to be sensible and prudent. And she would be. She wasn't going to waste Dad's legacy if negatives cropped up.

Yet neither was she going to discount her instincts. They may have misled her with Jason, but mansions and men were two different things.

And if she were a betting woman, she'd wager a month's salary from her previous job that Edgecliff was going to be a far superior match for her than Jason had ever been.

3

. . . .

"Bottom line, as legal agreements go, this one is about as straightforward as you can get." Eric Nash leaned back in his leather chair and steepled his fingers. "It also appears eminently weighted in your favor."

As the attorney Rose had recommended wrapped up his assessment of the proposed contract, Ashley homed in on his last comment. Apparently, she hadn't misread the startling clause she'd found in the document last night as she'd pored over it in her room at the Gull Motel after her meeting with Rose.

"You're talking about her bequeathing me her half of Edgecliff if we get past the two-year probation period."

"Yes. Along with her agreement to refund your investment if you don't."

"I knew about the refund, but my understanding from our correspondence was that I'd have the option to purchase her share upon her death. The bequest was a total surprise."

"The seventy-thirty profit split in your favor is also very generous."

"I know. I was expecting fifty-fifty."

The dark-haired man tapped his index fingers together, faint pleats marring his brow. "I'm not a real estate expert, but the property appears to be undervalued, given the number of acres involved. Coastal land here goes for big bucks, and from the rumors I've heard, the house is filled with valuable antiques."

"It is."

"So why a partnership versus hiring someone to run the place according to her specifications?"

The same question she'd asked in their initial email exchanges.

"Rose says she has the funds to give Edgecliff new life without a partnership deal, but not the energy or expertise. She wanted someone on board who would have a vested interest in the property long term, and she thought a partnership would ensure continuity in management. I think Rose is more interested in preserving the legacy of the estate than adding to her bank balance."

"In that case, it would appear you've lucked into a once-in-a-lifetime opportunity."

"I agree. So you didn't spot any red flags in the contract?" Ashley waved her hand toward the document on his desk.

"Not unless the renovations you plan to do are going to break the bank. Those are a fifty-fifty split. Is the house in decent shape?"

"It is, from what I can tell. I do want to have a structural engineer weigh in, though. Do you by chance have any recommendations?"

"As a matter of fact, I do. Stevens Design and Construction. In the interest of full disclosure, however, the owner is my wife." Eric's lips flexed. "Not that I promote or condone nepotism in general, but BJ's excellent at her job. She's an architect with a strong background in structural engineering. Besides, she'd kill for a peek inside that house."

"Sold."

Eric withdrew a business card from his desk and held it out. "Tell her I recommended her to you, and she'll move you to the top of her list. Maybe." His smile became a flat-out grin.

"I'll do that." She tucked the card in her purse. "You wouldn't happen to know any landscaping firms in the area, would you?"

"Greenscape may be a possibility. I don't have their number, but you could google them. Or ask BJ to put you in touch. She often deals with them when she does house additions that incorporate patios or decks. I know she's been impressed with their work."

Ashley jotted down the name. "You've been a tremendous help. Thank you for fitting me into your schedule on such short notice."

"That's one of the beauties of practicing law in Hope Harbor. Most matters aren't super urgent here. Makes for a wonderful pace of life. I highly recommend it. And you won't find a nicer bunch of people."

"Good to know." She stood. "I'll give your wife a call as soon as I round up lunch."

Eric rose too and crossed to the window that offered a view of the harbor and Dockside Drive. Peered north. "I think you may be in luck on the food front too. Charley's cooking today instead of painting."

She tipped her head. "You'll have to explain that."

"Charley's our resident artist. World famous, though you'd never know it to meet him. He also makes the best fish tacos this side of heaven. His stand is at the end of the street, next to the pocket park. You can't miss it."

"Thanks for that recommendation too. The cinnamon roll I had at the bakery this morning was phenomenal, but the energy boost it gave me is beginning to wear off. I'll call your wife after I sample those tacos."

"I'll let her know. Enjoy your lunch."

Once Eric showed her to the door and she stepped onto the sidewalk, Ashley had no trouble spotting the taco stand. But following her nose would have led her there anyway. Delicious aromas were wafting down Dockside Drive.

She set off at a brisk pace, passing Sweet Dreams bakery where she'd indulged in her high-fat, high-calorie breakfast. Yet despite her hunger, her pace slowed as she surveyed the scene and the peace of the bucolic setting that had charmed her this morning again seeped into her pores.

In the harbor, boats bobbed in the gentle swells. Planters filled with colorful flowers were spaced along the sidewalk above the cascade of boulders that led to the water. Across from the harbor, on the opposite side of crescent-shaped Dockside Drive, shops sporting bright awnings and flower boxes lined the sidewalk. At the far end of the street, which dead-ended at the river, a white gazebo graced the tiny park. The unhitched white food trailer beside the park, with "Charley's" spelled out in colorful letters above the serving window, appeared to be doing a brisk business.

As the savory aroma roused her appetite, Ashley picked up her pace.

Once in line, she tried to shush the rumble in her stomach as she watched two gulls circle a boat that was passing the long jetty on the left and the pair of rocky islands on the right that kept boats in the marina safe from the choppy waters beyond.

When she at last arrived at the window, the man behind the counter greeted her with a warm smile. "Sorry for the long wait. Everyone must want tacos today. One order?"

"Yes, please." She scanned the area around the window for a menu, but the sole piece of printed matter was a hand-lettered sign that said "Cash Only."

"If you're looking for a bill of fare, I don't

have one. I feature one kind of taco during each cooking session, with whatever fish catches my fancy after the boats come in. Flounder was the top choice today. That work for you?" He pulled two fillets out of a cooler and held them up.

"Sure."

The man adjusted the Ducks cap he wore over his long gray ponytail and set the fish on the grill before returning to the window. "I'm Charley Lopez. Welcome to Hope Harbor."

"Thanks. I'm Ashley Scott."

"Always happy for new folks to discover our little piece of paradise." He swiveled back to the prep area and began chopping red onion and cilantro as he spoke over his shoulder. "Have you had a chance to see much yet, other than Edgecliff?"

Ashley stared at his back. "How did you . . . did someone tell you . . . no one knows . . ." Her voice trailed off.

"I ran into the manager of the Gull Motel last night." Charley tossed the chopped items onto a griddle and sprinkled them with seasoning from a large, unmarked container. "She mentioned you'd checked in. First name only, but I did the math when you introduced yourself. She was quite intrigued by your visit to Edgecliff."

Okay, that made sense. During their brief exchange, she'd commented that she was here to see Rose.

But she hadn't expected the news to spread so fast.

As if reading her mind, Charley rotated toward her, his dark brown eyes twinkling. "It's hard to keep secrets in a small town. But on the plus side, we all have each other's backs. Not a bad trade-off."

"I guess not."

"How's Rose doing?"

He was on a first-name basis with the reclusive owner?

"Are you two acquainted?"

"We met a while back. On occasion, I stop in with an order of tacos for her." Charley pulled out three corn tortillas and laid them on the grill. Flipped the fish.

Hard as she tried, Ashley couldn't picture tea-drinking Rose Fitzgerald eating tacos or striking up a friendship deep enough with anyone to encourage impromptu visits.

"She seems fine." Enough said. Rose wasn't the type of person who would appreciate being talked about.

"The house is a gem, isn't it?"

"Yes."

"Empty, though. Love and laughter would bring it alive again." Charley began assembling the tacos.

Ashley squinted at him.

How much did he know about the purpose of

her visit? She'd told no one except her mother and Eric Nash, and it wasn't likely Rose had talked about their potential partnership with anyone other than her lawyer.

"I'm sure there was love and laughter there in days gone by."

"Without a doubt." Charley added a dollop of sauce to each taco, then started wrapping them in white paper. "I expect Rose would like to see that again. There's been too much sadness at Edgecliff."

"I agree. But she loves the place anyway. She says she has fond memories of childhood vacations spent there."

Well, shoot.

So much for being circumspect.

"Happy memories are a treasure that make hard days easier to bear. And they help keep bitterness at bay. Rose is an inspiring illustration of that. I admire her great capacity to find quiet joy amid trials and tribulations."

Ashley gave the taco chef a slow blink.

How well did he know the woman? Near as she'd been able to discern from the references Rose had provided and the research she'd done, the sole occupant of Edgecliff wasn't close to anyone now living.

"Would you like a bottle of water to go with your tacos?" Charley slipped the three packets into a brown paper bag.

"Yes. Thanks."

He added the beverage and slid the bag across the counter. "Enjoy."

"How much do I owe you?" Ashley opened her purse, still trying to wrap her mind around Charley's familiarity with Rose.

"First taco order for newcomers is on the house."

He was giving her a free lunch?

Frowning, she waved a hand toward the family group that had claimed a bench by the wharf. Clearly tourists, based on the Cardinals baseball T-shirt one of the younger boys wore. "Do you give free tacos to every first-time customer?"

"A newcomer is different than a customer." Charley began lowering the window. "Break time. Visit the lighthouse if you have a few minutes. Wonderful view from up there. And please tell Rose I said hello."

The window clicked shut.

For several seconds, Ashley remained by the shuttered taco truck, fingers crimped around the top of the paper bag.

That had been a strange encounter.

Then again, this trip had been filled with strange encounters.

An unsociable, chain-saw-wielding man at the gates of Edgecliff.

A reclusive owner who'd greeted her in turn-of-the-century attire.

Now a taco-making artist who knew an awful lot about a woman and an estate that, for most people, were shrouded in mystery.

Eric Nash had been the only normal person she'd met.

The aroma emanating from the bag tickled her nose, and Ashley wandered down the wharf. Claimed a bench. Twisted the cap on her water and pulled one of the wrapped bundles from the bag.

If Mom were here, she'd be uncomfortable with the whole setup. Anything that couldn't be explained with charts, graphs, tables, or diagrams was anathema to Jessica Scott.

In general, it would bother *her* to some degree too.

So why wasn't she more disconcerted? Nervous, even?

She unwrapped the taco as two seagulls fluttered down to the pavement beside her. Broke off a piece of fish and tossed it to one of the birds, who pecked it in half and pushed a portion toward his companion.

Sweet—and endearing.

Like Rose.

The woman's willingness to look to the future, and her desire to create a legacy of joy and love despite all the tragedy that had darkened her life, were touching.

Ashley poked a loose piece of red onion back

into her taco and spread a generous paper napkin on her lap.

As for Charley . . . the man was intriguing. Somehow he'd managed to get to know Rose. Yet it wasn't hard to figure out how he'd infiltrated the older woman's defenses. There was a quality about him that encouraged trust and confidences, and the quiet peace radiating from him was calming. Like a refuge in the midst of a storm.

The chain-saw-wielding guy? Different story. While he'd exhibited no ill intent during their encounter, there had been an off-putting, almost furtive quality in his manner. As if he had something to hide and couldn't get away fast enough. There'd been no redeeming qualities about their brief meeting.

Nevertheless, it was hard not to feel a bit sorry for the man. Someone that unsociable must have been hurt somewhere along the way. Like the abused pup she and Dad had found years ago, who'd nipped at them and refused to let them get close for weeks until they proved they weren't going to hurt him.

An odd analogy to come up with for a stranger, but it somehow felt apt.

Ashley bit into her taco, and as the tangy sauce, spicy seasoning, subtle sweetness of the onion, and savory grilled fish sent her taste buds into nirvana, she closed her eyes.

Eric Nash hadn't been kidding.

These tacos were heaven.

In fact, this serene little town with its inter-esting characters, beautiful setting, and sense of possibilities, also had a certain utopian appeal.

So once she finished her lunch, she'd call Eric's wife and the Greenscape company he'd mentioned and set up appointments to have them look Edgecliff over and give her their assessment and estimates.

Then she'd say a few prayers and hope what-ever numbers came back didn't nix the deal.

Because unless the maintenance records from Rose's lawyer indicated a pattern of major problems and expensive repairs, she was pretty certain Hope Harbor was about to become her new home.

David was calling.

Of course.

The surprise was that it had taken him this long.

Lips bowing, Rose took a sip of her tea, set the cup down, and pressed the talk button on her cell. "Good morning, David."

"Hello, Rose. I hope I'm not interrupting anything."

"Not at all. I'm having my afternoon tea on the terrace. It's a beautiful day at Edgecliff."

"I'm certain your view is much better than mine."

certain it is too." She may never have ~~in~~ her attorney's office, but no vista could surpass the vast sweep of sky and sea at Edgecliff. Especially on a day like today, with puffy white clouds studding a sapphire-blue sky and the Sitka spruce, pine, and hemlock trees soaring toward the heavens all around her. "You must visit again soon."

"I'd enjoy that. May I ask how your meeting with Ms. Scott went yesterday?"

"Very well. She appears to be a sensible and pleasant young woman, and her enthusiasm is contagious. I gave her the contract to review."

A moment of silence passed.

"Do you think that may have been a tad premature? I believe we discussed waiting until closer to the end of her visit to pass the document along."

"We did, but your background check on her was thorough. I don't believe we have any concerns on that score. Meeting her was more about seeing whether we clicked, which we did. I felt quite comfortable moving forward. But I won't sign until you and I have another discussion."

"Would you like me to talk with her too? Give you my impressions?"

Rose smoothed back a wisp of hair the capricious breeze had tugged free from the pins that restrained it. Windswept Way had earned its name. "I appreciate the offer, David, but I trust my instincts. With one exception, I'm not a bad judge of character."

"That was on him, not you, Rose. Everyone he swindled trusted him too. He fooled many people."

"Thank you for saying that. And for being not only a business and legal advisor but a friend."

"Your father was a valued client for many years. I'm glad we've continued that long relationship." A squeak sounded, as if he'd leaned back in his chair. "How much have you told Ms. Scott about your other activity?"

"Nothing. It's not relevant to our agreement, and I prefer to keep it confidential."

"If she accepts your offer to live in the carriage house, she could find out at some point."

"My quarters in the caretaker's cottage will be private and off-limits. However, if she proves to be as trustworthy and discreet as she appears, I may tell her about it down the road."

"I have every confidence you'll use sound judgment with that matter. If she has any questions about the agreement, don't hesitate to call me."

"Thank you, David. I'll do that. And I'll be in touch again soon."

"It will be a pleasure to hear from you, as always. Take care of yourself."

As they ended the call, Rose settled back in her seat and picked up her tea again.

What a dear man David was. And how fortunate that Papa had engaged him years ago. What would she have done without his indispensable advice and steady hand when she'd first arrived back here, distraught and scattered and grief-stricken? Thank heavens he'd been willing to assist with everything from legal matters to arranging household help and general property management.

And when her other activity, as he'd referred to it, had taken an unexpected turn, his astute advice and legal acumen had proven to be a godsend.

A boat appeared on the horizon, chugging steadily toward seas that could be calm or turbulent, toward weather fair or foul.

Much like the partnership she was poised to launch with Ashley.

If she took the plunge, would the venture soar or sink?

Only God knew.

But two things were certain.

She wasn't getting any younger—and with no descendants to pass the torch to, Ashley Scott appeared to be her best hope of preserving Edgecliff's legacy and restoring the joy that had motivated her grandfather to build it for his long-ago bride.

4

His hunch had been spot-on.

The woman whose image was indelibly etched in his mind was the person who'd called to set up this meeting on the grounds of Edgecliff and the potential co-owner of the seaside estate.

Jon eased back on the gas pedal of his truck and wiped one damp palm, then the other, on the denim of his jeans as he regarded her from behind the windshield.

She was waiting at the appointed spot, sitting on the steps of Edgecliff's front porch, head bent over an open folder. The morning sun cast a golden glow on her fair skin and highlighted the touch of auburn in her long, wavy hair as she tucked it behind her ear.

His pulse picked up, and the oatmeal he'd eaten for breakfast suddenly congealed into a hard lump in the pit of his stomach.

Blast.

Sweaty palms, racing heart, nausea—all the physical signs of stress he'd learned to tame were back. On steroids.

And it wasn't hard to figure out why.

The attractive woman sitting on the porch steps, whose bubbly personality had juiced his libido during their phone conversation, was the culprit.

All at once she looked up, as if she'd sensed his presence.

Too late to retreat.

Not that he would have, anyway. This job would be a plum one for Greenscape. A stellar credential that would boost the company's prestige.

So he'd suck it up and follow through with this meeting.

The mask he'd donned the day at the gate would be extreme for a face-to-face meeting even if he used his usual allergy mitigation excuse to justify it. But he did have other camouflage resources in his tool kit, as Kyle had pointed out.

Inching the truck forward, he settled his sunglasses on his nose, pulled his ball cap low over his forehead, and tugged the bandanna higher on his neck.

Too bad he couldn't cover his mouth too. But that would be overkill.

Besides, if Ashley Scott ended up hiring Greenscape, she'd see his face sooner or later. May as well give her a preview today.

She rose as he pulled around the loop in the drive, and by the time he picked up his clipboard and foldable measuring wheel, she was halfway down the stone walk.

Her step faltered, however, when he slid from behind the wheel and circled the hood of the truck.

She'd recognized him.

"Good morning. Ashley Scott, I presume." He kept his demeanor pleasant as he approached her.

"Yes. And you're the guy with the chain saw who came through the gate on Monday. Aka Jonathan Gray."

"Guilty. And I go by Jon."

She offered him a tentative smile as she resumed walking. "I have to tell you, your sudden appearance that day invoked visions of the old chain saw massacre movie. I'm not used to driving around in isolated areas alone on dead-end roads, and—"

Her gaze dropped from his sunglasses to the asymmetrical line of his jaw and the scar on his cheek that ran through and slightly distorted the left side of his mouth.

A flicker of shock dulled her eyes for a millisecond as her voice trailed off. So brief he'd have missed it if he wasn't watching. But it was there.

Like it always was the instant people got an up-close glimpse of his appearance.

And she hadn't even seen the whole picture.

Best to address her reaction straight-on.

"War injury. IED in the Middle East." He ran his left hand—the one with the two missing fingers—along the side of his chin.

Fixating on his hand, she moistened her lips. Swallowed. "I'm sorry." All of the bounciness and enthusiasm she'd exhibited during their phone call had evaporated.

"I came out of it better than most of my men. Only a few survived." And those who had were maimed for life. Like him.

"I'm so sorry."

Gut twisting, he took a long, slow breath and forcibly rechanneled his thoughts. This was not a subject he talked about. Ever. Bringing it up had been a mistake. "It's history now. Shall we discuss the job?"

"Um . . . sure. I was going to suggest we walk the grounds while we talk, but if you're not—"

"It happened a number of years ago. My leg has healed. Walking is no problem." His response came out stiff, and he relaxed his tone. "However, if you're concerned about my capabilities, there are a number of excellent landscaping companies in Coos Bay."

Despite the out he'd offered her, she wouldn't bail on the bid session. No one would in today's world, with discrimination suits a constant sword of Damocles for anyone who exhibited the slightest perception of bias. But there had been more than a few potential clients who'd passed on his bid later, despite the fact it was the lowest. They'd found his injuries too distressing to deal with. Not that they'd put their aversion into words, but it wasn't hard to read between the lines. Ashley Scott could be one of them.

So while the job she'd sketched out over the phone would raise the stature and profile of his business, it would be foolish to get his hopes up.

"No. No, of course not. BJ Stevens Nash gave you a glowing review."

"Is she involved in this project?"

"I hope so. We're meeting tomorrow to do a walk-through. The gardens are my priority today." She held out one of the two folders in her hand. "Those are copies of the garden plot drawings I mentioned on the phone, done by Rose's mother. I thought it would be helpful to consult them as we walked around."

He tucked the clipboard under his arm, took the file, and flipped through it. "Are you hoping to re-create these?"

"Not necessarily. I view them more as a starting place."

"Good. Some of these plantings would be high maintenance. Unless you intend to hire a full-time grounds crew, you may want to consider alternatives."

"A full-time crew isn't in the budget. Alternatives are fine. My goal is to create beautiful, low-maintenance gardens that will offer a photogenic backdrop for weddings, especially in the gazebo area."

"The gazebo is in ruins."

"It won't be after BJ rebuilds it, assuming all the costs shake out and we're able to proceed with this project. Shall we start there?" She motioned toward the side of the house and struck off.

He fell in beside her, assessing the grounds with an eye to more than his customary grass cutting as he took multiple photos with his cell.

The place did have immense potential for the sort of special event usage Ashley had in mind, but what magic had she used to convince a recluse like Rose to consider that? How had the two of them connected? Where did the woman beside him call home?

A dozen questions spun through his mind as they walked the grounds and discussed planting locations for hydrangeas, perennial flowers, spring bulbs, and dahlias, along with the possibility of a formal rose garden, but no opportunity came up to pose more personal queries.

As they ended their circuit back in front of the house, Ashley waved a hand toward the loop road. "There should be a garden in the middle of that too. Like in the old days. And flowers along the walkway to the porch."

He jotted more notes as he mentally crunched a few numbers. "You may want to do the landscaping in stages. The scope of this job is huge."

"In other words, very expensive." She bit her lower lip.

"Labor and materials don't come cheap."

"Can you itemize the different garden areas on your bid? That may help if I have to prioritize."

"No problem. What's your target date to be up and running?"

"The sooner the better. Weddings are booked far in advance, but deposits will help with cash flow. And smaller events book closer in. I should be able to launch the speaker program even faster. Realistically, I'm hoping for September 1. I'd like to start generating a revenue stream ASAP."

"Understood. The landscaping alone will take a chunk of change. I hope you have deep pockets."

"Not super deep, but I do have funds in reserve beyond the purchase price. Hopefully I can swing this and make it pay off. I'd hate to squander my inheritance, even though my dad would have loved this project." Her features softened, and a smile whispered at the corners of her generous lips.

He forced himself to refocus on the clipboard in his hand and the information she'd shared rather than her striking profile as she gave the grounds a sweep.

A bequest would explain why someone as young as Ashley had the resources to tackle this sort of venture.

What it didn't explain was her interest in a century-old home.

"Was your father a historian?"

"No." She redirected her attention to him. "Anthropology professor. I'm the historian in the family. But he was all about following your dreams." She swept a hand over the house. "And this is one of mine. A historic property to not only manage but own a piece of. Not that I ever expected it to come true. I don't think I'll believe it until I sign on the dotted line with Rose."

A tailor-made opening to ask a few questions.

"How did you connect with her?"

"The article in the *Herald*."

Ashley read the local paper?

Not what he'd expected.

"Are you from around here?"

"No. I was the event manager for an antebellum home in Tennessee. Unfortunately, a fire swept through and caused major damage. They kept the property manager on the payroll to oversee repairs and renovations, but the place is shut for the foreseeable future so yours truly found herself out of a job. A week after I was let go, I saw the article in the *Herald*, and the rest is history. Pardon the pun."

An adorable dimple appeared in her cheek, quickening his pulse, and Jon took a step back. "How did you, uh, happen to see a copy of the *Herald*?"

"Dad and I used to vacation here, and after our last trip I subscribed. The place has happy memories for me, and I liked the idea of staying connected through the paper. Who knew it would lead to this?"

"Sounds like serendipity."

"Or something more."

"Like what?"

"Divine Providence?"

Jon tried to mask his skepticism. A decade ago, he'd have accepted her answer as plausible, but that day in Kandahar had killed more than the four guys in his reconnaissance squad who'd perished.

Ashley cocked her head. "You don't believe in God?"

The woman had impressive intuitive powers.

"I didn't say that." How in the world had they gotten on this topic? "I'm just not sure the Almighty makes a habit of intervening in the human drama. Thinking you were led here as part of a celestial chess game could be a stretch."

She heaved a sigh. "You sound like my mom. She didn't buy my theory either."

"I take it she doesn't approve of your plans."

"Let's say she has a few doubts. She thinks I get carried away too easily."

"Do you?"

A twinkle glinted in her eyes, drawing attention to their fringe of lush lashes. "Sometimes. Not that I'd ever admit it to her. But much as I'd like to own a piece of Edgecliff, I'm not going to squander my inheritance. If the cost for the necessary work is too high, I'll walk away. With regret." She scanned the estate again. "I've already fallen in love with this place."

"Love isn't always enough to overcome obstacles." The bitter comment spilled out before he could stop it.

Mistake number two today.

As Ashley refocused on him, her expression quizzical, Jon shoved the folder she'd given him under the clip on his clipboard. Retreated another foot or two. "If there's nothing else you want to discuss, I'll take off and get working on these numbers."

Please don't let her pursue my stupid comment!

Apparently someone was listening to his silent entreaty, because she hugged her own folder against her chest and followed his lead. "No. I think we covered everything. If you have any questions while you work on the bid, let me know. I jotted my email address inside the folder. That will be the fastest way to get the numbers to me after I leave Friday. Unless you can have them ready before then?"

Not with his current workload.

"Early next week is about the soonest I can manage."

"Understandable, but hope springs eternal and all that." She offered him a sheepish shrug. "Patience isn't my strong suit either."

"I can understand why you're anxious. This

decision could be a game changer for your life. I also want to remind you again that I do employ ex-cons." He'd been up-front about that in their first conversation, and she hadn't balked, but if she was having any second thoughts, why waste time putting together a complicated bid?

"I remember. I assume you've checked all their references."

"Yes. And I've never had any trouble. They're all grateful for a second chance, and I trust them implicitly."

"That's good enough for me."

"In that case, I'll be in touch as soon as I have the numbers together."

"Thanks."

After a brusque nod that in no way betrayed the rush of warmth that had filled his heart at her acceptance of his crew, he turned and walked back to his truck. Slid behind the wheel. Glanced back.

Ashley hadn't budged from her spot on the sidewalk that led to the front door. She was watching him, no doubt wondering what had prompted his comment about love.

She wasn't alone.

Why had he made such a revealing statement? He never alluded to his romantic history with anyone. Including his sister. Despite her conviction that talking would help him heal, and her concerted efforts to get him to open up during her

70

regular calls, he always sidestepped the subject.

So what had happened back there with Ashley?

Give it a break, Jon. You know what happened.

Clenching his teeth, he jammed his key into the ignition. Yanked off his cap and threw it onto the seat beside him. Put the truck in gear and pulled away.

Fine. He knew.

Kyle's little heart-to-heart on Monday had forced him to acknowledge the loneliness he'd been trying to ignore for the past few months. With the sudden appearance of an attractive woman on his doorstep, it was no wonder the lack of love and romance in his life had begun to dominate his thoughts. Creep into his conversations.

Which was bad.

Because no one would want a man who was damaged goods. Especially a beautiful woman like Ashley Scott.

Those were the facts.

And much as he wished he could rewrite his past, it was as set in stone as the melancholy history of Edgecliff.

5

"This place is even more incredible than I expected."

As BJ Stevens Nash did a final three-sixty rotation in the foyer of Edgecliff, Ashley motioned toward the drawing room. "You want to sit while we discuss next steps?"

The other woman flipped her long blond pony-tail over her shoulder and grinned. "My jeans were not meant to get up close and personal with velvet tufted antique chairs. Would you settle for the stairs?"

"Whatever works for you."

Ashley followed her over, pulse picking up. While BJ had offered a few preliminary com-ments about the condition of the house during their walk-through, her bottom-line assessment over the next few minutes could make or break this project.

Once they'd each claimed a step, the woman got straight to business. "From what I can tell based on a cursory inspection, the house appears to be in excellent shape for its age. I also reviewed the maintenance documentation the attorney provided. No red flags popped up."

"That sounds promising."

"What I saw is encouraging, but I only did

a quick pass. To give you a more complete picture, I'll have to examine the infrastructure and exterior walls. I'll also need to evaluate the integrity of load-bearing walls, joists, beams, roofing, and foundation."

And any of those could be found lacking.

"How long will that take?"

"For a house this size and this old, I'll want a full day. I can schedule it for next week, if you want to proceed."

"Yes. I do." An inspection like that wouldn't come cheap, but the peace of mind it would buy was priceless.

"I'll slot you in. Now let's talk about other changes that will have to be made, aside from updates in the kitchen. How many people are you hoping to accommodate at weddings?"

"Using the historic house in Tennessee where I used to work as a guide, up to a hundred and fifty for a tented outdoor event and eighty for an indoor ceremony and reception."

BJ stopped jotting. "You're from Tennessee?"

"Not born and raised, but I've lived there for the past year. Why?"

"It was my home from the age of eight."

Ah. That explained the woman's faint southern accent.

"I thought I detected the hint of a drawl."

BJ gave her a quick smile. "Most people don't. You have a sharp ear." She tapped her pen against her clipboard and got back to business. "You may want to apply for National Historic Landmark status. That will give us a bit of leeway in terms of ADA compliance. I should be able to adapt two of the existing restrooms to accommodate requirements without sacrificing their historic character. We'll also have to add an ADA-compliant access ramp somewhere. The side door may work. It wouldn't be too obtrusive there and could be disguised with landscaping. Are you planning to use the ballroom on the second floor?"

"Yes. I was thinking most indoor ceremonies would be held there, with receptions on the first level."

"In that case, you'll need an elevator. That's a pricey item."

Ashley braced. "How pricey?"

When BJ gave her the number, she swallowed. "On second thought . . . we could hold off on using the ballroom, at least in the beginning. Outdoor weddings would require less alterations in the house."

"But your season for those would be limited here on the coast. The weather can be wicked in the winter."

"I've heard that." She watched a few dust motes dance in a rainbow-prismed beam of sunlight from the stained-glass window on the landing. Took a deep breath. "Assume we're having indoor weddings and itemize everything you recommend in terms of renovations and maintenance."

"Will do. Did you touch base with Greenscape?"

A natural segue to probe for more information about the scarred veteran who'd walked the grounds with her, his manner cordial but detached except for his terse, cynical comment about love.

"Yes, I did. The owner came by yesterday."

"Jon's a good guy." BJ slid her pen in her shirt pocket, as if preparing to leave.

Shoot.

Eric's wife was her most promising source of information about the enigmatic man whose wounds seemed to run deeper than the ones his protective coverings didn't fully conceal.

Maybe she could stall her long enough to ask a few questions.

"Have you, uh, done many projects together?"

"Quite a few since he set up shop eighteen months ago. His timing was providential. The owner of the landscaping firm I used to recommend was retiring, and none of his children were interested in the business. Jon ended up buying some of his equipment and picked up a few of his customers, including me. He's reliable, fair, thorough, and detail oriented. You won't regret hiring him." BJ stood.

Ashley rose more slowly.

While the man's work ethic was important, it didn't have any bearing on the questions that had been running through her mind for the past twenty-four hours.

Like . . . how serious had his injuries been? Where was he from? What had brought him to Hope Harbor? Why had he seemed so tense?

She couldn't ask any of those, though. Not straight out, anyway.

"He came across as very professional but a little prickly."

"Huh." BJ cocked her head. "I can't say I've ever noticed that, although he does tend to be quiet and reserved. And he does keep to himself. I imagine he's self-conscious about his scars."

"I can understand that. He told me they were war injuries."

"Seriously?" BJ tucked the clipboard under her arm, interest sparking in her eyes. "In all the months we've worked together, he's never mentioned that. I only know their source because Kyle, his foreman, let it slip once on a jobsite after Jon lost his grip on a balled tree he and another crew member were carrying. I wonder what prompted him to bring that up at your first meeting?"

Her reaction when they'd met, perhaps?

Hard as she'd tried to mask her shock, he'd picked up on it. The sudden stiffening of his shoulders, the resignation that dulled his eyes, the whitening of his knuckles as he'd gripped his measuring tool were proof of that.

"Actually, our paths had crossed once already under rather daunting circumstances." She gave BJ a quick recap of their encounter at the gate.

One side of the woman's mouth quirked. "I can see how a masked man carrying a chain saw on an isolated dead-end road could creep a person out. I wonder if he felt obligated to offer an explanation because he scared you at your first meeting."

Ashley folded her arms and leaned against the carved newel post at the bottom of the staircase, keeping her tone casual. "I have no idea." Nor did she have any idea what had prompted his remark about love near the end.

But no way was she bringing *that* up.

"Well, you may find out why he was so forthcoming if you end up hiring him. You'll leave the house key under the mat by the front door for me?"

"Yes. I'm meeting with Rose this afternoon, and I'll alert her you'll be stopping by."

"Watch for a report and preliminary estimate by the end of next week. It may take me a while to get final numbers, depending on how fast vendors respond and how much work I determine has to be done after I give the place a thorough inspection."

"I understand. Thanks for stopping by today."

Grinning, BJ pulled her truck keys from her jeans. "Believe me, it was my pleasure. I've been curious about this house for years. It was a treat to be able to see it up close, inside and out. Take care, and safe travels home tomorrow."

Ashley followed her to the door and continued onto the porch as the other woman strode down the walk and slid behind the wheel of her truck. Once it disappeared from sight around the bend that led to the leafy tunnel, she dropped onto the top step and wrapped her arms around her legs.

The past three days had been busy but productive. All that was left on her agenda before driving north to the airport early tomorrow morning was her meeting this afternoon with Rose, who'd kept herself scarce since their first chat over tea and scones.

Strange how fate had brought them together. A recluse and a woman on the rebound, separated in age by almost fifty years yet both wanting to start a new chapter in their lives.

Ashley propped her elbows on her knees and rested her chin in her palms as two seagulls circled overhead.

In many ways, Rose was as much of an enigma as Jon Gray. What did she do with herself here, day after day, with no one for company but seagulls and pelicans and the dolphin that liked to frolic offshore?

Such a solitary, lonely life.

Her solitude was on the cusp of evaporating, however. The place would be buzzing with activity if the deal went forward.

A big if at this point, though, and becoming bigger by the day. Assuming the house passed BJ's inspection, the necessary changes to bring it up to ADA commercial code would be expensive. And her potential landscaper had already warned her his work didn't come cheap.

Maybe she'd bitten off more than she could chew.

Wouldn't be the first time, as Mom liked to remind her.

The two gulls swooped lower, as if eager to get a closer look at the strange creature with hope in her heart and stars in her eyes who could be setting herself up for an epic—and very expensive—fail.

Except she hadn't signed any contracts yet. If the numbers were too intimidating, she could pass on the deal. Find work somewhere else. Give up the fanciful dream the *Herald* article had breathed life into.

Spirits drooping, she pushed herself to her feet.

A job that had gone up in flames.

A romance that had crashed and burned.

An opportunity that had blazed brightly but could be poised to fizzle out.

How depressing was that?

"Ashley, honey, don't ever let anyone take away

your dreams. They're worth more than gold. Remember what Thoreau said. If you've built castles in the air, that's where they should be. Now put foundations under them."

As the encouraging words her father had once shared echoed in her mind, Ashley straightened her shoulders and lifted her chin.

Dad was right. She was not going to give up.

Yet.

So she'd march into that meeting with Rose with all the confidence she could muster.

And hope the woman didn't see through her façade of optimism to the doubts undermining the excitement that had sent her on a cross-country trek in pursuit of a dream that might fade away like a Hope Harbor mist.

Her potential partner was worried about money.

As Ashley waved goodbye from the loop drive and climbed behind the wheel of her rental car, Rose wrapped one hand around the carved post that supported the porch and leaned against it.

The young woman who'd spent the past few days consulting with experts and soliciting bids hadn't voiced her concern, but subtext was easy to read if one listened with the eyes and heart.

How sad that the fate of so many dreams rested on the almighty dollar.

Thank goodness the trust fund Grandfather had left her—set up to prevent a husband from ever touching a dime, praise the Lord—and the sizeable bequest from Papa ensured she would never have to worry about money for the rest of her life.

Not to mention the extra buffer provided by her other source of income.

Ashley waved out the window as she approached the exit, and Rose's lips curved up as she responded.

Such a lovely young woman. And she didn't have to fret. If the vendors she'd consulted, all checked out and approved by David after a quick email from his favorite client, came back with bids that were out of her range, the agreement could be adjusted.

The rental car disappeared into the greenery, and Rose returned to the foyer. After locking the front door and detouring to the drawing room for her sweater, she continued through the house to the back, where the view was always a balm to the soul.

Pausing in the middle of the stone terrace, she surveyed the velvet-green lawn that dropped off sharply to the water, the ever-present boom of waves against the sea stacks muted behind the caw of seagulls soaring on the thermal wind currents overhead.

Perhaps she was being foolish, not creating a nonprofit entity that would assume control of the property under her management until her death, as David had advised. But if she'd chosen that course, the home to generations of Fitzgeralds would be run by strangers who came and went after she was gone. Who had no personal investment in or connection to Edgecliff. Who regarded their work here as a job and Edgecliff as their employer.

In the end, of course, it could come to that if Ashley got cold feet.

But she'd do everything in her power to pave the way for their partnership. Then she'd place it in God's hands. For as Papa had always said, if something was meant to be, it would happen.

A few dark clouds scuttled across the sky, obscuring the setting sun for a moment and adding a chill to the breeze.

Rose shivered and pulled her sweater tight around her body. The capricious coastal weather appeared to be on the verge of turning.

With one last survey of her domain, she reentered the house. Tea cleanup and dinner prep next, followed by an hour with Allison while her chicken baked in the oven. That would brighten her spirits despite the sun's sudden game of hide-and-seek.

And after her evening meal was finished, she'd wander over to the caretaker's cottage and end her day with the perfect companion.

Lucy Lynn.

6

"If I didn't know you, I'd think those dark circles under your eyes were evidence of heavy partying over the weekend. But since I do know you, I'm guessing you spent your so-called free time burning the midnight oil."

At Kyle's greeting bright and early Monday morning, Jon slid from behind the wheel of his truck, stifled a yawn, and scanned the jobsite. No sign yet of the other two crew members.

"I did put in a few extra hours." He reached back into the truck for his work gloves. "The bid for the Edgecliff job has a ton of moving parts."

"You really think the owner and her potential partner are going to shell out the big bucks it will take for the sort of work you told me about last week?"

"No idea. And it's a boatload of money, no matter how I slice and dice the numbers. But I want that job."

"Some outfits would cut corners to win a bid like this."

"Not my style."

"I know. And I agree taking the easiest or cheapest route is bad policy. A stunt like that may get you short-term results, but it will bite you in the long term. If I can help you out with anything at this early stage, let me know."

Jon began to close the truck door. Hesitated.

Should he pull Kyle into the bid process?

Sharing numbers with the crew wasn't SOP, but his foreman's jobsite input was often astute. And from everything he'd observed, the man was programmed for efficiency. Hadn't he come up with a clever idea that allowed them to reduce costs on their last job by 10 percent without sacrificing one iota of quality?

Decision made, Jon reached back into the cab and pulled out the draft of the proposal he'd labored over throughout the weekend, along with the notes he'd jotted during and after the tour of the grounds with Ashley.

If he wanted to give his foreman more responsibility, what better place to begin than by asking for his up-front input on a project that was vast in both scope and prestige?

"Why don't you read this over? See if you spot any major errors or opportunities. After all the hours I've put in on it, the numbers are beginning to blur on me. I could use a set of fresh eyes."

Kyle gave the papers Jon held out a once-over. "Are you sure? I mean, I'm usually a dirt-under-the-fingernails kind of guy. People have always tapped me for physical, not mental, work."

"Not to downplay your considerable contributions in sweat equity, but from what I've seen you also have a sharp mind."

A flush suffused Kyle's cheeks, and he shoved his fingers into the back pockets of his jeans. "I only have a GED, Jon. I never studied business and economics, like you did. And I don't have your fancy degrees in horticulture or landscape design."

"Don't discount on-the-job training. I've learned more in the real world than I ever did in school, even if my academic credentials did open doors. And one of the biggest lessons I learned was not to pass up opportunities." Jon waved the papers in front of him. "Going once, going twice—"

Kyle snatched the sheets and motioned toward two cars that were parking nearby. "The guys are here. We're ready to roll. You want me to look at this over lunch?"

"I'll get them going while you read through it. Find a quiet spot, and don't rush."

"Okay. I'll give it my best shot."

Jon started to turn away, but a hand on his arm stopped him.

"Thank you."

Kyle's choked words of gratitude, along with the deep appreciation in his eyes, tightened Jon's throat.

"I'm the one who should say thanks—and more often. You do great work. I'm lucky to have you."

He called up a grin. "Now take a gander at that and be ready to give me your two cents. You can leave the paperwork on the seat of my truck after you finish."

"I'm on it, boss."

Forty-five minutes later, when Kyle rejoined the crew, Jon waved toward several potted rhododendron bushes on the far side of the yard. "Let's get those in the ground while the guys finish up this bed."

He didn't bring up the bid until they'd hauled the bushes across the yard and picked up shovels. "Okay. Give me your top line." He positioned his shovel and pressed down.

"The job is big."

"The biggest I've ever tackled."

"You think the four of us can handle it?" Kyle put his shovel to work too.

"Not in Ashley's timeframe."

"Ashley?"

Warmth crept up his neck, and Jon focused on the hole he was digging. "Rose Fitzgerald's potential partner."

"Yeah, I know who you mean. You mentioned her name last week. But usually you keep it more formal with clients."

That was true. And he'd continue to be more businesslike with her in person.

But in his mind, she was Ashley. Had been from the moment she'd placed her slender fingers in his hand and given him a firm shake in front of Edgecliff.

"I'm talking to you, not her." He sank the blade of the shovel deep into the fertile earth. "Back to your question. She wants to be up and running ASAP. I'll have to bring on a couple more people. I was hoping to expand the crew at some point anyway."

"What about after this job is over, assuming we get it?"

"The Edgecliff project should help the business grow. As it is, I have to refuse too many bids because I don't have the personnel to get the work done in a timely manner. But that doesn't happen often enough to justify new hires. Adding to the crew shouldn't be a problem if we get this job, and more people on staff will also allow me to go after not only more, but bigger, projects. What else struck you?"

Kyle dug out another shovelful of dirt. "I like how you're proposing to salvage a fair number of the existing plantings rather than start from scratch. The rhododendrons, for example. Pruning them and stripping away the berry vines that are choking them rather than replacing the bushes will save your client serious dough."

"I know. The rhodies at Edgecliff have been neglected, but these babies"—he toed the one beside him—"can live for hundreds of years. Besides, antique plants go with an antique house."

"Makes sense." Kyle turned over another shovelful of dirt. "I liked your ideas for the planting bed in the middle of the loop road in front of the house, and I agree the gardens on either side of the walk leading to the porch should be colorful. First impressions and all that. But why not use some hostas there instead of all annuals? If you interspersed them with hardy annuals for season-long blooming, the client wouldn't have to replant everything each year. A little more expensive up front, but a cost saver in the future."

Also less maintenance in the long haul.

"Excellent idea. Anything else?"

As they dug and planted, Kyle offered several other suggestions that proved he had more to offer than dirt-under-the-fingernails type work, as he'd called it.

"I do have one final comment." Kyle finished filling in around his last bush, set the edge of the shovel blade on the ground, and rested one hand on top of the handle. "I'm not a numbers guy, but the prices seem on the low side."

That was true—and it wasn't surprising Kyle had picked up on it. While his foreman hadn't been privy to previous bids, the man had been working for him long enough to have a feel for the cost of both labor and materials.

Jon loosened the last rhododendron in its pot and removed it. "They're lower than usual, so our margin will be minimal. But the job should be worth a fortune in promotional value."

"Who's paying for all the renovations and restoration?" Kyle began spreading mulch around the bushes.

"Ashley didn't share those details with me."

Given her comments, though, at least a portion of the money was coming out of her pocket—and she didn't have limitless funds. Another incentive to pare the numbers back as much as he could.

Which his foreman didn't need to know.

"So how old is this Ashley?" Kyle sent him a sidelong glance.

Uh-oh.

This could get sticky.

"On the young side." He began loosening the roots with his fingers.

"How young?"

"Does it matter?"

"Not in terms of the job. I was just curious."

Jon bit back the *why* hovering on the tip of his tongue.

In light of Kyle's concern last week about his boss's hermit-like habits, the answer was obvious, if absurd. Kyle had seen him without any of his concealing paraphernalia. He, of all people, should realize the futility of harboring any far-fetched notions about matchmaking.

As the silence lengthened, Kyle arched an

eyebrow at him. "So is her age a state secret, or what?"

"We didn't exchange personal data." He pulled a twisted root free from the gnarled mess.

"An estimate would work."

The persistence he'd always admired in his foreman was coming back to bite him.

And the more he played dodgeball, the more suspicious Kyle would get.

"Thirtysomething." He kept his tone casual as he continued untangling knotty roots.

"Pretty?"

Oh yeah.

"That would be a fair assessment."

"Nice?"

"Pleasant." After she'd gotten over the shock of seeing his scars.

"Maybe you should lower the price even more."

He frowned at his foreman as he placed the rhodie in the hole and spread out the roots. "Why would I do that?"

"Working with this woman could have personal as well as promotional value. She may be able to coax you out of your cocoon."

Enough.

Gritting his teeth, Jon stood, jammed his shovel into the wheelbarrow of mulch, and swung it toward the newly planted bush, sending chunks flying Kyle's direction.

"Hey!" The other man jumped back.

"Sorry. You may want to step back, or you could end up with a faceful of my bark."

The man smirked. "Which, as I've learned, is worse than your bite. I'll go check on the guys."

"You do that."

Kyle sauntered off, shovel slung over his shoulder, whistling an off-key rendition of an old Sinatra classic.

Very funny.

But contrary to what Kyle thought, Ashley Scott hadn't gotten under his skin.

Yes, she was pretty. Charming. Engaging.

Yes, she'd awakened long-suppressed hormones that had kept him awake too many nights since they'd met.

Yes, she'd reminded him how lonely he was, despite Daisy's agreeable company.

But she was also off-limits.

All women were off-limits.

An image of the horror and disgust on Melinda's face when she'd come to visit him in the hospital strobed through his mind. She may not have broken up with him that day, but he'd known the Dear Jon letter was coming. It had just been a matter of time.

And not all that much time either. Less than two weeks. The actual note had been almost anticlimactic.

Jon filled in the hole with dirt, spread mulch around the base of the plant, and went in search of a hose to water the bushes. They'd need to be coddled after the shock of having their roots ripped apart. Watched over closely until they adapted to their new surroundings.

Not a bad parallel to his own situation five years ago.

Thank God he'd had Laura in those early, traumatic days. Without his sister's steadying hand and constant calls and visits, he might have given up. As Cal had.

His stomach twisted.

The world had lost a fine man the day Corporal Cal Mueller decided to leave all the pain and heartache and bleakness behind after the grievous injuries he'd suffered.

That kind of darkness could suck you in if there was no one to extend a lifeline, as Laura had for him.

Of course, there was also a downside to having a loving sister.

Now she thought she had carte blanche to butt into his life and offer advice.

Lips flexing, he soaked the plants. His kid sister was one of a kind.

Much as he loved her, though, no way was he ever mentioning Ashley during their conversations, whether he got the job or not. If Kyle had picked up on his interest, Laura would home in on it like metal to a magnet. In matters of the heart, she had weird ESP.

After stretching out the watering as long as he could, he rejoined the crew.

Thankfully, Kyle didn't bring up the Edgecliff job again or make any further insinuations about Ashley.

Yet Jon couldn't get either out of his mind.

Winning that job would be the break he'd been hoping for. The one that would put Greenscape on the map, draw in new clients, and set him up for long-term success.

As for Ashley—any man would have a hard time forgetting her. Beauty aside, she radiated energy and enthusiasm and hope. Her animation as she'd talked about her plans for Edgecliff had set off sparks in the air around her, and in her vivacious presence, impossible dreams had seemed within grasp.

Like finding a woman to love who could overlook all of his liabilities.

As if.

Gritting his teeth, he grabbed a hand trowel. Dropped to his knees. Jabbed the pointed blade into the garden soil.

If Greenscape got the job, Ashley would be his client. Nothing more. To hold out hope for anything beyond that was foolish. A beautiful woman would never want a man like him. He'd made his peace with that long ago, and letting a chance encounter disrupt his hard-earned serenity just because a bout of loneliness had left him vulnerable would only make his life miserable.

He plucked a lantana from the tray of annuals, set it into the hole, and mounded soil around it. With a bit of TLC, it should thrive here on the Oregon coast.

As he had, for the most part. Even without much TLC.

Yet as he watched Kyle pause to smile at his cell and take a quick call, it was impossible to deny the truth of what the man had said last week.

Having a special woman to come home to would brighten his days.

But wishing for things that could never be was an exercise in frustration. It would take a miracle for someone like Ashley to notice him for the right reasons.

And miracles had been in short supply since the horrendous day in Kandahar when life as he knew it had changed forever in the blink of an eye.

7

....

Ouch, ouch, and ouch.

Ashley lined up the three documents on the table in front of her, one beside the other.

BJ's bid, which had arrived an hour ago.

The three-day-old bid from Greenscape.

Her latest bank statement, showing the current balance.

Bottom line? Her grand plan wasn't going to work.

Even with Rose's 50 percent contribution for repairs and improvements, she didn't have the money to take this on. Close, but not quite— especially after factoring in living expenses. Granted, they'd be minimal if she took up residence in the apartment over the carriage house. Only food, gas for her car, adequate insurance. But she had to keep a modest amount in reserve to cover those items until Edgecliff was up and running.

So much for the fragile dream that had led her on an expensive wild goose chase to the West Coast.

Vision blurring, she gathered up the printouts on the table. Staring at the numbers wasn't going to change them, and there was nothing to question in BJ's thorough report or Jon's detailed and cost-conscious plans. Nor was there any obvious fat to trim.

Time to break the news to Rose.

Fighting back a wave of dejection, she opened her email, positioned her fingers over the keys, and—

Her cell began to vibrate on the table beside her, and she glanced at it.

Mom.

Dang.

Could her timing be any worse?

But on the plus side, a brief chat with her mother would give her an excuse to put off writing the thanks-but-no-thanks note to Rose for a few more minutes.

She picked up the phone. "Hi, Mom."

"Is that contract you sent me on the level?"

Ashley squinted at the blank email on her screen. "What?"

"The contract with the Fitzgerald woman. I had my attorney review it, and his comments landed in my inbox ten minutes ago. The terms spiked his suspicion meter as much as they did mine."

Double dang.

She should never have sent her mother the agreement Rose had proposed, despite Mom's insistence that more eyes on it were better than less.

"Why would you be suspicious? Everything's weighted in my favor."

"Exactly. Why on earth would this woman leave a stranger her half of a valuable property upon her death?"

"She doesn't have any family, and she wants the legacy of Edgecliff to continue with someone who has a vested interest in the estate."

"Oh, Ashley. No one does that. I think you're being played for a sucker. Like in that old movie . . . what was it? Oh yes. *The Money Pit*, with Tom Hanks. Have you ever seen it?"

"No."

"Well, this seemingly respectable older woman sells him and his girlfriend a house that appears too good to be true. And it is. It looks wonderful from the outside but is crumbling on the inside. She gives them a sob story about hating to part with it, which they fall for hook, line, and sinker, only to have one disaster after another hit. It was a total scam."

"This isn't a scam, Mom. Rose isn't like that."

"Tom Hanks and his girlfriend didn't think that older woman was either."

"That was fiction."

"Life imitates art. And it would be worse if it happened in real life."

Ashley leaned back and studied the crack in the kitchen wall of her apartment. The one her landlord had been promising to fix for months. "The house isn't falling apart. I've got the report in front of me from a very qualified contractor who did a thorough inspection. And while the attorney I consulted in Hope Harbor agreed the contract is unusual, he saw no red flags."

"Oh, sweetheart, he's a small-town lawyer. I'll bet he doesn't have any experience with these sorts of deals."

"He may live in a small town now, but he used to work for a major law firm in Portland that represented international corporate clients." She named the firm Eric had mentioned early in their meeting, when he'd given her a brief overview of his background. Perhaps to assuage any doubts *she* might harbor about the qualifications of a small-town attorney.

That news appeared to placate her mother.

"I do recognize that firm. It's a decent credential, so it's possible he knows what he's doing. But why would this woman be that generous? People don't do such things."

Maybe not in Silicon Valley.

But not everyone marched to the beat of the same drummer, and Rose had her reasons. Even if her mother would never understand them.

All of that, however, was a moot point at this stage and not worth arguing about.

"It doesn't matter, Mom. I got the bids for the work that would have to be done. I can't swing it."

A few seconds of silence passed.

"I know you're disappointed, Ashley, and I'm

sorry for that. But to be honest, I'm relieved you're not going through with this. There are too many strange aspects to the whole setup. You'll find another job you like, I'm certain of it. Or why not go back to school? Get an MBA. Launch a new career that has a decent amount of security and pays more than a pauper's wage. If you want to think about that, I'd be happy to loan you the tuition money. That way you wouldn't have to dip into your inheritance."

Sad but not surprising that her mom would offer to fund further education in a field she viewed as more stable and lucrative but hadn't asked how short of funds her daughter was for her dream project or offered to loan her the difference for that.

"I appreciate the thought, Mom, but I'm happy with my career in history. I'll find another job."

A sigh came over the line. "If you change your mind, the offer stands."

"Thanks."

"You want to come out in a few weeks for a visit? I can send you a ticket. A long weekend, maybe? We could go to the theater, the museums, eat out. I'll take you to my new favorite restaurant."

Where Mom would spend half the meal responding to work emails, like she had during their last get-together.

"Let me see where I am in my job search."

"All right. Just give me a little notice so I can clear my schedule. In the meantime, take care of yourself. Love you, sweetie."

"Love you back."

A true statement.

Even if she and her mother didn't have the kind of close relationship she'd shared with Dad, Mom loved her in her own way.

After saying goodbye, she set the cell on the table and positioned her fingers on the keyboard again.

It was time to let go of her dream.

Swallowing past the tightness in her throat, she began typing.

Dear Rose, I'm very sorry to have to tell you that . . .

• • •

. . . based on the attached bids, which I believe are fair, the necessary work is beyond my means. I'd hoped the funds I had would be sufficient and am deeply disappointed and sad that I can't manage the financial commitment.

Thank you for all your kindness and consideration during my visit and for the generous terms in the agreement you offered. I hope and pray you find someone else who can help you accomplish your goals for Edgecliff.

It was an honor and privilege to have had the opportunity to meet you and to visit your beautiful home and property. I will never forget the hours I spent there.

Wishing you all the best.

As she finished Ashley's email, Rose rested her elbows on her desk and interlaced her fingers.

The note wasn't a surprise, not after the young woman's obvious concern during their last meeting. The contractors must have warned her the bids would come in higher than she expected.

She opened the attachments. Read them. Jotted a few notes on the tablet beside her.

Then she picked up the phone and called David.

After a brief hold, he came on the line. "Good afternoon, Rose. How can I help you today?"

"It appears we'll have to get creative in my agreement with Ashley Scott."

He listened while she explained the situation and her proposed solution.

"Your idea may work, Rose, but I'd like to see the bids you have and think this through over the holiday weekend. The office will be closed Monday, but I can be back in touch Tuesday."

"That's fine. I want your honest assessment of this."

"Always." A beat ticked by. "This young woman must have made quite an impression on you."

"She did. Her résumé is outstanding, and her letters of reference were all very complimentary. I believe she'd bring commitment and enthusiasm to her role at Edgecliff."

"You seem determined to make this work, no matter what it takes."

"I wouldn't go that far, but I do believe in providence. And I'm willing to make concessions and meet her more than halfway. She brought new energy to Edgecliff while she was here, and this place could use a healthy dose of that." She picked up a pencil and doodled on the pad beside her.

"You do realize how much her plans will change the dynamics of your life. You'll lose much of your quiet and privacy."

"After seven years, I've had enough quiet to last a lifetime. Not that I'm planning to wander far outside the gates of Edgecliff, but seeing a few more people, even from a distance, holds a certain appeal. As for privacy, the caretaker's cottage will remain my domain. If I want to get away from people, all I have to do is close the door."

"You know, it may not be a bad idea to mingle once in a while. It has to be lonely out there, now that your father is gone."

She continued to doodle, mouth curving up. "Lucy Lynn keeps me entertained."

"That's not the same."

"It's enough, David. I appreciate your concern, but I'm accustomed to being by myself. I'm content to watch life from the sidelines."

"I'm sure you know what's best for yourself, Rose. You always have. Go ahead and send the bids and I'll be back in touch soon. Happy Fourth of July."

"Likewise, David. And thank you. You're a gem."

Once they ended the call, Rose forwarded Ashley's email to him, then typed a response to her future partner asking for a few days to consider the matter.

David would come back with sound suggestions, plus a few warnings, and she'd listen to them all. He always gave her comments serious and thoughtful attention.

But Ashley had lit a fire in her for this project, and it was going to happen.

Because while her high school days were long past, the Resolute Rose nickname that had appeared under her picture in the yearbook was as spot-on now as it had been all those decades ago.

This was so lame.

As the thump of hammering and the high-pitched hum of an electric saw filled the air on the quiet residential Hope Harbor street, Jon braked behind BJ's truck. Based on the cacophony of construction noise, her current house renovation project must be in full swing.

But just because he'd happened to spot her truck as he stopped at the corner didn't mean he should track her down to see if she'd heard anything yet about the Edgecliff project.

After all, it was possible she hadn't submitted her bid yet. Not everyone would labor over the weekend crunching numbers, as he had. Nor work late on a bid Monday night, as he had. But incorporating Kyle's input had taken a while, and he'd wanted to get the proposal sent off at the crack of dawn Tuesday morning.

He ought to be patient. Ashley would contact both of them once she'd made a decision.

As he lifted his foot off the brake to drive away, BJ came out the front door of the house, a piece of crown molding in hand. She spied him at once and detoured his direction, depositing the decorative millwork on two saw-horses en route.

"Hey, Jon." She lifted a hand in greeting. "You looking for me?"

"No. I was passing by and noticed your truck. Sounds busy in there." He motioned toward the house.

"We're reconfiguring the floor plan to accommodate a master bedroom suite, plus adding a sunroom. A medium-sized project—but nothing like the Edgecliff job would be."

Lucky for him she'd introduced the very topic he wanted to discuss.

"Heard anything on that yet?" He tried for a nonchalant tone.

"Nope. I don't expect to for a few days. I didn't send my bid off until this morning. It was a bear to put together, with all the vendors and suppliers I had to contact. You send yours in yet?"

"Tuesday."

"Wow." BJ's eyebrows rose. "You must have worked on it all weekend."

"Some." Like almost every waking hour.

"You think she and the owner are going to follow through on this? It's a pricey project."

"I don't know, but I got the impression they want to make it happen."

"Yeah. Me too. That house is phenomenal, isn't it?"

"I've only seen it from the outside."

"Well, trust me, they don't build 'em like that anymore." She tipped her head, scrutinizing him. "What did you think of Ashley?"

Jon rested his elbow on the window of his truck and tried not to squirm under her intent gaze. "She seemed pleasant."

"I agree. She mention any family to you, or significant other?"

That had come out of nowhere.

"No."

105

"I have a feeling she's unattached."

He tightened his grip on the wheel.

Why was everyone suddenly talking about relationship stuff?

"We didn't get into personal matters."

"Neither did we, but if you ask me, we could use a few more single women in town. The new guy up at Sandcastle Inn, for one, might like to meet her."

Jon frowned. "Don't you think matchmaking may be premature?"

"Not necessarily. He who hesitates, you know. Or so my husband always says whenever I'm vacillating over a decision." She smiled and motioned toward the house. "I should get back. If the Edgecliff job does pan out, we'll have to wrap this up fast. Ashley wants to jump on the project. See you around, Jon."

"Yeah. See ya."

While BJ strode toward the house, Jon put his truck in gear and aimed it toward his own jobsite.

At least BJ had answered his question about the status of the bids.

Unfortunately, she'd also passed on a bit of information that was as unsettling as waiting for word on the job. And for reasons far more elusive.

Why in blazes should he care if BJ tried to set Ashley Scott up with the guy at Sandcastle Inn, whoever he was? It wasn't as if his potential client had shown any interest in getting cozy with a certain landscaper—or ever would.

Jon flipped on his blinker as he approached the T-intersection. Braked at the stop sign. Hesitated.

He ought to turn right and get back to the jobsite. Lunch was over.

But he was the boss. If he needed a break to straighten out his head, he could take one. Like a quick detour to Pelican Point lighthouse.

Without further debate, he flicked his turn signal the other direction and swung left.

And if fate was kind, the fresh air, brisk breeze, and wide-open view on the headland would chase away his disconcerting jumble of emotions that were as tangled as the root balls of the rhodies he and Kyle had planted on Monday.

8

. . . .

Wow.

Double wow.

Ashley closed her eyes. Counted to three. Opened them again. Reread the email from Rose, containing a summary of the proposed new terms.

Terms that would allow the project to go forward.

Changing the profit split from seventy-thirty to sixty-forty seemed like a more than fair trade-off for Rose's willingness to fund 70 percent of the improvements instead of half. But it would be prudent to let Eric Nash weigh in before committing.

First, however, a quick response to the email that had done more to dazzle her than the distant fireworks she'd watched from her tiny balcony last night.

Yes!!!!! I absolutely want to reconsider. Let me talk to the attorney you recommended in Hope Harbor and I'll get back with you ASAP. I can't thank you enough for your willingness to find a creative solution to the problem.

Once she sent that reply off, she fished Eric's business card out of her Edgecliff file folder and tapped in his number.

Fortunately, he was in the office and available.

"I wondered what was happening with your project. BJ spent the weekend checking her phone messages and email every five minutes."

"The holiday slowed the process down. She and Jon Gray are next on my call list. The bids were out of my ballpark, but there's been a new development."

He listened as she explained the compromise solution Rose had proposed, waiting until she finished to comment.

"This deal keeps getting sweeter and sweeter for you. I can't say I've ever heard of a negotiation quite like this one."

"My mother thinks it's too good to be true."

"Not necessarily. Rose keeps a low profile, but from what I understand, she's been quietly philanthropic in the town, I know she's stepped in on occasion to donate to one of the Helping Hands programs or write a check if either of the churches in town has a special need. She was also a major contributor to a festival the town had last year. All very low-key, with no fanfare. In light of her generosity, it doesn't surprise me she'd be willing to spend extra dollars for a project that means a great deal to her."

"Can you think of any reason I shouldn't sign the agreement?"

"I'll be happy to review the amended sections, but if the language is as straightforward as the original, I see no downsides—assuming you haven't gotten cold feet about jumping into such a huge undertaking."

"No cold feet. I'll email you the new version as soon as I hang up, and I'll give BJ a call."

"She'll be over the moon. I'll have to pick up a celebration treat at Sweet Dreams after work. Expect to hear back from me within the hour."

After a final thank-you, Ashley ended the call and tapped in BJ's number.

The call rolled to voicemail, so she left a message asking the woman to get in touch at her earliest convenience.

She struck out with Jon too. When that call also rolled to voicemail, she left a similar message.

What a bummer that neither had been available to hear her wonderful news.

But in light of how interested both were in the project, they'd call the instant they got her message.

Until then, she had plenty to do. Unless Eric found an unanticipated glitch in the revised agreement, all it would take to get her new life rolling was a signed agreement with Rose and their signatures on the bids. Both could happen before this day ended.

Meaning she should put together a to-do list pronto.

And right at the top?

Hire a moving company ASAP.

Not that this would be a big job for them. Her tiny one-bedroom apartment wouldn't take long to pack up. She could be out of here fast—and with no regrets.

For as much as she'd enjoyed working in a Tennessee antebellum mansion, she was more than ready to launch a new chapter in her life as part owner of a historic clifftop estate on the Oregon coast.

This was it.

As the Tennessee area code registered in his log of missed calls, Jon's pulse stuttered.

Funny.

While the seven days since he'd sent Ashley his bid had dragged by like molasses, all at once he was in no hurry to get the verdict.

But delaying the inevitable wouldn't change the outcome.

Taking a deep breath, he played the message back and moved behind his truck, out of sight of the rest of the crew. They could handle cleanup alone for once.

The message was short. Just a request for a return call. But did he detect an undercurrent of excitement in her inflection?

Or was that wishful thinking?

Only one way to find out.

He placed the call.

She answered on the first ring. "Jon! You got my message."

"Yeah. Sorry for the delay. We were into heavy-duty digging, and I didn't want to get mud all over—"

"It's a go!"

His heart lurched. "You mean we got the job?"

"Yes! Well, not officially yet. I have to have my attorney give me the final green light and finish the paperwork with Rose, but I think all of that is more of a formality. I should be able to sign your bid today. How soon can you dive in?"

He tried to think past the euphoria that was muddling his brain. "Um . . . I can get everything rolling within a week, I think. How many of the itemized projects are we doing?"

"All of them eventually, but some have higher priorities than others. Like the front walk, circle drive, and gazebo area. You'll have to coordinate with BJ on the gazebo. That's the first project I want her to work on. Depending on her schedule, you may be able to get to it fast."

As Ashley continued to enthuse about the plans, her words tumbling over each other, Jon listened with one ear while he tried to wrap his mind around the fact that a once-in-a-lifetime job had dropped into his lap like manna from above.

He frowned.

No. Scratch the Bible analogy. God's hand wasn't in this. It was serendipity. Nothing more than sheer luck. Like the subscription to the *Herald* that had led Ashley to Edgecliff.

Still, however it had come about, landscaping the grounds of Edgecliff would be a stellar addition to the Greenscape portfolio.

". . . in touch by phone."

He tuned back in to Ashley. "Sorry. I missed that last comment. Cell phone service here can cut in and out."

"I said I don't want to delay the work until I'm on-site. We can stay in touch by email and phone."

"That's how I often communicate, even with clients who are in town." His choice, for the most part. But he left that unsaid. "When are you moving out?"

"As soon as I can pack up my place. I'm anxious to get there and settle in, but I think I'll spread the trip out over three days since it's a long drive alone."

A solo cross-country drive?

That didn't sit well.

But voicing his reservations could be interpreted as chauvinistic. At least in today's cell phone world, help would be a call away if she ran into trouble.

"I agree it would be safer not to push yourself."

"To tell you the truth, though, I'm so pumped I think I could jump in my car right now and do the drive nonstop—with energy left over!"

At her infectious animation, Jon's mouth bowed. Leaning one shoulder against the side of the truck, he watched as two seagulls that were a bit far afield from their usual foraging grounds at the harbor circled overhead. "Save it up. You'll need every ounce with all the ambitious plans you have."

"Trust me, I have energy to spare. And an exciting project doesn't consume energy, it creates energy. I imagine you felt the same when you launched your business."

Not quite.

"To a certain degree. But landscaping wasn't in my original plans."

Scowling, Jon straightened up as the words fell out of his mouth.

What had prompted *that* admission?

He never talked about the shattered dreams that had forced him to find a new direction, far off his original course. Only with Laura had he opened up, on rare occasion. And only after a ton of pushing and prodding on her part.

"Really? What did you intend to do?" Ashley's tone remained chatty and conversational. "I know your company is new, but I assumed you'd always been in the field. Your academic credentials are impressive, and I saw on the background information you supplied with your bid that you worked with another landscaper in the Portland area."

"That was just to gain field experience while I compiled those credentials. My plan after I left the service was to go back to school for a master's degree."

"In what?"

He was getting in deeper and deeper—but how could he dig himself out of this hole without being rude to a new client?

"Foreign affairs."

"Whoa! That's about as far from landscaping as you can get. What did you want to do with your degree?"

"Get a job with the State Department. I had my sights set on the diplomatic corps."

"No kidding?" Her manner was still bubbly. "I imagine that would have been exciting. Why did you change direction?"

He worked a rock loose from the dirt with the toe of his boot and kicked it. Hard. "Diplomatic work requires face-to-face interactions. Negotiating with foreign nationals, assisting US citizens who are traveling overseas, doing presentations and programs, representing the US at all kinds of public events. It wasn't a good fit after . . . after I got out of the service."

In the silence that followed his explanation, he tightened his grip on the cell.

Ashley appeared to be an intelligent woman, and it didn't take a genius to read between the lines of what he'd said.

A career in the diplomatic service that focused on one-on-one interactions wasn't an option for a man whose distracting appearance would get in the way of dealing with US citizens who needed assistance, comfort, and guidance—or with foreign nationals who had to be persuaded or won over or influenced.

"So you went with a second-choice career." Her tone had grown pensive.

"Second choice at the time, but in hindsight an excellent fit." No way did he want her sympathy. "Outdoor work has always appealed to me. After I got the appropriate credentials, I applied for a small business loan and hung up my shingle. Turns out I love what I do. And I couldn't have picked a more beautiful spot to live than the Oregon coast."

After a moment, she spoke again. "It's strange how unexpected events can lead us in directions we would never have anticipated, isn't it?"

As her quiet question hung in the air between them, the two gulls landed a few feet away and snuggled close together, watching him.

Her comment could refer to his war wounds or the fire at the place she'd worked, but a poignant undertone hinted that it wasn't only about either of their altered career trajectories.

"Are you talking about the fire?" If there was a more subtle approach to probe for information, it eluded him.

"That's one example." When she continued, the bounce was back in her voice. "Now I should let you get back to work. As soon as I have the green light, I'll text you."

She wasn't going to share anything more. And who could blame her, if her reference to an unexpected event was personal in nature? The two of them were almost strangers, after all.

"Thanks. I'll watch for it."

"And I'll look forward to working with you to give Edgecliff the gardens it deserves."

"It will be my pleasure, Ms. Scott."

"Let's dispense with formalities. Ashley is fine. Talk to you soon."

Jon signed off, slowly pocketing his phone as a smile tugged at his lips.

Working with Ashley would, in fact, be a pleasure. Her enthusiasm was contagious, and while she'd never be anything more than a client, spending time in the presence of a vibrant, beautiful, insightful woman would be a treat after two long, lonely years with only Daisy for company.

When he turned to rejoin the crew, Kyle was watching him with a wise-guy smirk from a few feet away.

"I take it that was Ashley."

Jon called up his most intimidating expression. The one he'd used whenever his squad got out of line. "Were you eavesdropping?"

"Not on purpose. I came over to tell you we finished the cleanup, and the guys took off. I caught the tail end of the conversation."

Bad news.

The tail end would have been sufficient to fan the flames of Kyle's sudden propensity to play Cupid, given the warmth that had crept into his voice as they ended their conversation.

Best to play this low-key, however.

"We got the job."

"I picked that up—among other things."

Jon planted his fists on his hips. If Kyle wasn't going to let this go, he'd have to address the situation. "What does that mean?"

"You sounded very friendly on the phone. Happy, even."

"Who wouldn't be happy, after being awarded a job like this?"

"Uh-huh." The other man grinned. "Unless you have anything else for me to do, I'm gonna take off. Sarah wants to drive up to the lighthouse tonight and catch the sunset."

"We're done for the day."

"You want to join us?"

Jon gave him a get-real look. "Are you kidding? Your bride would have my head if I intruded on such a romantic outing."

"Who said anything about romance? There's always a large contingent of locals and tourists up there in the summer to catch the best show in town—which you'd know if you ever ventured out in the evening and mingled a little. You must have romance on the mind."

"Go home, Kyle."

The man shrugged. "You're the boss. If you change your mind, though, give me a call." Jingling his keys, he walked to his car.

Jon waited until he pulled away, then slid behind the wheel of his truck and started the engine.

His foreman meant well, but his efforts were misguided. And his assumption about his boss's mindset was all wrong.

Romance wasn't on his mind. He could control his thoughts—more or less.

The problem was his heart.

That, it seemed, had a mind of its own.

9

As the organ launched into the final hymn for the Sunday service at Grace Christian Church, Ashley stood and sent a silent thank-you heavenward.

Tired as she was after the flurry of activity to close up her apartment, the ton of research she'd done on various wedding-and-special-event-related vendors in the Hope Harbor area, and the long solo drive across the country, everything had fallen into such impeccable alignment that it had to be divinely inspired.

And what more appropriate place to offer thanks than here, in the Almighty's house?

Once the last notes of the hymn died away, Ashley sat again in her pew while the congregants filed out. Anxious as she was to meet the Hope Harbor residents, the twelve days since Rose's new terms had sealed the deal had been nonstop. And her late arrival last night hadn't helped. Carrying on a lucid conversation in her present state of fatigue would be difficult, and first impressions mattered. It would be wiser to defer a meet and greet until she clocked a decent night's sleep.

When only a handful of people remained in the nave, she rose and headed toward the back. A few congregants were still in the vestibule, gathered in small groups, but she ought to be able to slip past them and—

"Good morning. Welcome to Grace Christian."

Drat.

So much for her discreet escape.

Tamping down her weariness, she turned to find the pastor approaching. "Thank you. It was a wonderful service."

"I'm delighted you joined us. Reverend Paul Baker. A pleasure to meet you." He extended his hand.

"Ashley Scott." She returned his firm handshake.

"Ah. It's nice to have a face to go with the voice from our phone conversation about Rose. What a pleasure to meet her new partner in person."

The taco chef who'd treated her to lunch on her last visit hadn't been kidding about the local grapevine.

"It appears news about the deal has preceded me."

A glint of humor appeared in his irises. "I doubt every single person in town is aware of it, but I expect a significant portion of the population is."

"Where did you hear it was a done deal?"

"From Marci Weber, the editor of the *Herald*. She ran into your contractor at the gas station, who mentioned she'd been tapped for the house updates. I imagine Marci will be in hot pursuit of a story once she hears you're . . . well, speak of the devil." He nodded toward a thirtysomething woman who was bearing down on them.

Ashley kept tabs on the redhead, who got waylaid by another congregant. "Given what I want to accomplish at Edgecliff, I'll take all the publicity I can get. It will generate both interest and customers."

"I doubt you'll have any trouble rounding up either. Edgecliff is legendary in these parts, and while I've never had the honor of visiting there, I understand the setting is sublime."

"It is. It's made for weddings. Or it will be, as soon as the gazebo is rebuilt and the gardens are in shape."

"I have to admit I was surprised by Rose's interest in such a project. Hard as I've tried to persuade her to attend services, she rarely leaves the property. And she never mingles with the townsfolk, despite repeated invitations to attend various events. Your powers of persuasion must be remarkable."

A man in a black shirt, black pants, and a Roman collar hustled toward them, the outside door closing behind him. "Better than yours, I imagine. Otherwise your congregation would be growing." A merry grin neutralized the jibe.

Reverend Baker shook his head. "My fellow cleric in town, Father Kevin Murphy from St. Francis." He folded his arms as the priest joined them. "He thinks he's funny. We try to humor him."

"I *am* funny. Ask my parishioners. I told a hilarious joke in my homily this morning."

"Preaching is not a stand-up comedy routine."

"There's nothing wrong with a touch of levity." The padre's eyes twinkled. "Don't you think God has a sense of humor?"

"He must have. You made it to ordination, didn't you?"

"Ouch." The priest winced, licked his left index finger, and drew it through the air. "You're one up." Then he held out his hand as Ashley tried to smother a chuckle. "Welcome to Hope Harbor."

She introduced herself while returning his hearty handshake. "I just arrived last night."

"Oh yes. I know all about your association with Rose. Welcome!"

The minister studied him. "Who filled you in?"

"Rose."

Reverend Baker did a double take. "When did you two become confidantes?"

"Some people appreciate my humor. I chat with her on the phone now and then. But I've only been to tea there once."

"You've had tea at Edgecliff?" The minister gaped at him. "Why haven't you ever mentioned that?"

"A *priest* knows how to be discreet about private conversations." He flecked an imaginary speck of lint off the sleeve of his shirt. "Rose and I became acquainted three years ago when the wind ripped off most of our roof in that ferocious winter storm we had. She made a generous contribution toward a replacement."

"But she's not Catholic."

"I believe her charitable support is nonsectarian. A lovely woman. Ah, Marci." He turned to the *Herald* editor as she joined them. "How nice to see you."

"Likewise, Father. Reverend." After giving both men of the cloth a cursory nod, she introduced herself to Ashley. "I heard you'd arrived."

Was there anyone who hadn't?

"Last night. Late."

"I told Ashley you'd most likely want to do a story about her venture," Reverend Baker said.

"Yes. This is big news for Hope Harbor."

"I agree. And from what I saw during my visit, Edgecliff will make a superb wedding venue." The padre clasped his hands behind his back.

Reverend Baker hiked up an eyebrow. "I didn't think Catholics believed in outdoor weddings."

"We don't. We like to maintain a sense of the sacred and keep a clear focus on the sacramental nature of marriage. A church setting is more conducive to that. But as you know, I have a deep appreciation for the beauty of God's handiwork. Nature can be very spiritual."

"My friend here does have a way with plants."

Reverend Baker tipped his head toward the priest. "The meditation garden at St. Francis is worth a visit."

"I'll second that. It's beautiful." Marci pulled out her cell.

"Thank you both." Father Murphy gave a tiny bow. "You're welcome to visit anytime, Ashley. Like Rose's generosity, our garden is also nonsectarian."

"I'll stop by soon."

The minister touched her arm and motioned toward a door off to the side. "I hope you'll join us for coffee and doughnuts in the fellowship hall. Even though my Catholic comrade here claims St. Francis has superior doughnuts, he often manages to show up at our door on Sunday during the social hour after one of our services."

"I'm not here for doughnuts." The priest gave an indignant sniff. "I came to pick up my copy of the minutes from our last Helping Hands board meeting—which I believe you were supposed to send out? However, as long as I happen to be here while doughnuts are being served, I may detour that direction and sample one. Would you like to join me, Ashley?"

"Thank you, but after my marathon drive, settling into my quarters and a nap are my highest priorities."

"Understandable. Please tell Rose I'll be in touch."

"I'll do that."

"I hope to see you again next Sunday." Reverend Baker once more shook her hand.

"That's my plan."

"If you ever get tired of this guy's sermons"—Father Murphy waved a hand toward the minister—"don't hesitate to swing by St. Francis. I can usually be counted on to liven up my preaching with a laugh or two."

"You might use a few Bible verses instead of jokes." Reverend Baker took his arm and tugged him toward the side door.

"I use plenty of Bible verses."

"Try not to mix up Elisha and Elijah again."

The priest heaved a sigh. "You're never going to let me forget that, are you? I was still getting over the flu, and I . . ."

As they disappeared from view and their conversation faded away, Marci grinned. "They're a hoot, aren't they?"

"I'll say. They're not like any clerics I've ever met."

"I hear you. But they've been best buds ever since Father Murphy showed up on the reverend's doorstep during our pastor's first week in town years ago with a box of golf balls and invited him to play a round. From that day on, they've had a standing tee time every Thursday. So when can we schedule an interview?" She opened the calendar on her phone, finger poised.

This dynamo didn't waste a moment in pursuit of a story, as Reverend Baker had predicted.

"Soon. I want to get the word out as fast as possible to generate interest. Money is going to be flowing out at a mind-boggling clip, and I need to begin refilling the coffers."

"Does Tuesday morning work?"

"That should be fine."

"I'll come out around ten. I can't wait to visit the house again. Rose served me tea on my first visit, but I only got to see the drawing room."

"I'll give you the full tour."

"Fantastic. Do you think Rose will join us?"

"I'll ask, but don't get your hopes up. She made it clear she wants to be a silent and largely invisible partner in this enterprise. If she declines, though, I'd be happy to pass on a few questions and she could email you answers."

"That'll work in a pinch."

Ashley tried to stifle a yawn. "Sorry. It was a long trip out. If I didn't have to drive again for a year, I'd be happy."

"You won't have to drive much at all here. Everything is close in Hope Harbor, and Coos Bay isn't far away if you crave a bigger-town fix." She twisted her wrist and scanned her watch. "Oops. Gotta run. My husband's on duty with our three-year-old twins, one of whom has the sniffles, and I promised not to linger. See you Tuesday."

She dashed toward the exit, vitality pinging in her wake.

Ashley followed at a much slower pace. Too bad she couldn't absorb a smidgen of the *Herald* editor's energy. How strange to be dragging at this hour of the morning.

But she'd be back in top form by tomorrow, ready to tackle the multitude of items on her to-do list. First up? An in-person conference with BJ, who also had boundless energy, and the intriguing landscaper who'd won the bid to restore the Edgecliff grounds and who seemed somehow in need of restoring himself.

Not her problem, though. Jon Gray was a contractor, nothing more, despite the tidbit of personal information he'd shared about his career choice during their first long-distance call. But in light of his subsequent cool, somewhat aloof manner, that had been an aberration.

Which was fine.

Romance wasn't in her plans with anyone, let alone a scarred veteran who hid his face behind camouflage and his heart behind a high wall.

Maybe someday, after Edgecliff was up and running and the wounds Jason had inflicted on her healed, she'd risk another relationship.

But until then, she intended to keep her distance—emotionally, if nothing else—from any man who entered her orbit.

Especially men who were clear from the get-go that they had no interest in her.

"I had a feeling I'd find you out here on this sunny afternoon."

At the greeting, Rose shifted toward the familiar voice as Charley Lopez appeared around the side of the house. "Now isn't this a pleasant surprise. Please, have a seat." She motioned to the empty chair across from her at the table on the terrace.

"Are you certain I'm not intruding? I understand a transformation is afoot out here, and I wouldn't want to get in the way of progress."

"No work is done on Sunday. Do I smell tacos?"

"You do indeed." He swung the brown bag to and fro as he approached. "This was my last order of the day. They should still be warm. And I brought you a slice of Eleanor Cooper's legendary chocolate fudge cake too. She sent a piece over for me today, but I saved it for you. I believe chocolate is one of your few vices."

"You know me very well." She eyed the plate covered in plastic wrap as he set it on the table. "That looks delicious. Who's Eleanor Cooper?"

"A longtime resident. Wonderful woman. You'd like her. I'd be happy to introduce you if you'd like to venture into town."

She ignored that as she pulled a wrapped packet

129

from the bag. Inhaled. "This smells divine."

"The highest praise. Thank you." He took a seat. "There's a bottle of water in there too, along with a plastic cup. I know swigging isn't your style."

Typical Charley. Always thoughtful.

She extracted the water and cup and spread a napkin on her lap. "I've been expecting you to visit."

"Why is that?"

"Because you know me better than most around here do." She picked up a stray piece of avocado and tucked it back into the taco. "I assume you're surprised by my decision to let strangers traipse around Edgecliff."

The weathered skin beside his eyes crinkled. "Pleased would be more accurate. Perhaps one of these days I can convince you to come into town for a taco. If you don't want to meet Eleanor, you could share a bench on the wharf with my friends Floyd and Gladys."

"My decision to open up Edgecliff doesn't mean I've decided to socialize, Charley. My conversational skills are on the rusty side."

"Not that I've noticed. But Floyd and Gladys won't expect you to talk."

"Why not?"

"They're seagulls."

A chuckle bubbled up inside her.

That sounded like Charley. He had an affinity

with the animal kingdom, just as he had uncanny insights about people—along with a remarkable ability to instill trust.

After all, only Charley would have been able to charm his way into her refuge seven years ago with a smile, a bag of tacos, and a heart that seemed to understand her pain and disillusionment and grief and desire for solitude.

And only he would have been able to convince her how much of a treasure Lucy Lynn was.

But the subtle campaign he'd launched a few months ago to entice her back into society wasn't going to work.

"I appreciate the thought, Charley, but I'm happy here. I have everything I want."

"That may have been true when you came back here to live with your father, but circumstances change."

She chewed slowly as she mulled over his comment. "I'm eighty years old, Charley. My needs are few."

"Everyone needs companionship."

"I'm too old to make new friends."

"No one is too old to make friends. You've become friends with Ashley, haven't you?"

"That's a business arrangement." She opened her second taco.

"Is it?"

"We signed a contract. We're partners, not friends."

"Hmm." He gazed out over the sparkling indigo sea, toward the far horizon. "I can see why you'd be taken with her. She's quite charming."

"You've met her?"

"She stopped by the stand one day during her first visit. Well, look who's come to call."

Rose stopped eating as two seagulls swooped down and landed on the stone wall of the terrace. "That's odd. I don't believe I've ever seen a seagull come this close to the house."

"And I don't believe I've ever seen Floyd and Gladys wander this far south. If you won't go to them, it appears they'll come to you."

These were the gulls Charley had been talking about a few minutes ago?

Rose squinted at them. Near as she could tell, they were identical to every gull she'd ever seen.

"How do you tell one gull from another?"

"All of God's creatures have unique personalities. Plus, Floyd has a nick in his beak and a black spot on his head."

She inspected them again, but they were too far away to discern details.

"You must have excellent vision."

"Or just the ability to recognize friends. That has more to do with the heart than the eyes." He refocused on her. "Like how you felt drawn to Ashley."

"I never said I was drawn to her."

"You didn't have to. You and I have known

132

each other for quite a long while. It would take a special person to convince you to let strangers enter your world."

"It's the price I have to pay to bring joy back to Edgecliff."

"And perhaps to yourself?"

She finished her taco. "You're quite the philosopher today."

"I don't philosophize. I observe."

"And what do you observe in me?"

He rested his elbows on the table and linked his fingers. "I see opportunities and possibilities."

"What does that mean?"

"I'm not certain. I imagine time will tell. How are the tacos?"

She wiped any stray sauce off her lips with a napkin. "Delicious, as always. But more than I can eat in one sitting."

"Save the other one for later. But you have to sample Eleanor's cake." He withdrew a plastic fork from the bag.

"I suppose I could try one bite."

She opened the plastic wrap, broke off a small piece, and put it in her mouth. Rich flavor exploded on her taste buds. "My. Whoever this Eleanor is, she knows how to bake a chocolate cake."

"Eleanor has many talents—and a fascinating story. You'd enjoy hearing it."

"You could tell it to me."

"Stories are always best heard from the source." He gave the grounds a sweep. "Where's your partner today?"

"Sleeping, I expect. The poor girl was exhausted after her long drive. I saw her leave this morning. Church, I'm guessing. When she came back, she disappeared into the carriage house and hasn't reappeared." She motioned in the direction of the structure that was around the side of the main house and hidden from view.

"So you've had the place to yourself."

"Except for Lucy Lynn. And I enjoyed every minute of it." It was important for him to understand that despite his gentle prodding, she had zero inclination to rejoin society.

"Speaking of Lucy Lynn, may I visit with her while I'm here? Catch up on her latest escapades?"

"Of course. It's always a delight to welcome you to the cottage." She indulged in one more large bite of cake and rewrapped the remainder.

"Also a rare privilege, for which I'm grateful."

She rose, cake in hand, and took his arm. "Rare friends deserve rare privileges."

"Thank you for that." He picked up the brown bag.

"The thanks are all on my end. If it wasn't for you, I wouldn't have Lucy Lynn."

"And the world would be a bit less bright."

As they strolled toward the cottage, the two gulls flapped their wings, rose into the air, and flew toward the carriage house.

Charley watched them, his expression pensive. "Curious."

"How so?"

"I expected them to head back to sea." He placed his hand over hers. "I believe interesting times are ahead."

He changed the subject then, but it was hard to concentrate on the conversation, thanks to an unfamiliar tingle tickling her nerve endings.

Could it be nervousness?

No. It was impossible to be nervous in Charley's presence. The man radiated peace and serenity.

It was more like . . . anticipation?

Yes, that was it.

This was how she'd felt the day she'd been accepted into the conservatory and the whole world had brimmed with potential.

But that had been almost six decades ago, when youth had been on her side. Before a less-than-happy marriage and scandal and death had tarnished her dreams and snuffed out any thought of bright, shining possibilities.

Strange that Charley would have mentioned the notion of possibilities today. Especially since he'd seemed to be referring to more than the transformation of Edgecliff.

135

"After you, Rose." He paused at the door of the cottage she now called home.

She twisted the knob and stepped inside. "You'll notice quite a few differences. Once I decided to move in, I did a fair amount of redecorating."

"I appreciate this peek into your inner sanctum."

"Lucy Lynn wouldn't have it any other way." She ushered him toward the back of the cottage and began to fill him in on all the latest developments.

It was fun to chat about Lucy Lynn with Charley. And safe.

Because her taco-making artist friend knew how to keep secrets.

10

He was early, but Ashley was earlier.

Emerging from the greenery that shrouded the entrance to Edgecliff, Jon eased back on the accelerator.

The female figure was too far away to see clearly, but at six thirty in the morning, it had to be her. His crew wouldn't be here for another hour. Nor would BJ's. He wouldn't have risen at the crack of dawn either, if he hadn't wanted to take a few measurements in the gazebo area before BJ's people descended.

However, spending one-on-one time with Rose's partner hadn't been in his plans.

The first rays of sun peeking over the hills to the east gilded her slender form, and as she lifted her face toward the heavens, his pulse hitched.

Blast.

That kind of adolescent reaction was crazy.

It was also unprofessional, immature, pointless, and pathetic. Ashley Scott was his client.

Period.

Clamping his jaw shut, he pressed on the gas again.

He had to get a handle on his emotions. Shove any that were inappropriate into the darkest corner of his heart with all the others he'd stowed there over the past few years.

And he would.

Soon.

But since his misbehaving heart wasn't listening at the moment, that probably wasn't going to happen today. Until it did, all he could do was try to corral his unruly hormones.

Ashley turned as he swung into the circle drive, shaded her eyes against the sun, and lifted a hand in greeting. Rather than walk over to meet him as she had at their last encounter, she waited near the gazebo site while he parked, sipping from a lidded mug.

After tugging down his baseball cap, adjusting his sunglasses, and pulling up the scarf around his neck as high as possible, Jon slid from the cab. Clipboard in hand, he crossed the lawn to join her.

"Good morning." She smiled as he approached, the warmth in her tone chasing away the early morning chill. "I didn't expect to see anyone out here at this hour. Our meeting with BJ is at eight, right?"

"Yes. I wanted to get here early and take a few more measurements around the gazebo. What's your excuse for being out and about at the crack of dawn?"

She made a face. "I think I have jet lag—minus the jet. The time change must have messed with my circadian rhythm. If yesterday is any indication, I'll be dragging by six o'clock tonight even if I manage to sneak in a nap. On the plus side, I didn't have to commute to get here early, like you did."

"It's not much of a commute. I could walk it if I didn't have equipment to haul."

Her eyebrows rose. "You live around here?"

"Yes. Next house down on Windswept Way. I was walking home the day you saw me with the chain saw."

"Ah. Now your appearance out of nowhere and your disappearance down the road make sense. My nerves have yet to recover. A masked man with a chain saw is more than a little scary." A cute dimple dented her cheek.

He tried not to stare at it. "Sorry about that. But you'd have been more scared if I hadn't been wearing the mask." He motioned toward the gazebo area. "Why don't I go ahead and—"

"Are your scars really that bad?" She wrapped both hands around her mug as she asked the quiet question.

He froze.

So much for his attempt to move on to less personal subjects.

"Depends on your perspective." He forced up the corners of his mouth. "My sister says the shock value wears off fast, but she isn't exactly impartial." Nor did she have any idea how difficult it was to live with surreptitious peeks, shocked expressions, and sometimes outright gawking.

Especially for someone used to being stared at for far different reasons.

"Sometimes family members are more honest than strangers."

He took that opportunity to point the spotlight back at his client.

"You have opinionated siblings too?"

"No. Only child. But I have an opinionated mother who isn't thrilled with my new venture." She swept a hand over the house and grounds.

"What's her beef with it?"

"Not just with this. With my whole career choice. It's hard for a high-paid Silicon Valley executive to understand why anyone would be drawn to a low-paying job in history."

"I take it you two don't get along."

"On the contrary. For two people who live in different worlds and have different priorities, we have a decent relationship. I know Mom loves me, so I accepted long ago that she'd never understand my passion for this field. Do you get along with your sister?"

"In general."

"But you don't think she's being honest about the scars?"

They were back to that.

He gave a stiff shrug. "Her opinion is honest. I'm not certain it's valid."

"You could always ditch the disguise and see what happens."

His stomach clenched, and despite his effort to maintain a neutral inflection, a touch of resignation crept into it. "I know what would happen. They'd make people uncomfortable." Or worse.

"How can you be sure of that?"

The image of Melinda's sudden and total loss of color during their first meeting after the accident in the handful of seconds before she lost her lunch strobed across his mind.

"Experience."

Parallel creases appeared on Ashley's brow. "I can see how scars might shock people at first, but once they got to know you, your appearance would be less important."

She and Kyle must be on the same wavelength.

That's not how it had worked with Melinda, though, and she'd known him well before shrapnel ripped through him.

"What sounds logical in theory doesn't always pan out in real life."

"Mmm." She sipped from her mug as she regarded him. "I expect there's an element of vanity involved too."

Vanity?

Frowning, he pulled the brim of his cap lower.

He'd never been vain, even back when his appearance had mattered.

Had he?

No. Not that he could recall.

But could vanity be a factor in his decision to cut himself off from the world now? Had he become a hermit to keep other people from feeling awkward—or because he was self-conscious and embarrassed . . . and vain?

As the silence between them lengthened, pink spots bloomed on Ashley's cheeks. "Sorry. That was too personal. I don't know what came over me. In the future, I'll stick to my area of expertise and stop dabbling in psychology." She hefted her mug. "I need a refill. Would you like a cup?"

"No, thank you."

"Go ahead and take your measurements while I get another java infusion. Hopefully that will activate both my brain and my diplomacy. Be back in a few minutes."

With that, she pivoted and sped toward the house. As if she couldn't escape fast enough.

For a full minute after she disappeared around the side, toward the carriage house, Jon remained where he was, mind whirling.

What had just happened here?

One minute they'd been talking about land-scaping around the gazebo, the next about his scars and his rationale for masking up and maintaining a low profile.

Conversations like that weren't going to help him keep his distance from his new client.

Meaning they couldn't happen again.

But while he could continue to hide his physical wounds going forward, somehow Ashley had managed to unmask his invisible scars. The ones left by Melinda as well as the ones he'd inflicted on himself.

Like self-pity and isolation and loneliness and resignation and resentment and a host of other unhealthy emotions.

All the ones he'd stuffed away in that dark corner of his heart and tried to ignore while he told himself that despite all his trauma, he'd gone on to lead a productive life.

Which was true.

But it wasn't the life he'd envisioned. It lacked the human connection that infused a person's days with joy and laughter and love.

Jon exhaled. Removed his sunglasses. Massaged the bridge of his nose.

Maybe Kyle and Ashley and Laura were right.

Maybe hiding out here on Windswept Way with only Daisy for company was as disfiguring to his psyche as the scars were to his face and body.

Maybe he should begin reaching out. Test the water. See if he could establish a few tentative connections.

Not of the romantic variety, of course. It would take a special woman to see past the ugly evidence of his injuries to the man underneath.

A woman who probably didn't exist.

Yet as he slowly put his sunglasses back on and began taking measurements at the gazebo site that would host countless weddings in the years to come, a tiny spark of hope that refused to be extinguished flickered to life in his heart.

What on earth had gotten into her?

Hands braced on the sink in her new home above the carriage house bay that now held her car, Ashley took a long, slow breath of the salty air drifting in through the open window.

Bringing up Jon's scars had been a huge breach of etiquette, even if he'd cracked open the door with his remark that they were scary.

But she should have let that comment pass.

Why hadn't she?

Outside the window, a pair of gulls in close formation wheeled and dipped on the wind currents, out for a romp together on this beautiful morning. On the ground, two squirrels played a game of tag, zipping among the trees.

God's creatures enjoying each other's company and companionship.

She picked up her mug from the counter. Wandered over to the coffeemaker.

People were supposed to be like that too. It wasn't normal to cut yourself off from the world, as Rose and Jon had.

At least Rose was open to a bit more human interaction, or she wouldn't have signed on for the plan to welcome the public to Edgecliff on occasion.

Jon, on the other hand, showed no such inclination.

Sad. And oddly bothersome.

Huffing out a sigh, she filled her cup with the dark brew.

Why should she care about her landscaper's private life? After all, if he wanted to live in a Covid-like quarantine, complete with masks and social distancing, that was his business, not hers.

And in truth, his attitude wasn't difficult to understand despite her inappropriate remark about vanity. Anyone who'd suffered injuries that left scars even half as bad as he'd intimated his were could have their confidence shaken, and a bruised self-image was difficult to overcome.

As she well knew.

Memories of her senior prom came flooding back, and Ashley took a sip of coffee. Grimaced. Stirred in half a teaspoon of sugar to curb the bitter taste.

Strange how more than a dozen years later, thinking about that night could still make her wince. Yes, she'd gone through with the event and managed to act as if the hideous black eye from her rollerblading fall hadn't bothered her, but she'd cringed inside at every stare. Instead of her peers noticing her knockout dress and elaborate do and acrylic nails with glitter polish, her shiner had taken center stage.

What a disaster her prom had been.

But it did give her a tiny taste of what Jon lived with day after day.

Except unlike his scars, her eye had healed and life had returned to normal.

What if she'd had to keep the black eye forever?

Ashley shuddered.

Having to look at it every day in the mirror and endure the unwanted attention it would generate could have damaged her psyche. Driven her to live in a self-imposed exile, as Jon had done. Like her new business partner, the landscaper she'd hired had an understandable justification for keeping his distance from society.

And trying to push either Rose or Jon past their comfort level was wrong, no matter how altruistic her intentions.

If Rose wanted to hide out in the caretaker's cottage, as she'd been doing except for a quick visit late yesterday with a welcome plate of scones, so be it.

And if Jon wanted to keep people at arm's length, that was his choice—and his loss.

From now on she would refrain from venturing into restricted territory with either of them.

Mashing her lips together, she gripped her mug and marched out the door.

She was through being Miss Buttinski.

Since Jon was still measuring when she returned, she waited off to the side until he finished and joined her.

"Not much to see yet, is there?" She motioned toward the concrete pad that would form the foundation for the gazebo, calling up a too-bright smile.

He didn't return it.

"The concrete has to dry and set before they can begin construction. That takes about ten days."

"BJ told me that. Impatience is one of my faults."

"I haven't picked up many of those yet." Before she could digest that comment, he flipped open a folder and pulled out a schematic of the gazebo and gardens. "I had a few additional ideas for the landscaping to share with you. Does now work?"

"Absolutely."

"I know you wanted a short, manicured boxwood hedge around the gazebo, but Japanese holly may be a wiser choice. Boxwoods don't like being this close to the ocean. We can put lower-growing annuals in front of the hedge for continuous color. It would look like this." He angled the printout her direction, and she moved closer.

As he continued to explain his vision for the site that would be the location for many of the weddings at Edgecliff, Ashley tried to concentrate.

But the scent of a very masculine aftershave swirling around her was super distracting.

So were the long, lean fingers holding the diagram inches in front of her and the broad shoulder that brushed hers as Jon pointed out the various plant groupings while he discussed his proposed alterations from the bid.

He had a pleasant voice. Mellow. Deep. Calm. Composed. All qualities that had been evident during their phone conversations, but much more apparent in person, with him standing mere inches—

". . . unless you disagree?"

Whoops.

How was she supposed to answer a question she hadn't heard?

Curses on her inappropriate mind wandering.

"Um . . . sorry. I zoned out for a second." She lifted her mug. "The caffeine is taking a while to kick in today."

Lame—but it was all she could come up with on the fly.

Thankfully, he didn't question her explanation.

"I was saying that I think we should widen the stone path leading to the gazebo, in case one of your brides decides to go with a Scarlett O'Hara–type dress."

"Those aren't popular anymore."

"Styles could change."

She wrinkled her nose. "Let's hope hoopskirts never come back into vogue. Comfort trumps fashion in my book."

He gave her long fleece sweatshirt and leggings a swift once-over and retreated a few steps. "I try to plan for all contingencies. Adjustments later can be expensive."

Dollar signs flashed through her mind, helping her refocus.

"I'm open to any modifications that will conserve cash now or in the future, as long as they don't impact the ambiance I'm trying to create. Here's an alternate idea. Why don't we forego the path entirely? As long as the grass is kept manicured in that area, a paved path shouldn't be necessary. And a grass aisle would also give us more flexibility." Not to mention the fact that it would save a fair number of dollars. Hardscaping didn't come cheap. "We could always add the stone path later if I decide we need one."

"That'll work. Are you on board with my other ideas?" He lifted the schematic.

"I think so." Even if she hadn't heard all of his suggestions. But the preliminary designs he'd sent with his bid had been impressive. If he'd made adjustments, they'd been well thought out. "May I keep a copy to review again later this morning?"

"This one is yours." He handed it to her as a car

appeared at the entrance and crunched down the road. "That's Kyle, my foreman. I'll introduce you as soon as he parks. Any other questions?" Jon turned back to her.

Oh yeah. A dozen. None of which were appropriate or business related.

Like . . . what color were the eyes he hid behind those dark glasses?

She frowned.

Where on earth had that come from?

Dipping her head, she pretended to brush dust off her pristine leggings.

Who cared about his eye color? The only man's eyes she'd ever noticed were Jason's.

She snuffed out an image of the baby blues that had sucked her in and spit her out. Gritted her teeth.

Jon's eye color was of no concern to her.

And the tiny tingle in her nerve endings had nothing to do with attraction.

She was done with men for the foreseeable future.

"No. No questions." When Jon cocked his head at her sharper-than-intended tone, she softened it. "You were very thorough. I'm impressed with all the designs. I can tell you put a lot of thought into them."

"This is a beautiful place and a plum job. It deserves an extra effort." The car parked in the circle drive, and Jon motioned the driver over as the man opened the door and stood. "Either Kyle or I will be on-site while the work is underway here. Probably both of us, most days. But if I'm not available, don't hesitate to speak with Kyle."

As the foreman joined them, Jon did the introductions.

Kyle held out his hand and gripped her fingers in a firm clasp. "It's a pleasure. Jon's told me about you."

What did that mean?

With most of her landscaper's features covered, it was impossible to tell. But from the flat line of his lips as he spoke to his foreman, it was clear he didn't appreciate the man passing along that tidbit. "You ready to work?"

It wasn't a question.

"The crew's not here yet."

"We'll get started without them. I want to tackle the circle garden today. Ashley, we'll regroup at eight after BJ arrives." Without waiting for a reply, he strode toward the front of the house.

Kyle watched him, his expression . . . amused?

Why? What had he found funny in that exchange?

"I guess we're clocking in early today." Kyle shifted toward her with a grin. "He can be a tough taskmaster. Watch out, or he'll put you to work too."

"Not happening. I have a whole list of appointments today with vendors who may be interested in recommending Edgecliff for weddings and other events. I'll escape before I can be recruited to wield a shovel. Jon said one of the two of you would always be on-site, so if you ever need to speak with me, try the carriage house or the main house. Or call my cell." She motioned toward the caretaker's cottage, tucked farther back among the coniferous trees, on the fringes of the property. "That's Rose's domain. Consider it off-limits."

"Got it. But I expect Jon will be here most days, given all the opportunities this job represents." He hooked a thumb toward his boss. "I better get over there. When the man says it's time to work, he expects all hands on deck."

As Kyle walked away, Ashley pretended to study the new gazebo garden rendering while keeping surreptitious tabs on the two men.

Once Kyle reached his boss, they talked for a moment. After glancing her direction, Jon fisted his hands on his hips and leaned toward Kyle, his words too faint to hear. But Kyle's laugh in response carried clearly in the quiet air before he walked toward the truck. A few seconds later, Jon followed.

Within minutes, they were hard at work marking the perimeter of the garden that would grace the center of the circle drive.

Ashley lingered as long as she could, but with nothing to do until BJ arrived, she had no excuse to hang around outside. The guys would think she was watching them, and earning a reputation as a micromanager wouldn't be wise.

Garden rendering in hand, she returned to the new digs that were a huge upgrade from her old apartment. And the smell of fresh paint, the pristine carpet, and the spic-and-span appearance that had greeted her Saturday night were the nicest welcome Rose could have given her, as she'd told the woman during the scone delivery on Sunday.

Her new partner might not be into socializing, but her effort to put out the welcome mat was a clear indication she had a kind and empathetic heart.

It was possible Jon did too, despite his aloof manner. Just because he kept people at arm's length didn't mean he wasn't a caring person. In fact, every instinct in her body told her he was.

But it was hard to get a definite handle on a person without being able to look into their eyes. Whatever color they were.

And in light of the dark shades Jon never removed, it appeared the window to his heart would remain firmly closed.

Which dampened her spirits on this otherwise bright and sunny day—for reasons she refused to ponder.

11

Why was a strange car parked next to his house?

And why hadn't Daisy run up to greet him, as usual, at the end of his workday?

Setting the brake in his truck, Jon surveyed his backyard and the wooded area beyond.

Nothing but the wind in the spruce trees broke the peaceful stillness.

Where was the owner of the car? And where was Daisy?

As if on cue, a happy bark sounded from the woods. Seconds later, Daisy raced toward him.

Jon climbed out of the truck and bent down to give the pooch a pat. "Hey there, girl. How did you—"

His voice petered out as a familiar figure emerged from the thick copse of evergreens.

"Aren't you going to say hello to your one and only sister?"

As Laura called out the question, he stared at her and rose. "What are you doing here?"

"That is not an acceptable greeting, big brother." She jogged over and threw her arms around him. Squeezed.

He squeezed back, still trying to come to grips with her unexpected appearance. "It's great to see you."

"Much better." After holding tight for another moment, she backed off and scrutinized him. Gave an approving nod. "You're looking good. Outdoor work agrees with you. And the scars have faded quite a bit since I last saw you."

Not true, but she meant well.

"Thanks for the pep talk."

She squinted at him. "You don't believe me?"

"The scars are never going away, Laura."

"I didn't say they were gone. I said they've faded. The change may not register with you because you look at your face every day in the mirror, but I haven't seen you since you set up shop here. There's a definite improvement. If you'd ever let anyone take your picture, you could compare and see the difference."

"Cameras and I parted company long ago. So what are you doing here?"

Thankfully she got his message and dropped the subject—for now.

"Can't a girl visit her brother?"

"You know you're always welcome. But why didn't you tell me you were coming? What if I'd been gone?"

One of her eyebrows rose. "Do you ever go *any*where?"

She had a point. Not that he'd admit it.

"What if I had?"

She shrugged. "I'd have made myself at home until you got back." She pulled his spare key from the pocket of her jeans. "I knew where you stashed this, thanks to the emergency information you sent me. But I assumed you'd be back about now, and I only arrived an hour ago. While I waited, I turned off the electric fence and borrowed your buddy here for a hike through the woods to see the ocean. A rare treat for a gal from Colorado." She bent down to pet Daisy, who lapped up the attention. "Your friend seemed starved for companionship. She must get lonely out here by herself all day."

"I give her plenty of attention in the evening, and she enjoys chasing the squirrels while I'm gone. You going to tell me what inspired you to trek out here from Colorado?"

"A camping trip."

"You came out here to camp?" He scanned the grounds. "Are Bill and the twins with you?"

"No, they are not. And no, I did not come out here to camp. Bill and the boys decided to go camping, and I declined their gracious invitation to join them. No ticks and chiggers and pit toilets for me, thank you very much. So rather than sit at home alone, I decided to take a week of vacation and visit my dear brother, since he never visits us."

"I've been busy starting up a business."

"I realize that. Another reason I decided to come to you."

He pulled off his baseball cap and forked his

156

fingers through his hair. "I wish you'd told me about this."

"Sisters are allowed to barge in. Besides, if I'd shared my plans, you'd have said not to come."

She knew him too well.

"The thing is, I just started a huge job. I'm not going to have much time to entertain you."

"No worries. I knew you'd be busy, and I can keep myself amused. Have rental car, will travel." She waved a hand toward it. "I mapped out an ambitious itinerary. It would be wonderful if you could join me for a day or two, but if not, we can spend the evenings together. Unless you have other social engagements?"

"Nothing on the schedule this week."

She sighed. "That's what I figured. How long are you going to live like a monk?"

"Hey." He tried for a teasing tone. "Did you come out here to sightsee and catch up or to badger me?"

"All of the above."

"No badgering allowed on these premises."

She waved his comment aside. "Sisters are allowed to badger. You want to go somewhere and have dinner? My treat."

"Why don't we eat here? You must be tired after traveling for hours, and I was on the job at the crack of dawn today. Literally. I've got salmon in the fridge. I could throw it on the grill and bake a couple of potatoes."

"You have salad and fresh vegetables?"

"No salad, but I've got frozen beans and broccoli."

"How come I knew that?" She smirked at him. "Lucky for you I stopped at a market a few miles from here and stocked up on provisions. But only enough for two meals. We're splurging on restaurant food for the rest of our dinners. I eat at home every night, where I'm both the chef and the referee for food fights. I deserve a few peaceful meals cooked by someone else, cleanup included."

"I can cook for you—cleanup included."

"No offense intended, Jon, but you are not a Cordon Bleu chef. Heck, you're not even a fast-food-caliber chef."

"I've improved."

"Glad to hear it, for your sake. But I still want to eat out. If you spend the evening cooking, it will be hard to have any in-depth conversations. Trust me, I know. Our kitchen is a madhouse at dinner."

"There aren't eight-year-old twins running around here."

"More's the pity." After giving him a pointed look, she commandeered his arm and tugged him toward the house. "I want quality visiting time while we eat decent food neither of us has cooked, tonight being an exception. I'll admit I'm tired after traveling all day. But beginning tomorrow, you and I are going to have long talks over dinner."

"About what?" As if he couldn't guess.

"Anything and everything. Your business, this new job you mentioned, how you like living in Oregon . . . romance."

"There's nothing to discuss on the romance front."

"We're going to talk about that too."

Jon stifled a groan.

Much as he loved his sister, she could be as dogged as a seagull following a fishing boat.

But she was only going to be in town a week. He could dodge and weave for that long. Try to appease her by coming up with a few creative dinner locales that didn't involve sit-down restaurants. Tell her about his business, give her a peek at Edgecliff, perhaps steal away from work for a few hours and take her up to Shore Acres State Park. She'd enjoy the gardens there.

All he had to do was listen to whatever she had to say, agree to take it under advisement, and change the subject. Should be simple.

After all, how much could she disrupt his life in a mere seven days?

Everyone was gone for the day.

Half hidden behind the drapery in the dining room of the main house, Rose kept tabs on the cloud of dust approaching the tunnel of foliage at the entrance. Foliage that was destined to come down soon.

As Ashley had explained during the daily briefings they'd agreed on and launched today here in the kitchen after the crews left, the entrance would be more impressive—and welcoming—if the tangle of concealing brush and the warning signs were removed.

Hard to argue with that logic, even if the greenery and those notices had done an excellent job discouraging visitors.

Now, however, the time had come to again welcome guests to the gracious home that had once known much happiness. Meaning changes had to be made.

Ashley's car disappeared from view, and Rose let the drape drop back into position.

At last she could visit Allison in privacy.

Her cell phone began to ring as she crossed the foyer toward the parlor, and she pulled it from her pocket. Smiled.

David. Checking up on her, no doubt.

She put the phone to her ear and greeted him as a kaleidoscope of rainbow colors danced across the floor, courtesy of the sun beaming through the stained-glass window on the landing. "Good evening, David. I didn't expect to hear from you again this soon."

"I thought I'd call and see how you're adjusting to all the activity at Edgecliff and to your new quarters. Living in the cottage has to be quite different than living in the house."

"I still spend a fair amount of time in the house. I'm here now, as a matter of fact. Ashley gave me a briefing in the kitchen a few minutes ago on our project. And the cottage is cozy. Plus, I have Lucy Lynn close by there. So far, it's all been working out fine."

"Glad to hear it. I'll have to drive over soon and see the progress."

"You're welcome anytime. Eugene isn't that far away. Give me a day's notice and I'll have a batch of scones waiting."

"I'll hold you to that. Any special plans for the evening?"

She continued toward the parlor. "I'm going to spend an hour with Allison."

"A pleasant end to the day."

"Always."

"I'll let you go, then. Remember to call me if anything comes up that we should discuss. Anytime."

"You know I will. And thank you for following up. It's a blessing to have such a conscientious attorney. I'm sure all your clients appreciate your diligence. I don't know what I'd do if you ever retired."

"Sixty-five is ten years away. I intend to remain on the job at least that long. And after all these years, I'd like to think we've become more than business associates."

"Indeed we have, David. I don't know what I would have done without your wise counsel, savvy advice, and friendship."

"You would have been fine. You're a smart, strong woman who knows what she wants. This latest project proves that. As does Lucy Lynn."

Lips curving up, Rose pushed the end of the pocket door that was peeking out of the wall between the parlor and foyer back into its hiding spot. "Charley Lopez gets the credit for Lucy Lynn."

"I must meet him on one of my visits."

"With enough warning, I may be able to arrange that."

"I'd enjoy that, along with a taste of those tacos you always rave about. Now I'll let you get to Allison."

"Thank you again for calling—and for caring, David."

"My pleasure on both counts."

As they rang off, Rose moved across the parlor in the quiet house. Ashley had said she had a meeting this evening with a wedding planner in Coos Bay to pique the woman's interest in Edgecliff and encourage her to recommend it as a venue. That meant her partner should be gone two hours, minimum.

A generous window to spend private time with Allison.

● ● ●

Well, shoot.

Ashley stopped at the end of Windswept Way and riffled through the folder on the seat beside her.

The revised schematic of the gazebo gardens Jon had given her this morning wasn't in there.

She'd have to go back and get it.

Could be worse, though. What if she'd been halfway to Coos Bay when she'd thought of it?

After scrutinizing Highway 101 both directions, she pulled out and executed a wide U-turn.

Accelerating back toward Edgecliff, she kept a tight grip on the wheel as she navigated the narrow road, paying no attention to the few houses scattered along the isolated stretch. Nor did she slow as she passed the driveway closest to Edgecliff's entrance, as she had on her more leisurely first trip.

Who cared if Jon lived there? It wasn't as if he would ever invite her to visit.

She didn't ease back on the gas pedal until she passed through the iron gates and hit the gravel drive that led to the main house. Going too fast on this type of surface would be foolish. Speeding would not only reduce her traction and control but kick up small rocks that could chip her paint.

And her older-model Civic had to last five more years. Minimum.

Rather than circle around back as usual, she

parked in the loop drive. It would be faster to dash around the side of the main house and up the stairs to her apartment in the adjacent carriage house.

Purse in hand, she slid from behind the wheel, zipped across the front lawn—and came to an abrupt halt as beautiful, classical music seeped through the walls of the house and floated through the air.

Ashley stared at the ornate structure.

No one should be in there. BJ was gone for the day, and other than her contractor, only she and Rose had keys.

The piano notes died away as the piece wound down, and silence descended.

Ashley hesitated.

Should she call Rose, see if she knew what was going on?

Yes. Excellent idea.

She dug her cell out of her purse and punched in the woman's number.

After four rings, it rolled to voicemail just as the music started again.

This piece, she recognized.

Clair de lune.

Ashley tightened her grip on her purse as visions of the woman in white and spectral music quickened her pulse.

But that was ridiculous.

The house wasn't haunted, and she didn't

believe in ghosts. There was a flesh-and-blood person in there. Guaranteed. And no one who flawlessly played such evocative classical music could be dangerous, even if her erratic respiration didn't appear to be convinced of that.

Tamping down her nerves, she dug out her key and crept up the steps. Tiptoed across the porch. Inserted the key in the lock and gingerly twisted the handle. After cracking the door wide enough to slip inside, she entered the foyer.

Here, the music was pure and ethereal—and it was coming from the parlor. The room where a large, antique upright piano occupied a prominent position.

Hugging the wall and staying in the shadows, Ashley continued toward the edge of the pocket-door slot and peeked around.

No ghost after all.

It was Rose at the keyboard of the elaborate instrument.

And wow, could she play.

Mesmerized, Ashley remained frozen in place as the woman put her whole body into the expressive piece, imbuing the haunting strains with poignant emotion and throat-tightening tenderness filled with longing and echoes of remembered joy.

It was masterful. Memorable. Moving.

Almost like looking into the woman's soul.

As the last notes died away, Ashley exhaled.

Though she hadn't made a sound, Rose must have sensed her presence because all at once, her posture stiffened. After a moment, she turned.

Warmth seeped into Ashley's cheeks.

Although she had full access to the house, she suddenly felt like an intruder. Or worse, a voyeur.

"I . . . I'm sorry, Rose. I forgot the schematic for the gazebo garden, and when I came back for it, I heard the music and thought I should investigate. I didn't mean to intrude or invade your privacy."

For a few seconds Rose didn't speak. But at last she offered a gentle smile. "It's all right, Ashley. I knew someone would discover my love for Allison sooner or later, with all the activity at the house."

"Allison?"

Rose rested a hand on the keyboard. "My mother always called her Allison. She was made by the Allison Piano Company in England in 1910. It was the first item my grandfather bought for the house. My grandmother was an accomplished pianist, according to my father."

"That talent must run in the family. Your playing was exquisite."

The older woman brushed her fingers over the ivory keys. "Music has given me tremendous comfort through the years. That's one of the reasons I wanted access to the house when it wasn't in use."

"How did you learn to play like that?"

"I began taking lessons as a child and discovered I had a natural aptitude for the instrument. When I was accepted at the Boston Conservatory, I had grand plans for a life on the concert stage and world tours."

Rose had trained to be a professional pianist at a prestigious conservatory, aiming for a performing career?

"What happened?" The question was out before Ashley could stop it.

Rose twined her fingers together in her lap, the whisper of a sad smile bowing her lips. "Life. It takes years to establish a name in the classical music world, but I was making progress until I met my husband. Love—or in my case, infatuation—can derail plans. He dazzled me with his continental manners and smooth talk and extravagant gestures."

"And you gave up performing?"

Her shoulders rose. "I didn't think it would be forever. He convinced me to stop traveling while we settled into married life. But it's very hard to regain lost momentum in that business, and my heart wasn't in it anymore after I discovered I'd been duped. Turns out my husband didn't want a famous or successful wife. He wanted someone wealthy and pretty and talented who could entertain the clients he courted. Love wasn't in the equation."

"Why did you stay with him?"

Rose smoothed a wrinkle from her skirt. "Pride, plain and simple. My mother never liked him. She warned me I'd regret the marriage. It was hard to admit she'd been right. And by then, my career was over anyway."

"I'm so sorry." Ashley's throat tightened. "That was a huge loss. Your playing is amazing."

"Thank you, my dear. I did continue to play for myself, and I took in an occasional student, which was rewarding. Music has tremendous healing power." She tapped her watch. "If you linger much longer you'll be late for your appointment."

Yes, she would.

Yet she hesitated.

Rose seemed so alone, sitting here in the empty parlor with no one to listen to her remarkable playing but the imaginary ghosts of Edgecliff. "Would you like to . . . I mean, I know you don't go out much, but why don't you ride along with me? The scenery is beautiful, and you could stay in the car, and we could . . . we could stop on the drive back for ice cream somewhere."

The woman's expression softened. "That's very kind of you, my dear, but I'm content here. And I have Allison for company." She stroked the polished mahogany of the massive piece.

No surprise she'd rebuffed the impulsive offer, but it hadn't hurt to try. And one of these days, maybe the woman would accept such an invitation.

"I'll let you get back to playing, then. I assume you'd like me to keep Allison a secret?"

Rose waved the offer aside. "It's not really a secret. There's just never been anyone out here to hear my music, except my father. And Charley. He stopped by once while I was playing. But he has superb discretion. I doubt he told anyone." Her mouth curved up. "If people find out, it's not a problem, but I see no point in spreading the word. It isn't as if I'm planning to book any gigs for myself."

"I understand." Ashley eased toward the door. "I'll see you tomorrow for our briefing session."

"I'll look forward to it. Drive safe."

While Rose swiveled back to the piano, Ashley returned to the front door and let herself out. As she crossed the porch, the strains of *Moonlight Sonata* followed her, the quiet opening notes muted by the walls of the house.

In less than five minutes, she was back in her car and crunching toward the gate, revised schematic tucked into the folder beside her.

Just before she entered the foliage tunnel, she glanced back at the house, where a cloistered woman with incredible talent spent her days finding solace in music for all the blows life had dealt her.

It was heartbreaking.

But with all the activity at the estate now, perhaps some of the joy and laughter Rose hoped to restore to Edgecliff would also find its way into her life.

And if the opportunity presented itself, maybe . . . just maybe . . . a certain historian could help renew Rose's existence just as she was renewing the place that the last Fitzgerald called home.

12

"By the way, Jon, Ashley was looking for you this afternoon. I answered her questions as well as I could, but I think she prefers to talk to you." Kyle passed the basket of biscuits to Laura. "Help yourself. Sarah made plenty."

Jon shot Kyle a silent warning across the dinner table in his foreman's apartment.

The man ignored him.

"Don't mind if I do. The pizza Jon got us last night was excellent, but it can't compare to this feast." Laura took a biscuit.

Jon kept an eye on Kyle as he responded to his sister. "Frank makes the best pizza this side of the Rockies. It's one of my favorite takeout places." Not just because the pizza was first class either. The dim interior and crusty, taciturn owner were also a winning combination. "And I gave you a world-class view, didn't I? Better than any restaurant."

"I'll concede that the panorama from Pelican Point lighthouse was amazing, even if the two cackling seagulls serenading us while we ate left a bit to be desired in the ambiance department. So who's Ashley?"

A bite of flaky biscuit got caught in Jon's throat.

Of course his sister would pounce on any mention of a female.

He should never have let Kyle talk him into this cozy dinner. Latching on to the invitation just to avoid a restaurant meal had been a huge mistake.

Before the other man could respond, Jon jumped in. "She's my client on the big job I told you about."

"You never mentioned her. Only Rose, the recluse." Laura inspected him as she buttered her biscuit. "I thought Rose was in charge of the project."

"We never see her. Ashley's our contact." Kyle avoided eye contact despite the glare Jon aimed his direction. "Nice woman. Pretty too. But I doubt she'll stay single long, once the local bachelors start seeing her around."

Laura stopped eating. "She's single?"

"We don't know that." Jon stabbed the last piece of chicken on his plate with his fork.

"Yes, we do."

Jon scrutinized him. "How did you turn up that nugget?"

"She doesn't wear a wedding ring. And I've never seen a guy hanging around Edgecliff."

"That doesn't prove she's single. Maybe her husband is wrapping up loose ends in Tennessee before he joins her."

"Nope. Sarah called while Ashley and I were

talking. I told Ashley we were newlyweds and asked if she was married. She said no."

"That's very interesting." Laura took a bite of her biscuit. "How old is she?"

"Early thirties is my guess. What do you think, Jon?" Kyle's tone remained conversational, but humor glinted in his eyes.

So much for taking what had appeared to be the easy way out of a restaurant meal.

His foreman was going to hear about this tomorrow.

"Estimating ages isn't my forte. Sarah, Kyle promised a spectacular dessert. I've been thinking about it all day, after sampling the treats you send with him to our jobsites. What are we having?"

After regarding him and her husband, the sweet brunette picked up his cue. "An almond fudge torte with raspberry sauce. Honey, why don't you help me clear?" She nudged her husband, seated beside her at the small, round table.

"Sure."

"I'll help too." Jon rose and picked up his plate and Laura's.

"Oh no. You're a guest." Sarah tried to relieve him of his excuse to delay a conversation with his sister.

He held on tight to the plates. "No. Laura's a guest. I'm a boss. I'd like to help."

"In that case . . ." Kyle sat back down. "Our

kitchen's tiny. Three's a crowd in there. I'll keep Laura company while you two tote out the plates."

Kyle with Laura, one-on-one, where his sister could grill him about Ashley?

A disaster waiting to happen.

But after volunteering for KP, he was stuck. All he could do was clear as fast as possible and try to retake his seat before too much damage was done.

Unfortunately, Sarah also commandeered him to carry in the plates of dessert, and cutting the cake felt like a slow-motion exercise. As she carefully sliced it, did a fancy drizzle over each serving, and artistically placed a few fresh raspberries on each plate, he tried to keep one ear cocked to the conversation in the adjacent dining room.

Too muffled to pick up.

At last, dessert in hand, he rejoined his sister and foreman.

The speculative once-over Laura gave him wasn't reassuring. Nor was Kyle's fixation on gathering up a few biscuit crumbs from the tablecloth.

At least no one mentioned Ashley again during the remainder of the meal.

His reprieve, however, ended less than half a minute after he and Laura pulled away from Kyle's house and headed home.

174

"When are you going to give me a tour of the Edgecliff grounds, like you promised?" His sister twisted toward him on her seat, studying his profile in the dark.

He should never have dangled that in front of her, hoping it would appease her if he begged off on dinners at sit-down restaurants.

"I don't know if I can make that happen. I have a number of stops on my schedule tomorrow, so I won't be on-site much. Friday I thought I'd take you up to Shore Acres State Park. And you're leaving Sunday."

"You could give me a tour on Saturday."

"I don't think the work crews are welcome on the premises on weekends."

"You could ask. I bet Ashley wouldn't mind."

It was impossible to miss her slight emphasis on his client's name—or its significance.

Kyle had filled her head with stupid ideas.

"I don't want to impose. Besides, Rose wouldn't appreciate strangers wandering around her property."

"There will be hundreds wandering about once the place is up and running as a special events venue and museum."

"We're not there yet. And I expect she'll stay sequestered while other people are around."

"Does this mean you aren't going to give me a tour?"

"Let's see how everything goes. If I can block

out a spare hour on Friday before or after our trip to Shore Acres, I'll take you over." But there would be no spare hour. He'd make certain of that.

"Kyle says Ashley is nice."

He let that pass.

"Well?" She poked his arm.

"Well what?"

"What do you think?"

"She seems to be."

"What's wrong with getting to know her better?"

Jon squeezed the wheel. "She's a client, Laura."

"She won't be forever."

"I don't date."

"Why?"

"Come on, Sis. Get real."

"I am getting real. You are way too sensitive about your scars. I never thought you were vain, but maybe I was wrong."

"It's not about vanity."

"Are you sure?"

He blew out a breath. "You sound like Ashley."

The instant the words left his mouth, he cringed.

Though the car was dark, Laura's intent scrutiny was almost palpable. "You've talked to Ashley about your scars?"

"No." He gave her a quick recap of their first encounter. "She admitted to me later that the

176

mask and chain saw had scared her, and I told her she'd have been more scared if I hadn't been wearing a mask."

"Is that when she called you vain?"

"Not exactly. Besides, it doesn't matter. I don't think—"

"I'd like to meet this woman."

Not happening. Ever.

"She's hard to pin down. Most days she's out and about." And he'd confirm her absence if Laura managed to strong-arm him into giving her a quick tour of the premises.

"Mmm." His sister settled back in her seat. "You should take a serious look in the mirror, Jon."

"I have." He was all too familiar with the scars and the asymmetry of his features. No, it wasn't the stuff of horror movies anymore, but it wasn't anywhere close to normal either.

"Just because Melinda couldn't deal with—"

"Laura." He was done discussing this. If it took a bit of shock value to end the conversation, so be it. "The first—and last—time she saw me after the accident, she puked."

Several moments of silence ticked by.

"You never told me that." Laura's voice was laced with tears. "I'm so sorry."

"Don't be. It's history. But my days of appealing to the opposite sex are over."

"I think you're wrong about that. You may not

177

be a chick magnet anymore, but believe me, the women who were drawn to you in those days aren't the type you'd want to spend the rest of your life with anyway. True love goes a lot deeper than superficial appearance."

"Says the prom queen who led the cheer squad and married the football-hero-big-man-on-campus after college."

"So I haven't walked a mile in your shoes. I get that. But I can imagine how awful it would be to lose your physical self-image. You—the real you, the you that matters—hasn't changed, though. And the right woman would be able to see past any physical flaws and love the real you."

He called up a smile. "You always were a dreamer."

"Sometimes dreams come true."

"Hold that thought. Now let's talk about plans for the rest of the week."

Thankfully, she let him guide the conversation for the remainder of the drive home, but as they parted for the night, she gave him an extra-tight squeeze. "You know, I bet if Melinda saw you now, she'd be sorry she walked out."

Not likely. But why waste any brainpower on what-iffing?

"Thanks. Sleep well."

"You too."

They parted in the hall, and Jon continued

toward his room. Veered toward the master bath. Flipped on the light and faced the mirror—a rare occurrence, except while shaving.

Judging his current features by his pre-roadside-bomb appearance was pointless. He'd never look like he had five years ago.

Nevertheless, compared to the early days there was noticeable improvement. The surgeons had done a remarkable job patching him up. He'd been spared the burns and traumatic brain injuries many in his squad had suffered, thanks to his location farther from the explosion. But the shrapnel that had pierced and shattered his jaw, ripped off two fingers, taken most of the vision in his left eye, and left a mottled mass of white scars from forehead to chin, down his neck to the top of his body armor, and along his left arm and leg, had altered his appearance forever.

He wasn't a pretty boy anymore, and he'd never win a spot on *The Bachelor*.

But he wasn't horror-movie material either. Not like he'd been in the beginning, when the sight of him had turned Melinda's stomach.

The question was, were Kyle and Laura right? Was it possible people would be able to overlook his obvious physical imperfections and see into his soul and heart?

There was only one way to find out.

Ditch his disguise. Let the world see his scars and wait for a verdict.

His pulse spiked, and he gripped the edge of the vanity.

Vanity.

There was that word again.

Maybe he *was* vain.

After all, the face staring back at him wasn't bad enough anymore to scare people, despite what he'd told Ashley. Yes, it would draw curious looks, but he could live with that. And Hope Harbor was small. It wasn't as if he'd be meeting new people every day. Once residents got used to his appearance, it was possible they wouldn't pay any attention to his physical flaws.

He forked his fingers through his hair and straightened up.

Going cold turkey would be difficult, but why not drop his concealing paraphernalia one item at a time? The scarf could go first. Getting rid of that annoying scrap of cloth would be a pleasure.

Armed with that plan, he pulled out his toothbrush and got ready for bed.

He'd wait until Laura left to implement his multistage shedding strategy, though. While she was here, he had another challenge on his hands.

Now that Ashley was on his sister's radar, he'd have to find an excuse to keep Laura away from Edgecliff.

Far away.

Because introducing them wouldn't be smart. Laura would ask too many questions. All tactful, naturally. Laura knew how to be discreet—with other people.

But she was also insightful. A beneficial skill in her role as an employee ombudsman for a major company, but a definite negative for him in her role as sister. If Kyle had picked up on his interest in Ashley, Laura would be all over it in minutes. Or less.

He squeezed the toothpaste onto the bristles, coaxing the last dribs out of the almost-empty tube.

There were only two days left in the workweek. He'd already nixed tomorrow with his legitimate errand excuse. He did have several suppliers to visit. And the visit to Shore Acres State Park on Friday would be a worthy substitute for Edgecliff.

It was a decent plan.

Laura would continue to pester him about Ashley, of course. But if he could keep the two women apart for the next three days, his sister would be winging home to Colorado on Sunday.

And with more than a thousand miles separating her from him, and communication confined to calls and emails, she'd have to resort to advice rather than action.

A far safer and more manageable situation.

As long as he got through the next three days unscathed.

13
....

"Sorry I'm late. And thanks for your willingness to change our appointment from Tuesday to Thursday."

Ashley pulled the door to the main house wider and ushered Marci in. "No worries. A sick three-year-old takes precedence over a newspaper article. How's she doing?"

"Improving. Whatever bug she picked up did a number on her, though. She hasn't been sleeping at night, and neither have we. Thank the Lord I have a capable assistant at work who is more than up to the task of running both the paper and my PR business if I'm not there."

Ashley's ears perked up. "You have a PR business too?"

"Yep. That's what pays the bills. The *Herald* feeds my journalistic soul, but in a town the size of Hope Harbor, a biweekly newspaper doesn't provide a living wage."

"Let's sit in the drawing room." Ashley motioned toward it, digesting this new information. "Do you do websites in your PR business?"

"Absolutely. I pull in a designer sometimes, depending on the complexity of the project, but most often we do them ourselves. Why?"

"Edgecliff needs a website, and that's not my area of expertise. After we finish with your questions for the article, can we talk about that?"

"I'm always happy to discuss new projects." Marci perched on one of the tufted chairs and surveyed the room. "Rose isn't joining us?"

"No. Sorry. I tried."

She sighed. "Disappointing, but I can't say I'm surprised. To tell you the truth, I was shocked she agreed to the first interview."

"When it comes to protecting her family's history and heritage, she's all in."

"Your partnership with her proves that." Marci withdrew a sheet of paper from her notebook and held it out. "Since I didn't expect her to show, I put together a list of questions, like you recommended. It would add a lot to the story if she answered even a few."

Ashley took the sheet. "I'll pass it on and try to convince her to contribute."

For the next hour, Marci peppered her with questions. She continued the friendly inquisition during the tour of the house and grounds while she oohed and aahed over the furnishings and the gardens that were beginning to take shape.

As they ended back in front by the porch and settled on a time for a follow-up meeting about the website, a UPS truck rumbled down the drive.

"Impeccable timing for you to accept a

delivery." Marci motioned toward the vehicle as she stowed her pen.

"I doubt it's for me."

"Who else would be getting packages?"

Ashley waved in the direction of the caretaker's cottage. "Rose. There have been several deliveries this week."

"No kidding?" The truck veered off the loop drive in front of the main house and trundled around to the back on the single lane road that led to the carriage house and cottage. No hesitation. As if the route was very familiar. "How much stuff does a recluse need?"

"Apparently more than you'd imagine."

"Curious." Marci pulled out her keys. "Thanks for the tour. And I'll be certain to mention the open house you're planning to host for area wedding and special event vendors. I know you've already sent out invitations, but our circulation isn't bad, and a few more businesses may express an interest in attending."

"That would be great. I'm all for drumming up as many bookings as possible."

"Are you planning to have any entertainment at the event?"

"Hmm." Ashley folded her arms. "I hadn't thought of that, but it's not a bad idea."

"Music always adds ambiance. I can imagine a harpist, or a string quartet, or a jazz combo."

Or a woman who played superb classical music

184

on an antique piano, perhaps dressed in period attire.

Her pulse picked up.

Wouldn't it be fantastic if she could convince Rose to come out of hiding long enough to participate?

A huge if.

But it was worth pursuing.

"You've just given me a brilliant idea."

"Happy to be of assistance." Marci offered her a mock salute. "And I've got you down for tomorrow morning at nine to talk about the website. Here or at my office?"

"I'll come to you."

"Bring the garden renderings, and any historic photos you think would be appropriate, along with the copy you've been working on. I took a ton of pictures today that should be fine for an initial website. We can jazz it up later if you want more glitz."

"Basic is fine for now. My main goal is to get it up. Like you said, we can always add bells and whistles."

"You ought to set up social media sites too. Document the progress as this place begins to take shape."

"On my list."

"We could also handle that for you."

Ashley flexed her lips. "I'm trying to do everything I can on my own to conserve cash at this stage. But hold that thought for the future."

"You got it." Marci jingled her keys. "I'm off to work from home for the rest of the day while I play nurse."

As Marci climbed into her car, the UPS truck rumbled back out.

Curious, as Marci had noted.

The grocery deliveries from town were understandable. So were the visits from the cleaning crew that kept the main house immaculate and also tended to Rose's cottage.

But what would a woman who lived an isolated life be ordering that required frequent UPS deliveries?

If she went down to the cottage now to talk about her idea for the open house, would she get a peek at the package?

Not that she was nosy or anything.

Yet the Rose riddle was intriguing. Who would ever imagine that a world-class pianist lived on these isolated grounds? Or that a woman known as a recluse would strike up an unlikely friendship with the taco-maker in town? Or that the last living Fitzgerald had a deep well of kindness that had gone untapped these past seven years, save for the care she'd given her father and her quiet generosity when needs had arisen in Hope Harbor?

Invading the woman's privacy, however, would be wrong. Rose had been clear from the beginning that the cottage would be her domain, and all communication would be by phone, email, or during their daily briefing sessions in the main house.

Ashley blew out a breath.

Rose's willingness to stay hands off and let her run the whole shebang was flattering, but how was she supposed to help her partner reconnect with the world when the woman gave her no opportunities to do so?

Yet one had just dropped into her lap—and she'd call up every argument she could think of to persuade Rose that classical music wafting through Edgecliff would be a huge selling point. One that would make the open house guests more receptive to using or recommending the estate for special events, which in turn would help bring joy and laughter back to these walls.

And perhaps to Rose herself.

Was that Laura walking down the gravel drive toward Edgecliff, with Daisy in tow?

Yeah, it was.

Jon muttered a few choice words.

"Isn't that your sister?" Kyle came up beside him, wiping his forehead on the sleeve of his shirt as the early afternoon sun heated up the late July Thursday.

Daisy gave a happy yip and strained at the leash, propelling Laura forward.

"Yes."

"What's she doing here?"

Best guess? Coming for the tour she wasn't confident he'd provide.

Leave it to Laura to take matters into her own hands. Especially if she had an agenda.

Like getting a glimpse of Ashley.

His stomach clenched.

This visit was not going to end well.

Jon glanced toward the house. No sign of his client. But she'd been on the grounds all day today, according to the Edgecliff version of the *Herald*—aka Kyle. Per his foreman, she'd spent most of the morning giving the editor of the real *Herald* the grand tour.

"Hey. What's she doing here?" Kyle prodded his arm as he repeated the question.

"I have no idea." *Liar, liar.* "But I'll find out." And head her off at the pass.

Leaving Kyle behind, he strode away from the gardens on either side of the walkway that led to the house and hurried toward his sister.

They met in the circle drive.

"What's up?" He paused in front of her, blocking her path.

"I decided to take Daisy for a walk."

"Why this direction?"

"I saw your truck pass by the house and figured you'd be here. I was hoping to kill two birds with one stone—a doggie walk and a tour."

"I'm only here to drop off flats of annuals and hostas."

"Can't you spare a few minutes to give your sister a quick peek?" She leaned sideways to look past him and raised her voice. "Hi, Kyle!"

"Hey, Laura."

Jon didn't turn around. "Not today. I have another errand to run, and I won't be back until—"

"Jon!"

At the summons from Kyle, he shifted toward the man. His foreman motioned toward Ashley, who'd come out the front door and was descending the steps.

Talk about rotten timing.

But Kyle could handle her questions. His first priority was to hustle Laura out of here ASAP.

He refocused on his sister. "If we still have light after our trip to Shore Acres State Park tomorrow, I can try to work in a tour here and—"

"Is that Ashley?"

She leaned to his left again to peer at his client.

Tempted as he was to lie, that wasn't his MO.

"Yes. She must have business to discuss. Why don't you go on back to the house and—"

"I'll wait." She smiled around him at Ashley and waved.

No doubt Ashley had waved back.

Now what?

He could leave Laura standing here, but Ashley

would ask about her. How would he explain his reluctance to introduce them?

With limited options, this was a lose-lose scenario all around.

He exhaled.

May as well suck it up and do what any normal person would do under the circumstances. At least if he was hovering over the two women, the situation couldn't get too far out of hand.

He hoped.

"I'll introduce you. Come on."

Leaving Laura to follow in his wake, Jon dodged Daisy's taut leash as his canine friend lunged forward.

Ashley smiled as they approached. "I didn't mean to interrupt, but I had a few questions. If you're busy, I can ask them later, or tomorrow."

"I'm not too busy." He did the introductions quickly.

"Welcome to Edgecliff." Ashley swept a hand over the house and gardens as she addressed Laura. "Who's your friend?" As she bent to give the dog a pat, the pooch snuggled close to her leg, then rolled over for a belly rub.

"This is Daisy, Jon's housemate." Laura dropped down and joined in the canine lovefest. "Isn't she a charmer?"

"I'll say."

"I decided to take her for a walk, and since Jon had promised to give me a tour—"

"Ashley, you said you had some questions?" Jon nudged his sister, and she wobbled. When she grabbed the hand he offered, he pulled her up. Fast.

Ashley stood too. "Yes. I was going over the plans for the gazebo garden again, and I noticed—"

"Hey, boss!"

What now?

Jon pivoted toward one of the members of the landscaping crew assigned to the gazebo area. "Yes?"

"We have questions."

More bad timing.

"Kyle, you want to handle that?"

"Can't. They already ran their questions by me, and I said you'd have to answer them. An executive decision is required."

"You go on, Jon. I'll wait for you." Laura petted Daisy again.

He faced her. "Or you could go back to the house. I'll be busy the rest of the day."

"What about my tour?" Before he could respond, Laura turned her charm on Ashley. "My big brother has been promising me a peek at the grounds, but I'm leaving Sunday and he hasn't had a spare minute to show me around."

Her ploy was obvious.

But angling for an invitation wasn't going to work.

"I told you tomorrow may—"

"I'd be happy to show—"

As he and Ashley spoke simultaneously, Jon took his sister's arm and locked onto her gaze. "Let's plan on tomorrow. Ashley's busy, and she and I have business to discuss."

"Actually, I have a free hour and my business can wait. You have more urgent issues to deal with." She motioned toward his landscaping crew waiting by the gazebo for direction.

Laura smirked at him. "Run along, dear brother. I can see I'm in excellent hands. And I know I'll get a much better tour from Ashley than I would from you."

"What about Daisy?" A lame, grasping-at-straws excuse to nix an Ashley-led tour, but nothing else came to mind.

"You can clip her leash to the porch railing while we're inside, if you like." Ashley tipped her head toward the house.

"That'll work. See you back at the house later, Jon."

Without giving him a chance to protest, she started toward the house. Ashley fell in beside her, the two women already chatting like old friends.

"They seem to have hit it off." Kyle watched them ascend the steps.

Yes, they did.

Unfortunately.

Because if his sister clicked with Ashley, taming his sister's sometimes unruly romantic streak during the remaining three days of her stay would be a full-time job.

14

"You want me to do what?" Rose stared at Ashley from her chair at the kitchen table in the main house as their daily briefing wound down. Surely she'd misunderstood.

Ashley shifted in her seat and twined her fingers into a tight knot on the table. "It was Marci's idea, actually. The *Herald* editor. She brought it up while she was here today for the interview, and I thought it was inspired."

"You told her I play the piano?"

"Oh no!" Ashley's reassurance was swift and fervent. "I haven't shared that with anyone. She just thought music would add to the ambiance of the open house. Having you play was my idea."

Rose was shaking her head before Ashley finished. "Impossible. I don't perform anymore."

"But you could. Your playing is superb. And it would be much better than a hired harpist or string quartet. The guests would love it. And you wouldn't have to interact with them. We could rope off that part of the room, and your back would be to the people while you played. I was also hoping to convince you to wear the vintage outfit you dug out of the attic for my first visit. That would be the icing on the cake!" Ashley was glowing with enthusiasm.

Rose glanced out the window, toward the vast expanse of sea sprinkled with diamonds in the late afternoon sun, no more brilliant than the sparkle in the younger woman's eyes.

It felt wrong to throw cold water on her plans. But stepping back into the spotlight was out of the question.

Shoring up her resolve, she shook her head again. "I'm sorry. I can't. People would come just to gawk at the recluse, and I've had enough of that to last a lifetime."

"Not if we don't tell people in advance you'll be playing." Ashley leaned forward, earnest and intent. "No one has to know about the entertainment until they arrive. And I don't have to share your name if anyone asks. But they may not. Most of the guests aren't from Hope Harbor and won't know much about the history of the house. You could remain anonymous, if that's your preference. I think they'll simply be charmed by your attire and swept away by your playing."

As Rose studied the other woman, a tiny tingle ran through her. The kind she used to experience, back in her concert days, as she waited in the wings to be announced.

How strange, after half a century, that the idea of once again playing for an audience would produce a tiny adrenaline rush. Bring back a flood of memories from the days when sharing her music with an appreciative audience buoyed her spirits and left her on more of a high than any of those mind-altering drugs favored by young people today.

But she was too old for such fancies. Spending hours alone with Allison was sufficient.

She leaned forward and touched Ashley's hand, gentling her voice. "I'm flattered by your invitation and kind words, but my performing days are over."

"Why?"

"I'm eighty."

"So? Your playing is timeless."

The stubborn set of Ashley's chin indicated she wasn't going to give up without a fight—an impressive quality that had been evident since their first exchange of letters.

Admirable as persistence was, however, it wasn't going to work in this case. Nevertheless, it was clear she'd have to try a different dissuasion tactic.

Rose rested one hand atop the other on the table. "How long will this open house last?"

"Two hours."

"I don't have the energy to play that long."

"Only the first hour is in the house. We'll move outside after that. Under the tent if it rains, but hopefully it will be a beautiful day. Your part would be finished after the first hour. And I'll rope off the whole room if necessary to keep the people far back. Please, Rose. Your music would add magic to the event."

She steeled herself to the plea in Ashley's expression. "I'm sorry, but I'm not prepared to play in public." She slid her chair back from the table, stood, and forced up the corners of her mouth. "I do think music would enhance the ambiance, so if you want to hire the harpist or string quartet you mentioned, you have my full support. Is there anything else we should discuss today?"

"No." Ashley's shoulders drooped. "Same time tomorrow?"

"I'll be here. Have a pleasant evening." Rose crossed the room and let herself out the back door.

In the waning daylight, she strolled down the gravel path toward her cottage, breathing in the invigorating air while surveying the panoramic vista from the small piece of terra firma claimed by the Fitzgeralds long ago.

Her domain.

Such a blessing to have this beautiful, peaceful retreat to call her own. Yes, she'd opened the gates to others now, but most evenings this view, this serenity, would be hers and Ashley's alone.

And what a lovely young woman to share it with.

Rose paused to watch the aerial acrobatics of

two gulls, their movements synchronized as if choreographed.

Charley's birds, perhaps?

Her lips twitched.

Only the man himself would know. But those two birds had been amusing the day they'd dropped in during his visit on the terrace. Floyd and Gladys, he'd said. A seagull couple.

She continued toward her cottage, the notion of couples leading her back to Ashley. Strange that her young partner hadn't caught any man's fancy by now. Or vice versa. She was beautiful and vivacious, smart and conscientious. Yet other than an occasional mention of her parents, she never referenced any friends or previous beaus.

Could there be a romance gone awry in her past? One far less public than the Warner fiasco and divorce, but possibly as disheartening?

If so, she hadn't let it dampen her zest for life. And she seemed determined to inject a portion of that zest into her partner with the preposterous idea about playing at the open house.

Rose waved off a bothersome bee that apparently thought her purple blouse was a new flower to be investigated.

Whatever on earth could have made Ashley think a woman who'd left society behind would be receptive to such a suggestion? Much as she'd once enjoyed performing, at this stage of life she didn't need anyone to validate her playing or boost her ego with applause. It was enough to play for her own pleasure.

But what about the pleasure it might give others?

Rose jolted to a stop a few steps from the cottage door. Frowned.

That was a different take on the situation.

It was true that in the past people had enjoyed her playing. Her father, certainly, in his final years, but also her audiences when she'd been young and ambitious and passionate about sharing her talent with the world.

Was it possible she was being selfish? God had blessed her with an exceptional aptitude for music, after all. Yes, she'd honed it with diligent practice and dedication, but the talent was a gift. Was it wrong not to share it with others?

And was it also wrong to say no to Ashley, who'd worked so hard to bring their vision to life? Whose lights burned late every night in the carriage house as she gave this project all of her energy and enthusiasm?

Rose took a deep breath.

Maybe she owed more to this endeavor than her generous financial commitment.

Maybe she owed it a piece of herself.

Maybe, to use one of her father's favorite phrases, she should put some skin in this game.

As that idea sent down tentative roots, she slowly continued to the cottage, grasping the support beam on the tiny porch when the ground beneath her seemed to shift.

Agreeing to Ashley's proposition would require a huge leap outside her comfort zone. One she'd never planned to take.

But her offer to cordon off the whole parlor had been both smart and compelling. Venturing back into the world of real people couldn't get any safer than that.

She stepped up onto the porch and swiveled back to look at the grand Victorian lady in the distance. Her haven. The house she'd intended to occupy alone until the good Lord called her to her eternal home.

Yet her decision to preserve the family heritage had trumped her desire for solitude. Giving up a modicum of privacy to bring life and laughter to those walls and these grounds had been worth the sacrifice.

Would sharing her music with others also be worth the sacrifice of public exposure?

Rose rested a hip on the railing of the tiny porch, weighing the pros and cons as a flicker of excitement licked along her nerve endings at the prospect of playing for an audience again.

And there wasn't much risk. She could enjoy the thrill of performing again with relative anonymity. Be part of the gathering without mingling. Most people at events like an open house paid scant attention to the background music anyway. It tended to register on a peripheral level, setting a mood. This wouldn't be a concert.

It would, however, be a performance. If she was willing to venture outside the insulated little world she'd created at Edgecliff.

A light came on in the long-unused carriage house, an unexpectedly comforting sign of life after months of sharing the property only with passing birds and squirrels.

And really, wasn't that sufficient? Why stir the pot any more than she already had? Remaining in the shadows would keep her life placid and predictable.

Except . . .

She lowered herself to the rocking chair.

What had Charley once said about that very subject? The day he'd explained to her why he kept an irregular schedule, painting in solitude some days, cooking and conversing at his stand on others.

All at once his voice echoed in her mind.

"Predictability has its virtues, but too much routine can get stale and bland. A touch of spice is as essential for life as it is for my tacos."

An observation applicable to many situations. Including her own.

Her taco-making friend had made a comment about shadows once too, hadn't he? Something about how they were helpful for people who wished to hide, but that true freedom came only in sunlight—even if it entailed risk.

Brow furrowed, Rose stood and moved to the railing again, where the light from the carriage house was more visible.

Should she stay sequestered and safe in the shadows, or step into the light and dance with danger?

When no answer came to her, she turned away from the carriage house and slipped inside the cottage.

Perhaps a few minutes with Lucy Lynn would help clarify her thinking.

But this wasn't a decision she'd finalize tonight. It deserved serious pondering for a day or two.

And once she did settle on a course, she'd have to pray it wasn't one she'd live to regret.

"What do you mean, you and Ashley are going to tea?" From the passenger seat, Jon whipped his head around as Laura dropped that bombshell.

His sister continued to tool down 101 in her rental car as if she didn't have a care in the world.

That made one of them.

"Am I not speaking English?" She sent him an amused glance. "I mean exactly what I said. We're going to tea. On Saturday. At Bayview Lavender Farm. I invited you to join me earlier in the week, if you recall, and you nixed the idea. Since tea should never be taken alone, I asked someone who would appreciate the ambiance."

"Get real, Laura. Can you see me juggling a dainty china cup and eating cucumber sandwiches?"

"No, but I did offer. I expect I'll have more fun with Ashley anyway. Men tend to gulp down the food at a tea and are ready to leave in twenty minutes. We women like to have long chats over our scones and sweets."

A scenario that sent a cold chill rippling through him.

"Laura." He injected a warning note into his voice.

"What?"

"I want you to butt out of my love life."

She snorted. "There's no love life to butt out of, as far as I can see."

"I'm serious."

"So am I." She flipped on her blinker and hung a left onto Bluff Avenue, the scenic road into town. "I hope you're hungry."

Not anymore, now that it was clear where they were going.

The Myrtle Café was the sole sit-down restaurant in town, and it had been packed every time he'd peeked in during his tenure here. Sitting elbow-to-elbow with locals before he'd psyched himself up for that kind of exposure was bound to result in a case of severe indigestion—assuming he could choke his food down.

"Not very. I had a late lunch while I was running around today, and I hear the Myrtle has generous—"

"We're not going to the Myrtle, even if I've become addicted to their spinach quiche."

Jon squinted at her. "There aren't any other restaurants in town."

"Depends how you define restaurant. I have tacos on my mind."

She was taking him to Charley's?

"I thought you wanted to eat at sit-down restaurants for dinner while you were here?"

"I did. But have you taken me to any yet?" She arched her eyebrows at him, then directed her attention back to the road that curved around the bluffs.

A wave of guilt crashed over him.

No, he hadn't. They'd had two dinners at his house from the provisions she'd brought, venturing out only for a home-cooked meal at Kyle's apartment and takeout pizza at the lighthouse.

He did owe her a meal at a real restaurant.

"Why don't we go up to Coos Bay and—"

"I'm fine with Charley's. We'll claim a bench or grab the picnic table in the gazebo, if it happens to be empty. Since it's obvious you don't want to eat at a sit-down restaurant, I'm not going to force you. I didn't come to Hope

Harbor for the food anyway." She hung a right onto Dockside Drive and motioned toward Grace Christian Church as they passed. "You ever go to services anymore?"

He squirmed in his seat. "Not lately."

Like not in five years.

"Wouldn't hurt. Might help."

"With what?"

"With getting your life back on track."

"My life is already on track."

"You sure about that? Because as I recall, one of your goals back in the day was to have a wife and family."

He wrapped his fingers around the strap of the shoulder harness. "Sometimes plans have to be altered."

"And sometimes they don't. Detours can involve delays and route adjustments, but the destination doesn't have to change—unless you get so lost you give up." She sent him a quick but pointed look. "I never thought you were the type who gave up, big brother."

"Who said anything about giving up?"

"Actions speak louder than words. But I'm betting the right woman could change your mind."

He erased the image of Ashley his brain conjured up. "I'm not discussing this."

"Fine." She motioned ahead with her hand. "We're in luck. A vacant parking spot near Charley's is a rarity in my limited experience."

She sped up and swung in. "You want to get the food while I secure a seat?"

He surveyed the stand. For once there was no one in line waiting for a taco fix. Too bad that hadn't happened more often, or he'd have become a regular customer. "I can do that. But Laura . . ." He touched her arm as she reached to open her door. "Leave me out of the discussion during your tea with Ashley on Saturday."

"That's a tall order. You're our link."

"I have every confidence in your ability to direct the conversation to less personal topics. Promise me you'll do that."

"I can promise to try—but what if she asks questions?"

Not out of the realm of possibility, in light of the ones she'd posed the day he'd told her about his scars.

"Tell her I like my privacy, and that in the interest of sibling harmony you can't talk about me."

"Taking any mention of you off the table would be weird." She tapped a finger against the wheel. "How about a compromise? I can promise not to discuss the accident or anything not publicly known that happened afterward."

He could live with that bargain.

"Deal. But try to steer the conversation away from me."

One side of Laura's mouth rose. "You think Ashley will try to guide it that direction?"

He gritted his teeth. "I didn't say that. I'm more worried about the direction *you'll* guide it. I'm picking up matchmaking vibes."

"You're imagining things." She gave a dismissive wave. "Besides, matchmaking doesn't work unless there's interest on both sides. So far, I've only picked it up on your end."

For some reason, that observation didn't sit well.

"I never said I was interested." His response came out sounding peeved, and he reined in his annoyance. "As I keep reminding you, she's a client."

"Uh-huh." She subjected him to a knowing once-over and opened her door. "Get the tacos. I'm staking a claim on the picnic table that was just vacated."

She was out the door in a flash and jogging toward the pocket park behind the taco stand.

Jon exited the car more slowly and readjusted his scarf, shades, and baseball cap while he walked toward the stand.

As he had on past visits, Charley greeted him with a beaming smile. "Welcome back, Jon. I'm happy to see you out and about on this beautiful evening."

The aroma emanating from behind the counter jump-started his appetite. "My sister didn't want to go back to Colorado without another taste of your tacos. She picked your stand over a sit-down restaurant."

"I'm flattered. Two orders?"

"Yes."

"I've enjoyed chatting with her on her two visits here this week." He pulled fillets out of a cooler and set them on the grill. "How goes the Edgecliff project?"

No surprise Charley knew he'd gotten the job. Nothing stayed a secret in Hope Harbor, especially from the taco-making artist.

"We're getting there, but we have a long way to go. Restoring the grounds of an estate that large is a challenge, made more difficult by years of neglect."

"I can understand that." Charley chopped up red onion with deft fingers. "Bringing ruined gardens back to life, restoring the beauty that was once there, requires vision and patience and plain hard work." He angled sideways. "I'd say you're well-equipped for that job."

As their gazes met, Charley's dark eyes seemed to see straight into the depths of his soul.

Jon's heart stumbled.

Were they still talking about landscaping?

Before he could ponder that question, Charley turned away and tossed the onion onto the griddle. "How's Ashley?"

"Um . . . fine."

"An admirable young woman. She'll be good for Rose."

Jon did a double take. "You know Rose?"

"We became acquainted not long after she arrived in Hope Harbor. She brews a wonderful cup of tea, and her scones are to die for. Stiff competition for the ones at Bayview Lavender Farm."

"You've been to Edgecliff?" The man was full of surprises.

Charley spoke over his shoulder. "Naturally. I'm her taco supplier."

"But I thought . . . that is, she has a reputation as a sort of . . . recluse. I didn't think she socialized."

"She doesn't seek out the company of others, if that's what you mean, but I don't believe she turns away the few people who come to visit her. Don't you two ever talk while you're there cutting her grass?"

"No. I've seen a curtain move on occasion, and I wondered if she was watching me. But she's never come out. I assumed she didn't want to interact."

"It's easier to hide behind curtains sometimes."

Or masks . . . or scarves . . . or sunglasses . . . or caps.

Charley didn't say that as he flipped the fish, but the words hovered in the air nonetheless, as real as if they'd been spoken.

Or was he imagining a message that wasn't there?

The town's resident sage set six corn tortillas

on the grill and flashed him a smile. "Will you give Ashley my regards? And Rose too, if you have the opportunity?"

"Yes."

"I'll have to get up there soon and see the progress that's been made." He shook open a brown bag and set it beside him, then began assembling the tacos. "Marci from the *Herald* says everything appears to be coming together. The open house should be a smashing success."

No need to ask how he knew about that. The man had his finger on the pulse of everything that happened in town.

"Let's hope it brings in business. Ashley and Rose are spending a fortune on the renovations."

"How could it not, with all the energy and enthusiasm Ashley has poured into this project? It's refreshing to see someone with such passion for her work. The world could use more of that. Success doesn't always have to be measured by the almighty dollar." He finished wrapping the last taco and slid it into the bag, along with two bottles of water.

Jon fished out his wallet and extracted cash to cover the tab. "But dollars do pay the bills and put food on the table."

"I agree money is a necessary evil, but it doesn't feed the soul. Nor does hiding behind curtains. And now I'm off for a stroll on the beach as this day winds down. Enjoy your tacos." He reached over his head and pulled down the roll-up shutter that closed off the serving counter, ending the conversation.

For a long moment, Jon remained where he was, the savory smell of the tacos tickling his taste buds.

It appeared his dinner order had come with a generous side of philosophy.

Sort of like his last visit had, early in the spring on a blustery day, when he'd complained about the wind and the fog-reduced visibility on the roads.

What had Charley said then?

Something about how a shift in the wind could usher in a welcome change, clear away fog, and let the sun shine through so the road ahead was clearer.

There were certainly winds of change blowing at Edgecliff, bringing fresh air and new life to the isolated and insulated estate.

He rounded the taco stand and struck out for the tiny park and the picnic table Laura had claimed.

Perhaps there were winds of change blowing in his life too, now that he'd decided to ditch his disguise and begin making a few forays into town, thanks to prodding from Kyle and Laura.

But whether those winds would usher in a sunny day or unleash a new tempest remained to be seen.

15

Laura was already seated when Ashley arrived at the Bayview Lavender Farm tearoom and was shown to their table.

"Sorry I'm a few minutes late." She slipped into the chair across from Jon's sister. "I got stuck on the phone with the caterer for the open house I mentioned while I showed you around Edgecliff. She had quite a few questions."

"No worries. I've been enjoying the relaxing view." Laura swept a hand over the rows of blooming lavender bushes outside the window. "You should too. I'm guessing you could use a little downtime."

Ashley exhaled and looked over the serene scene. "You're right. I've been going nonstop since Rose and I signed on the dotted line, dealing with more than a few challenges and naysayers."

"Who's been giving you grief?"

Oops.

If Mom hadn't called on the heels of the caterer, she'd never have let that slip.

She unfolded the lavender linen napkin and draped it across her lap. "Let's just say my mother isn't gung-ho on this project." She gave Laura a three-sentence explanation. "But my dad would have approved."

"I'm glad of that. Supportive parents are worth their weight in gold."

At the tinge of melancholy in the comment, Ashley studied her. "I take it your parents fall into that category."

"Yes, they did. They're both gone now." She swallowed. Brushed a bead of moisture off her water glass. "They were flying with another couple to a weekend getaway six years ago. Their friend was an experienced pilot, but for reasons never determined, they didn't clear the trees at the end of the runway. No one survived."

Shock rippled through Ashley. Hard as it had been to lose Dad, at least he hadn't been taken in a tragic accident.

"I'm so sorry."

"Thank you. They were wonderful people." Laura sniffed and sipped her water. "Would you like to see their picture? We took a family shot the Christmas before the accident. It's the last one I have of the four of us."

"Yes. Please."

While Laura dug out her cell, the tearoom owner approached. "Welcome again." She set menus on the table. "This is our selection of tea. I'll be back in a few minutes to take your order and answer any questions."

As the woman departed, Laura finished scrolling through her phone and held it out. "From happier times."

Ashley took it, and though she gave Laura's parents a quick glance, it was the tall, dark-haired man standing beside them that drew—and held—her attention.

It had to be Jon.

And whoa! While Jason had been handsome, her ex-beau came in a distant second in the hot department to the brown-eyed man smiling into the camera, whose chiseled jaw, flawless features, and confident bearing were the stuff of Hollywood.

Going from this to whatever lay under the camouflage he'd layered on after the accident would be devastating. No wonder he—

"People always said I resembled my mom."

As Laura spoke, Ashley pried her gaze off the image of Jon and compared mother and daughter. "Yes, you do. The similarity is remarkable." She examined the older couple. "They look like nice people. The kind you'd welcome as neighbors or friends."

"They were. I was blessed to have them as parents." She held out her hand for the phone.

After committing Jon's image to memory, Ashley gave the cell back. "I get the feeling the four of you were close."

"Very. Jon and I still are. More than ever, with Mom and Dad both gone. I also have Bill and the boys to fill in the gaps. I wish Jon had someone too." She tucked the phone back in her purse.

"I imagine the injury had a huge impact on his life, beyond derailing his plans to go into the diplomatic service." If she made a few comments about him, Laura might offer information without her having to ask specific questions.

The other woman hiked up her eyebrows. "He told you about that?"

Whoops.

In light of Jon's reticence, she probably shouldn't have mentioned anything he'd shared with her.

She lifted one shoulder, as if the disclosure was of no consequence. "It just came up in conversation."

Laura's expression was difficult to decipher. Skepticism? Curiosity? Satisfaction? Approval?

All of the above?

The owner returned for their tea order while Ashley tried to analyze her companion's demeanor, but it was hard to interpret the vibes wafting her way as they both settled on the house specialty—lavender lemon.

After the woman departed, Laura picked up the conversation. "I think it's fair to say his life took a dramatic turn. When you're as handsome as Jon was, with a fellow model for a fiancée, such a radical change in appearance would have huge consequences."

Fellow model?

Fiancée?

"You didn't know that part of his background?" Laura appraised her with discerning brown eyes that were a match for her brother's in the photo.

"No." Somehow she found her voice.

The tearoom owner returned with a loaded three-tier stand filled with savories, scones, and sweets, but Ashley was too busy trying to absorb Laura's news to do more than half listen to the owner's description of each item.

Jon had been a model. Engaged to a woman as beautiful as he was handsome.

The kind of injury he'd suffered would be hard enough to stomach for the average person, but for someone who was used to being in front of a camera? A man with silver-screen looks, whose larger-than-life photo may have appeared on billboards?

No wonder he took refuge behind a disguise. Perhaps as much to hide his face from himself as from others.

And if vanity also played a role, as she'd mentioned to him, there was valid justification.

While Laura helped herself to one of the tiny croissants filled with lavender-studded chicken salad, Ashley took a cucumber sandwich and set it on her plate.

"I'm sorry for all your family has been through in the past few years." The words were inadequate, but she infused her tone with heartfelt compassion,

"Thank you." A brief cloud passed over the features of her new acquaintance. "I won't lie. It's been tough. Tougher on Jon. In addition to the grief over Mom and Dad, he had to contend with both a broken body and a broken engagement." She sighed. "I wish he didn't live hundreds of miles away. I'd worry less if he had a close friend or two nearby, but as you may have realized, Daisy is his main source of companionship."

"I'm sure he could make friends if he wanted to. I haven't been here long, but Hope Harbor appears to be a very welcoming town."

"I picked that up too." Laura waited until the owner poured their tea before continuing. "But to be welcomed, you have to be willing to be approached or do the approaching yourself. If I were staying longer, I'd encourage Jon to do that. It's harder from 1,200 miles away." She shook her head and took a sip of tea. "It's such a shame. He's a terrific guy. The kind of man who sticks by a friend through thick and thin. You won't find anyone more loyal or caring or conscientious. Did he tell you about Daisy?"

"No. We haven't had many conversations, and most are work related."

"A pity." Laura didn't elaborate on that succinct reply, instead returning to the subject of his dog. "He adopted her from a rescue shelter in Colorado while he was recovering from his injuries. I convinced him to move there after he was released from the hospital, when he needed a lot of help. You should have seen the poor thing back then. She'd been abused and wouldn't let anyone get close. But Jon worked with her until he earned her trust, showing incredible patience and compassion. And look at her today. She's a happy, healthy, well-adjusted dog who adores her owner."

Another insight into her landscaper's character.

If he'd been that kind to an animal in distress, it was easy to imagine the compassion and care he would lavish on a person who'd won his heart.

"My dad and I had a rescue pup once too. She was well worth the effort to win over. Daisy is one lucky dog."

"That she is." Laura dabbed the napkin at the corner of her mouth. "The thing is, the accident didn't change who Jon is inside, and people who take the time and make the effort to get to know him will see that. If anything, he's more compassionate than ever." She put her napkin back in her lap. "And now, enough heavy talk. We're here to relax. Try the mini chicken salad sandwich. It's fantastic."

For the remainder of the tea, their conversation spanned a wide range of topics. But it didn't return to Jon.

Unfortunately.

Yet what they'd discussed had been enlightening. In the course of those first few minutes, she'd learned more about the wounded landscaper than she had in all her encounters with the man himself.

By the time she parted from Laura outside the tearoom an hour and a half later, Ashley had reached a firm conclusion.

Jonathan Gray was a man she'd like to know better.

And that verdict had nothing to do with the sparks that had skittered along her nerve endings the day he'd leaned close to show her his revised ideas for the gazebo garden.

Oh, come on, Ashley. Who are you trying to kid?

Huffing out a breath, she pulled the keys from her purse and stalked over to her Civic.

Fine.

Jon did have a certain magnetism, despite his scars and camouflage, even if she wasn't in the market for romance.

But beyond that, he also seemed as if he could use a friend, as Laura had confirmed. Why couldn't she offer him that at least?

He'd have to be receptive to such an overture, though, and he'd given no indication he was.

So what could she do to get past the barriers he'd—

Wait.

She stopped beside her car. Frowned.

When had her mission in Hope Harbor morphed from creating a historic special events venue and museum to include helping Rose—and perhaps Jon? Didn't she already have an overflowing plate?

Yes.

Meaning she ought to forget about the two isolated people who seemed in desperate need of the warmth and joy that only human contact provided.

Yet as she slid behind the wheel and pointed the car back toward Edgecliff, her mind was already scrambling to come up with new strategies to persuade Rose to play at the open house and to convince a wounded warrior to accept the hand of friendship she planned to offer.

Someone was playing the piano.

Jon slowed his pace in the circle drive in front of Edgecliff as the muffled notes wafted through the darkness. The piece was classical and vaguely familiar, filled with a deep emotion that clutched at his heart.

It could be a recording, but based on the light filtering around the curtains in the room to the left of the front door where he'd once spotted a piano through the window, it was more likely a live performance.

If so, it had to be Ashley. After all, in the many hours he'd spent on this estate over the past two years, never once had music seeped through the walls of the stately, silent house.

And wow. She was good. Better than good. He might not be a musician, but he could recognize exceptional.

The melody followed him to the gazebo, growing fainter as his distance from the house increased. But once he had his forgotten phone in hand, he returned to the mansion.

Music continued to fill the night. A different selection, but also stirring and evocative.

Could he sit on the steps of the porch and listen for a while? No one would miss him at home. Laura had gone to bed at nine in anticipation of her dawn rising tomorrow to catch her flight, so what was left of the evening was his. As long as he didn't have a Saturday night date, why not end his day with a private concert?

He approached the porch quietly, but as he lowered himself to one of the treads, a slight movement drew his attention.

Someone was sitting in the solitary rocking chair on the front porch, in the shadows, head tipped back.

In the gentle glow of light from around the curtains, it took him but a moment to identify the profile.

It was Ashley.

So who was the pianist?

He hovered halfway down, suspended.

Stay or go?

If he stayed, he'd have to alert Ashley he was here. Watching her clandestinely would be impolite. Or worse.

But sitting here alone in the dark with her, listening to music that stirred the soul, might not be wise. Not if he wanted to keep his distance. Maintain the vendor/client relationship. Follow the smart course.

Did he?

What a ridiculous question.

Of course he did.

Which meant he had to leave.

As he straightened up, the rocking chair creaked and she leaned forward, posture taut, an almost palpable tension emanating from her. "Jon?"

The question was tentative, as if she wasn't certain of his identity.

Understandable, since he'd left his cap, glasses, and scarf at home. Why bother with them when darkness provided excellent cover? Especially since he hadn't planned to run into anyone.

"Yes. Sorry I startled you. I left my phone here earlier, while I was watering a few of the more fragile annuals we planted. I came to get it, heard the music, and walked closer to listen."

She relaxed back against the chair, her features obscured by the dimness. "You seem to be making a habit of scaring me." Amusement feathered the edges of her words, lightening the atmosphere.

"Trust me, it's not intentional." He motioned toward the house. "Who's playing?"

"Rose."

Given that the property was occupied only by the two women, that made sense. But still . . .

"I have to admit I'm surprised."

"You and me both. I heard her a few days ago, and for a brief second I thought maybe the place was really haunted." She set the chair rocking, a hint of laughter in her tone. "I'm trying to convince her to play at the open house, but I'm getting nowhere."

He shoved his fingers into the pockets of his jeans. "From what I know about her, your campaign may be an exercise in frustration."

"I'm finding that out."

"So what are you doing out here at this hour of the—"

"Oh." Ashley stopped rocking, breathing the single syllable as the music shifted yet again. "Puccini. 'O Soave Fanciulla' from *La Bohème*."

"You know your opera."

"Thanks to Dad. We used to listen to recordings on our road trips. He loved classical music." A wistful note crept into her voice. "Why don't you sit? This is too beautiful to miss."

After a brief hesitation, he lowered himself to the step.

Ashley fell silent as Rose played, and he sat back against the column that supported the roof, tuning in to the melody within the house. Even the muffling effect of the walls couldn't diminish the power of the soaring notes.

Not until the last one died away did he speak. "Do you sit out here in the dark every night and listen?"

"No. I'm never certain when—or if—she'll play. But I saw her cross the lawn from the cottage about twenty minutes ago and had a feeling she was coming to visit Allison."

Jon cocked his head. "Who?"

"The piano." Though it was too dark to see her features, the smile in her voice was clear as she explained the name. "It's such a shame she won't share her gift with others."

"From what I understand, she hasn't been part of the world for years. I imagine playing in public would be a huge leap for her."

"But I've made it as safe as possible." She described the arrangement she'd proposed. "It's not healthy for someone to be that cut off from meaningful human interaction."

Silence fell between them as he digested that comment.

Was she talking about Rose, or was her remark also directed at him?

And since when had he begun looking for hidden meanings behind people's comments?

Rose launched into a tune he recognized, and Ashley spoke again, her surprise clear in her inflection. "That's unexpected. I've never heard her play anything but classical music. This is from—"

"*The Phantom of the Opera*—'All I Ask of You.' "

"You know your musical theater."

His lips curved as she parroted his comment back at him. "No, but I've seen that show." Under duress, after Melinda dragged him to a production. While she'd been far more impressed by the dramatic extravaganza than him, this heady, romantic melody had stuck with him. As had the lyrics, which had ended up capturing all he'd yearned for during the rough, early days of his recovery.

All he still yearned for.

A world with no more night—and someone to lead him from his solitude.

Someone like the woman sitting a few feet away.

His throat tightened, and he forced air into his lungs.

"It's an amazing piece of theater, but I prefer happier endings." Ashley's usual upbeat vibe was subdued.

"Life doesn't always provide those." His reply came out choked.

"I know."

He stiffened. No missing that inference. She was talking about him and the accident. Implying she knew what it was like to go through what he'd endured. But no one did. No one had any idea how—

"Jason taught me that."

What?

He peeked at her under cover of night. Her head was bowed, her focus apparently turned inward. To an unhappy ending of her own.

This wasn't about him after all.

Jon took a long, slow breath.

When had he grown so self-absorbed, so touchy, so quick to assume everyone pitied him that he'd become blind to other people's pain?

He forced himself to shift gears.

Her comment invited follow-up, but what could he say? If she wanted to talk about personal matters, she should choose someone she knew well.

Except she couldn't yet have made any close friends here. And considering the mother/daughter relationship she'd described, it was doubtful her mom would be a confidante.

But she must have someone she could talk to. A vibrant woman like Ashley would draw friends like a light drew moths. She could call one of them if she wanted to hash out painful subjects.

Yet her sad admission begged for a response.

For an invitation to unburden her soul if that's what she needed to do. Anyone with an ounce of compassion would offer as much.

The moisture in his mouth evaporated, and his pulse picked up.

You can do this, Gray. Just spit out the question.

Curling his fingers around the edge of the tread, Jon spoke as the muted melody filled the night. "You want to talk about him?"

The question hung between them, dangling in the night air, until heat flooded his cheeks.

So much for trying to be empathetic. Instead, he'd put her in an uncomfortable—

"I've never told anyone what happened."

And why should she start with him? A vendor who was a business associate, not a friend.

Pushing could be a mistake.

Yet all at once, he wanted to know her story. Wanted to know what kind of man would hurt a radiant woman like Ashley, who carried sunshine in her smile and kindness in her heart.

A man who'd spawned a surprisingly intense anger deep within him.

"I take it he was your boyfriend?" The question spilled out before he could stop it.

The music swelled to a crescendo as silence fell between them, filled with unasked questions and unexpressed emotion.

He'd overstepped.

Wiping his palms on the denim stretched taut

227

against his thighs, he stood. "Sorry. I didn't mean to pry. I should go. It's getting late, and—"

"Wait."

He froze, a sudden wave of panic engulfing him.

Maybe pushing hadn't been smart. There was risk if she opened up. He could get sucked in. Begin to care for her. Set himself up for another rejection.

And despite the loneliness that had been plaguing him of late, falling for—and losing—another woman would be worse.

The safest strategy was to cut this conversation short and walk away.

A course he intended to follow as soon as he could formulate an excuse to leave and convince his uncooperative feet to get into gear.

16

Jon was going to walk away.

And she should let him.

Talking about Jason would be hard. And what purpose would it serve?

Except . . .

Ashley gripped the arms of the rocking chair.

Hadn't she, mere hours ago, decided to offer him the hand of friendship? And how better to let him know she'd like to deepen their relationship beyond vendor/client status than by trusting him with a hurtful secret?

As he eased toward the darkness beyond the porch, a wave of panic swept over her. The window of opportunity was closing. Fast. If she didn't act, it would slam shut within seconds.

"Wait." The repeated request came out strangled, and she swallowed. "Please."

He hesitated, but every taut line of his body said he was primed to disappear into the night.

It was now or perhaps never.

She cleared her throat and took the plunge. "If you have a few more minutes, I could use a sympathetic ear."

He shoved his hands into his pockets and remained where he was. "Wouldn't you rather talk about this with a friend? Someone you have a history with?"

He was trying to bail.

Not surprising, but an ego hit nonetheless. Her skills with the male species must be as sadly lacking as her persuasive powers, in light of her failed attempts to convince Rose to play at the open house.

"I don't have any close friends. My parents shared custody, so I spent the school year in one state and summers in another. None of my grade school friendships survived. I lost touch with my high school friends after we graduated and went our separate ways. I was a commuter student in college, which isn't conducive to forming friendships. Being a nose-in-the-book studious type doesn't lead to many friendships either."

"What about career friends?"

"The series of positions I had kept me on the move while I inched closer to my dream job in Tennessee, where Jason occupied my time. Until he didn't." She exhaled as Jon edged deeper into the shadows. She'd have to give him an out. If he didn't want to stay, coercing him into lingering would accomplish nothing. "If you don't want to listen to my sad tale, I understand."

He froze. "I didn't say that."

"Your body language does. You seem poised to flee."

After a few moments, he slowly returned to the

porch and reclaimed his seat on the step. "I can listen."

She released the breath she'd been holding.

First hurdle on the path to friendship cleared.

Gathering her thoughts, Ashley set her chair in motion again. "This is . . . it's hard to talk about."

"I get that."

Yeah, he would, if his fiancée had thrown him over.

"Let me go back to your earlier question. Yes, Jason was a boyfriend. One I believed was destined to become more." She leaned her head back against the tall rocker and looked up at the stars twinkling through the diaphanous furls of fog beginning to swirl through the night.

Several seconds ticked by.

"How did you two meet?"

It was a natural follow-up question, but based on the lag, Jon had had to dig deep for it. As if he was pulling his conversational skills out of the dusty corner of an attic.

"At a society soiree held on the grounds of the historic house where I worked. One of those charitable affairs where people pay five hundred bucks or more for dinner to support a worthy cause. I was there in a professional capacity, as part of my job coordinating special events. He was a guest. We chatted, he called, we started dating. I thought I'd found my dream job and my dream guy in one fell swoop." She gave a humorless laugh. "Wrong. About the guy, anyway."

"He didn't end up being Prince Charming?"

"More like a frog." She rocked harder as all the repressed hurt came surging back. "He began canceling dates at the last minute, always for what seemed to be valid excuses. He had to work late on a hot project. His boss had tapped him for an unexpected business trip. A promising client was in town and had to be wined and dined."

"None of that was true?" Jon's voice was quiet, but there was a hard edge to it.

"I imagine some of it was. He did have a busy, high-profile job in investment banking. But I doubt most of his excuses were legit. And the last one sure wasn't." Another wave of pain washed over her, along with a heaping dose of humiliation.

Jon twisted toward her, his features masked by the darkness, his posture relaxed. Yet there was leashed anger in his inflection. "What happened?"

"Another last-minute out-of-town meeting came up—on his birthday. I canceled the dinner reservation I'd made but decided to at least give him a memorable homecoming. So I got a giant happy birthday banner, a bunch of balloons, and garland and went over to his house to decorate his garage door. It was a rear-entry job, and I wanted him to be surprised when he pulled in. Except I was the one who was surprised."

"He was home." Jon's flat tone suggested he already knew the ending to her story.

"Uh-huh. And not alone. There was a BMW convertible in the driveway. At first, I wondered if someone had stopped by to check the house and get his mail while he was gone, but through the privacy hedge in back I could see him sitting on the edge of his pool. A blond was wrapped around him like an octopus, and there was some heavy stuff going on."

"Did you confront him?" The steel in his manner returned.

"No. I've never been the confrontational type. I waited for him to call me. Two days later, he did. He stuck with his out-of-town story until I told him what I'd seen."

"Did he try to backpedal?"

"On the contrary. He was brutally honest." Thank goodness the darkness hid the blush of mortification on her cheeks. "He said that when we met, he'd been getting over a breakup and needed someone to fill the gap until he found a new girlfriend. After he met Debra—the blond—he strung me along until he was certain she was the one. He said he'd been planning to break up with me in the next few days."

Jon muttered an unintelligible phrase. "There's a term for men like him."

"I know, and it's not fit for polite company."
She tried to inject a light note into her reply
but couldn't quite pull it off. "To rub salt in the
wound, he said he could never fall for someone
whose biggest thrill in life was rooting through
dusty archives and uncovering arcane facts of
history. In other words, a boring loser." Hard
as she tried to remain in control, the last few
syllables wavered. Worse yet, a sniff escaped.

Dang.

Crying hadn't been in her plans. She was past
that with Jason. He didn't deserve any more of
her tears.

"Hey." Jon leaned toward her, extended a hand
. . . then pulled it back. "I'm sorry he hurt you.
And the way I see it, there was only one loser in
the scenario you described—and it wasn't you."

The husky timbre of his voice tightened her
throat again.

"Thanks for that." She groped in her pocket
for a tissue. Swiped at her nose, forcing back
the tears. "But I do lead a boring life by most
people's standards. Contacting Rose, and coming
out here to start over, is the biggest risk I've ever
taken."

"I don't think your life is boring. You're
doing what you love, and it shows. Tackling the
Edgecliff project required vision and enthusiasm
and daring and initiative, and from what I've
seen, you have an endless supply of those."

Warmth radiated through her, chasing away the slight chill in the evening air. "Thank you for that too."

"Just stating the facts." His reply came out a tad gruff.

Pressure built behind her eyes, and she leaned forward. "Can I tell you something?"

A beat ticked by.

"Okay." Though he didn't sound too certain.

"My experience with Jason kind of soured me on romance, but it's nice to know there are guys out there like you who are genuine and honorable." Even if his fiancée hadn't appreciated him.

A few more beats passed before he responded.

"Thanks."

At his flat, perfunctory reply, she peered at him in the dark. "What? You don't believe I think that, or you don't believe you're genuine and honorable?"

He lifted one shoulder. "You don't know me well enough to make that judgment."

"You don't have to know someone forever to get a sense of who they are. I have positive vibes about Laura too, and we've only spent a handful of hours together."

"She's easy to read."

"And you're not?"

"I have a few more layers." He folded his arms, leaned back against the column, and changed the subject. "She said you had fun at tea but didn't offer much beyond that."

Ah.

He was fishing for information about their conversation. Curious how much his sister had shared.

She should give him a top line. To pretend Laura hadn't passed on a few key pieces of information would be disingenuous.

"Yes, we did. But we also had our serious moments. She told me about your parents. I can't begin to imagine how difficult it would be to cope with a loss like that."

Despite the distance separating them, she could hear his long, slow exhale over the achingly tender chords of the music. "It was hard. We had a great relationship."

"I could tell that from the picture she showed me of the last Christmas you all spent together. Everyone looked so happy."

His posture stiffened, but he didn't comment on the photo. "What else did you two talk about?"

"Daisy, and how you adopted her."

"Did she tell you about Melinda?"

Ashley frowned. "Who?"

"The woman I'd planned to marry."

"Oh. She mentioned a broken engagement but few other details." Resting her elbows on the arms of the chair, Ashley continued with a comment rather than a question. "I assumed the incident in the Middle East was a factor in the breakup."

Her carefully phrased statement was as diplomatic as she could make it, giving Jon the option of opening up about his own failed romance or changing the subject.

But as Rose launched into Puccini's "O mio babbino caro," Ashley prayed the emotion-laden melody would touch his heart and help convince him to trust her with his secrets as she'd trusted him with hers.

Surrounded by soaring notes of poignant music and tendrils of fog curling through the night air, Jon took a deep breath.

He could shut down this conversation. Respond with a simple yes, fabricate an excuse to leave, and disappear into the darkness.

But if he wanted a world with no more night, he'd have to step into the sunlight sooner or later. Risk exposure. Share his secrets.

Until now, nothing had enticed him to do that. Not the increasingly oppressive solitude, or the prospect of years ahead filled with empty days and nights, or the lack of physical human warmth in his daily life.

Yet for the first time in half a decade, he was tempted to talk about the trauma that had led to his shattered engagement and derailed his plans for the future.

Maybe it was the stirring music wafting through the air.

Maybe it was the growing need to assuage the chronic loneliness that had begun to chip away at his soul.

Maybe it was the not-so-subtle nudge from Kyle and Laura to get back into circulation, expand his social circle beyond Daisy.

More likely, though, it was the sympathetic, receptive woman sitting a few feet away in the dark who filled the night with a light more luminous than the glow provided by the silver moon playing peekaboo with the fog.

The question was, did he have the courage to do what she'd done minutes ago and bare his heart?

"You know, I think the fog is getting thicker." Ashley's observation was a touch too bright. As if she'd sensed his indecision in the long stretch of silence between them and decided to do the shutting down herself. "During my short tenure here, I've already learned how fast it can disorient. I wouldn't want you to get lost going home."

She was giving him an opportunity to escape.

But despite the sudden terror nipping at his courage, he didn't want to take it.

Pulse spiking, he sucked in air.

He should talk to her. Baring his soul under the cloak of darkness was about as safe as it got. She'd told him her story, and turnabout was fair play. Unless he wanted to send a strong I'm-not-interested-in-getting-to-know-you message.

A message that would be a lie.

The truth was, he did want to get to know her.

And to do that, he'd have to crack the door and let her in.

Resting his forearms on his thighs, he laced his unsteady fingers. Tight. Stared at his knuckles. "I can find my way home through the fog. My brick-and-mortar home, anyway. But it's not always as simple to find your way home in life. Especially after someone you love walks out, as you know."

The creaking ceased, indicating she'd stopped rocking. "I'm not certain I do. Not to the same degree you do. Jason and I weren't engaged."

"You expected to be."

"Yes, but I'm beginning to realize I mistook infatuation for love. Jason was handsome and wealthy and polished, and I was flattered someone like him even noticed me, let alone asked me out. I guess the stars in my eyes blinded me to his real character. Or more accurately, lack of character. The breakup would have been much worse if my infatuation had been real love and we'd been engaged, like you were." She started rocking again. "Laura said your fiancée was a model."

"Yeah." He continued to focus on his linked fingers. "Did she tell you how we met?"

"No."

"Did she tell you I used to model too?"

"Not directly. I think she assumed I knew."

He loosened his interlocked fingers, flexed them to restore circulation, and leaned back against the column again. "It was a fluke, how it came about. An advertising executive in our town saw me in a high school play when I was sixteen. She approached me afterward and asked me to have my parents contact her if I was interested in a modeling gig for a print ad campaign she was putting together for a new beverage product. She said I had the look she was after."

"That must have been flattering."

"Probably not as much to a guy as it would have been to a girl. And I wasn't interested. I stuck her card in my pocket and forgot about it. My mom found it while she was doing the laundry later that week."

"She encouraged you to follow through?"

"Yes. She knew I was getting ready to apply for a summer job and thought this was worth investigating. As usual, she was right. The pay was excellent compared to what my buddies were earning at fast-food joints or doing yard work or selling popcorn at the movie theater. The first job led to another, which led to an agent, which led to more gigs that helped put me through college."

"Sounds glamorous."

"The glamour aspect is highly overrated."

"Did you enjoy it?"

He shrugged. "It was just a job to me. An easy one. And the money was good. But it wasn't what I wanted to do with my life, even before the accident. I already had the State Department in my sights."

"So how did you end up in the army?"

He lifted his head, following the flight of a pelican as it sailed across the moon through the sinuous whorls of fog. "I figured military service would be a helpful credential for government work, and at the risk of sounding hokey, after enjoying the liberty so many people in the world don't have, I wanted to do my part to help promote and preserve freedom in places where it was threatened."

"That doesn't sound hokey to me." Her response was serious and earnest. "It sounds generous and brave and admirable."

Heat suffused his cheeks. "Don't give me too much credit. If I'd known how it was going to end, I wouldn't have enlisted or re-upped."

"I stand by my comment. You knew the risks when you did both."

"In principle. But I was one of those guys who was convinced he was invincible. Melinda worried about the danger more than I did."

"How did you two connect, anyway?" Ashley began rocking again.

"On leave. I was back in the States, stationed at

241

Fort Benning between deployments, and I came home to Atlanta for Christmas. My old agent was having a holiday party and invited me. Melinda was there, and we clicked. Since Fort Benning was only about a hundred miles away, we made that drive often."

"I imagine she was beautiful."

At Ashley's wistful tone, Jon shifted toward her. Surely she wasn't insecure about her own appearance, not with those killer eyes and generous lips and glorious hair that glinted with auburn highlights?

But a breakup could do serious damage to an ego, as he well knew. And if hers needed bolstering, he could oblige without stretching the truth a fraction of an inch.

"In a theatrical sense. She was into clothes and makeup and glitz. But with the perspective I've gained over the past five years, I've come to recognize and prefer substance over fluff. Vision and enthusiasm and daring and initiative and a host of other qualities in addition to physical beauty create a much more appealing package."

Other than the background piano music, silence descended.

Crud.

He'd said too much. Boosting her ego was fine. Implying he had romantic inclinations by repeating his earlier description of her wasn't.

How was he supposed to dig himself out of this hole?

Thankfully, Ashley came to his rescue. Rather than comment on his faux pas, she asked another question about Melinda—though there was an undertone to it, and a breathiness, that was hard to decipher.

"So you two fell in love through a semi-long-distance relationship."

"Yes. Eight months after we met, and six weeks before I was redeployed to the Middle East, we got engaged. We were supposed to be married a month after I got back. Instead, just days away from discharge, I ran into the IED. That was the end of a lot of things. Including my relationship with Melinda."

"She broke the engagement just because you were injured?" Shock vibrated in the air between them.

"If you'd seen me in those early days, you'd understand."

"No. I don't think I would. You don't desert someone you love." Her declaration was laced with passion and indignation. "It's all about for better or worse, right?"

"We hadn't taken that vow yet."

"Do you think she'd have stuck with you if you had?"

Jon squinted at the moon, barely visible now beyond the mist.

That wasn't a question he'd ever pondered.

But in light of Melinda's reaction the day she'd seen his injuries, and the speed with which she'd fled, maybe not.

Was it possible the appeal of a handsome soldier, and the allure of exotic travel to distant locations as a diplomatic spouse, had been higher in her priorities than love? After all, her career as a model had plateaued. None of the high-profile runway gigs she'd coveted had materialized. Print ads and a few commercials paid the bills, but it wasn't the lifestyle she'd once confided she aspired to.

"Jon, I'm sorry." Ashley's apology was subdued and contrite. "That was out of line. I didn't mean to offend you."

He shifted gears and refocused. "No offense taken. But your question isn't one I've considered. To be honest, I'm not certain about the answer. I'd like to say yes, but in hindsight I don't know. The life she would have had was nothing like the one I'd promised her."

"What happened wasn't your fault, though. And your life was altered forever too. It seems to me that once you commit to someone, you have to be ready to adapt to changed circumstances."

"In my case, that also included a changed appearance."

"But you healed."

"Not without scars. I'll never again look like that picture Laura showed you."

"I don't mean to be trite, but the old saying is true. Beauty is only skin deep."

"Tell that to a model who relies on her face to put bread on the table. I can't honestly say I blame her for her repulsed reaction at our first meeting after the accident. I was horror-movie worthy."

"You've hinted on more than one occasion that you still are."

Yeah, he had. But according to Laura, that perception was off base.

"I may have exaggerated. The doctors did a remarkable job patching me back up, considering what they had to work with, and the scars have faded somewhat. But I'll never be a model again."

"Most of us aren't to begin with. And those who never met you pre-accident won't have anything to compare to. Why not give people a chance?"

Same message Laura and Kyle had sent. Even Charley had intimated that he should stop hiding behind masks and scarves and sunglasses and caps.

Was there a secret plot to push him to reenter society?

The last notes of an unfamiliar melody died away, and a few moments later the light went out in the room on the left, giving him an excuse to change the subject. "I think our concert is over."

"I guess so." But she remained seated, as if reluctant for this interlude to end.

He could relate.

With the fog thickening, however, it could be dangerous to linger. Despite his assurance to Ashley that he could manage the walk home without a problem, it was easy to get lost when the road ahead was unclear.

The time had come to leave.

Calling up every ounce of his self-discipline, he pushed himself to his feet. "I should go."

"I suppose it *is* getting late." She stood too. "Thanks for listening tonight. It was a treat to have someone to talk to. I love what I'm doing at Edgecliff, but sometimes it gets kind of lonely. I mean, Rose is here, but she keeps to herself."

Pressure built in his throat at her melancholy tone. "I hear you. It gets lonely at my place too. Daisy's fine company, but her conversational skills are limited."

She took two tentative steps toward him, putting herself almost within touching distance if he stretched out his arm. "Maybe sometime, if you have a few spare minutes, we could do this again."

"Maybe we could." He dipped his chin to hide his features in case her night vision was sharper than his.

"Friends?" She extended her hand.

Fingertips tingling, he regarded it.

How could he resist the offer of friendship with this woman, who radiated energy and enthusiasm and caring? Who brightened the world with her presence?

Slowly he lifted his hand. Stretched it out. Captured her delicate fingers in his. "Yes."

And perhaps, if God deigned to grant this wayward son of his a favor, it might become more down the road. After Ashley put her failed romance with Jason to rest. After they got to know each other. After he found the courage to let her see him in daylight. Assuming she didn't turn tail and run, as Melinda had.

A big assumption.

Because while his appearance these days was less shocking and scary, it would take a miracle for a beautiful woman like Ashley to be able to see past his scars and—

She squeezed his fingers, and a powerful yearning swept over him. So strong it was impossible to resist the urge to squeeze back . . . and ease closer.

Under the cloak of fog and darkness, it was hard to see her features. But his other senses more than compensated. Her faint, fresh scent, with a hint of floral that spoke of warm summer days, soaked into his pores. Her skin was soft and silky against his calloused palm. Her respiration was as rapid as his own.

After five years on the sidelines of the relation-ship game, it was possible his instincts were rusty. But if he was reading her signals right, she was receptive to a kiss.

It was too soon for that, though.

Or was it?

Why not give her a sweet memory to mitigate her reaction when she saw him in daylight and remind her that underneath his scars, his heart had an immense capacity for passion and tenderness?

Pulse thundering, he tugged ever-so-slightly on her hand, urging her toward him. If she resisted, he'd back off.

If she didn't?

Tonight could launch a whole new chapter in his life—and mark the end of the solitary confinement he'd consigned himself to during his lonely tenure in a town with a name that promised so much more.

17

Good heavens.

Was that a man and woman holding hands on her front porch, or was the mist playing tricks on her eyes?

As Rose pulled the front door wider and peered into the darkness, her question was answered.

The two people jerked apart and swung toward her.

They were real.

And while it was impossible to read the woman's expression in the dim light and fog, there was no question about her identity.

"Gracious, Ashley. You startled me." Rose stared at her while the man melted back into the shadows at the base of the porch.

"I could say the same." Her hand flew to her chest, and she offered a laugh that sounded forced.

"I don't often find people on the front porch at this hour of the night—except one Halloween a few years back. But a call to the police chief took care of that problem. I don't think such drastic action is necessary tonight, though."

Not by a long shot.

Unless she'd misread the situation, a kiss had been imminent.

"No. Definitely not. It's just me and, uh, Jon. You know, the man who cuts your grass. Also our landscaper."

And a bit more, in light of their interrupted almost-clinch.

Could there be a budding romance on the Edgecliff grounds?

Rose studied the man on the fringes of the porch, who was no more than a shadowy outline. "We've never met. My legal advisor handles the contracts for that sort of work."

"Oh. Well . . ." Ashley offered a vague wave his direction. "This is Jonathan Gray. We were, uh, saying good night."

"I'm sorry I interrupted. Good evening, Mr. Gray. It's a pleasure to make your acquaintance."

"Jon is fine, and it's nice to meet you too."

His husky response came across as sincere, but he kept his distance.

Why?

All at once, a comment David had made when he'd hired the man's firm echoed in the recesses of her mind. Something about supporting a wounded veteran who was launching a new business.

Were war injuries the reason he always wore a cap and glasses and that neck covering she'd noticed while peeking through the windows as he worked? Were they also why he remained in the shadows tonight?

And how had he and Ashley gotten to the kissing stage in less than a month?

Hmm.

Her partner was certainly old enough to make her own decisions about men, and the meticulous plans and accounting records she shared during their daily meetings indicated she had a precise and clear-thinking mind, but hormones could short-circuit even a smart woman's brain.

A lesson she'd learned to her detriment, with disastrous consequences.

Perhaps it would be wise to get to know this young man. To protect her investment, if nothing else.

She pulled her sweater tighter around her. "I came outside to sit for a few minutes, but I didn't realize fog had descended. It's quite thick tonight."

"Yes. We were talking about that while we enjoyed the concert."

Warmth flooded Rose's cheeks. "You were sitting out here in the dark listening? Why didn't you come inside?"

"I didn't think you wanted an audience."

"An audience of strangers, no. Friends, on the other hand, are always welcome to listen. That includes you, Jon."

"Thank you." His head swiveled in Ashley's direction, then back toward her. "But it's a shame not to share your talent with others. If your playing could reel in someone like me who knows nothing about classical music, imagine what it could do for people who already appreciate it."

Rose tried without success to read Ashley's face. If she'd told him about her open house recruitment campaign, it was possible he was trying to lend a hand. Help convince a reluctant pianist to take the plunge.

Sweet, and rather endearing, but she wouldn't let such efforts influence her decision.

"I don't play in public anymore."

"That's too bad." Jon eased farther back into the shadows, leaving his features more hidden than ever. "It's like putting a lamp under a basket, to paraphrase a Bible verse my mom used to quote."

If the man knew his Scripture, there might be less to worry about in terms of his involvement with Ashley.

"Yes, I'm familiar with that one. From Matthew." The very verse she'd been thinking about since Ashley had asked her to play at the open house, along with the parable about the talents. Not that she intended to bring that up or discuss the matter further tonight. A change of subject was in order. "I think I'll forego my plan to sit on the porch. It may be more prudent to go back to my cottage before this fog gets any worse."

"Why don't I walk with you?" Ashley moved toward her. "It would be easy to trip in the dark."

Rose opened her mouth to decline. Shut it. Following the narrow gravel drive that led to the cottage wouldn't be difficult to do alone, but why not give these two young people an excuse to extend their evening?

"Your company would be most welcome. Thank you. Perhaps Jon will walk with us too, in case we run into a ghost or two."

"I'm not too worried about that." Ashley's lips twitched.

"If ever you were to encounter one, though, this would be the place, wouldn't it?" She swept a hand over the mist-shrouded grounds. "But it won't be a problem tonight. The resident ghost isn't doing any haunting this evening. She confines that to Halloween."

"You've seen a ghost here?" Ashley's eyes widened.

Rose gave a soft laugh. "No, my dear. I *am* the ghost here. After the incident on Halloween, I initiated a new ritual. Every year, on that night, I dress in a long white gown, walk past the windows carrying a candle, and play the title song from *The Phantom of the Opera* on Allison— with the window open. I decided to give any ghost-seekers a thrill and fuel speculation about spectral sightings. It's been quite amusing."

A male chuckle rumbled in the darkness. "That sounds like a scheme my sister would dream up. After we got too old to dress up and

253

traipse through the neighborhood for candy on Halloween, she turned our garage into a haunted house for the local kids. I was always recruited for one of the more gruesome roles."

"I believe I'd like your sister." Rose gave him a smile he likely couldn't see in the darkness.

"Everyone does."

"May I call on you for an escort? Not to diminish Ashley's strength, but she's a slip of a thing and I'd welcome a sturdy arm to hold on to on my trip back to the cottage."

He hesitated, but only for an instant. "I'd be happy to walk you home."

"Wonderful. Let me lock up first. Why don't we cut through the house and I'll activate the security system by the back door?"

Jon eased farther into the darkness. "I'll circle around and meet you there."

He didn't want the light to shine on his face.

Gracious.

How bad did he look?

Evidently bad enough to keep him in the shadows, which was a shame.

But who was she to criticize people who shunned the spotlight?

"That will be fine. Ashley, come along and help me check the lights." She took the other woman's arm and guided her inside, locking the door behind them. "Why don't you circle left and I'll go right? We can meet up in the kitchen."

Two minutes later, when they rendezvoused, Ashley appeared less flustered. "No lights on my side."

"Nor on mine." Rose strolled over to the security system control panel and flipped open the door, keeping her inflection casual. "I didn't realize you'd become such close friends with our landscaper."

"I haven't. We're, uh, just getting acquainted. He came by tonight for the cell phone he forgot earlier and we, uh, ran into each other."

"I get the feeling he's on the skittish side."

"He is. He was injured in the Middle East and usually wears a cap and sunglasses to cover the scars, but he didn't expect to run into anyone here tonight." She glanced toward the back door. "I was surprised he agreed to walk you back to the cottage. He won't be able to keep his distance."

"Well, it's dark and foggy out—and he may not care if *I* see his scars."

Ashley frowned. "Maybe I should slip out a different door. I don't want to make him uncomfortable."

"That's very considerate, but it's possible he'd like to continue the conversation I interrupted. Why don't you join us?"

"No." She shook her head, a hint of panic flaring in her eyes as she backed toward the hallway. "I'm ready to call it a night. If you'll give me a minute to leave through the terrace door, I'll lock it behind me."

"Don't you want to say good night to Jon?"

Ashley continued backing away. "You can pass that on for me, if you wouldn't mind."

"Not at all."

With that, her partner fled.

An apt description. That girl was running scared.

And that wasn't all bad. Getting carried away with romantic fancies could lead to heartache, especially if you fell for the wrong person. She was wise to be wary.

After the green light on the security panel indicated Ashley had slipped out, Rose armed the system and crossed to the back door.

Her attempt to give the two young people a chance to extend their evening after her ill-timed interruption may have failed, but it wouldn't hurt to have a few minutes one-on-one with Jon. That would allow her to do a more thorough assessment.

He was waiting in the shadows as she exited and locked the door. "Ashley went on ahead to the carriage house. She asked me to tell you good night."

"Thanks for passing that on." His relief was obvious.

Apparently Ashley wasn't the only one running scared.

She extended her arm, and after a moment he emerged from the fog and grasped her hand, still staying as far away as possible.

"Watch the step." He dipped his chin and motioned toward the ground.

"I'll be careful."

Once she was on level terrain, he crooked his elbow. "Even after two years here, I haven't gotten used to the fog."

"It can be quite intimidating." She slipped her hand through his arm as they set off. "Where are you from?"

"Born and raised in Atlanta."

"Ah. I thought I detected a slight southern accent."

"You have an excellent ear. There isn't much left."

"I knew someone once from the South." No point in telling him her husband had been raised in Alabama.

"I consider myself an Oregonian now. By the way, Charley Lopez asked me to give you his regards."

"Thank you. He's such a dear man." A light came on in the carriage house as they passed, and Rose motioned toward the ghostly glow in the fog. "Ashley's another dear person. She came along right when I needed someone like her in my life. God was watching out for me, I think."

"Or it was a lucky coincidence."

She looked up at him. Whatever physical scars he bore were impossible for eighty-year-old eyes to discern in the dark and mist, but his jaw was somewhat asymmetrical.

His scornful tone, on the other hand, was crystal clear. A definite indication his scars were more than skin-deep.

"You don't believe in God's providence?"

"Let's just say I haven't seen much evidence of it."

"Yet you quoted the Bible."

"Correction. My mother quoted the Bible. I was relaying what she told me."

"So you're not a believer?" She might have to rethink his suitability for Ashley.

"I didn't say that. But God and I haven't communicated in a while."

"Ashley goes to church every Sunday."

"My sister does too."

"Church attendance is a fine habit."

"Do you go?"

Touché.

"God and I have an understanding."

Several seconds passed before he responded. "My mother also used to remind us not to cast the first stone unless we were without sin." His manner was conversational, but his message hit home.

Fighting back a niggle of guilt, she motioned to the path. "Watch your step." A warning as much for herself as it was for him. She didn't know his history, didn't know what had driven a wedge between him and God. It was wrong to judge or criticize or jump to conclusions. "There's a small rut in the drive about here that we should avoid."

"Thanks for the warning. Ruts can be dangerous."

In more ways than one, as Charley had reminded her.

She tightened her grip on his arm and redirected the conversation. "In case you didn't know, Ashley has been trying to convince me to play the piano at the open house next weekend."

"She mentioned that. After tonight, I can see why. I hope you'll reconsider."

The light from the carriage house was swallowed up by the fog as they approached the cottage. "I'm giving it more thought."

"Makes sense. Any big step should be carefully considered."

His pensive tone suggested he was talking about more than a piano concert.

When they reached her small porch, Jon reclaimed his arm and moved back.

"Thank you for the escort." She motioned toward the fog. "Will you be able to navigate in this pea soup?"

"I'm used to walking the route to my house. Sleep well."

With that, he pivoted and disappeared into the mist.

Rose didn't linger outside. Even after years of living on the coast, the combination of fog and darkness was unsettling. Maybe because her mother had perished on a night much like this one after wandering too close to the perilous precipice on the perimeter of the estate.

Truly, it wasn't safe for anyone to be out and about on such a night.

But Jon had been confident about finding his way back to his house, if not to God. Or perhaps even Ashley.

As she closed and locked the door behind her, Rose flipped on a light.

Much better. In the cheery, cozy cottage she now called home, the disorienting fog felt far away.

But the decision about the open house loomed, chasing away thoughts of slumber despite her later-than-usual bedtime.

A cup of tea and a visit with Lucy Lynn should help clear her mind, though.

After taking off her sweater, she ambled through the living room toward the kitchen, straightening the poster she'd recently hung that bore the words she read every day.

Never look back.

Wise advice. Yesterday couldn't be changed. Today was almost over. But tomorrow?

That held promise—and possibilities.

Thanks to Ashley.

Lips curving up, she opened a cabinet and selected a bag of soothing chamomile tea.

From the day that young woman had appeared with her energizing vision for Edgecliff, life had become much more interesting. In fact, it had expanded to include more of everything. More people. More activity. More excitement.

And both she and Lucy Lynn had benefitted from it, even if the path ahead wasn't as predictable or clear-cut as it had once been.

She filled a mug with water, added the bag, and slid it into the microwave.

One thing for certain.

The seed Ashley had planted about playing at the open house hadn't fallen on fallow ground. It had taken root and was sprouting leaves.

Whether it would continue to grow and flourish remained to be seen. By morning, it was possible it would wither and die.

Yet as she waited for her tea to brew, Rose knew deep in her soul that wasn't going to happen. Unless a severe case of cold feet undermined her courage, she was going to take a giant leap of faith and play at the open house.

And hope her bold decision didn't come back to haunt her far more than any imagined ghost at Edgecliff ever had.

18

Jon was avoiding her.

Shading her eyes, Ashley scanned the workers scrambling to get the gazebo and grounds ready for the open house that was a mere forty-eight hours away.

Her landscaper was nowhere to be seen.

As usual.

And who could blame him for his disappearing act, after the impulsive almost-kiss last Saturday? The one that had kept her awake far too late for the past five nights.

Even now, days later, thinking about the magnetic-like force that had drawn them together sent her pulse skyrocketing.

The music . . . the fog . . . the feel of otherworldliness in the mist-shrouded landscape . . . all of those had joined forces to transport them to another dimension for those few brief seconds.

There was no discounting a healthy dose of hormones in the mix either.

Whatever the factors that had sent them spiraling toward a kiss, the combination had been potent.

She sighed.

No wonder Jon had delegated Kyle to run interference for him on the job ever since. He must be as embarrassed by the near miss as she was.

And who knew where it would have led if Rose hadn't interrupted?

A delicious shiver rippled through her, and she clamped her lips together.

That was inappropriate. She wasn't in the market for romance. Not after Jason's betrayal. Nor did she have time for dating and all its attendant demands. She was already juggling too many plates.

There had been one positive outcome from that evening, though.

Rose had agreed to play the piano.

Unfortunately, the week had gone downhill from there with a string of crises, from delayed delivery of bathroom fixtures in the women's powder room to a scramble to book an emergency housecleaning session to deal with the drywall dust that had left a fine white film on everything.

At least those issues had been resolved.

But while the subcontractor Jon's firm had hired to lay the gravel for the parking lot had done the prep earlier in the week, no rock had yet been put down—and someone needed to get on that ASAP. With the possibility of rain in the forecast for Saturday, a finished lot was essential. Traipsing through mud to get to the front door would *not* make a favorable first impression on her guests or generate bookings.

Kyle appeared in the distance, phone to his ear, and as he walked toward the round garden in the center of the circle drive, Ashley waved to catch his attention.

He acknowledged her summons but continued to gesture as he spoke to whoever was on the other end of the line, his body language communicating agitation.

Uh-oh.

Another glitch in her inaugural event would bump the blender in her stomach from pulse to purée.

As Kyle's conversation dragged on, a truck turned in at the entrance that had been excavated from its Sleeping Beauty tangle of brush, vines, and thorns.

Jon.

Her heart stuttered, and she scuttled back into the shadows of the porch, out of sight.

Which was ridiculous.

She was thirty-two years old, for pity's sake, not sixteen. So she and Jon had almost kissed. So what? They were both adults. They'd both been in other relationships. All they had to do was attribute the lapse to the ethereal ambiance that night and move on.

Heck, it was possible he already had. That he hadn't been avoiding her at all but instead was slammed trying to coordinate the huge amount of work still to be done by Saturday. For all she knew, he'd forgotten about the incident days ago.

She should do the same.

Too bad her heart wasn't listening to that logic.

When Jon parked the truck and slid out of the cab near Kyle, his foreman shifted the phone aside, spoke to his boss, and motioned her direction.

Forcing up the corners of her mouth, Ashley sidled out of the shadows and raised a hand in greeting.

After a moment, he reciprocated. Then he spoke again to Kyle.

The other man shook his head and pointed to his phone.

Left with no choice, Jon approached her from the other side of the circle garden. As he drew close, the air whooshed out of her lungs.

His usual sunglasses were in place, but the scarf and cap were gone, leaving his face on almost full display.

Rather than meet him halfway, she gripped the edge of the bannister and held on tight.

Don't stare, Ashley. Be discreet. Don't do anything to make him feel self-conscious. Steel yourself to however bad it is.

As that mantra looped through her mind, he reached the end of the walkway in front of the house. Paused. Lifted his hand and removed his glasses.

Even from fifty feet away, down the long stone path bordered by the lush gardens his crew had installed, hints of the damage he'd suffered were visible.

The late morning sun cast a sheen on the white scars stippling the left side of his face and neck, and his jaw was . . . wrong. Without the scarf to disguise it, the misshapen appearance, though not dramatic, was far more apparent.

He bore very little resemblance to the man in the photo Laura had shown her.

And as he slowly began to walk toward her, the full extent of the damage began to click into focus.

The scar she'd noticed on his cheek during their first meeting was, in fact, a network of pocked blemishes that ran from his forehead to his chin, down his neck . . . and who knew how much farther?

Mercy.

What must he have suffered if this was how he looked five years after the explosion?

Pressure built behind her eyes, and she gritted her teeth. Dammed up her tears. Letting them leak out could send a very bad message.

By the time he stopped at the bottom of the steps, the brilliant sunlight mercilessly high-lighting the evidence of his injuries, she'd done her best to rein in her emotions and erase any evidence of distress.

"Kyle said you flagged him down. What can I help you with?"

Her brain tried to process Jon's question.

Failed.

Did he expect her to disregard his discarded camouflage?

But that was like ignoring the elephant in the room.

Even if he'd been able to attribute their near-kiss to a foolish mistake and brushed it aside, how could she not mention the bold step he'd taken after the story he'd shared with her Saturday night?

"Ashley?"

At his prompt, she moistened her lips and prayed she wasn't making another mistake. "You aren't wearing your cap and glasses and scarf."

The uninjured side of his mouth quirked up, but his tone was serious. "On the advice of someone I trust."

She blinked.

Was he talking about her or Laura? Or both?

Before she could respond, he spoke again. "But it may have been a mistake. I think I've shocked a few people. Present company included."

"I'm not shocked."

His gaze dropped to her hands.

She looked down. Her knuckles were bloodless as she gripped the railing.

Heat suffused her cheeks, and she pried her

fingers loose. "You prepped me for your appearance. I'm more shocked that you let go of the disguise so fast." A slight stretch of the truth, but not a total fabrication.

"It was time." He rested a hand on the bottom newel post of the railing. The one that was missing two fingers. "I got tired of living behind a mask. I did warn you it wasn't pretty."

She forced her balking legs to carry her forward, studying him as he stood at the base of the steps. "Yes, you did. And no, it's not." She wasn't going to lie. "But the damage also isn't worthy of a horror movie. Or even Rose's haunted house."

"I'm not certain about that. This three-fingered man, who's legally blind in his left eye, also has major scarring here." He swept a hand down his left arm and left leg. "It would be enough to scare some people."

She digested the news about his vision issues as she lifted her chin. "I'm not one of them."

"Good to know. What did you want to ask Kyle?"

That was it. He was getting back to business, with no mention of Saturday night.

But if he didn't want to talk about it, forcing the issue could be a tactical error. Besides, the ditched disguise was plenty to deal with for one day.

"I wanted to get an update on the parking lot."

"That's where I was this morning. I thought an in-person visit would light a fire under them. They'll be here by two o'clock. I don't think they wanted to tangle with a guy who looks like me." Again, he hitched up one side of his mouth. "There may be some utility to my appearance on the business side as an intimidation factor."

He was joking about his scars?

That was a positive sign. Wasn't it?

"Whatever works. I have to have a parking lot by Saturday."

"It will be ready. And now that BJ's crew has finished the gazebo, we'll be able to get the plantings done around the base. You'll be all set."

"That helps my stress level. And I have good news too. Rose is going to play."

A genuine smile brightened his features. "I'm glad to hear that."

"I think your encouragement made the difference. She's mentioned you in several of our conversations since Saturday."

His gaze locked on to hers. "Saturday was . . . memorable."

Her respiration went haywire.

Was he talking about the impromptu concert or the almost-kiss?

If it was the latter, all at once she wasn't ready to deal with it.

"Yes. Rose is an amazing p-pianist. She used to play for a living."

After regarding her in silence for a few beats, he motioned toward the side lawn. "I want to check on the progress by the gazebo. I'll see you later."

Without waiting for a response, he strode away.

As he disappeared around the side of the house, she drew a shaky breath and gripped the railing again.

For a woman who didn't like loose ends, she hadn't handled that very well. If Saturday night was on his mind, like it was on hers, they were going to have to discuss it sooner or later.

But first she had to digest and adjust to his appearance sans disguise.

No, his scars weren't horror-movie caliber anymore. She hadn't lied about that. But it was easy to see how they could have been in the beginning. Even now, years later, they would attract second glances. As anything outside the normal range did.

Except this was normal for him now.

And it always would be.

Hopefully, once people got used to his appearance, they'd be more interested in what was under his skin than on his skin.

But it was impossible to deny that the scars were off-putting. At the very least.

A gust of wind tousled her hair, spurring her to turn back to the house and head for the door. Standing around worrying about how her reaction would affect their relationship while there was a huge list of chores to do wasn't productive.

But no matter what other problems she grappled with for the rest of this day, one would be front and center in her mind.

What was she supposed to do about her growing feelings for a man who looked nothing like the Prince Charming of her dreams but whose courage and persistence in the face of adversity and overwhelming odds put that fairy-tale hero to shame?

"Jon! Wait up!"

At the summons, Jon pivoted away from the mailbox outside the Hope Harbor post office, letters poised halfway to the slot.

Charley waved at him from halfway down the block, his usual smile in place.

His stomach bottomed out.

The coast had been clear when he'd parked beside the box and slid out from behind the wheel, so where had Charley come from?

Who knew?

But the last thing he needed today was another shocked reaction, especially after his earlier encounter with Ashley at Edgecliff.

Yet how could he be rude to a man who'd never shown him anything but kindness and understanding?

After dropping his bill payments into the box,

he braced, swiveled, and lifted a hand in greeting. "Afternoon, Charley."

"I'm glad I spotted you." The taco-making artist stopped in front of him. If the exposed scars shocked him, his placid features gave no indication of it. "I was in the mood for a café de olla from The Perfect Blend." He motioned toward the coffee shop a few doors down. The one Jon had been tempted to try on numerous occasions but had never worked up the courage to set foot in. "I was hoping to find someone to join me. Can I tempt you to take a break for a few minutes? Coffee shared with a friend always tastes better."

Venture into a public place without his disguise?

No way.

The construction and landscaping crews at Edgecliff had gotten past his scars after several days of seeing him without his disguise, but the initial shocked stares and averted gazes had nicked away at his confidence. And Ashley's distraught expression an hour ago hadn't helped, despite her efforts to moderate it.

Maybe his decision to dispense with his camouflage in one fell swoop rather than piecemeal had been premature.

"I'm on a tight schedule this week, trying to tie up a bunch of loose ends before the open house at Edgecliff."

"I imagine you are. That will be quite an event. I understand Rose is going to play."

Jon frowned.

Hadn't Ashley said she was keeping Rose's identity under wraps?

"I don't think that's widely known."

"I expect not, but Rose and I stay in touch. I was glad to hear she'd decided to venture into the world again, if only on a small scale. It isn't healthy to cut yourself off from people, although I do understand the merit of taking small and safe steps." He adjusted the brim of his Ducks cap, his demeanor warm and encouraging.

Was Charley talking about Rose? Or was that comment directed at him?

The town sage picked up the conversation without giving him a chance to respond. "The Perfect Blend will be winding down for the day. It closes at one, you know. I expect there are few customers inside at this hour."

In other words, venturing inside should be low risk.

And he'd been wanting to try the place for months. The coffeemaker at his house produced a serviceable mug of caffeine, but anything other than straight java was beyond its capabilities.

His taste buds began to tingle at the thought of a barista-brewed treat.

"I see I've tempted you." Charley's smile widened. "Let me introduce you to the most authentic Mexican coffee this side of the border. My treat."

"That's a hard offer to refuse."

"Then don't." The man swept a hand toward the shop in invitation. "I guarantee you won't regret it. Zach's created a peaceful oasis that de-stresses everyone who walks through the door."

"Sold."

He fell in beside Charley, but as they struck off down the street, the knot in his gut tightened. Despite his companion's reassurance, there was risk here. Even if the shop was empty of customers, a barista would be behind the counter.

Best plan?

Claim a seat in a far corner and let Charley order for them.

But his fellow coffee lover had other ideas.

As they entered the shop, Charley lifted a hand in greeting to the tall, midthirtyish man behind the counter. "Hi, Zach."

"Afternoon, Charley." The man stopped wiping the nozzle on the espresso machine and checked his watch. "You're getting your caffeine fix late today."

"My muse had me up early and working through breakfast. A café de olla would hit the spot before I open the stand for the day. For my friend here too. Have you two met?"

"No." The man set down the rag and extended his hand. "Zach Garrett."

Legs stiff, Jon walked forward and returned Zach's firm clasp as he introduced himself.

"Zach's the owner." Charley extracted a wallet from his pocket and counted out bills. "Great space, isn't it?"

Charley's comment gave him an excuse to avert his face from the discreet perusal the other man was giving it.

A gallery of close-up, poster-sized nature shots graced the walls, with tables tucked in between them and around a freestanding fireplace in the center. The design was clean, simple, and restful, as Charley had promised.

"Very nice."

"Have a seat and I'll bring your drinks over as soon as they're ready. You have your pick of tables at this hour." Zach waved a hand over the shop and set about preparing their coffee.

"I'm partial to that spot." Charley indicated a table near the fireplace. "On a chilly day, it's the most coveted seat in town."

"That works." Anywhere away from the harsh light of the afternoon sun streaming in through the picture window was fine with him.

Jon followed him over, claimed a chair, and exhaled.

That hadn't been too bad. Other than Zach, the shop was deserted. And while the owner had noticed his scars, he'd recovered from any initial shock fast.

Perhaps others would too.

Like Ashley.

Once she got used to his appearance, maybe it wouldn't be the stumbling block to romance he'd always assumed it was. After all, the sparks flying Saturday night hadn't been one-sided. As far as he could tell, she—

"Well, look who's here on this bright afternoon."

Charley's comment pulled him back to the present as two golf-shirt-clad, fiftysomething men engaged in a heated debate entered the shop.

He stifled a groan.

So much for sharing a quiet, one-on-one cup of coffee with Charley in relative anonymity.

"Ah. My favorite clerics." Zach continued working as he greeted them. "You two are later than usual today."

"Blame it on Kevin. He insisted on searching for every ball he hit into the rough—and we're talking lots of balls." The more slender man rolled his eyes.

"Hey! Golf balls are expensive." His jolly-faced companion pulled out his wallet. "Ministers must be paid more than priests, if you can afford to lose as many balls as *you* do. We'll have the usual, Zach."

Charley leaned across the table and lowered his voice, humor glinting in his irises. "Our town pastors, Reverend Baker and Father Murphy. The padre is the one with the wallet. They have

276

a standing tee time on Thursdays and an ongoing friendly rivalry. But you'll never meet two finer men or better friends."

"I don't discuss money." Reverend Baker gave a disdainful sniff.

"You sure spend enough of it. Those high-end doughnuts you serve after Sunday services are pricey. And they don't hold a candle to St. Francis's homemade ones."

"I'm not debating doughnuts with you again." Reverend Baker skirted around his companion and approached their table. "Hello, Charley. I see you were in the mood for a late coffee too."

"I'm introducing my friend to The Perfect Blend. Have you met Jon Gray?"

"Only by phone." The minister extended his hand, and Jon rose to take it. "Your company did a fine job with the landscaping around our fellowship hall last year."

"Thank you."

"Two café de ollas." Zach set their drinks on the table as the minister moved aside and Father Murphy joined them.

Charley repeated the introduction.

"Happy to meet you." Father Murphy pumped his hand, exhibiting no reaction to the scars other than a brief flicker of surprise, followed by compassion, in his eyes.

"Being a landscaper, you should drop in at St. Francis and see the meditation garden my

Catholic counterpart has created." The minister nodded toward his golfing buddy. "His talent on the greens may be questionable, but he does have a green thumb with plants and flowers."

"Thank you for that backhanded compliment." The priest gave his fellow cleric a smirk. "But please do stop in, Jon, if you're passing by. All are welcome to seek refreshment in my little slice of paradise."

"Drinks are ready, gentlemen," Zach called out from behind the counter.

"Would you like to join us?" Charley stirred his coffee with the cinnamon stick in his brew.

"No can do. I have homily prep on my schedule this afternoon." Father Murphy pulled out his car keys.

"And he needs every hour he can get for that task." Reverend Baker's lips twitched.

"Very funny. I happen to have it on good authority that a pastor who shall remain nameless cited the wrong verse last Sunday while preaching about the good Samaritan."

Reverend Baker arched his eyebrows and folded his arms. "Who told you that?"

"I have my sources."

"You mean spies."

Father Murphy shrugged. "A source by any other name . . ."

"For the record, it was a mere slip of the tongue. I corrected it immediately."

"I would hope so. I would suggest you bone up before our next Bible trivial pursuit event." The padre winked at them. "You two enjoy the rest of your day."

After adding a similar sentiment, the reverend followed his friend out.

They were still razzing each other as they pushed through the door.

"They're quite a pair. They'd be a great stand-up comedy team." Charley motioned toward the untouched coffee on the table. "Give that a stir with your cinnamon stick and let me know what you think."

Jon did as instructed, took a sip . . . and exhaled. The brew was sweet, black, and strong, with a hint of spice from the cinnamon.

"Now this is a cup of coffee."

"Glad you like it. All the other drinks are exceptional too. You'll have to come again."

Charley kept the conversation centered on general chitchat after that, and by the time they parted in front of The Perfect Blend fifteen minutes later, the tension in Jon's shoulders had eased.

This unexpected social engagement hadn't been too bad. None of the four Hope Harbor residents who'd seen his scars had overreacted.

On the other hand, they weren't typical either. If Zach really did have a female barista with triple-pierced ears and spiky, rainbow-hued hair, as Kyle had mentioned once, a scar-faced man would be nothing more than a blip on his radar. And clerics were no doubt schooled to mask their shock. Otherwise, no one would seek their counsel. As for his host today, Charley had been Charley. Kind, empathetic, and always accepting.

Meaning the coffee shop excursion hadn't been the best test of going public with his appearance.

It was, nevertheless, encouraging.

For if those four could so quickly get past his looks and proceed to more important matters, maybe others could too.

Whether a woman—Ashley in particular—could make the quantum leap from acceptance to attraction, however, remained to be seen.

But in a town with the name of Hope Harbor, perhaps anything was possible.

19

This was a disaster.

From her spot on the puddle-dotted terrace, Ashley stared over the Edgecliff grounds as dawn transitioned to day under a leaden sky.

The gazebo was undamaged, despite the high winds that must have raged last night, as was the open-sided white tent adjacent to it, where refreshments would be served later today at the open house. But a huge section of one of the large spruce trees had splintered off and crashed into the chairs that had been arranged in rows by the gazebo to simulate a wedding setup. Those that hadn't been crushed or buried under needle-bedecked boughs were strewn about. And smaller branches littered the lawn Jon's crew had manicured yesterday.

Dare she look in front of the house?

"Oh my."

As Rose spoke behind her, Ashley's throat tightened. After all the stresses of the past week, after all the work she'd put into the open house, this was too much.

"I knew rain was predicted last night, but I didn't hear anything about high winds." Somehow she choked out the words. "And how could a tree that was supposed to act as a windbreak break instead?"

"The wind can be capricious on the coast, and the storm was bad. Much worse than usual for July." Rose touched her arm. "Is there any other damage?"

"I don't know. This is as far as I got."

"Let's cut through the house and check the front."

Rose walked over to the back door, unlocked it, and disarmed the security system before Ashley could get her feet in gear.

The other woman was already halfway to the foyer when Ashley entered, and she hurried to catch up, steeling herself as Rose twisted the knob and opened the front door.

It wasn't good.

Two of the new hanging ferns had fallen, spewing potting soil across the pristine porch. Another large branch had blown into the circle drive, blocking it. Tree debris littered the lawn, freshly planted center garden, and new gravel parking lot.

Ashley grasped the edge of the door to steady herself as she surveyed the damage. "How could I have slept through all this?"

"You've been running around nonstop for weeks and working late into the night, if the light burning in the carriage house at all hours is any indication. Exhausted people eventually cave."

"I wasn't supposed to cave until after the open house." Panic clawed at her windpipe, cutting off her air supply. "How am I supposed to clean all this up before the caterer gets here in five hours?" She tried to focus, to put together a mental to-do list, but her brain had become sludge.

"You may want to call the caterer first. I imagine they have more chairs."

Ashley turned away from the scene of devastation, pulling out her cell as she lurched toward the kitchen. "More chairs are the least of my problem. The beautiful grounds are one of our biggest selling points, and they look like a tornado has—"

"Ashley."

She halted and swiveled back. "What?"

"I believe your knight in shining armor may be arriving. Not on a white charger, but in a white truck."

What?

She hurtled back to the door.

Jon's Silverado was trundling down the drive, an open trailer attached.

"Why would he be here at this hour on a Saturday?"

"You'll have to ask him." Rose withdrew into the house. "I think I'll brew a pot of coffee. I expect we'll all need an energy boost to get us through the next few hours."

The truck stopped on the far edge of the circle

drive, and Ashley pushed through the door. As she clattered down the steps, Jon slid out of the driver's seat and pulled a chain saw from the trailer. He was already striding toward the gazebo area when she called out to him.

He swung back as she trotted over.

"What are you doing here?" She stopped a few feet from him.

One of his eyebrows rose. "Good morning to you too."

Heat bloomed on her cheeks. "Sorry. Good morning. Why are you here?"

"Have chain saw, will travel." He tipped up the blade and wiggled it.

"But it's Saturday. Most people sleep in. And how did you know about this?" She swept a hand over the carnage.

"I swung by an hour ago. I figured there'd be a few issues, and I had a feeling you'd be freaking out."

God bless this man!

"That about nails it. But I wasn't up as early as you. My panic is of more recent vintage. I'm guessing you didn't sleep through the storm, like I did."

"That's not an option if you have a dog who hates bad weather and howls with the wind. She was very vocal last night."

Meaning he likely hadn't had much sleep.

"Listen, you must be tired. I can't ask you to—"

"You didn't ask. I volunteered. Kyle will be along within the hour, after he rounds up a couple of our people."

Pressure built behind her eyes. "How can I ever thank you?"

He gave her a lopsided grin. "Save me a few of your caterer's fancy treats. I want to take a shot of them and send it to Laura. She thinks all I eat is cereal and frozen dinners."

"Done. Would you like me to deliver them to your place later?"

"Not necessary. I'll stop by and pick them up."

"Okay—but a sampling of appetizers doesn't come close to compensating you for going above and beyond. Why don't I pay you time and a half for weekend work?" The extra expense would ding the budget short term, but the longer-term negative economic impact would be worse if her guests left with a bad impression.

"The crew would appreciate that. I'll comp my services in exchange for the food. I better get rolling, or we'll still be in cleanup mode when your guests arrive." He started walking toward the gazebo again.

"Jon."

Once again, he stopped and turned.

"I hope you know how grateful I am."

In the murky light of early morning, it was impossible to read his expression. But the warmth in his husky voice wrapped around her like a comforting embrace.

"I'm glad I could help."

With that, he pivoted and strode across the lawn toward the gazebo.

And even though he was wearing jeans rather than chain mail and carrying a chain saw instead of a lance, in the soft, golden, just-past-dawn glow he looked as heroic and chivalrous as any knight from the fabled Round Table.

The woman was still watching her.

As Rose launched into her final piece to close out the inside part of the open house, she cast a surreptitious glance into the small mirror she'd placed on the piano, positioned to give her a view of the milling crowd.

No one was paying attention to her or her playing. As expected, the guests had been too busy inspecting the house and the artist renderings Ashley had placed on easels in the various rooms, showing how the space could be set up for a wedding or reception or presentation or cocktail party.

All except the fortysomething woman who'd claimed a seat at the entrance to the roped-off drawing room thirty minutes ago and had remained there for the duration, her attention riveted on the piano, the music—and perhaps the pianist.

Rose's fingers glided over the familiar keys while her mind spun out possibilities.

Could she be a reporter who'd somehow heard about the entertainment and the identity of the pianist, then finagled an invitation? Someone who was hoping to do a follow-up on the scandal? Who wanted to dredge up all the ugliness and shine a spotlight on the woman who'd withdrawn from the world to an isolated seaside estate?

That was possible. Because if she was here to check the place out as a potential event venue, she wouldn't have glued herself to a chair by the door.

Fortunately, the rope had kept her at bay. And once the musical portion of the event was finished, it would be easy to slip out the discreet door at the back of the room and escape through the kitchen.

Behind her, Ashley began rounding up the crowd in the foyer and shepherding them out the front door, toward the gazebo.

Her audience of one angled toward the activity. After a brief hesitation, she rose.

Moments later, Ashley joined the woman, motioned toward the door, and waited until she disappeared into the crowd before sending a thumbs-up in the direction of the piano.

Rose acknowledged the signal with a nod and kept playing.

Bless that girl for watching out for her.

287

Less than three minutes later she finished her final piece with a flourish, and once the last note died away, silence greeted her. The hum of conversation in the house had ceased. Everyone was gone. Quiet and privacy had been restored.

A smile playing at her lips, she closed the cover on the keyboard.

Her gig had gone well.

It hadn't been like the old days, on a concert stage, with everyone paying rapt attention to her performance. But the pressure had also been less. She'd been able to play with all the emotion in her heart, no worries about mistakes or critics or disappointing an audience that was tuned in to every note.

Lips still bowed, she swung around on the bench and rose. A late lunch would hit the spot. Eating prior to a performance, even one like this, had never been part of her routine, and old habits died hard.

She picked up the small mirror and strolled toward the side door.

Ashley would save her a few goodies from the catering fare, but until then, half a turkey sandwich would fill the—

"Excuse me."

At the summons, she froze. Slowly rotated back.

The blond woman who'd been watching her

was in the foyer, on the other side of the velvet rope, a notebook clutched against her chest.

Rose's mouth flat-lined.

The interloper must have hung back and tucked herself into a corner to avoid detection, planning to swoop in once the house was deserted.

"I believe the gathering has moved outside." Rose backed toward the door as she spoke, her words stiff.

"I know, and I'm sorry to disturb you. But I wanted to . . . I had to tell you how much I enjoyed your music, and there wasn't an opportunity while the crowd was in here. Besides, I didn't want to interrupt your playing. It was impeccable—and moving."

Either the woman was an excellent actress, or the catch in her voice was genuine and her compliment sincere.

Rose slowed. "Thank you."

"I used to play too. Never like you, but music always gave me comfort."

Rose stopped.

That sounded familiar. As did the woman's poignant tone.

Yet earnest as she appeared to be, her praise and emotional reaction could be a ruse. A savvy journalist could wheedle her way into almost any situation. Like the reporter who'd pretended to be a neighbor and come knocking at the door after she and Mark moved to a smaller town in the wake of the scandal. She'd even had the gall to snap a few photos with her cell phone once Rose got suspicious and began to slam the door in her face.

Was this woman in that camp?

"May I ask what brought you here today? I understood that the guests were special event vendors."

"Yes. I do chair covers, up in Coos Bay." The blond shifted her weight from one foot to the other. "Those are the coverings that slip over folding chairs to make them fancier for parties."

"I'm familiar with the term." Maybe the woman was legit. A true music lover, not someone with a devious motive. Assuming the worst about people had never been her style in the old days. What would it hurt to give her the benefit of the doubt—while keeping a safe distance, of course? "I'm glad you enjoyed my playing."

"It made me wish I could take it up again. Just for myself, though. Not to play in public, like you do. I bet you're booked solid."

Was this visitor to Edgecliff really unaware of her identity?

Perhaps. There was no trace of guile in her demeanor.

Rose took a small step back toward the piano. "No. I don't perform. Today was an exception."

Shock flattened the woman's features. "Seriously? But you seem so professional."

"I was once. Long ago."

"You could be again."

"That's not in my plans. I was doing a favor for someone today."

"Lucky them. And lucky us, who got to hear you play." The woman pulled a card from her purse and held it out. "I'm Mindy Jackson, by the way."

After a brief hesitation, Rose crossed the room and took the card. If this woman was an imposter, she'd gone to a great deal of trouble. The card appeared to be legit. "It's nice to meet you." But she didn't offer her name in return. "If you enjoy playing so much, why don't you go back to it?"

"I wish I could, but I don't have five minutes to call my own these days, what with trying to establish my business and raising a teenage daughter alone. Plus, I don't have a piano any-more." She gave Allison an appreciative scan. "That one's a beauty."

"It's been in this house for many years." Rose studied her. Was she a widow? Divorcée? And why didn't she have a piano anymore? Since it would be impolite to ask any of those questions, she settled for one less personal. "What piano did you have?"

"A Baldwin. My parents gave it to us for a wedding present."

"Did your daughter play too?"

"No. She was more into ballet, until the lessons got too expensive. Now she does sports at school, and she seems okay with that. But I miss the piano." Mindy gave the antique upright another longing look.

Sounded like she and her daughter had fallen on hard times.

"I hope you can get back to it one day."

"Thank you. As rusty as I am, though, I'd need brush-up lessons. And those definitely aren't in the budget."

"Life can be difficult if finances are tight." A fact she could appreciate in principle if not in practice, thanks to the trust fund money from Grandfather and Papa's bequest, which had provided a cushion until Lucy Lynn came along.

But this woman obviously didn't have a safety net.

"Yes." Mindy tucked her hair behind her ear, distress tightening her features. "And it's harder when someone you trusted is the reason."

A quiver of shock rippled through Rose.

Had this woman also been betrayed by her husband?

"I know what that's like." Rose reached out and touched her arm. "I've been there."

As the admission spilled out, her pulse stuttered.

Why on earth would she share such a private piece of information with this stranger?

Mindy's eyes began to shimmer, and her breath hitched. "Was it . . . did your husband . . . did he lie to you too?"

At the broken question, a host of painful memories stirred to life in a dark corner of her heart. "Yes."

"That's how it was with Frank. I had no idea he had a gambling addiction. Before I realized what was going on, he'd lost all of our savings, and his credit cards were maxed out. The house and cars were repossessed, and we had to sell everything. Including the piano."

A story of broken dreams and disillusionment almost as sad as her own.

"I'm so sorry, my dear."

"Thank you." Mindy sniffed and pulled a tissue from the pocket of her slacks. Dabbed at her lashes. "I did give him a chance to undo the damage. I said if he got help, we could try to start over. He agreed, but within a month he was gambling again. I couldn't put my daughter through any more upheaval, so I . . . I divorced him."

"I can understand that. Does he stay in touch with her?"

"No. Two months after the divorce became final, he was killed in a car accident." Her eyes began to shimmer. "He'd never been much of a drinker, but his BAC was way over the limit. On top of everything else, I also had to deal with a boatload of guilt. I'll always wonder if it was the divorce that drove him to alcohol and led to his death."

"You're being too hard on yourself. He created the mess by the bad choices he made."

"I know that in theory, but some days it's hard to convince myself of that." She sniffed and swiped at her lashes. "Anyway, at that point, I decided to move to Coos Bay for a new beginning. With my daughter ready to start high school, the timing was good to relocate."

"How long ago did all this happen?"

"Almost three years. And launching a new career after being a stay-at-home mom has been tough. But if my business keeps growing, someday I may be able to afford another piano."

Rose wove her fingers together. Tight. After years of playing it safe, of staying away from strangers, it could be a mistake to let this woman infiltrate her defenses.

But she'd taken a risk with Ashley, and all the outcomes up to this point had been positive.

Why couldn't they be again?

Without further second-guessing, she freed her fingers and unlatched the velvet rope that blocked access to the room, clearing the path for Mindy to enter. "Would you like to play a piece on this one?"

Her fellow music lover looked at Allison, yearning and hesitation mingling in her eyes.

"My skills are awfully rusty. And I'm a rank amateur next to you. Besides, the owner may not appreciate a stranger playing it."

"The owner won't mind. And this isn't a competition. Forget I'm here. Play for the pleasure of the music."

"This would be such a treat . . ." She chewed on her lower lip.

"Go for it, as you young people like to say."

After an infinitesimal pause, Mindy set her notebook on the chair she'd occupied earlier, wiped her palms on her slacks, and approached the piano.

"This is a beautiful instrument." She ran her fingers over the satiny wood and lifted the keyboard cover.

"Yes, it is—and it's meant to be played. Go ahead, sit down. I'll wait over there." Rose indicated her favorite tufted chair.

Without further encouragement, Mindy slid onto the bench, flexed her fingers, and positioned them on the keys. After doing a few scales, she launched into a piece of Baroque music that was often included in beginner and intermediate repertoires.

As the familiar strains of Bach's "Minuet in G" filled the room, Rose leaned back to watch and listen.

Considering how long it had been since Mindy last played, the flow was smooth, with only a few missteps. Her execution was adequate, but her staccato and legato techniques had room for improvement.

On the plus side, her posture was excellent and her hands were controlled, with minimal extraneous movement. She kept her wrists level, her fingers straight, and she played with the tips.

Most important of all, based on her expression of utter joy, she was savoring every note.

When she finished, Mindy exhaled and swung around on the bench. "That was such a treat. I know I made a ton of mistakes, but just having my fingers on the keys again fed my soul."

"I thought you did fine."

"I hit quite a few wrong notes. And the trills were shaky."

Actually, they were mordents—but the difference was irrelevant for this discussion.

"Those require practice to execute smoothly."

"I used to be able to do them." She stood. "Maybe I will again someday. If my finances ever allow, a piano and more lessons are high on my priority list." She retrieved her notebook and tucked it under her arm. "I suppose I should join the group outside. Refocus on business."

"I'll let you out." Rose stood, crossed to the foyer, and flipped the lock on the front door. "Good luck with your chair-cover venture. I'll pray that a piano is in your future."

"Thank you for that—and for the concert. It

brightened my day." The woman extended her hand.

Rose took it, gave her fingers a firm squeeze, and pulled open the door.

Once Mindy left, Rose reset the lock and headed toward the side exit that would allow her to slip out and return to her cottage without attracting attention.

But first she paused in the doorway of the drawing room, fingering the card in her pocket as she regarded Allison.

It was a shame Mindy wasn't able to find comfort in playing anymore. The mental health benefits of producing beautiful music could be a lifesaver, as she knew firsthand.

All at once, the stirrings of an idea began to percolate through her mind.

Hmm.

It did have possibilities—if she was willing to sacrifice an even bigger chunk of her privacy than she had this afternoon.

Yet today's leap had produced no negative repercussions. On the contrary. It had made someone's day and whetted her own appetite for further, if limited, engagement with the human race.

And as she wandered toward the door to let herself out and return to her secluded cottage, her mind was already weighing the pros and cons of taking a step that as recently as last month would have been unthinkable.

20
....

Her mother was here?

As the last open house guests began to mosey toward the parking lot, Ashley did a double take.

Yes, the woman who'd emerged from the black sedan parked in the circle drive in front of the house was Mom.

But why had she come?

After bidding the final wedding planner good-bye, Ashley hustled across the lawn, toward the drive.

As she approached, her mother lifted a hand in greeting, her usual put-together appearance and composed demeanor a tad askew.

"I thought you weren't coming." Ashley closed the remaining distance between them in a few long strides, leaning into the hug her mother offered.

Inviting Mom to attend the event had seemed like a polite gesture after her frequent calls to check on the progress at Edgecliff—and the sanity of a daughter who would embark on such a wild scheme—but it had been no surprise when she'd passed. Jessica Scott's packed calendar didn't have a slot for inconvenient travel that wasn't business related, or overnight stays in towns the size of Hope Harbor.

"I had a last-minute opening in my schedule and decided to surprise you. But my flight was fog-delayed, and after I picked up my rental car in North Bend, I sat in traffic for an hour, thanks to a major pileup on 101 north of here." She scanned the tent, where the catering company had already begun to load its vans. Grimaced. "I missed it, didn't I?"

"Yes. But I wouldn't have had time to visit while everyone was here anyway. Now I can give you my full attention. How long can you stay?"

"My flight leaves at one tomorrow."

Ashley quashed a pang of disappointment. "That's a fast trip."

"I have a crammed schedule on Monday."

Naturally.

But at least Mom had shoehorned her in for twenty hours. That counted for something.

"Let me see if the caterers have any questions, and then I'll take your luggage to the carriage house and give you a tour."

"Could we eat first? Breakfast was hours ago."

"Of course. I can scrounge up some leftovers from the caterers."

"No. Let's go out. My treat. You choose the place."

"The pickings are slim, unless you want to drive all the way back to Coos Bay."

She dismissed that idea with a flip of her hand. "No, thank you. I've had my fill of car trips for the day. Aren't there any restaurants in the little town I passed a few miles from here? Hope Harbor?"

"One. A small café. And the tacos from the stand on the wharf are phenomenal if the owner is cooking."

Her mother wrinkled her nose. "I don't want street-truck food. Is the café decent?"

In other words, was it upscale?

"It's not fancy, and the menu is simple, but everything I've had has been tasty."

"That will have to do." She nodded toward the catering crew. "Go ahead and finish up over there. Business comes first."

Ashley bit back the dissent poised on the tip of her tongue. "Give me five minutes. Why don't you drive around back and park by the carriage house? I'll join you there."

"Sounds like a plan."

As her mother returned to her car, Ashley hurried back to the tent to wrap up loose ends.

Five minutes later, she found her mother waiting at the carriage house door that provided access to the second floor living quarters.

"Everything squared away?" Mom already had her overnight bag in hand.

"Yes." She unlocked the door, took the bag, and ushered her up the stairs, mentally running through a to-do checklist. There was only one bedroom, so she'd have to change the linens.

Also stock the bathroom with fresh towels. And what was in her fridge for breakfast? Should she stop for provisions in—

"I didn't realize your space was this small. I should have booked a hotel." Her mother paused at the top of the stairs to survey the compact living/dining room.

"It can accommodate two people for one night." Ashley set her mother's bag on the floor. "When we get back, I'll tidy up the bedroom for you."

"Where will you sleep?"

"I have a futon that converts to a bed." Thank goodness she'd brought it with her from Tennessee instead of consigning it to the pile of items she'd donated to charity.

"I don't want to put you out of your bed."

"I'll be fine for one night. Let's go eat."

Mom didn't argue.

Nor did she comment on the spacious, manicured Edgecliff grounds as they drove toward the cleaned-up entrance, now vine and foliage free.

Which must mean she'd found something to dislike.

Ashley let her direct the conversation during the drive and throughout their meal. In between texts, emails, and a phone call that couldn't wait, Mom grilled her on expenditures at the house and asked a few questions about today's event. But mostly she talked about an upcoming business trip to London and the hot new musical she'd seen on her last visit to New York.

Typical Mom.

She continued to hold forth as they wrapped up their meal and during the drive back to Edgecliff. Ashley half listened as she made a mental list of follow-up calls to several vendors who'd expressed an interest in recommending the venue to a current client.

Only as she set the brake did she tune back in to her mother, smiling through the fatigue that was beginning to set in. "Would you like a quick tour of the house?"

Indecision flashed across her mom's face . . . but then she acquiesced. "Yes. The outside gives me an idea of what to expect, but I suppose I should see the inside too."

Not the most enthusiastic response, but again, typical Mom. Unless the topic or item under discussion was in her sphere of interest, she'd never been able to muster up much enthusiasm for it.

Even if it meant the world to her daughter.

So the circuit would be short and sweet.

Ashley showed her through the rooms, offering an abbreviated version of the spiel she'd developed for real tours after spending hours researching the history of the house and its contents, with much input from Rose.

Mom dutifully trailed behind her until they

ended up back in the foyer where they'd begun.

"And that concludes the ten-cent tour." Ashley fished out her keys. "Any questions?" There wouldn't be. Mom had zero interest in history.

"No." She surveyed the space. "It's an impressive house, but everything is very old."

Ashley curbed an eye roll. "That's why it's a historic property."

"It's hard to imagine anyone living here in this day and age, though. Or spending their life in such an old-fashioned setting."

Another jab at her daughter's lifestyle.

Let it go, Ashley.

"Well, no one lives here now." She summoned up a smile. "And the carriage house I call home has been updated, as you've seen." Nothing on the scale of Mom's high-rise condo, with its sleek fixtures and white walls and modern art, but it was comfortable and cozy.

"Yes. Your quarters are very cute. But it's also isolated here. Don't you get lonely?"

"No. The place is buzzing with activity during the week. There are a ton of construction and landscaping people on-site. And Rose lives here too. It's too late to introduce you to her today, but I could ask her to come over tomorrow."

"That would be fine." Mom studied her. "I do want what's best for you, Ashley. And I do want you to be happy."

There was a *but* coming.

"I appreciate that."

"But I don't know how you'll ever meet anyone living in such isolation."

"Are you referring to a man?"

"Yes. I doubt anyone like Jason will ever show up in a place like this."

"I certainly hope not."

At her vehement response, her mother's eyes narrowed.

Oops.

Bad mistake.

No one but Jon knew the details of their breakup. With Mom, she'd confined herself to saying it hadn't worked out.

Too bad she'd gushed about him ad nauseam at the beginning.

"He sounded like a suitable match." Mom continued to scrutinize her. "You said he was handsome, had an impressive job, took you to classy places."

It was time to spill the truth. Otherwise, his name would keep coming up.

"He was and he did. But he also had zero class or integrity. He was seeing another woman on the side."

Pleats reappeared on Mom's forehead. "Are you certain about that?"

"Yes." And that was all she was going to say on that subject. "Why don't we go back to the carriage house? You must be tired after your trip, and I want to spruce up the bedroom before you turn in." She pulled the front door open and angled back toward the foyer, motioning for her mother to exit. "I'll set the alarm and meet you in back. At least there's no rain or fog this evening. You shouldn't get lost on—"

Her mother jolted to a stop on the porch and stared toward the drive.

Ashley swung around.

Jon stood at the bottom of the steps. Come for his promised fancy food samples, no doubt.

"Hi." She eased out beside her mother and called up a teasing tone. "You must be hungry."

He didn't respond. Nor did he move.

At the weird vibes wafting through the air, her levity faded.

"Um . . . this is my mom. She came up to surprise me for the open house. Mom, this is Jon Gray. He's responsible for the beautiful grounds here."

Neither spoke.

"Mom." Ashley gave her an elbow nudge.

But it was Jon who at last broke the silence, speaking as he backed off. "Nice to meet you, Ms. Scott. I should go. I don't want to interrupt your visit." He turned and strode away.

"Jon! Wait! What about your food? I have it for you in the carriage house."

"I'll get it tomorrow." He called the response

over his shoulder and kept walking. "Enjoy your evening."

Ashley crossed the porch, stopping at the top of the steps as he picked up his pace. "That was bizarre. I've never seen him act like that."

When her comment didn't produce a response, she swiveled back.

At the shock and revulsion contorting her mother's face, Ashley's stomach knotted.

No wonder Jon had fled. This was exactly the kind of reaction he'd been afraid of provoking if he removed his camouflage.

But Mom's repugnance was over-the-top.

Struggling to keep her temper in check, she marched back across the porch. "Why are you staring at him like that?"

Her mother pressed a hand to her chest. Swallowed. "What . . . what happened to him?"

"He had a close encounter with an IED in the Middle East five years ago."

"Ah. That would explain it."

"Staring is rude."

"I expect he's used to it by now."

The twist in Ashley's stomach tightened. "Would you ever get used to it? Do you know how hurtful that kind of reaction would be? How self-conscious it would make someone?"

Head cocked, her mother appraised her. "I thought you said this man was a groundskeeper?"

"No, I didn't. He's a landscaper. I contracted

with his firm to refurbish the Edgecliff grounds and gardens."

"Why was he here on a Saturday night? And what was that reference to food all about?"

Ashley folded her arms.

Jessica Scott hadn't risen to the top of a highly competitive profession without possessing strong instincts and an ability to cut to the chase in any situation. It wasn't surprising she'd picked up more than basic humanitarian concern in her daughter's impassioned defense.

She needed to tone down the emotion and keep her comments about Jon business focused.

"We had a bad storm here last night. The grounds were littered with debris this morning. As a courtesy, Jon showed up at dawn to restore order before the open house. To express my thanks, I promised to save him samples of the fancy food we served."

"Why would a contractor do hours of work for free?"

"I paid his crew time and a half."

"But not him."

If her mother hadn't been a business executive, she'd have made a formidable prosecuting attorney.

"No."

A few seconds passed.

"Why don't we sit for a minute?" She motioned to the two adjacent rocking chairs.

"I thought you were tired."

"This won't take long." Mom chose a chair and sat.

Meaning she wasn't going to budge until her daughter complied.

Posture taut, Ashley perched on the edge of the second chair.

Her mother began to rock. "You know, a man doesn't make a special trip to someone's home on a Saturday night at this hour just to collect a plate of food."

"It wasn't much of a trip. He lives down the road."

"Ashley, you've only been here a month." Her mother gave her The Look. The one she always used when she'd concluded her follow-your-heart daughter was on the verge of making a mistake.

"I know."

"You're fresh out of a bad relationship, based on what you told me tonight."

"I know."

"There's a certain rebound danger in situations like that."

"I'm past the rebound stage with Jason, Mom."

"That's reassuring. But living in an isolated place like this has to be lonely. It could prompt you to seek companionship in the wrong places."

Her mother's tone was gentle, but the implication nevertheless made her bristle.

"What do you mean by wrong?"

"Well, I'm sure Jon is a fine, hardworking man. But he's a landscaper."

"Who also happens to be highly educated. His credentials were on his bid. He has three degrees to my one."

"Oh." That news stopped Mom—but only for a moment. "That's impressive. But you're a beautiful young woman. With your looks and intelligence, you could have your pick of men. You don't have to settle for whoever is available in this godforsaken spot."

Settle?

Ashley's irritation morphed to anger, and she vaulted to her feet. "First of all, you're jumping to too many conclusions. Jon and I are friends, nothing more. And second, from what I've seen of him, any woman would be lucky to win his affections."

"So you *are* interested."

"I didn't say that."

"You didn't have to. I know you. Plus, I've picked up a few people skills through the years. Besides, a woman doesn't defend a man as heatedly as you've defended him if she's not interested in more than friendship."

"What if I am? And I'm not saying I am. That's a rhetorical question. Are you implying he wouldn't be good enough for me?"

"I'm just reminding you there are other fish in the sea. Jason may have had clay feet, but there are plenty of men out there with his assets, minus his liabilities."

She fisted her hands on her hips. "How can you dismiss Jon after an exchange that lasted less than a minute? All you learned about him is that he's scarred."

"Physical scars can lead to psychological scars."

"Only if other people make them an issue. If they judge someone by what's on their skin instead of what's in their heart."

Her mother stood too. "Not everyone has Hollywood looks, Ashley. But can you say in all honesty that those scars don't bother you? That when you look at him, a little part of you doesn't cringe inside, despite all the fine qualities he may have? That they diminish any attraction you might feel for him?"

"I didn't say I was attracted to him."

"You're not answering my question. And you don't have to answer it for me. But you should answer it for yourself before you let this go too far. I think your landscaper is interested in cultivating more than your gardens, and you could be setting him up for a hard fall if you lead him to believe you care and then don't follow through. That would be far worse than a stare from a stranger. Shall we call it a night?"

Without waiting for a reply, her mother descended the steps and strolled toward the adjacent carriage house.

After giving her a head start, Ashley set the security system, locked the door, and followed her.

She wasn't leading Jon on.

Was she?

All at once, the answer was unclear.

Of course she wouldn't mislead him intentionally, but in hindsight, it was impossible to know who'd initiated that almost-kiss a week ago. She could have been the one who'd leaned in a fraction, sending a message she was receptive to a lip-lock.

The only thing she knew with absolute certainty was that she'd been all in, thanks to the music and fog and intimate darkness. Not to mention Jon's admirable character and kindness. Every one of those elements had played a role in generating the sparks that had flared inside her.

But his appearance hadn't been among them.

That was the truth of it.

Had the scene transpired in the light of day, and without a soaring romantic score, would the sparks have been as strong? Or would the scars have been a turnoff?

She blew out a breath and kicked at a stray pine cone, a leftover from last night's storm missed by the grounds crew.

For someone who'd preached about beauty being skin deep, it was disheartening to realize she might be too shallow to put that adage into practice in her own life.

There was no getting around the fact that his scars were disfiguring and somewhat off-putting. No matter how beautiful his heart was, his face would always be unattractive. That wouldn't matter much in the context of casual acquaintances or friendships. People could get past appearances eventually in those kinds of relationships.

But romance was different. It had a physical component, one that required a visceral attraction. The magnetic buzz had definitely been there last Saturday night, but his features hadn't been on full display. And the scars below his neck had remained hidden.

Unless she could look at him in broad daylight and feel the same spark, Mom was right.

Encouraging his interest would be worse than unfair. It would be cruel.

Sighing, she joined her waiting mother at the stairs to her apartment.

And as she unlocked her door, she reached a decision.

Until she determined whether Jon's appearance was a deal breaker, she'd be friendly. Nothing more.

Starting tomorrow.

Because hurting this man who'd already endured more than his share of disappointment and rejection wasn't an option.

21

Laura was calling.

While Daisy romped at his feet on the sand to the beat of the up-tempo ringtone that came nowhere close to mirroring his mental state on this Sunday afternoon, Jon weighed the cell phone in his hand.

He was *not* in the mood to talk to his sister. Not after his encounter with Ashley's mother last night.

As two seagulls soared on a wind current above him, circling higher and higher in a spiral against the cobalt blue sky, an image of the woman's expression that had seared itself in his mind materialized.

Her shock hadn't been as profound as Melinda's. Nor had she thrown up. But her revulsion had been clear.

And not unexpected for someone who hadn't been schooled to brace for a jolt.

The minimal response from the clerics and barista and Charley a few days ago was the outlier. After all, they were locals who'd likely heard about his history and been more or less prepared for his appearance.

Ashley's mother's reaction was what he could expect for the rest of his life from strangers.

And that had forced him to face a hard truth.

He took a deep breath as the distant boom of the surf against the sea stacks offshore reverberated through the air.

Difficult as it was to deal with revulsion personally, subjecting a woman he cared about to curious stares and bewilderment whenever they were out in public together, directed at her by people who wondered how she could find someone like him attractive or appealing, would be worse.

That kind of scrutiny would be a constant and selfish burden to impose on anyone.

End of story.

Including the fantasy he'd begun to concoct about himself and a certain historian with sparkling eyes and vivaciousness to spare.

The phone stopped ringing, and he slid it back in his pocket, heart heavy. Letting himself get carried away had been foolish. He knew better. It would be him and Daisy against the world. Period.

After giving his faithful canine companion a pat, he retraced his steps through the woods that separated his house from the beach. He could always return Laura's call later, after he—

He stopped as the music kicked in again. Exhaled.

His sister's persistent streak hadn't abated in thirty years.

"Should I answer, Daisy?"

Social animal that she'd become, the pup gave a happy yip.

"Yeah, you're right. If I don't answer, she'll keep calling until I do." As had become her habit since the bomb incident.

He pulled out the phone, put it to his ear as a childish wail sounded in the background, and injected as much enthusiasm as he could muster into his greeting. "Morning, Sis. I take it the campers have returned."

"Thursday night. Covered with chigger and mosquito bites, assorted bruises and scratches, and poison ivy. Can I run away to your place again?"

"You're always welcome."

"I'll hold you to that if it gets too bad around here. Listen, I won't keep you, but I wanted to see how your first foray to church went."

Whistling for Daisy, who'd taken off in hot pursuit of a squirrel, he started walking again as he debated how to answer that question.

Too bad he'd told her about his plan to slip into an early service today. But the decision had seemed reasonable after his encounters at The Perfect Blend and the evening he'd spent with Ashley listening to an impromptu concert.

It didn't seem reasonable anymore. Not after last night.

Opening that can of worms with his sister, however, would be a mistake. A simple explanation would have to suffice.

"I didn't go."

"Why not? I thought you said—hold a minute." She issued a few muffled instructions about wiping shoes and washing hands, then returned to the conversation. "What happened?"

"You know the Edgecliff open house was yesterday."

"Yes. Ashley told me about it."

"We had a storm Friday night. The crew and I assembled at dawn to do cleanup. It was a race to the finish. I was pulling out of the entrance with the last load of debris as the first car turned in for the event. I was beat."

True enough. But that hadn't stopped him from walking back to Edgecliff to pick up his treats last night.

Another piece of information Laura didn't need to know.

"You could have rested in the afternoon."

"I had work to do around the house."

A few silent seconds crawled by as he side-stepped a downed, broken limb. Another casualty from Friday night's storm.

"What aren't you telling me?"

Time for dodgeball.

"If you want details of the event, I can't help you. I wasn't on the guest list. The weather cleared up and the place looked great, so I assume it went—"

"That's not what I mean, and you know it. What's the real reason you didn't go to church?"

"Laura . . . let it go." He injected a warning note into his tone since diversionary tactics weren't working.

She ignored it. "Something happened to make you gun-shy again, didn't it?"

"Since when did you become a psychologist?"

"I'm a sister. I know you even better than a psychologist would."

"That's a scary notion."

"Ha-ha." A huff came over the line. "You're not going to tell me, are you?"

"There's nothing worth telling. No big news, no shocking revelation to share. Everything here is status quo."

"The status quo stinks—and I thought you were about to change it. How's Ashley?"

At the abrupt change of topic, he frowned and halted. "What?"

"It was a simple question."

"She's fine, as far as I know. I imagine she's tired, though. She insisted on helping us with the cleanup all morning, then had to host the open house. On top of that, her mother showed up at some point."

"Ouch. From what she shared about their relationship, I bet that jacked up her stress level.

I got the impression her mother doesn't approve of the whole Edgecliff project."

"I picked that up too."

"Did you get to meet her?"

He massaged the bridge of his nose. "I left the property at noon."

"She wasn't there yet?"

"If she was, I didn't see her."

"Then how do you know she showed up?"

He'd walked straight into that one.

"I, uh, had to run back there later in the day. Ashley and her mother were on the porch."

"So you did meet her."

"It was a brief exchange." He started forward again.

"What was your impression of her?"

"I was only there for a minute. I didn't want to intrude on their visit, so I—"

He froze as he emerged from the woods and Ashley rose from the seat she'd claimed on his patio to lift a hand in greeting. Daisy made a beeline for her, all four legs pumping.

"So you what?"

At Laura's question, he refocused on the conversation. "Can I, uh, call you back? Something just came up that I have to deal with."

"Is that legit or a ploy to shut me down?"

"It's legit. I'll call you later."

"I'll hold you to that. Give Daisy a pat for me."

"I will. Talk to you soon."

He lowered the phone and moved forward, shifting his features into neutral as he approached his unexpected visitor.

"Hi." He stopped several feet away from her. "This is a surprise."

"It shouldn't be." She gave Daisy a final tummy rub and straightened up. "I owe you appetizers, and they won't improve with age." She tapped a white box on the table beside her. "I wish you would have let me get them for you last night. I hope you weren't counting on them for dinner."

Yeah, he had been. But cereal was always a reliable fallback.

"I didn't starve. I have food in the house, despite what my sister thinks."

"Unless you're a gourmet cook, these will be tastier. The mini quiches and chicken skewers were my favorites. Don't forget to nuke the ones that should be hot."

"Got it. Thanks for the delivery."

"It wasn't a long trip. But you're lucky you came back when you did or I might have been tempted to steal one of your fruit kabobs." The humor in her demeanor faded as she moistened her lips and tucked her fingers into the front pockets of her jeans. "I also wanted to apologize for my mom last night. I'm sorry if she made you feel self-conscious."

"No worries. It's not the first time I've shocked someone, and it won't be the last."

"She overreacted."

"No. She *re*acted. You can't blame people for an auto-response. My face isn't as bad as it used to be, but it will always draw attention. That's the reality. How long is your mom staying?"

Ashley's brow puckered at the change of subject, but she didn't press him. "She's already gone. It was a fast trip. Her calendar opened up at the last minute and she decided to drop in unannounced."

"Did she like Edgecliff?"

A shadow passed over her eyes, indicating her mother had been less than enthusiastic. "It's not her cup of tea. But she did enjoy having tea with Rose. The three of us met up in the kitchen this morning for half an hour before Mom took off."

"How did the open house go?"

Ashley lit up. "Fantastic! Rose was a hit, and everyone seemed impressed and interested in using or recommending the property as a venue. I've already had three queries for smaller events in the fall. As long as you and BJ stick to your schedules, we should be in business by September 1."

"I can't speak for BJ, but we're on track to finish. Probably sooner than anticipated unless you want to proceed with Phase 2 now."

"No. That will have to wait until we have cash flow. The parking lot is functional, if not pretty, and we can rope off the edge of the lawn to keep guests contained and safe until the ground cover and perimeter gardens along the cliff edge can be put in."

"In that case, we'll be out of your hair by the end of the week."

"But . . . you'll continue to do regular maintenance on the lawn and gardens, right?"

"We didn't bid on that."

"Would you?"

"Yes. I'll work up a proposal and get it to you this week."

"Thanks." She offered him a tad-too-bright smile. "It will be nice to see a friendly face around the place on a regular basis. I don't have many friends here yet, and Edgecliff is an isolated location. A girl can always use another friend."

Message received.

She wanted to be friends, nothing more.

Meaning he wouldn't have to worry about trying to protect her feelings if she happened to have any romantic interest in him.

Good news.

But if that was the case, what was with the pang of disappointment echoing in the empty, cavernous chambers of his heart?

"Unless you don't want to be friends."

At Ashley's uncertain addendum, he put his own question aside.

"No. We're already neighbors. I don't see why we can't be friends too." He propped up the corners of his mouth and motioned toward the white box on the table beside her. "Thanks again for the delivery. I'll enjoy those for lunch."

She took his hint and retreated a step. "I'll let you dive in. I should be going anyway. I have a ton of chores waiting for me back at Edgecliff." Yet she hesitated, as if hoping he'd invite her to stay and sit with him while he ate the treats she'd brought.

That was a serious temptation. Chatting with her while he sampled yesterday's party fare would be the best treat of all.

But despite the assurance he'd given her, mere friendship might be beyond him. He could be friendly to her, but being a friend was different than mere sociability. It involved sharing and caring and laughing together and loyalty and cheering each other on, along with a host of other things that deepened relationships.

The truth was, if he did too much more of that with this woman, he'd be on dangerous ground.

Maybe some guys could be just friends with a woman who attracted them, but he wasn't one of them.

And Ashley attracted him.

Big time.

So the safest course was to be cordial acquaintances rather than friends, keep his distance as much as possible, and confine their discussions to business during any meetups.

When he didn't respond, she lifted a hand in farewell and backed farther away. "See you around."

"Count on it. Edgecliff will require regular maintenance."

With a brief nod, she pivoted and strode down his driveway, disappearing behind the trees a minute later as she walked down Windswept Way.

Leaving him with a box of treats he no longer wanted.

And wishing for a treat that hadn't been on her caterer's menu, but which he'd come close to enjoying eight nights ago on a mist-shrouded porch with a background score worthy of a chick flick.

That had not gone well.

As Ashley plodded back down the road to Edgecliff, shoulders slumped, she shoved her hands in her pockets.

Seeking Jon out to set the stage for friendship while she tried to determine if his appearance would be a stumbling block to romance had seemed like a smart plan last night. But it had been predicated on the assumption he was interested in romance, as Mom had concluded.

As she herself had concluded after their porch encounter a week ago.

If that take was accurate, though, he'd given no indication of it today. On the contrary. His actions and demeanor had implied romance wasn't even on his radar.

Maybe her mother's worries about his interest and her own angst about whether his scars could snuff out any sparks between them had been much ado about nothing.

Because there sure hadn't been any sparks a few minutes ago.

Her hair blew into her face, obscuring her vision, and she shoved it back.

His scars weren't the culprit today on her end, though. It was just hard to feel warm and fuzzy about a guy who, overnight, had dialed down the heat and posted large keep-out signs.

Not that he'd been rude or anything. Far from it. His manner had been cordial. Pleasant. Polite.

In other words, night and day from the ardor he'd displayed during those few moments on the porch last weekend. Suggesting that brief interlude had been an aberration prompted by the intimate setting and unusual atmosphere.

She skirted around a pothole in the road.

Whatever had caused him to back off, his lack of interest solved one problem. She didn't have to invest any brainpower—or heart power—trying to determine whether his appearance was a stumbling block, or if getting too friendly would end up hurting him.

Good news, right? One less worry on her already overflowing plate.

She should be happy.

So why wasn't she?

A drop of cold rain plopped onto her nose, and she jerked. Lifted her chin.

Good grief.

When had all those gray clouds moved in? The sky had been blue during her hike to Jon's house an hour ago.

The coastal weather did have a tendency to be moody, though, as she was fast learning. It could be sunny one minute, foggy the next, and apt to change with little or no warning.

Sort of like her relationship with Jon.

Another raindrop landed on her cheek, and she broke into a jog. If the skies opened, she'd be soaked. There was no cover between here and Edgecliff.

Less than a minute later, the sudden beep of a horn sent her veering to the side of the road.

As she swiveled around, Charley waved through the window of a vintage silver Thunderbird with a white top.

"Getting in your daily exercise?" He stopped beside her.

"Not exactly. I was, uh, making a delivery."

"Did Jon forget one of his tools?"

325

"How did you . . . I didn't realize you knew he lived out here."

"He mentioned it once."

"What are *you* doing in this neck of the woods? Your taco customers will be disappointed to find a shuttered stand on a Sunday afternoon."

"I closed when the clouds arrived, after I made an order for Rose." As the rain picked up, he motioned toward the passenger seat. "Why don't you let me give you a lift back? Otherwise you'll be taking a shower and doing your laundry in one fell swoop." He flashed her his megawatt smile.

She examined the sky again.

It was darker than ever, and the angry clouds appeared poised to dump their load of H_2O at any moment.

"I think I'll take you up on that."

She circled the car, and he pushed the door open for her from the inside, transferring the brown bag of tacos from the passenger seat to the floor.

"I'd say my arrival was timely." He put the car in gear and swept a hand across the windshield, where large drops of rain were beginning to pepper the glass.

"Must be my lucky day."

"Luck is overrated."

"You don't believe in luck?"

"I believe everything happens the way it's supposed to, though often that's only apparent in hindsight. What do you think of Bessie here?" He patted the dashboard.

"You named your car?"

"This one's special."

She surveyed the pristine interior. "How old is she?"

"Came off the line in 1957. Long before you were born."

"She's in excellent condition."

"She wasn't when I got her. She'd been banged up pretty bad. People took one look at all her scratches and dents, turned up their noses, and walked away. But I was more interested in checking out her inner workings, and they were sound. Everything else is cosmetic."

An image of Jon flashed through her mind, but she did her best to erase it.

"You had her restored?"

"No. I did it myself. It took two years, but the effort was worth it. Despite all the hard knocks Bessie took, she's reliable, resilient, and a rare find."

Also like Jon?

She squinted at Charley.

Were his comments supposed to be an analogy, or was she reading more into them than he'd intended?

He glanced over at her, his expression guileless. "How did the open house go?"

"Fine." She switched mental gears. "Everyone

was enthusiastic, and I've had several queries already."

"I'm not surprised. Edgecliff is another rare gem that will benefit from TLC, like Bessie did. I thought about you yesterday morning, after that storm we had. I wondered if it had caused any damage." He guided the car through the open gates at the entrance to the estate.

"A little." She gave him a quick recap. "But Jon showed up at the crack of dawn to clear out the debris."

"That sounds like him."

"Do you know him well?" Maybe she could glean a few more insights about him from the town sage.

"I wouldn't say that, but we do chat during his infrequent stops at the stand. I imagine you've seen more of him in the past month than I have in the two years he's lived here."

"Mostly from a distance. He doesn't get too close."

"I expect there are reasons for that." He swung onto the circle drive as the rain drummed against the roof of the car.

"Yes." She plucked at a tiny piece of fuzz on her jeans. "I can't imagine what it must be like to live with such a devastating injury."

"It has to be difficult—and lonely."

"Without a doubt. Getting past appearances can be hard."

"Yes, it can. But as most people learn the hard way, a beautiful or handsome face doesn't always translate to a beautiful heart or soul."

"I know." Thanks to Jason, the golden boy with the tarnished character.

Charley passed in front of the house and turned onto the small road that led to her quarters and Rose's cottage. "Jon's done a fine job sprucing this place up."

"Yes, he has."

"Please tell him I said hello when you see him next."

"I'll do that. But the Phase 1 landscaping projects here are winding down. I doubt he'll be around much." And given his attitude today, the probability was high he'd send others from his crew to do the routine maintenance.

"He's not far away, though. A friendly visit on occasion wouldn't be out of line."

The very notion she'd broached to Jon.

Yet he hadn't been all that receptive. Nor as warm as usual during her impromptu visit.

Was it because he'd picked up on her message that she wasn't ready to jump into romance, or had his attitude shift already been in place even before her visit?

Who knew?

"I'm not certain he wants visitors, Charley." She unlatched her door as he stopped the car.

"Sometimes people are afraid to ask for what they want."

At his quiet comment, she twisted toward him. His eyes were kind—and astute. As if he'd sensed her turmoil and wasn't judging her for it. Somehow that gave her the courage to take the opening he'd offered. "But what if they want more than you're able to give?"

"Most people only want a chance."

"I didn't get that impression today. It felt more like a brush-off."

Charley pursed his lips and studied the terrain through the front window, where the steady rain was obscuring the familiar landmarks. "If that's true, I wonder what the reason would be?"

Ashley forced her mouth into a curve. "He may have decided he doesn't like me all that much."

"You really think that's the reason?" Charley turned back to her.

"What else could it be?"

"An intriguing question to ponder on this rainy afternoon." He indicated the bag on the floor at her feet. "And now I'm off to deliver those to Rose. Otherwise she'll be eating cold tacos."

Her signal to leave.

"Thanks again for the lift."

"Anytime."

She pushed open the door, slid out, and dashed toward the carriage house while Charley rolled on toward Rose's cottage.

But long after he disappeared, his comments lingered.

Did Jon want a chance with her? And if so, why had he erected barriers between them today? What had spooked him?

No clear answers presented themselves.

So as she opened her laptop to number crunch and take care of open house follow-up, she added a prayer for guidance to her afternoon schedule.

Because she could use all the help she could get figuring out whether Jon's appearance was an insurmountable hurdle to a romantic relationship, as her mom had warned, or simply a minor facet of his persona that had far less to do with lasting love than the content of his heart, mind, and soul.

Yet if Mom's assessment did prove to be wrong, another puzzle remained. The one Charley had zeroed in on today.

If Jon hadn't backed off due to lack of interest, what had prompted his withdrawal?

And once she discovered the answer to that question, what could she do to change his mind?

22

Maybe this was a mistake.

Stomach flip-flopping, Rose set her cell phone back on the desk beside her in the cottage and twisted her fingers together.

What had seemed like an inspired idea three days ago suddenly felt risky. And much too big a step after years of keeping her distance from society and confining her in-person interactions to a few trusted friends.

Even Charley's encouragement during his taco drop-off on Sunday afternoon and David's endorsement during their phone chat earlier today couldn't corral the butterflies that had taken flight in her stomach.

"What do you think, Lucy Lynn? Yea or nay?"

The precocious five-year-old smiled back at her. Trusting her to do the right thing, as usual.

But sometimes it was hard to be certain what that was.

"You know, I believe you need a bow in your pretty hair." She cocked her head and assessed the girl. "Shall we try a red one today? It should be lovely with that navy-blue sailor dress." She leaned forward and added it to Lucy Lynn's hair. Nodded. "Yes. Red was an excellent choice."

Too bad all decisions weren't as easy.

She eyed the phone. Heaved an annoyed sigh.

Dithering was ridiculous. It was possible nothing would come of her call anyway. But kindness was never wasted. At the very least, she'd brighten that young woman's day. And if she positioned the offer as a trial run, she could cancel the arrangement if it didn't work out— as both Charley and David had mentioned. Two trusted friends who knew her story and had never given her bad counsel when she'd solicited their opinions or advice.

Taking a deep breath, she stood. "I'll be back in a few minutes, Lucy Lynn, and we'll finish up for the day."

She picked up the phone, exited the cottage, and settled into the rocker on the front porch that offered an expansive view of the house and grounds.

In the distance, the tent company was taking down its contribution to Saturday's open house. The landscapers were pruning more bushes and trees. And in the back of the main house, the construction crew was building a discreet ADA compliant ramp by the side door, where it could be camouflaged with bushes.

Everyone was engaged in meaningful work.

As she was.

It wasn't as if her life lacked purpose, after all. Being entrusted with Lucy Lynn was a great responsibility.

But she had room in her schedule for other projects—like Mindy Jackson.

Pulse picking up, she pulled the woman's card from her pocket and tapped in the number.

A female voice answered after three rings. "Picture Perfect Chair Covers. How may I help you?"

"Am I speaking with Mindy?"

"Yes."

"This is Rose Fitzgerald, the pianist from the open house at Edgecliff on Saturday. Do you have a minute to talk?"

"Oh." Surprise raised the woman's pitch. "How nice to hear from you. Yes, I have a few minutes."

"I won't keep you long, but I have a proposition for you. After I quit playing piano professionally, I offered lessons to a few select students. I do have the credentials to teach." She gave Mindy a quick recap of her conservatory education and the faculty she'd studied under. "I thought lessons could be beneficial for both of us. If you're interested, of course."

Dead silence.

As Rose waited for a response, Ashley appeared on the terrace in the distance and homed in on Jon's employees at work on the far side of the property.

At last Mindy spoke. "I'm sorry. I'm just . . . taken aback. I'd love to accept, but as I mentioned on Saturday, finances are very tight, and I—"

"Oh, there wouldn't be any charge. I should have made that clear up front."

Another pause.

"But . . . I don't understand. Why would you do this for free?"

"There would be compensation of a different kind. I like teaching. And I would enjoy getting to know you. I realize your time is stretched thin, though, so if you can't squeeze lessons in, I—"

"No! I'll find a way to make this work. Except I don't have a piano to practice on."

That had been the one flaw in the plan from the beginning. Coos Bay was too far away for Allison to be a practical practice option.

There was, however, one possible solution.

"I did think about that, and I have a suggestion." In the distance, Ashley shaded her eyes with her hand and did a slow pivot. As if she was searching for someone. "Most churches have a piano. If you attend one on a regular basis, it's possible you can get permission to use their instrument to practice on until you can buy one of your own."

"My daughter and I do attend a local church." A note of excitement and a touch of hope crept into her inflection as she continued. "I've chatted with my pastor after services on occasion. I could ask him."

"Is he aware of your personal situation?"

"Not in any detail."

"He may be more receptive if he knows a bit of your story. Assuming you're comfortable sharing that with him, of course."

"I think I would be. He comes across as very kind and empathetic, and I know he's had sorrow in his own life. I believe he lost his wife a few years ago. I'll call him and see if I can stop by in the next day or two to discuss it with him."

Smart. Face-to-face meetings were always wise if favors were being requested.

"You can let me know the verdict whenever it's convenient." A hummingbird darted to the feeder on her porch, its reddish-orange throat glinting as it hovered in the sunlight to draw sustenance from the nourishment she'd provided.

"I will. Where would the lessons be?"

"At Edgecliff."

"You mean . . . on the antique piano?"

"Yes."

"You must have influence with the owners."

Rose's lips flexed. "You could say that. I'm one of them. Edgecliff was built by my grandfather, and I've lived here for many years."

"You live in that beautiful house?" The question was hushed and tinged with awe.

"Not since Ashley and I became partners and decided to open it to tours and special events. But I do live on the grounds."

"Wow. Now I'm even more amazed by your offer. How many students do you have?"

"You'll be the first in many years. I have other interests that keep me busy. But your situation struck a chord with me and nudged me to reach out."

"I'm glad you did. Thank you!"

"Don't thank me until we get the details worked out. A practice piano is essential."

"I'm on it as soon as we hang up. I'll call you the minute I have news." She exhaled. "I can't believe this. It's like an answer to a prayer. Being able to not only play the piano again but also improve my skills would be such a blessing."

"And teaching you would be a blessing for me. I believe this will be a win-win. If we can work out all the details, let's give it a trial run and see what we both think."

As they ended the conversation and rang off, Rose leaned back in her chair. So far, she'd been batting a thousand with her ventures back into society. First Ashley, now Mindy. Who would be next?

A figure emerged from around the corner of the main house. A man.

Rose squinted at him.

Was that Jon?

Hard to tell from this distance. The darkness had masked his features the night Ashley introduced them on the porch, and prior to that he'd always hidden behind sunglasses and caps and neck coverings.

It could be one of his crew.

The man stopped at the under-construction ramp and chatted with the workers for a few moments, then stepped back and gave it a once-over. Perhaps to weigh a few tweaks to the landscape design?

After taking a measurement, he started to walk toward the back of the house but jerked to a stop the instant he spotted Ashley on the terrace.

She was focused again on the work being done on the far side of the property, unaware of his scrutiny as he backed into the shadows.

Ah.

It had to be Jon. Only a man running scared would avoid a woman he was attracted to.

And he was attracted to Ashley, no doubt about that. With eight decades of living under her belt, she was long past the stage where crazy hormones could lead to the angst of unrequited longing. But that didn't mean she'd lost the ability to recognize it.

That young man had it bad.

But those scars of his could be a game changer . . . or not, depending on the maturity of the woman involved.

Was Ashley up to the task?

From all indications, she was. But while acumen in business matters and strong people skills often led to professional rewards, they didn't always translate to success in romantic relationships.

There was only one way to find out if they did in this case.

Those two young people needed to hash out whatever roadblock was keeping them apart, or the potential between them would fizzle faster than spent fireworks on the Fourth of July.

And since that roadblock appeared to have arisen after her inopportune appearance on the porch, she ought to do her part to try to help them address it.

That goal front and center, Rose pushed herself to her feet and set a course straight down the narrow lane toward the house.

Perhaps Ashley and Jon weren't meant to be together. But as Charley had reminded her over tacos two days ago when she'd mentioned Mindy, opportunities to do good deeds were gifts. A chance to put the golden rule into action.

And if her instincts were correct, her action today could very well lead to other action—with a potential long-term payoff Ashley and Jon would thank her for in the years to come.

As Jon turned away from the terrace, preparing to escape before Ashley spotted him, Rose smiled and waved at him from halfway down the road to her cottage.

Blast.

It would be rude to return the wave and run off. Especially if Charley's contention was right, and her reputation as a recluse was prompted in part by the fact that few sought her out.

Rebuffing a friendly gesture from her would be worse than rude.

But if he lingered, Ashley could wander over.

He glanced back toward the terrace.

Maybe he could chat with Rose for a minute without Ashley spotting him if he took cover behind one of the bushes on the side of the gravel lane.

Armed with that plan, he skirted around the house and tucked himself beside a bush as she drew close. "Afternoon, Rose."

"Jon." If his exposed scars shocked her, she didn't let on. But Ashley could have prepped her for his appearance. "Did you enjoy the samples Ashley saved you from Saturday's party?"

A flush crept over his cheeks. "She told you about that?"

"Not until I came across her in the kitchen, packing the box. She said you'd asked her for a few."

"For the record, I'm not a moocher."

"Perish the thought." She waved his comment aside. "That was small recompense for all the cleanup you and your crew did. Dozens of potential clients came that day, and first impressions are very important."

"Yeah. I know." Fighting back a surge of melancholy, he propped up the corners of his mouth. "I understand your performance was a highlight."

"According to whom?"

"Ashley. She stopped by my house to drop off the box of food."

"That was sweet of her."

"Uh-huh."

"She's a very nice woman."

"Yes." If Rose was expecting him to sing her partner's praises, she was going to be disappointed. Just because she'd witnessed their almost-kiss didn't mean he had to provide any details about their relationship.

"May I be honest with you, Jon?"

Uh-oh.

Those kinds of questions never led anywhere good.

"I guess so." What else could he say?

"I've been feeling bad ever since the Saturday night I interrupted you two on the porch, after I finished playing. My entrance was poorly timed."

"No." He shook his head. "It was spot-on. We needed to call it a night. Music and moonlight and mist can carry people away." Why dance around the facts? Rose had obviously figured out what was going on.

She adjusted the sweater draped around her shoulders as she considered him. "Are you certain the ambiance was responsible?"

"Yes."

"Why?"

Good grief. How had he gotten into a discussion about his love life with an eighty-year-old recluse? He had to shut this down fast and put an end to any romantic fantasies she might be harboring about love blossoming on the grounds of her ancestral home.

"Ashley and I just met a few weeks ago, Rose. I think she was happy about the interruption."

"She did disappear faster than a nervous mole crab on the beach." Rose leaned closer and lowered her voice. "Between you and me, I believe she's rather gun-shy of romance."

Had Ashley told her about Jason?

He slid his hands into his pockets and kept his tone casual. "Why do you say that?"

"Well, she's a beautiful woman in her thirties, but she's never mentioned a boyfriend. I expect there's a story there."

So Ashley hadn't shared that piece of her history with Rose.

Nor would he. If she wanted her partner to know about her ex, she should be the one to divulge it.

"Could be."

"I expect the right man could change her mind, though."

He met her gaze straight on. "In case you have any inclination I could be that man, you're wrong. She's made it very clear she's interested only in friendship."

Rose narrowed her eyes. "Those weren't the vibes I picked up on the porch."

"It's possible your intuitive powers are off."

"No, I don't think so. You may find this hard to believe from the perspective of youth, but while faces may wrinkle, hearts don't. On the contrary. They become more sensitive to nuances with age. If you want my opinion, she was running scared that night."

He shoved up one corner of his mouth. "Wouldn't you be scared if a guy who looks like me almost kissed you?" Why not be honest?

Rose pursed her lips. "You think your appearance is why she's skittish?"

"I'm not exactly handsome."

"No. It's clear you've suffered a traumatic injury. Ashley told me it was battle related."

Another subject he wasn't inclined to discuss. "Yes."

If Rose was put off by his curt reply, she didn't let on. "I'd describe you as intriguing. And anyone who looked close would also see the kindness in your eyes—and the integrity." She continued to inspect him. "Have you given Ashley a chance to look close?"

A muscle spasmed in his cheek. "She saw me Sunday, when she brought the appetizers to my house." His voice sounded stiff even to his own ears. "And during her visit, she made it clear her interest was confined to friendship."

"Friendship can lead to much more."

"Not unless both parties are receptive."

"You don't think Ashley is?"

"I wasn't referring to her. I'm not interested in where, as you put it, a friendship could lead."

She scrutinized him for a moment. "May I be honest again?" Without waiting for a response, she continued. "I don't think you're being honest with *me*. My romantic fancies are all in the past, but I still recognize them in other people. I'd wager my beloved Allison that you're very interested in where a friendship with Ashley could lead."

Jon stifled a groan.

This conversation was going from bad to worse.

"People can be interested in a lot of things they never pursue." He twisted his wrist and scanned his watch. "I should run. I've got another job to bid on today." Not for two hours, but Rose didn't know that.

"And it appears I have a delivery." She motioned toward a UPS truck as it rounded the corner of the main house and rumbled toward them down the gravel lane. "But I'll leave you with one thought." She fixed her keen gaze on him. "Deciding what's best for other people may seem noble, but it can also be presumptuous and lead to regrets all around. Enjoy the rest of your day."

With that, she walked back toward the cottage, the UPS truck following in her wake.

A cloud of dust wafted toward him, and Jon retreated around the side of the house.

Farther away from Ashley's sight.

Yet as he plodded back to his truck, Rose's final words continued to echo in his mind.

How could she have discerned that his rationale for keeping his distance from Ashley was motivated by a desire to protect her? And why would she imply that such a selfless act was misplaced?

More important, had shutting Ashley out on Sunday been a mistake?

All of those questions deserved serious thought.

And until he came up with answers, it was safer to keep his distance so he didn't make any more tactical errors he could end up regretting for the rest of his life.

23

·····································

"You're going to give piano lessons?" Ashley did a double take as her Thursday briefing with Rose wound down. A piano discussion was on her agenda too, but it could wait until Rose offered a few details about this surprising news.

"Yes." Her partner folded her hands on the kitchen table and explained how she'd come to meet Mindy.

"I remember her." Ashley called up a vague image of the blond who'd seemed reluctant to move outside at the vendor event. "I didn't realize she'd stayed in the house."

"You did a superb job corralling everyone, but in hindsight I'm glad she managed to elude you. I brought it up today because I don't want you to worry about these lessons interfering with any of your plans. I've already told Mindy we'll have to be flexible with our schedule to accommodate events here."

Ashley waved aside Rose's concern. "I think the lessons are a wonderful idea. Will she be coming here to practice too?"

"No. She lives in Coos Bay. But she was able to work out an arrangement with her minister to practice on the piano at her church."

"Sounds like an ideal setup all around." Ashley

tapped the stack of papers in front of her into a neat pile. Considering how well Rose's performance had gone at the open house, and her willingness to give a stranger piano lessons, it was possible the next-to-last item on the meeting agenda today wouldn't be too hard to sell after all. "I do have two other topics to discuss with you. The first is also piano related. As I've told you, I had numerous compliments on your playing last Saturday."

A faint tinge of pink bloomed on Rose's cheeks. "I appreciated you passing those on. I have to admit that having an audience again was more satisfying than I expected."

"I'm glad to hear that. Because I've had two inquiries about your contact information and availability."

Rose blinked. "Availability for what?"

"To play at events here. One is for a small wedding that will be held on the terrace, followed by a cocktail party. The other is for a twenty-fifth anniversary dinner in the drawing room and foyer. Both requested that you wear vintage attire, like at the open house."

"Goodness." Rose's flush deepened, and her hand fluttered to her chest. "I can't believe people want to hire me to play."

"Why not? They used to."

"That was decades ago."

"But you never stopped playing, and it shows.

Otherwise people wouldn't be clamoring to book you. And look how you captivated Mindy."

"I'll admit I'm flattered by all the compliments, but paying engagements at my age? I don't know . . ."

Yet the spark in her eyes said she was tempted.

Ashley leaned forward and touched her hand. "Why not do this, Rose? Your skills are ageless, and I doubt the guests will know who the pianist is in advance. It's not as if you have to worry about unwanted publicity."

"When are the events?"

"Early September."

"May I think about this overnight?"

"Of course. And if you decide to accept, don't underprice your services."

"Oh, I wouldn't be doing it for the money."

"I realize that. But based on my experience in Tennessee, you deserve top dollar."

Rose's lips curved up. "Thank you for that. What's the other matter we have to discuss?"

Ashley took the top sheet off her stack of papers. "I asked Greenscape—Jon's company—to give us a bid on regular lawn and garden maintenance. Kyle, his foreman, passed this on to me today." She handed it to Rose. "If you'd like to review it overnight, feel free. But I think it's fair."

The other woman gave it a quick scan. "In light of the amount I was paying for regular grass cutting, I don't believe this is out of line. Especially after you factor in all the gardens that have to be attended to now. I'm fine with this." She passed it back.

Ashley set it on top of her pile. "I'll let him know—or tell Kyle if I don't see Jon." The latter was more likely, given that she'd caught no more than a glimpse or two of him all week, and always from a distance.

"Aren't he and his crew still working here?"

"Yes, but they should be finished by tomorrow. I think Jon's been popping in to monitor progress, but I expect he has other jobs lined up that require his attention now that the Phase 1 work here is done."

"I've enjoyed meeting him. He seems like a very nice young man. We had a lovely chat on Tuesday."

That was news.

"What about?" Ashley kept her manner casual as she straightened the edge of the paper stack.

"Oh, this and that. Your name came up."

Her breath got stuck in her throat. "In reference to . . . ?"

"The night you two sat on the front porch and listened to my concert."

Her cheeks warmed. "He talked about that?"

"Only after I brought it up. I wanted to apologize to him for interrupting."

"That wasn't necessary." She tried for a dismissive tone. "There wasn't anything to interrupt."

"That's not how I saw it."

Heat surged up her neck again.

Memo to self: never underestimate Rose's perceptive abilities.

"I suppose we may have gotten a bit carried away by your music. It was lucky you came out when you did."

"That's what Jon said."

Well, shoot.

Maybe the sparks really had fizzled on his end.

"There you go." Somehow she managed to hang on to her nonchalance.

"Except I don't think he was being honest. He likes you, you know."

No, as a matter of fact, she didn't.

"I'm not certain about that. I mean, he's polite and cordial, but he hasn't done anything to indicate he's interested in picking up where we left off on the porch."

"I expect most men need a little encouragement. Jon perhaps more than most."

Hard to dispute—and she hadn't given him any the day she'd delivered the appetizers.

Not a subject she wanted to discuss with Rose.

"He didn't need much the night of our private concert."

Rose's expression grew speculative. "I wonder what could have happened in the interim to dampen his interest?"

Her Sunday visit, for one.

But he hadn't been all that warm and welcoming even before she'd started dropping the friend word.

"I don't know. I've only talked to him twice since that night. And the first exchange, when he stopped by the house Saturday night while Mom and I were on the porch, was very brief."

"He met your mother?"

"Yes." Ashley ran a finger along the uneven grain in the kitchen table. "It was kind of . . . awkward. I think Mom made him uncomfortable. She, uh, stared at him."

"Ah." A look that was hard to decipher passed across Rose's face. "I wonder if that could be related to his change of heart."

Ashley squinted at her. "How so?"

"Why not ask him? You and Jon are adults, well able to handle an honest discussion. And putting fears and concerns on the table is better than spending sleepless nights trying to guess how another person feels." Rose pushed her chair back and stood. "I'll let you know by tomorrow about playing at those events. Enjoy your evening."

As her partner slipped out the door, Ashley set her elbow on the table and propped her chin in her palm.

Not much chance of that, with Jon on her mind.

Should she do as Rose had advised and initiate a conversation with him about their relationship?

Explain why she wanted to confine it to friendship for a while?

Or would admitting she needed time to determine whether his appearance could be a stumbling block to romance be too honest and hurt him more?

That would be awful.

Ten minutes later, no closer to a course of action, Ashley armed the security system and exited.

Best plan at this muddled-mess stage?

Pray for guidance—and hope the Almighty came through before any ardor Jon might still feel evaporated forever, like a Hope Harbor fog swept away by a relentless wind.

The parking lot at St. Francis church was deserted.

Almost.

But the two cars occupying spots near the entrance weren't anywhere close to the meditation garden in back, so the coast should be clear.

Jon rolled past the cars and continued to the rose-bedecked arbor topped by a sign that said "All Are Welcome."

If this place was half as peaceful and contemplative as Reverend Baker had claimed, perhaps it would help him work through the questions Rose had planted in his head about Ashley.

He gave the adjacent church a pensive perusal as he parked.

Once upon a time, he'd have sought guidance by chatting with the Almighty. But the long radio silence between them was hard to bridge.

The garden would have to do.

And maybe, there in the shadow of his house, God would take pity on a wayward son and give him a blinding flash of insight. Even if that son wasn't willing to venture inside.

He could hope, anyway.

Jon set the brake, opened the door—and froze halfway out of the truck as a radiant bride, hand in hand with her groom, emerged from the arbor.

A photographer with an assistant came out behind them and proceeded to pose the joyful couple under the cascade of roses as their laughter floated across the parking lot.

Jon's throat tightened.

Talk about rotten timing.

He eased back onto the seat, keys clenched in his fingers.

Hard as he tried to be happy for the newlyweds, the scene reminded him too much of all that was missing in his own life.

What might always be missing, unless he was willing to subject a woman he cared about to lifelong scrutiny and pity.

Rose had implied that his decision to back off wasn't necessarily the noble course, but wasn't protecting those you cared about always the honorable choice?

The very question he'd come here to seek an answer to today.

But the trip was a bust.

As soon as the wedding entourage left, he was out of here. A visit to the garden wouldn't be very helpful in light of the sudden funk that had descended over him.

Within a handful of minutes, the photographer wrapped up and the small group traipsed toward the cars near the front door, the bride's wispy veil trailing behind her, held aloft by the gentle breeze.

As the couple got into their waiting car, the photographer and assistant stowed their equipment in their own vehicle. Minutes later, both cars pulled out of the lot.

His cue to leave as well.

He reached toward the ignition just as Father Murphy walked through the rose arbor.

When the cleric caught sight of him and lifted a hand in greeting, Jon groaned.

He was stuck again, like he'd been the day Rose waved to him at Edgecliff.

Rather than get out of the truck, though, he started the engine and drove over to the padre, rolling down his window en route.

"Good afternoon, Jon," Father Murphy greeted him as he braked. "I thought that was you across the lot. What brings you here on this beautiful Saturday?"

"I was going to visit your garden, but it was occupied."

"Ah yes. Wedding photos. Most brides and grooms stop here after the ceremony for a few shots before following the guests and the rest of the wedding party to the reception or other scenic locales for more pictures. It's all yours now." He swept a hand toward the entrance.

"I think I'll come back another day. I was only planning to stay a few minutes, and the photo shoot ate into those."

"I hear you. We all run on tight schedules these days, don't we? If you could spare five minutes for a bit of free advice, though, I'd appreciate it. I put in a sword fern a couple of years ago that flourished in the beginning but now appears to be under stress. I was going to call the nursery where I bought it and talk to an expert, but a bird in hand and all that." He grinned.

It was impossible to refuse the jolly cleric.

"I can take a quick look, but I'm not a fern specialist."

"I guarantee you know more than I do. I'm a self-taught amateur. Let me show it to you." He trotted toward the entrance.

Jon followed more slowly. Yet once he entered Father Murphy's little piece of paradise, as the man had called it, the serenity seeped into his pores and loosened the taut muscles in his shoulders.

As he followed the priest down the meandering, circular stone path, he gave the space a slow, appreciative perusal.

Annuals and perennials were tucked among hydrangeas, rhodies, and other bushes, producing a pleasing palette of varying heights. The soft splash of water from a fountain in the middle mingled with birdsong to create a soothing background that muffled the sound of any traffic beyond the arbor. Two wooden benches were tucked into the greenery at discreet intervals, one beside a statue of Saint Francis of Assisi.

The overall effect was restful and refreshing.

By the time he caught up with Father Murphy, the garden had worked its calming magic and boosted his lagging spirits.

"There it is." The priest pointed to the tall fern near the back of the garden. "I've babied it all along, but I must be doing something wrong."

The limp fronds were proof of that.

"It does seem to be struggling." Jon studied the plant from the path, then motioned to the garden. "May I walk over to it?"

"By all means. I trust you not to crush my plants. But feel free to step on as many weeds as you like."

Jon moved into the garden and examined the plant up close. Checked out the base. Felt the soil. "How much do you water this?"

"Every day if it doesn't rain. I know ferns like to be kept moist."

Jon pushed aside a small amount of mulch and worked his finger into the soil.

Problem solved.

He stood and rejoined the priest. "You're right about ferns and moisture, but too much of a good thing can be bad. The water is cutting off oxygen to the feeder roots and drowning the plant. Overwatered sword ferns are also particularly susceptible to a fungus called *Phytophthora cinnamomi*, which causes the frond wilting you see here."

Dismay flattened the priest's features. "Is it too far gone to save?"

"I don't think so. This species is on the hardy side. My advice is to water it less and amend the soil around the roots with compost to improve the drainage."

"I'll take care of that as soon as I finish my Masses tomorrow. Thank you for the excellent counsel."

"My pleasure."

The priest shifted his attention to the plant and shook his head. "Just goes to show how we can kill something we love with kindness. All with the best intentions, of course, and in the interest of keeping it safe. I expect I should let hardy plants fend for themselves instead of assuming I know what they need to flourish."

Jon frowned.

Father Murphy was talking about plants, but his comment could also be true about people.

Like Ashley.

Was he killing any possibility of love between them because he wanted to protect her and keep her safe? Because he was trying to predict what would help her thrive instead of recognizing she was a strong woman and letting her make her own choices?

Was that what Rose had meant when she'd implied his selfless act was misplaced?

"You seem in deep thought, my friend."

Jon transferred his gaze to the padre, whose kind, caring demeanor invited confidences.

"Sorry. I do have a few things on my mind."

"You've come to a perfect place to think." He indicated the garden. "But you're also welcome anytime at Mass."

"I'm not Catholic, Father." He stared at the ground, nudging a stray pebble off the path with the toe of his boot. "To tell you the truth, I'm not much of anything anymore."

"Ah. You and God are on the outs." There was no recrimination in his voice. No reproach. Instead, the priest's tone was conversational and matter of fact.

Jon lifted his head. "My lapsed faith doesn't bother you?"

"The word *bother* often implies annoyance, and that doesn't fit this situation. It does sadden me to see anyone distanced from God, but I understand how it can happen. The blows life deals us and the mistakes we make can drive a wedge in what should, in an ideal world, be a relationship of total trust and acceptance on both sides. God lives up to his part of that bargain, but we humans often fall short on both counts."

"Blows and mistakes pretty much nail it for me, Father."

"That combination can certainly erode faith for many people. If you have a few more minutes, I could share with you a story I often tell people who come to me seeking guidance and comfort."

At this point, there was no hurry to leave. And if the priest could offer even a sliver of insight or direction, it was worth hanging around.

"I have a few more minutes."

"Shall we sit by St. Francis?" Father Murphy motioned toward the bench beside the statue. "I've been on my feet all day, and five o'clock Mass isn't far off."

"Sure." Jon walked over to the bench and claimed one side.

The priest settled in next to him. "My Protestant colleague, Paul, claims I have a tendency to run off at the mouth, so in the interest of brevity I'll rein in my propensity for embellishment." He winked and smiled. "This story goes back to my early years as a priest. A young man came to me, conflicted about a woman he'd fallen in love with. It was an opposite-side-of-the-tracks story. She was from a prominent family, and he came from an impoverished, broken home. He'd also gone to prison for a burglary in which a man was killed. Not by his hand, but he believed in his heart he could have stopped that shooting."

Jon rested his arm on the back of the bench. "How did two people from such different backgrounds meet?"

"By chance—or not, depending on how much credence you give Divine Providence. They both volunteered at a food bank. And the more they got to know each other, the more he came to love her. But even though he'd turned his life around, he didn't feel worthy of her love because of the mistakes he'd made that cost a man his life."

"What did you tell him?"

"I reminded him that we're often a harsher judge of ourselves than God is. He knows we're not perfect. All he expects is that we acknowledge our failings, learn from our mistakes, try to do better, and trust in his mercy and love. I believe I reassured him on that score, but he was also afraid the stigma of his past would hurt the woman he loved if they got involved."

Jon's pulse skittered at the similarities between this story and his.

"Don't you think his concerns were valid?"

The priest offered him a gentle smile. "Wanting to protect those we love is always admirable—unless we overreach. I'm not an expert on romance, but I believe the most loving thing we can do for those we care about is respect their free will and trust them to make their own choices rather than decide what we think is in their best interest. Or its best interest, as my experience with the sword fern proves."

Rose and the padre appeared to be tracking the same direction.

"What happened with this couple?"

"They celebrated their twenty-fifth anniversary last year." A fan of crinkle lines radiated from the corners of the priest's eyes before he grew more serious. "Not that they haven't encountered challenges, you understand. There have been quite a few bumps along the road. But their deep, abiding love for each other and their strong faith have kept them on track."

Deep, abiding love and strong faith.

Jon let out a slow breath.

That's what he wanted.

But both had eluded him.

He flicked a wayward ant off his jeans, lifting his finger to examine the muck under his nail from poking around the base of the struggling fern. It would take diligent scrubbing to remove the wedged-in dirt, but with sufficient effort he could restore his nail to pristine condition.

Perhaps he could do the same for his soul, with God's help.

As for Ashley . . . maybe he'd overreacted the day she'd appeared at his house with the appetizers. It was possible she hadn't been shutting the door on romance, just setting a slower pace. Shouldn't he give her the opportunity to clarify that?

Mind whirling, he looked over at the priest. "You've given me a lot to think about, Father."

"And you've saved my fern. I'd call us even." He rested a hand on his shoulder. "May I offer you a blessing?"

"Please."

Jon bowed his head as the priest asked for God's guidance and grace, then made the sign of the cross.

Three minutes later, as they parted and Jon returned to his truck through the rose-bedecked arbor and under the "All Are Welcome" sign, his spirits rose.

He'd come to this place seeking, but not expecting, direction.

Yet God had put a Catholic priest in his path. A man from a different church than he'd attended growing up, but whose strong faith and insights had provided the very guidance he'd sought.

Guidance he intended to follow come tomorrow as he started a new chapter with God.

And with Ashley.

24

As the final hymn wound down at the early Sunday service, Ashley leaned around to pick up her sweater from the seat.

Froze.

Was that Jon in the last pew, half in the shadows?

She draped her sweater over her arm and reached for her purse, giving him a scan in her peripheral vision.

The clothes were a disconnect. In all their encounters, he'd worn jeans and a sweatshirt or denim jacket. This guy's broad shoulders showcased a tailored sport coat and crisp dress shirt, and his dark gray slacks were as far from blue jeans as you could get.

She squinted.

It could be him. The build was right. But he didn't—

The man edged into a beam of light spilling through the high windows that lined the nave and lifted a hand in greeting.

Her lungs locked.

It was Jon.

The GQ version.

This was how he must have looked in his

modeling days, except for the face. Even from a distance, the mottled skin on the left side and the asymmetry of his features were apparent.

Despite those physical aberrations, however, the tall, toned physique and powerful shoulders gave him a commanding and potent presence.

Ashley responded to his greeting but waited until the aisle cleared to exit the pew, giving him plenty of opportunity to escape, if that was his plan. Cornering a guy in a public place, especially a guy who didn't want to be cornered, would be awkward.

But he didn't leave.

Rather than making himself scarce, as he'd been doing all week, he remained at the back of the church while she ambled up the aisle.

As if he was waiting for her.

Her pulse picked up.

Maybe, if he was willing to chat for a few minutes somewhere outside in privacy, she could follow Rose's advice and broach the subject of their relationship. Have an honest but diplomatic discussion about her concerns.

Because given the flutter of butterflies in her stomach as she approached him, the scars that were on full display today weren't necessarily the deal breaker for romance her mother had assumed they'd be.

When she drew close, he joined her in the aisle.

"Good morning." She offered him an encouraging smile. "This is a surprise. I thought you and God were on the outs."

"We've mended our fences. Or, I should say, I've mended mine."

"I'm glad to hear that." Especially if romance was in the cards for them. There were enough challenges in any relationship without adding differences in faith to the mix.

"May I walk you out?" He motioned toward the exit.

"Sure. Thanks."

He fell in beside her as they left the main body of the church and entered the vestibule. If he was aware of the curious but discreet peeks directed at them by the congregants gathered in small groups, he gave no indication of it.

Yet the fact that he didn't make eye contact with any of them could mean their perusal had registered and he didn't want to encourage engagement.

Because he wasn't ready to subject himself to up-close scrutiny, or because he wanted to spend a few private minutes with her and preferred not to be waylaid?

Perhaps both.

Reverend Baker waved at them over the heads of the people clustered around him, but following Jon's example, Ashley kept moving as she responded. There'd be no opportunity in here to talk about anything of a personal nature or have a one-on-one chat.

Once outside, Jon nodded down Dockside Drive. "Would you like to stroll over to Sweet Dreams and get a cinnamon roll? We could claim a bench and enjoy the view of the wharf while we eat."

Her heart flip-flopped.

He was asking her on a date? Well, maybe not an official date . . . but an impromptu social get-together sort of qualified as a date.

Didn't it?

Unless she was misreading him, the slight uncertainty in his manner, along with the tiny spark of warmth—and hope?—in his brown irises, gave her the answer.

And if he was offering her a tailor-made setup to have a discussion about personal matters, refusing would be crazy.

"A cinnamon roll would hit the spot. Pick one slathered in icing for me."

Some of the tension in his features eased, and he hitched up one side of his mouth. "Do I detect a sweet tooth?"

"Guilty as charged."

"You're not alone. I like sweet things too." His gaze locked on hers.

Pulse tripping into fast-forward, she wrestled down a sudden urge to fan herself.

Was he flirting with her?

Without giving her a chance to ponder that question, he ushered her out the door and fell in beside her as they crossed the parking lot, taking her arm to skirt a broken piece of pavement. "Watch your step."

At the touch of his lean fingers, a zing ricocheted through her.

Attraction, pure and simple.

That was a positive sign—and further evidence her mother's assumptions had been out of whack. While someone like Jon wouldn't appeal to Mom, it didn't appear the elder Scott had passed her romance prerequisites on to her daughter.

Chatting eye to eye with Jon on the bench, though, should tell her once and for all whether his appearance was a zing zapper.

Jon veered off from the parking lot onto Dockside Drive, lifting his hand to acknowledge the toot from Kyle's horn as his foreman pulled out of the lot. "Thanks for awarding us the maintenance job at Edgecliff. Kyle gave me the signed bid Friday." He motioned toward the car disappearing down the street.

What?

Now he wanted to talk about business?

Her spirits nose-dived.

Maybe this wasn't a date after all. It was possible he just wanted a friend nearby while he navigated a maskless public gathering.

Shoving up the corners of her lips, she draped

her sweater over her shoulders to ward off the morning chill. "I talked it over with Rose. We both agreed the price was more than fair."

"I'm glad to hear that. The maintenance chores will help keep the extra crew I brought on for the big job busy until our work volume ratchets up. That's already happening, by the way. Courtesy of Edgecliff. Thank you again for giving me that opportunity."

"You had the credentials."

"Credentials aren't always enough to win bids."

"Why not?" She glanced over at him, shading her eyes against the rising sun as they strolled along the sidewalk above the sloping bank of boulders that led to the water.

"My appearance unnerves some potential clients."

Shock rippled through her. "They told you that?"

"They didn't have to. I knew we had the lowest bid, but I could sense their discomfort during our initial meeting to discuss their project. I did the math."

Anger bristled through her. "That's crazy. Why should they care about anything other than your work ethic and skills?"

"They shouldn't." His tone remained calm. As if he'd long ago accepted the unfairness of such skewed judgment. "But we live in a world where appearances not only count but exert tremendous influence. Anyone who's different in any way carries baggage, even in our so-called tolerant and inclusive society."

"That stinks."

"It's reality. I've learned to live with it in the business world." He paused, and when he continued the tenor of his inflection had changed from matter-of-fact to measured. "The real question is, could someone associated with me on a personal level learn to live with that kind of fallout?"

O-kay.

He'd definitely switched out of landscaper mode, left work behind, and appeared as ready to discuss their relationship as she was.

She took a steadying breath as they approached Sweet Dreams bakery. "I'm glad you brought that up. I've been wanting to—"

"Hold that thought." He raised a hand. "Before we launch into heavier topics, why don't you claim that bench?" He indicated one a few yards ahead. "I'll get the coffee and cinnamon rolls so we can fortify ourselves with caffeine and sugar while we talk. That work for you?"

"I'm in."

"How do you like your coffee?"

"Generous cream and two sugars."

His eyebrows arched. "Wow. You really are a sugar addict."

"Yes, but I also have self-discipline. I know how to enjoy my treats in moderation."

"I can see that." He gave her trim figure a leisurely, appreciative head-to-toe.

No question about it. The man was flirting with her.

"I'll, uh, save the bench." She gave a vague wave that direction.

"I won't be long."

With that, he crossed the street and headed for the bakery.

Ashley watched until he disappeared inside, then continued to the bench and sat, a tiny trill racing through her.

Based on the tingle in her fingertips and Jon's new, more amorous attitude, things were looking up on the romance front.

Meaning the conversation she wanted to have might not be as hard as she'd expected. Less so if she was honest about her reaction to him this morning and her growing conviction that the concerns Mom had expressed were off base.

Most encouraging of all, Jon seemed to have dealt with whatever hurdle had caused him to back off all week. Whether he'd share what that stumbling block had been remained to be seen, but as long as he'd—

"Ashley! I thought that was you."

At the greeting from an all-too-familiar voice,

her jaw dropped and she swung around. Gaped at the sandy-haired man sauntering across the street, a disposable cup in hand.

"Jason?"

"None other." He joined her and tapped the back of the bench. "May I?" He gave her the engaging smile that had once turned her insides to mush but now simply turned her stomach.

Somehow she managed to formulate a coherent response as he sat without waiting for her response. "What are you doing here?"

"I needed some R&R, I had a ton of frequent flyer miles, this is a beautiful part of the country, and you're here. I was going to wander up to Edgecliff this afternoon and surprise you."

This wasn't making any sense.

"Are you saying you came here to see me?"

"Why not? We were an item for a while."

"You dumped me."

He gave a mock wince. "That may be a bit harsh."

"Harsh is precisely how you treated me." She stood. "I have no interest in talking to you."

"Now, Ashley." He rose too, his cloying, placating tone setting her teeth on edge. "I traveled thousands of miles to see you."

"Why? What happened to your blond friend?"

He gave an indifferent flip of his hand. "She's history. I realized not long after you left that she wasn't for me. After we split, I got to thinking about all the fun we had and decided to pay you a visit."

"How did you find me?"

His lips curled into a cocky grin. "Your former boss was a sucker for sweet talk. I was hoping you and I could give it another go."

The gall of the man was hard to fathom.

"Until you find someone else who's less boring and more adventurous, like the blond who entertained you on your birthday? No, thank you."

"Oh, now, Ashley honey, don't hold that against me. I wasn't thinking straight that night. I'd had a few too many martinis."

Ashley swallowed past her disgust and squared her shoulders. "Go back to Tennessee, Jason. We're done."

"Let's not be hasty." He edged closer. Too close. "Why don't you give me another chance to—"

"The lady said move on."

As Jon issued the measured but firm directive, he circled the bench and stood beside her, juggling a tray containing the two cups of coffee and a white bag.

Jason did a double take as he looked between the two of them. Then the curl returned to his lips, this one the snarky variety. "Who's your friend?"

Ashley gave him her most withering glare. "There's no need for introductions, since you're leaving and I doubt our paths will ever cross again."

A muscle ticced in his cheek, and his jaw hardened. "You used to be more polite than that."

"I don't have to be polite to people who use me." She edged closer to Jon. "Not when there are far worthier people to spend time with."

He gave Jon a derisive once-over. "Are you telling me you'd choose scarface here over me?"

Ashley sucked in a breath, her stomach knotting at Jason's crudeness and abject cruelty.

How could she ever have thought this man was worthy of her affection, let alone her love?

She checked on Jon.

He continued to focus on Jason, his expression impassive. If her former beau's callous and brutal insult had affected him, he was hiding it well.

"Let's have our coffee somewhere less crowded, Jon." She slipped her arm through his.

"Ashley, you can't be serious." Jason's eyes froze over. "Is this the kind of man you're willing to settle for?"

Settle.

The same word her mother had used.

And it didn't sit any better today than it had then.

She tugged her arm free of Jon's, planted her fists on her hips, and got right in Jason's face.

"Let me tell you something, Mr. Smooth Talking Cheater. Jon has more integrity and character and courage and kindness in one finger than you have in your whole body."

Jason gave him another disparaging survey, lingering on his left hand. "He's missing a few of those too."

Anger coursed through her, so violent she began to shake. "You know what, Jason? For the first time in my life, I'm tempted to use language that would shock my father. Except you're not worth violating my standards for."

A crimson stain spread across his cheeks, and he grabbed her arm. "I came thousands of miles to see you. The least you could do—"

"Let her go." Jon's hand shot out to grip Jason's wrist.

"Stay out of this."

"I said, let her go. Now." Jon's voice was quiet but deadly.

"And what if I don't?"

Jon didn't respond, but all at once Jason's complexion paled. Seconds later he released his hold on her, jerked his hand back, and rubbed his reddening wrist.

"You overstepped." He flexed his fingers.

"No. You did." Jon urged her back, putting himself between her and Jason as he set the tray on the bench.

In case there was trouble?

Man, this was not how she'd expected this day to—

"Morning, folks." One of the Hope Harbor police cruisers stopped beside them, Chief Lexie Graham-Stone behind the wheel. "Everything okay here?"

Ashley looked at Jon, who looked at Jason.

When neither responded, she spoke. "We're fine. Just chatting with a former acquaintance of mine, who's leaving now." She lasered Jason a pointed if mute message.

For a moment he stared her down. Then, muttering a curse that scorched her ears but was likely too soft for the chief to hear, he flung his disposable cup into a trash container and stalked down the street.

The chief watched him for a few seconds before transferring her attention back to them. "You sure everything's under control?"

"Yes." Jon continued to keep tabs on Jason. "We've got it covered."

She sized him up, nodded, and took her foot off the brake. "You two enjoy the rest of your day."

As she rolled down the street, Ashley exhaled. "Sorry about that."

"No need to apologize. The blame for that scene is all on him."

"I can't believe he'd be so rude and unkind. Or arrogant enough to think he could stroll back into my life and pick up where we left off, despite what he did. How could I ever have thought he was potential husband material?"

"Guys like him know how to use charm and flattery to their advantage when it suits their purposes."

"And I fell for it hook, line, and sinker." She shook her head in disgust.

"That's because you don't go around expecting people to use or mislead you. I'm sorry he disillusioned you about men."

"No worries. I won't let that experience stop me from appreciating the real deal." She slipped her arm back through his, sending a clear message. "Shall we go back to Plan A and have our cinnamon rolls and coffee?"

He picked up the tray, his brow pinched. "Do you mind if we pass today? A residual effect of my injuries is headaches, and I've got one coming on. My appetite is gone."

For cinnamon rolls—or romance?

The implication was the former. Yet every instinct in Ashley's body said it was the latter. That today's altercation had shifted the landscape of their relationship yet again.

But if his head really was aching, now wouldn't be ideal for a discussion about that.

"I'm sorry about the headache. A rain check is fine."

"I'll walk you back to your car."

He didn't speak much as they retraced their

route, responding to her comments with the briefest of replies. Nor did the grooves on his forehead abate.

At her car, he held out the tray. "You can give one of these to Rose if you don't want both."

"You may be hungry later."

"I don't think so." He plucked his coffee out of the holder. "I can use the caffeine, though. Go ahead, take these home."

"I wish we'd been able to share them on the wharf." She relieved him of the tray.

"Some things aren't meant to be." He took a step back. "Drive safe going home."

As he turned and strode to his truck on the other side of the lot, pressure built in Ashley's throat.

It was possible Jon was just upset by the encounter with Jason and wanted space to regroup. She could use a few minutes to pull herself together too. Given all that had happened, a heavy discussion today could have been a mistake.

But as she slid behind the wheel and the sweet, spicy scent of cinnamon swirled around her, she had a sinking feeling their interrupted coffee date wasn't what he'd been referring to in his last comment.

That instead, when it came to things he suddenly didn't think were meant to be, the two of them were at the top of his list.

25

"So how'd it go with Ashley yesterday?"

As Kyle spoke behind him, Jon closed his eyes and squeezed the measuring wheel he'd pulled from the truck seconds ago.

Why, of all weeks, had his foreman decided to switch from his usual late service at Grace Christian to the early one?

And why had Kyle and Sarah left just as he and Ashley struck off down the sidewalk on Dockside Drive?

At least he'd prepared a speech for this expected query as he stared at the dark ceiling into the wee hours and debated how to respond to the text Ashley had sent yesterday afternoon.

Shifting his features into neutral, he turned. "Morning."

"Back at you." His foreman grinned. "Why didn't you tell me you were going to church yesterday? You could have sat with us."

"I didn't decide until the last minute. And I thought you preferred the late service."

"We usually do, but we were both awake and decided to get up early. I didn't see you as we walked out."

No doubt because he'd stayed in the shadows until Ashley approached up the aisle.

"I was in the last row."

"I'm still surprised we didn't spot you. So where were you and Ashley off to?" He waggled his eyebrows.

"We were thinking about having coffee together but ended up going our separate ways." End of speech.

Kyle's humor evaporated. "What happened?"

"Long story." He motioned toward the stark new deck at their latest jobsite, in need of softening with bushes and plants. "I want to double-check my measurements before we start digging."

As he closed the truck door and began to walk away, Kyle caught his arm. "Hey. Was that go-your-own-way temporary or permanent?"

Of course his number one guy would push for more information.

"Doesn't matter. It's not a good fit."

"For you or for her?"

"Her." Why not be honest? Kyle had already picked up on his boss's interest.

"So you decided you'd do her a favor and back off."

Jon clenched his teeth.

Had he and Rose and Father Murphy all compared notes and decided to launch a unified attack?

"One of us has to make the smart choice."

"You don't think Ashley's capable of that?"

Jon shrugged. "Emotions can muddle people's thinking."

"She strikes me as levelheaded."

"I'd agree with that in general."

"But not in terms of you."

He unfolded the measuring wheel, giving the rote task more attention than it deserved. "Let's just say I'd prefer not to put her in a position where she always has to defend me—or her decision to be with me."

"Ah. This is about *your* preferences."

"No." He frowned at Kyle. "I'm thinking of her."

"You know"—Kyle crossed his arms—"if I tried to decide for Sarah what was in her best interest, she'd have a fit."

"Sweet Sarah? Somehow I can't picture that."

"Don't let her fool you. There's steel under that sweetness. And I mean that as a compliment. She's strong and decisive and doesn't take kindly to anyone trying to control her life."

"Yeah?" Jon didn't try to hide his skepticism.

"Yeah." Kyle hoisted the shovel he'd been leaning on to his shoulder. "Here's a primo example. I was a goner for her after a handful of dates, and I could tell she liked me too. But I didn't think it would be fair to saddle her with an ex-con. Too much baggage. So I stopped calling. When she tracked me down to find out what was going on, I was honest. And I'll never forget what she said."

A few beats passed.

Jon expelled a breath. "You're going to make me ask, aren't you?"

Kyle grinned. "That's what storytellers do. They build suspense."

"Fine. I'll ask. Lay it on me."

His foreman sobered. "She said, 'I know what I want. I also know the price, and I'm willing to pay it. Because you're worth every penny.'" Kyle's voice scratched, and he dipped his chin. Cleared his throat. "I'm not certain that last part is true, but I do know love can work miracles. And in our experience, it's also smoothed out the rough spots we've hit."

The same takeaway in Father Murphy's tale.

"I heard a similar story not long ago. But I'm nowhere near love."

"You know what they say—a journey of a thousand miles begins with a single step. If you ask me, you're already way past the starting point."

"No comment. But thanks for giving me a few things to think about."

"Hey, what are landscaping foremen for, if not to plant a few seeds?" Kyle blinked away the shimmer in his eyes as his sunny demeanor returned. "You want me to get the guys rolling?" He motioned to the two crew members who were parking across the street.

"Yeah. Thanks. I have a couple of messages to respond to."

One in particular.

As Kyle greeted the two men and waved them toward the bushes loaded in the back of the truck, Jon moved off to the side and opened Ashley's text message from late yesterday afternoon.

> Hope your headache is gone. I haven't eaten the cinnamon rolls yet. If you're hungry later, stop by.

He should have responded, but after the encounter with her ex, *bummed* hadn't come close to describing his mood.

Especially since he'd had such high hopes that yesterday might be the beginning of a new, less lonesome chapter in his life.

But letting one unpleasant confrontation rattle him could be a mistake. It would be foolish to close and lock a door until he worked through the implications of what had happened.

Besides, if nothing else, he owed Ashley the honest discussion he'd hinted at during their truncated semidate yesterday.

He positioned his thumbs over the keypad and began to type.

> Sorry for the late response. Was wiped out all day yesterday. Enjoy the cinnamon rolls, but let's think about

scheduling a trip to The Perfect Blend later in the week.

His finger hovered over the send button for several seconds. Then he pressed it before he could chicken out.

It wasn't as if his message was that risky, after all. It hadn't contained any promises. It merely kept the door open.

But would he walk through?

Up for debate.

Because despite all the stories he'd heard and the guidance he'd received, the truth was that while most people wouldn't be as blunt and rude and offensive as Jason, in an Instagram-perfect world there would always be a stigma in certain circles on those who associated with people who were less than perfect. It wasn't right, but it was reality.

And while Ashley had held her ground yesterday with Jason, would the constant need to justify her choice, if she did choose him, wear her down until love was no longer enough to smooth out any of the rough patches that would surely lie ahead?

She was not going to get sick.

Not with a million items on her to-do list before the first event debuted at Edgecliff in less than a month.

And not with an afternoon coffee date tomorrow in town with Jon that would be the highlight of her Friday.

However, her uncooperative body wasn't in sync with her resolve.

Trying without success to find a more comfortable position in bed, Ashley groaned and peered at her watch.

Only eight fifteen in the evening, with the whole long, dark, and likely sleepless night ahead to get through.

Would it help to try to eat a light meal? The few bites of dinner she'd choked down last night were long gone.

But the mere idea of food sent a wave of nausea through her.

She pushed her hair back from her damp face as another pain shot through her midsection.

Mercy.

Whatever bug she'd caught was a doozy.

Too bad the urgent care center in town was closed. And too bad she'd waited this long to decide a trip there would be prudent.

If she could hang on until it reopened tomorrow, though, she'd be first in line to—

"Ashley?" The muffled query came as a rap sounded on the door at the base of the stairs. "Are you up there?"

Rose.

Gritting her teeth, she pushed herself into a

sitting position and swung her legs over the side of the bed. Hand pressed to her stomach, she rose and stumbled toward the bedroom door.

"Ashley?" A hint of panic elevated Rose's pitch.

"I'm coming."

She inched through the living room, half bent over, hanging on to every piece of furniture she passed. Paused at the top of the stairs she ran up and down a dozen times each day with nary a thought.

Now the prospect of navigating them felt as overwhelming as a hike down the cliffs surrounding Edgecliff.

She wrapped her fingers around the post at the top. "Rose, I'm, uh, not feeling too well. What can I do for you?"

"I came over to check on you. You looked peaked earlier. I have my spare key with me. May I come up?"

"I don't want to give you any germs."

"I've lived eighty years. I've got hardy genes. Do I have permission to enter?"

Why use up her waning energy arguing?

"Yes." Ashley shuffled over to the couch and sank down.

A few seconds later, the key rattled in the lock, the knob turned, and Rose charged up the stairs with remarkable speed and agility.

She stopped at the top to inspect her partner.

"Oh my. You look worse than you did at our meeting after BJ's crew left today—and that's saying a lot."

Ashley's stomach began to churn, and she wrapped her arms around her middle. "Lucky I have a healthy ego." She tried to inject a touch of humor in her tone but couldn't quite pull it off.

"How long have you been sick?"

"I woke up feeling rocky yesterday." Bile rose in her throat.

Oh, crud.

She was going to upchuck.

Clapping a hand over her mouth, she pushed herself to her feet, stumbled to the bathroom, and barely made it in time to empty the contents of her stomach into the toilet—what little contents there were.

When she stopped heaving, Rose spoke from the other side of the door. "Have you called a doctor?"

"I don't have one here yet." She wiped her mouth on a towel, but the acrid taste lingered on her tongue.

"Do you have a fever?"

"I don't know. I don't have a thermometer either. I never get sick."

"You're sick now. Are you planning to stay in there?"

"No." What could be left to throw up?

Still doubled over, she twisted the knob on the door and tottered out on shaky legs.

Rose took her arm and led her back to the couch. Helped her sit. Laid a hand on her forehead.

"You're warm. Not burning up, but hotter than you should be. How often have you thrown up?"

"Once. You witnessed the inaugural event."

"What hurts?"

"My stomach. I'll go to urgent care tomorrow if I haven't improved."

Rose's forehead crinkled. "Waiting may not be wise. I think you should go to an ER."

Another pain pierced her stomach, and she gasped.

Maybe Rose was right.

But how was she supposed to get there? Driving was out of the question.

"Why don't I call Jon? He could take you up to Coos Bay." Rose sat beside her.

"I hate to bother him with this."

Rose touched her arm. "I don't think he'll consider it a bother. Not in an emergency. He's our neighbor and friend."

And perhaps more, if all went well.

"Okay. My phone's in the bedroom, on the nightstand. If you'll get it, I'll call him."

Rose was off in a flash, and in less than half a minute, she returned to hand off the cell.

Trying to quell the renewed roiling in her

stomach, Ashley scrolled through her contacts and placed the call.

Five rings in, it rolled to voicemail.

"He's not answering." She hung up.

"Why didn't you leave a message?"

"What's the point in worrying him if he's not in a position to help?"

Her stomach revolted again, and she wrenched herself to her feet as Rose pulled out her own phone. "What are you doing?"

"Making an executive decision."

Ashley had no idea what that meant.

But as she staggered back to the bathroom as fast as her wobbly legs allowed, two concerns were top of mind.

Reaching the toilet before the Vesuvius in her stomach erupted again.

And figuring out how she was going to survive for twelve long hours until the urgent care center in town opened again.

26

A date with Ashley tomorrow.

Could there be a better end to his week?

Mouth curving up, Jon leaned out of the shower and grabbed a towel off the rack. After giving his hair a vigorous rub, he stepped out, finished drying off, and twisted his wrist to see his watch.

Only eight forty-five. Too early for bed, too dark for a walk down to the water with Daisy.

Why not dive into the suspense novel that had been languishing on his nightstand since Laura sent it to him for his birthday two months ago? A high-stakes story might help take his mind off tomorrow's real-life high-stakes encounter.

Yet while much depended on what Ashley had to say, it was hard to snuff out the flicker of hope that multiple people and incidents had sparked to life in his heart.

Maybe they were right, and all his fears were—

Jon cocked his ear.

Was that a siren? On Windswept Way?

Could be—though that would be a first during his two-year tenure. Never had an emergency vehicle disrupted the placid stillness of the off-the-beaten-path byway he called home.

The wail increased in volume.

No question about it. One of his few, secluded neighbors must require assistance.

He moved into the bedroom and pulled on his jeans. Tugged a sweatshirt over his head.

Froze when two emergency vehicles raced past, their flashing lights ricocheting off his blinds as Daisy barreled in and sidled up to him with a whimper.

Heart stumbling, he shoved his bare feet into his shoes, snatched up his keys, and raced toward the door.

There was only one occupied property between his house and the cliffs. Meaning someone at Edgecliff was in trouble.

Most likely Rose, given her age.

Or else there was a fire.

Neither scenario was good.

And whatever was going on there, the two residents shouldn't have to handle it alone when they had a friend and neighbor nearby.

Once in his truck, he floored it down the dark, narrow road, tearing into the Edgecliff entrance a minute later.

A Hope Harbor police car was parked in front of the main house.

Jon took the drive too fast, spewing rocks in his wake, and slammed on the brakes in a spurt of gravel.

At least there was no visible smoke coming from the house.

But where was the other vehicle that had gone by?

He vaulted out of the truck and raced over to the uniformed man, who held up a finger while he finished his phone conversation.

The instant the officer tucked away his cell, Jon introduced himself. "I live at the next property down the road and heard the sirens. I know the owners and came down to see if I could help."

"Officer Jim Gleason. Happy to make your acquaintance." The man held out his hand. "I think everything is under control. The paramedics are taking care of the emergency."

Jon returned his firm clasp. "Is Rose okay?"

"Why don't we walk back and find out? I parked here to keep the drive clear for the ambulance."

Jon fell in beside him as they circled behind the grand Victorian, but his step faltered when he spotted the ambulance.

It was parked by the carriage house.

The air whooshed out of his lungs.

Before he could reinflate them, Rose exited—confirming the conclusion he'd already reached.

She wasn't the one who needed medical assistance.

Jon sprinted toward her, leaving the officer behind.

The instant she caught sight of him, she hurried over, hand extended. "Oh, Jon. I'm glad you're here."

He cocooned her cold fingers between his. "What happened?"

"Ashley's sick. She tried to call you before I panicked and dialed 911, but no one answered."

"I must have been in the shower. What's wrong with her?"

"I haven't a clue." She gave him a quick recap of her partner's symptoms. "She thinks it's a bug or virus, but I didn't like the stomach pain. She couldn't even straighten up. The paramedics are up there with her. I was in the way, so I came down."

"Let me see what I can find out."

As he started toward the stairs, his arm was taken in a firm grip.

"Why don't you let me get the lowdown?" The officer's directive was friendly but firm. "It could be tight quarters up there, and the paramedics need room to work."

Without giving him an opportunity to argue, the man strode toward the stairs and disappeared.

Jon scowled after him. "If he's not back in three minutes, I'm going up."

"I won't try to stop you." Rose's inflection was resolute. "In fact, I may go with you. They'll have to kick us both out."

Angling his wrist, Jon focused on his watch as he waited the longest three minutes of his life and tried not to freak out.

It was a losing battle.

"Jon." Rose touched his arm. "I believe someone is coming down."

Seconds later, the officer rejoined them.

"They're getting ready to transport. Is there
anyone we should notify? Someone who could
meet her at the hospital in Coos Bay?"

"Her mother lives in San Francisco. I have
her phone number as an emergency contact, and
I'll be happy to give that to you. I don't believe
Ashley has any other close relatives." Rose
turned to him. "Are you aware of anyone else,
Jon?"

"No. But she has me." He directed his next
comment to the officer. "We're friends."

"I'm sure she'll be happy to see a familiar face
at the hospital, but they'll have to get in touch
with someone who can speak on her behalf if
she's not able to communicate. I'll take that
number, Ms. Fitzgerald."

She pulled out her cell and scrolled through her
contacts. Recited the number as the paramedics
maneuvered the gurney through the door.

Jon broke away from the duo, hurried over
to the emergency crew as they approached the
ambulance—and almost lost his dinner at his first
glimpse of Ashley's pallor and the lines of pain
contorting her features.

"Jon?" Her glazed eyes fixed on him, prodding
him to take her hand.

"Yes. I'm here."

"Th-thank you for coming."

At the hitch in her voice, pressure built in his throat. "You don't have to thank me. This is where I want to be. I'll follow you to the hospital. You'll be fine."

"We need to move." One of the paramedics shouldered him aside.

After giving her fingers a squeeze, he released them.

Once the paramedics loaded her into the ambulance, he plucked the driver's sleeve as the man headed around the side of the vehicle. "What do you think is going on?"

"You family?"

"No."

"You'll have to talk to her or an authorized relative. Sorry. HIPPA rules tie our hands."

Jon knew all about government red tape after living it every day in the military, and he didn't like it any better now than he had then.

"Fine. I'll do that. Where are you taking her?"

The guy rattled off the information, then continued to the front of the vehicle while Jon rejoined Rose and the cop. "Rose, I'm going to follow them to the hospital."

She lifted a hand and touched his cheek. "I knew you would. I'd go with you, but it could be a long night—and while the spirit is willing, the flesh is weak. Will you call me, though, as soon as you have any news? No matter the hour?"

"Yes. Try not to worry."

"I'd say the same to you, but I don't think either of us will rest easy until we know what's going on." She reached for his hand, gave it a squeeze, and transferred her attention to the officer. "I wonder if I might impose on you to walk me back to my cottage. It's quite dark, and I wouldn't want to fall and have to call 911 twice in one night."

"I'll be happy to, ma'am."

They all moved off the road as the ambulance drove down a few yards and executed a wide U-turn that took the vehicle off the gravel and onto the grass.

As soon as it rolled past them, Rose and the officer struck out for her cottage while Jon took off at a jog for his truck.

And for the first time in years, other than the conversation he'd had with God at church last Sunday, he prayed.

For Ashley.

For himself.

And for a chance at a future that was tantalizingly close, but which could wither and die as quickly as tender spring blossoms succumbed to an unexpected frost if Ashley took a turn for the worse.

If they'd taken her appendix out, why did her shoulder hurt? Why was she still sick to her stomach? And why did it feel like she was on a boat?

Ashley pried open her eyelids, watching from flat on her back as the ceiling above her moved.

No.

The ceiling wasn't moving.

She was moving.

Or her bed was.

All at once, the gurney hung a left, and she fisted the sheet in her fingers, trying to keep the world from tilting.

"Hello, Ashley." A face loomed into her field of vision. "I'm Caroline. I'll be your nurse here on the surgical floor for the next few hours. We're going to get you settled in bed and then we'll talk more. Okay?"

" 'Kay."

That was the easiest answer, even if she wouldn't be doing much talking until the cotton cleared out of her head. But she did want answers. Whatever the surgeon had told her in recovery had disappeared into an anesthesia-induced fog.

The nurse and an aide took care of the transfer to the bed with practiced efficiency, but that didn't keep the maneuver from hurting. Hard as she tried to stifle it, a moan slipped out.

"Sorry about that, sweetie. You'll be sore for a

few days, but there are meds to help with that." The nurse went about hooking up equipment and checking monitors.

"My shoulder . . . hurts too." She had to focus on forming every word.

"Residual gas from the CO_2 used to inflate your abdomen. It will dissipate in a day or two. You were fortunate. The appendix didn't rupture, and the laparoscopic procedure will expedite recovery. The doctor said he'd be in to see you after he's finished with his current patient, since there was no family to talk with immediately after the surgery."

Family.

Had someone called Mom?

"Did anyone . . . contact my . . . mother?"

"I'll find out. I do know you were able to sign all the necessary papers yourself, though, so they may not have."

"Is my . . . phone . . . here?"

"No, but you can use mine."

At the familiar masculine baritone, Ashley turned her head toward the doorway.

Jon stood on the threshold, holding a disposable cup.

So she hadn't imagined his promise to follow her here as they'd prepared to load her into the ambulance.

Warmth radiated through her.

He crossed to her in a few long strides, circling

around the nurse to the other side of her bed while the woman gave him a perusal.

If she was shocked by his appearance, she didn't let on, but the scars, bloodshot eyes, and hair sticking up in all directions—as if he'd toweled it dry and never bothered to comb it—would likely startle the average person.

"Why don't I give you two a few minutes alone while we wait for the doctor to stop by?" The nurse adjusted the IV line and made a quick exit.

"How are you?" Jon wrapped both hands around his coffee cup as he assessed her, the purple smudges under his lower lashes testifying to his stress and fatigue.

"Grateful I survived." She forced herself to concentrate, willing her sluggish brain to kick into gear. "If I'd known it was appendicitis, I'd have gotten help sooner."

"You're lucky it didn't rupture." He tipped his head toward the door. "I overheard the nurse give you a quick recap. No one would tell me anything."

"I'm sorry." She held out her hand, and after a nanosecond hesitation he engulfed her fingers in his solid, comforting grip. "I'd have given them permission to talk to you if I'd been thinking straight."

"No worries. I'm just glad there were no complications. If you can manage it, you may want to call Rose. I promised her an update, but all I was able to tell her was that you were in recovery. Hearing your voice would reassure her."

"I should call Mom too." The last wisps of fog evaporated from her brain.

He set his coffee down and pulled out his phone. "Who first?"

"What time is it?"

"A little afer five."

"Oh, Jon. You've been up all night."

He gave her a weary smile. "No sweat. I got used to all-nighters in the military. Besides, it's hard to sleep when someone you care about is in trouble." Without waiting for her to process that comment, he held up his phone. "Your mom or Rose?"

"Rose. If no one's called Mom, she's still in bed, and she doesn't appreciate having her beauty sleep interrupted unless it's an emergency."

"This qualifies."

"No. Last night was an emergency. Today is a postcrisis debrief. Would you dial for me?"

He scrolled to Rose's number, placed the call, and held out the phone. "You want me to wait outside while you talk to her?"

"No." She ought to tell him to go home. He had to be dead on his feet. And she would. Soon. But not quite yet. "Why don't you sit and have your coffee?"

The speed with which he caved confirmed his exhaustion.

"I'll wait over there." He motioned toward a chair in the corner, picked up his java, and left her alone to talk to Rose.

Her partner answered on the first ring. "Jon? I've been waiting and waiting for your call. I haven't done more than doze all night. I should have gone up there with you and—"

"Rose, it's Ashley. I'm using Jon's phone."

"Oh, my dear!" She exhaled. "I've been worried sick. Tell me how you are."

She filled her in on the diagnosis and what little else she knew at this stage. "I don't expect they'll keep me long, since it wasn't open surgery."

"Wonderful news! When you come home, I want you to spend the first couple of nights in my cottage where I can keep close tabs on you."

Pressure built behind Ashley's eyes. "You don't have to do that, Rose. I don't want to invade your space. I know you value your privacy."

"You're not invading if you're invited, and friends are always welcome. I should have asked you in weeks ago. Please say you'll stay."

"I'll tell you what. I haven't talked to my mom yet. Let me see how that goes. If she insists on coming up, I'll be covered."

"Fair enough. Can you give me your room number so I can call you directly?"

Ashley lowered the phone. "Jon, do you know what my room number is?"

He recited it, and she passed it on.

"So Jon's still there?" Rose sounded pleased.

"Yes." She peeked over as he tipped his head back against the wall and let his eyelids drop closed, the harsh hospital lights highlighting every worry line in his face.

"Good man."

"I agree."

"I'm happy to hear that. You should have seen him last night. He was beside himself. A basket case."

Jon, a basket case?

Telling—and endearing.

"Thankfully the crisis is over."

"Amen to that. You may want to send him home to get some sleep now that you're out of danger."

"That's my plan."

"I'll call you later for an update if I don't hear from you."

"Thanks, Rose." As she ended the connection, she glanced over at Jon. "She seems relieved."

"That makes two of us. You certain you don't want to call your mom?"

She heaved a sigh. "I suppose I should. She gets up at six thirty anyway. An hour of lost sleep shouldn't be that big of a deal."

After tapping in her mother's number, Ashley settled back on the pillows.

Six rings in, a groggy voice answered. No surprise. Mom was never fully awake until she downed two cups of coffee.

Ashley gave her the news in a handful of sentences.

Her abbreviated report was met with silence.

"Mom? Are you there?"

"Yes. Did you say appendicitis?"

That was all she'd picked up?

"Yes, but I'm fine. I'll be out of the hospital in a day or two."

"Hospital?"

Ashley counted to three and repeated what she'd already said.

"Give me a minute while I sit up and let that sink in." A sound of shuffling came over the line. "Is the number you called from your hospital room?"

"Um . . . no." She lowered her volume. "Jon's here. I borrowed his cell."

Several seconds ticked by.

"Jon, the landscaper?"

"Yes."

"So he's more than a vendor after all."

"I hope so."

"Ashley . . ." The warning note from their prior conversation on this subject was back. "Don't rush into anything."

"Never."

"We'll talk more in person. I'm supposed to leave Sunday for London, but let me see if I can reschedule that trip and come up there."

"You don't have to do that, Mom. Rose invited

me to stay with her after I'm released. We've got it covered."

"I don't know . . . I think I should come up."

But her hesitancy suggested she was willing to be convinced otherwise. Heaven forbid personal obligations would disrupt her professional calendar.

"I'll be fine, Mom. We'll stay in touch by phone. You can come up for a visit if you have an opening in your schedule after the London trip."

"Well, if you're sure you'll be all right . . ."

"I'm sure. I'm in good hands." She locked on to Jon's gaze as she passed on that assurance, sending what she hoped was a clear message.

Because while their up-close-and-personal tête-à-tête at the coffee shop later today wasn't going to happen, she'd been around this wounded warrior enough to know he was stealing her heart—and that the sterling qualities of *his* heart added to his appeal far more than fleeting physical attributes ever would. For while bodies aged, the beauty of a kind and caring heart never dimmed.

Jon's eyes warmed, and when she held out the phone after signing off from her mom, he rose and rejoined her.

Their fingers brushed as he took it, and once he put it in his pocket, she twined her fingers with his again.

"Thank you for being there last night and for

staying with me through this whole ordeal."

"You're welcome. And I'll come back as soon as I take care of Daisy and clock a couple hours of shut-eye. Kyle can cover for me at the jobsite today."

He was leaving?

Of course he's leaving, Ashley. The man is beat, and he has other obligations. Suck it up and let him go.

Quashing her selfish impulses, she called up a smile. "You should sleep more than a couple of hours. And I don't want to take you away from work. How's this for a compromise? Text or call later today, and give me a ride home when I'm released. Hopefully tomorrow."

"But don't you want anything from your apartment? I could ask Rose to put a bag together for you."

"I'm fine for a short stay. The shorter the better. Go home. Sleep. Work. Call."

One corner of his mouth twitched. "You drive a hard bargain."

"Not to hear my mom talk. She thinks I'm a pushover. And maybe I am—for a sweet deal." She squeezed his fingers.

Jon's eyes darkened, but before he could respond, a man wearing scrubs entered the room and approached the bed.

Drat.

Could his timing have been any worse?

"Good morning, Ashley. We talked earlier, but I won't hold it against you if you don't remember."

"I have a vague memory of our discussion. Very vague."

"Not surprising, given your condition. I wanted to bring you up to speed on treatment and prognosis. May I speak in front of an audience?" He nodded toward Jon.

"I was about to leave, so—"

Ashley tightened her grip on his fingers. "If you can spare five more minutes, I'd be grateful. My brain isn't firing on all cylinders yet, and I'd like someone I trust to hear this. All part of that sweet deal I mentioned."

His Adam's apple bobbed. "I'll stay."

The doctor briefed them, but Ashley only half listened. It was hard to engage her brain with her hand in Jon's firm, reassuring clasp. But the surgeon left with a promise to see her again prior to her discharge—tomorrow, if all went well—and answer any questions that came to her in the interim.

"Daisy awaits. And not very patiently, I expect." Despite his words, Jon didn't let go of her hand. Indicating he was as reluctant to leave as she was to let him go.

But Daisy's needs were more urgent than hers at this point.

"You should go home."

"I know." He forked his fingers through his

hair, his frustration evident. "That talk we keep trying to have doesn't seem fated to happen."

"It will happen, but this isn't the time or the place. You can give me another rain check."

"Done. Why don't you pencil me in for a week from tomorrow? Block out the whole afternoon."

"I'll write it in ink. But does that mean I won't be seeing you between now and then?" She tried for a teasing tone, but a hint of disappointment slipped through.

"Consider me on call for chauffeur duty, starting tomorrow when you're released. And I'll drop by in the evenings. But let's hold the discussion until you're on the mend. In the meantime, just so we're clear on the subject matter to be discussed, I'll leave you with this to ponder."

Keeping her hand enfolded in his, he slowly leaned down and claimed her lips in a kiss that was gentle and caring and careful, but also filled with the promise of passion to come.

Long before she was ready for it to end, he backed off, touched her cheek, and disappeared out the door.

Leaving yearning and hope and a delicious tingle of anticipation in his wake.

Next Saturday couldn't come fast enough.

And hopefully nothing else would intervene to postpone yet again a discussion that could open the page on a new and exciting chapter in both their lives.

27

He shouldn't have kissed her yesterday.

Fingers clenched around the steering wheel, Jon pulled into the hospital and drove toward the main entrance in Kyle's borrowed car.

It would have been wiser to wait until they had their talk before introducing any physical affection, but after the harrowing events of Thursday night, how could he have left the hospital without giving her a concrete indication of his feelings?

The kiss had more than done the trick, and as far as he could tell she'd been all in.

That made two of them. The adrenaline surge on his end when their lips melded hadn't subsided for hours.

Problem was, now too many emotions—and hormones—would muddle their thinking. And they both needed clear heads while they discussed their relationship.

So until they had that conversation, he had to stay hands off.

Even if that would require him to call up every ounce of his willpower and self-discipline.

Jon pulled up at the hospital entrance, put on his flashers, and slid from behind the wheel. His call to alert Ashley he was ten minutes away should mean an aide would escort her out soon.

Less than sixty seconds later, a scrubs-clad young woman pushed a wheelchair through the door, the passenger hidden behind a huge flower arrangement.

The florist had obviously followed to a T his instruction to go all out.

Jon circled the car and waited for them.

As the wind picked up, Ashley peeked around the garden in her lap. "New car?"

"Kyle's. I assumed climbing in and out of my truck would be less than comfortable for you at this stage."

"I like a man who thinks ahead and plans for all contingencies." The warmth radiating from her smile soaked straight to his core.

Hands off just got twice as hard.

"Ready to go home?" His voice rasped.

"More than."

While he stowed her flowers and a plastic bag with the hospital logo on the back seat, the aide got her settled in the car. She was already buckled in when he retook his place behind the wheel.

As he twisted the key in the ignition, he gave her a swift perusal. With each call yesterday, she'd sounded stronger and perkier and more like herself, but the old adage was true. A picture was worth a thousand words. Color had returned to her cheeks, the sparkle was back in her eyes, and energy emanated from her.

The last vestiges of tension in his taut muscles released.

Thank you, God.

The expression of gratitude came unplanned and unbidden, but it was straight from the heart.

He put the car in gear, pulled away from the curb, and flipped on his wipers as rain began to pepper the windshield. "I talked to Rose this morning and gave her our ETA. She's chomping at the bit to have you back."

"And I'm anxious to be back." She scanned the sky. "Those are seriously black clouds."

"The wind shifted an hour ago. A major front is rolling in." He frowned at the churning heavens. "Bad timing."

"Why?"

"We've got a big job half installed, with piles of dirt sitting around and holes dug. On top of that, we put mulch down at another site yesterday. A torrential downpour won't do us any favors."

"Is there any damage control you can do in advance of the storm?"

"We're on it. I have a crew at both locations as we speak."

"You should be there too, shouldn't you?"

At the dismay in her tone, he glanced over. "I will be. But I had other priorities this morning."

"I could have taken an Uber or Lyft home."

"No, you couldn't. They're not available out here."

"A cab, then."

"An unnecessary expense when you have a chauffeur willing to work gratis." He shot her a grin. No sense both of them worrying about the potential havoc the incoming storm could wreak on the in-progress jobs.

"I'll owe you after this."

"Next Saturday will be repayment enough."

Her face lit up. "I've been thinking about that. Where are we going?"

"You'll have to wait and see."

She huffed out a breath. "You know patience isn't my strong—" A powerful gust rocked the car, and she grabbed the dash. "Wow. This is nasty."

Yeah, it was. He tightened his grip on the wheel as the wind buffeted the Nissan and rain began to pound against the windshield, slowing to a crawl once he swung onto 101.

For the next twenty-five-plus miles, driving required his total concentration as he battled to keep the car on the road. Standing water on the pavement also made the trip dicey. Hydroplaning into a tree or a ditch wasn't on his morning agenda.

Ashley fell silent too as the tumult engulfed them, her fingers laced tight in her lap.

By the time he turned onto Windswept Way, the knots of tension in his shoulders had not only returned but grown to epic proportions. While the drive had been taxing, who knew what carnage had been wrought at the jobsites?

Mother Nature's rampage didn't bode well for a relaxing weekend. Nor one where he'd likely see much of his passenger.

Not until he pulled through the Edgecliff gates did Ashley speak. "What a homecoming."

"You'll be safe and sound soon."

"I'm already safe and sound. I have been since you followed the sirens here Thursday night."

At her quiet, heartfelt comment, he looked over.

The tenderness in her eyes about did him in.

Lucky the wheel required both of his hands or he'd already be tempted to break his hands-off rule.

"Let's not get ahead of ourselves. We still need to have that talk."

"Words are fine, but the language of the heart is more powerful."

Despite his plan to play it cool and cautious until all the hurdles to a relationship were cleared, it appeared Ashley had other ideas. If her attitude today was any indication, she was already way past the starting point of their journey—as Kyle had claimed his boss was.

While that was encouraging, they nevertheless had hard facts to face. And until they did, he couldn't let himself get carried away.

At least not any more than he already was.

"Hold that thought." He circled around the back of the main house and crept down the gravel lane toward Rose's cottage, where light spilled from the windows. As they approached, Rose opened the door. "She must have been watching for us."

"Like during my first visit." Ashley lifted a hand in greeting to the woman, but it was doubtful she could see the gesture through the downpour. "Except that day she barely cracked the door. And she stayed in the shadows. We exchanged several comments before my charm convinced her to open it enough to let me in."

Ashley's tone was teasing, but he remained serious. "You do have a remarkable ability to convince people to open doors." Without giving her an opportunity to respond, he motioned toward Rose. "Your welcoming committee awaits."

The older woman had moved onto the small porch, an umbrella in hand.

"She's going to get wet if she comes out in this."

"Crack your window and tell her I have an umbrella. I'll walk you in."

Ashley did as he asked once they drew alongside the porch, and Rose acknowledged Jon's offer with a wave. Yet while she retreated closer to the house, she remained on the porch instead of seeking shelter inside.

"Let's do this fast so neither of you gets too

damp. Sit tight. I'll take the flowers and the rest of your stuff in first."

He braked, reached into the backseat, and pulled out the large golf umbrella a previous tenant had left at his house. Using an elbow to hold it in place against his side, he managed to transport the plastic bag and flowers to Rose's porch without doing too much damage to the posies.

"My. Those are beautiful." Rose gave the arrangement an admiring scan as she pushed the door open for him. "You can set them on the kitchen counter if you like. Let me take your umbrella."

He handed it over, wove through the cozy cottage, and deposited everything in the kitchen before rejoining her. "Now for the patient."

"How is she?" Rose peered through the curtain of water as she gave him back the umbrella.

"She looks great, but I'm glad you'll be watching over her for a few days."

"I am too. She's become very precious to me."

"You're not alone."

"That's what I thought." She gave him an approving nod. "Let's get her inside, out of the storm."

He opened the umbrella, returned to the car, and positioned it over Ashley's door. She took full advantage of the elbow he lent her as she got out of the car.

"Thanks for the assist." Her voice was strained

and a mite breathless. "I guess I'm more sore than I expected."

"That doesn't surprise me. Stay close while we walk to the door."

She didn't need any encouragement. And as she tucked herself beside him, it was the most natural thing in the world to drape a protective arm around her shoulders while they negotiated the much-too-short path.

So natural he had to force himself to release her and step back once they reached the shelter of the porch.

"Would you like to come in, Jon?" Rose spoke around Ashley as she gave her temporary houseguest a hug. "I have tea and scones waiting, but I'll make you coffee if you prefer."

"I wish I could, but I have to check on a couple of jobsites." He transferred his attention to Ashley. "I'll call you later."

"I'd like that. Thank you for everything."

"My pleasure."

Fighting back the temptation to accept the invitation in her eyes for a goodbye kiss, he pivoted and returned to Kyle's car. With a final wave, he executed a U-turn and rolled back toward the Edgecliff exit.

Rose and Ashley faded from view in the heavy rain within seconds, but long after he lost sight of them, Ashley's image remained vivid in his memory.

She wasn't a woman any man with a lick of sense would easily forget or let get away. Which said volumes about Jason. None of it good.

Yet a big question remained.

Would the sparks arcing between them survive their pending, pivotal discussion . . . and the big reveal he was planning during their Saturday date?

"Let's go in before this mist soaks through our clothes. We don't want to add pneumonia to appendicitis."

As Rose took her arm, Ashley sent one more glance after Jon's disappearing taillights and allowed herself to be led inside. "Thank you again for offering to let me invade your privacy, Rose. I'm sure I'd be fine in the carriage house, but I do think I'll sleep better with someone close by for the first night or two."

"Of course you will. We're all more relaxed when people we care about are near. I know I've slept better since you moved onto the property." She closed the door behind them.

"To tell you the truth, beautiful as Edgecliff is, I don't know how you managed to live out here by yourself after your father died. Weren't you lonesome?"

"A bit. But Charley stopped by on a regular basis, and a few other people in town visited on occasion. I also have acquaintances and friends in other places who keep in touch." The corners of her mouth rose a hair, and a twinkle glimmered in her irises. "And Lucy Lynn has kept me entertained for many years."

Ashley looked past Rose, to the illustrated poster on the wall behind her. It featured a winsome little girl wearing a backpack, her hair blowing in the breeze as she marched past a sign with two arrows. One was labeled "yesterday." The other, pointing the direction the girl was going, said "tomorrow." Underneath were three words.

Never look back.

It was a Lucy Lynn poster, featuring the iconic little girl who graced greeting cards, stationery, tote bags, T-shirts, and a host of other merchandise.

"I'm a Lucy Lynn fan too. I've never seen that illustration, though."

"It's new. And I'm more than a fan. That's the original artwork." She motioned toward the poster.

"Are you a collector?" A hobby like that could explain Rose's comment about the girl keeping her entertained.

"Not quite. Let me show you to your room." She led the way toward the back of the house. "As soon as there's a break in the rain, I'll get whatever you need for tonight from the carriage house."

Puzzling over Rose's reply, Ashley followed along behind her. "If you're not a collector, did someone give you the poster?"

Instead of answering, Rose opened the last door down the short hall, entered, and motioned her in.

One step over the threshold, Ashley froze.

There was an opened sofa sleeper against one wall, but this wasn't a bedroom.

It was an artist's studio.

As she gaped at the drafting table positioned in the corner, where illumination from a large lamp on a swivel arm was supplemented with natural light from two windows . . . surveyed the dozens of colored pencils and markers neatly arranged in upright slots on one side of the table . . . scanned the countless Lucy Lynn images that graced the walls . . . the truth began to sink in.

She turned to stare at the older woman. "You're Lucy Lynn."

"No. But I created her."

"Wow." She gave the room another sweep, trying to digest that piece of news. "You're famous."

"No again. Lucy Lynn is famous. I'm anonymous—by choice." She straightened the edge of the comforter covering the sofa sleeper. "I hope you won't mind sharing her room for a few nights. Shall we have our tea?" Rose turned.

"Wait." Ashley touched her arm, mind spinning.

"You can't drop a bombshell like that and not let me ask a few questions."

"You may ask all the questions you like over tea. If you want to freshen up, I put clean towels on the vanity for you. The bathroom is across the hall. Why don't you meet me in the kitchen when you're ready?"

With that, she retraced her steps.

Ashley did make a quick stop in the bathroom, but in less than five minutes she entered the small, cheery kitchen to find Rose setting a teapot on the table, along with a plate of scones.

"That was fast." Rose tapped the back of a chair at the table for two. "Have a seat. I went online to see what your post-op menu should be. Scones aren't on there, but I didn't think a few bites of comfort food could hurt. I'll stick to the recommended menu after this."

"Scones and tea sound wonderful to me." Ashley eased into the chair, trying not to cringe.

Rose poured their tea, sat, and took a scone. "I can almost hear the questions tumbling through your brain. Ask away."

"Does anyone know about your connection to Lucy Lynn? Other than the company that produces the products, I mean."

"David and Charley. Both are the soul of discretion."

"Your attorney I can understand. But why does Charley know?"

419

"Lucy Lynn wouldn't exist if it wasn't for him." Rose took a sip of her tea. "I've always had a knack for drawing, and after my career as a pianist faded, I began to doodle. About twenty years ago, Lucy Lynn appeared one day out of the blue. A true godsend—literally, I believe. She became my faithful companion and a much-needed positive force in my world. A ray of hope and brightness when days were hard."

"How does Charley fit in?"

"About a year after I moved back here, I sent him a hand-drawn card to thank him for his occasional taco deliveries and friendship. He thought it was quite charming and offered to contact a professional acquaintance who had connections in the greeting card world. The rest, as they say, is history."

"But Lucy Lynn is so much more than greeting cards." In truth, with all the merchandise out there, she was an industry unto herself.

"Yes. And that never ceases to astound me." Rose's lips curved up again. "I had no idea people would come to love her as much as I do. At the beginning, I thought a small line of greeting cards from my large backlog of ideas and sketches would keep me occupied and allow me to be part of the world but not in the world. No one was more surprised than I when the line grew from greeting cards to other products. Fortunately, David handles the business details for me. Now drink your tea or it will get cold."

Ashley dutifully picked up her cup and took a sip. "I assume all those UPS trucks that come through here are business related."

"A fair number are. I send off drawings, they send back proofs and merchandise samples and prototypes."

"Wow again." All these years, the woman everyone considered a recluse had been leading a secret life. Part of, if not in, the world, as she'd said.

It boggled the mind.

"I believe I've surprised you." The twinkle was back in Rose's eyes.

"That would be a gross understatement. I'm flabbergasted."

"You're also only the second person in Hope Harbor to learn my secret."

"I promise it's safe with me." She exhaled. "I can't tell you how impressed I am."

Rose waved that aside. "Don't be. The talent is God-given. I take no credit for it. But I've been blessed to find an outlet that lets me share it with the world."

"I feel honored to be trusted with your secret." Ashley touched the woman's hand. "Thank you.

"I should have told you sooner. As for thanks, I should thank *you*."

"For what?"

"Having you here has been revitalizing for both

me and Lucy Lynn. I'd become far too insular. All the changes you've instituted, and all the people you've brought into my life, have given me fresh inspiration. In fact, I have a new piece I want to show you. Give me two minutes." She rose and disappeared into the hall.

While Ashley waited for her to return, she nibbled at her scone and continued trying to wrap her mind around Rose's startling revelation.

The mistress of Edgecliff was both an accomplished pianist and a renowned illustrator who'd somehow managed to stay under the radar in a wired world.

It just went to show that there was often more to people than appearances might indicate. Hidden depths and dimensions only trust and time would reveal.

A lesson well worth applying to her relationship with a certain landscaper.

Rose returned, an illustration board in hand. "I finished this one yesterday. You're the first to see it." She turned it around and rested it on the table.

Ashley set her cup down and gave the drawing her full attention.

In the rendering, the precocious little girl sat on a wicker chair holding a puppy. Not a cute, cuddly, fluffy puppy, but the ugliest puppy Ashley had ever seen. The ears were lopsided, one shorter than the other. Fur the color of soiled snow, with dirty-hued patches that looked as if the poor pup had been sprayed with mud by a passing car, stuck up in all directions like a cowlick on steroids. The eyes were crooked.

But the puppy's appearance was secondary to the emotion in the illustration.

For as Lucy Lynn cuddled the tiny pup in her arms, warmth and devotion and adoration took center stage as they gazed at each other with a pure, absolute, mutual love that tightened Ashley's throat.

The quote from Gibran at the bottom wasn't even necessary, but it did capture the message in one simple sentence.

Beauty is not in the face; beauty is a light in the heart.

Ashley blinked the mist from her vision. Sniffed.

She didn't have to ask where Rose had gotten the inspiration for her latest illustration.

He lived down the road.

"I love this, Rose."

"I hoped you would." She set the illustration aside. "I thought of Jon while I worked on it."

"That's what I figured."

"He seems to be a fine young man. One who hasn't let the hard hand he's been dealt harden his heart. That takes grace and courage and wisdom."

"I know." Mouth flexing, Ashley wrapped her hands around her mug. "And since you shared your secret with me, I'll let you in on one of mine. We have a date next Saturday."

Rose smiled and reached for her hand. Gave it a squeeze. "It would take an exceptional woman to look past Jon's appearance and see the caring heart inside, but I knew you were special the day we met. I hope the date goes well. Now let me warm up your tea."

As Rose busied herself with that task, Ashley took a bite of the tender scone, anticipation over the upcoming date sending a delicious tingle through her despite Jon's clear let's-proceed-with-caution signals.

If he was still unsure about whether she could live with his physical flaws despite all the messages she'd been sending, she'd clear up those concerns fast. After all, she'd seen his face. Been with him in public and experienced the discreet, curious stares—not to mention the outright rudeness of her former beau. She could handle all of that. None of it had the power to diminish his appeal.

So unless he was hiding some deep, dark secret, the odds should be small that anything else he shared would have the power to snuff out the spark of attraction that had ignited into a steady flame.

28

This was the day.

Jon pulled through the Edgecliff gates and rolled toward the circle drive, a spurt of adrenaline generating a buzz in his nerve endings when he spotted Ashley waiting for him in front of the main house.

"She's a sight for sore eyes, isn't she, Daisy?"

From the backseat, his loyal companion gave a woof.

"I'll take that as a yes."

Despite the distracting view ahead, he managed to keep the truck on the road. But man, not seeing much of her all week had been tough. Who knew that mitigating the fallout from last weekend's foul weather would require such long hours?

Perhaps the enforced absence had been a blessing in disguise, though.

Because on the couple of occasions he'd dropped by in the evening for a chat on the front porch of the Victorian, keeping his hands to himself had been a major challenge. Even if that was the safest and fairest course until they got past today's hurdle.

Ashley stood and waved as he drew closer,

dressed as he'd requested. Her jeans, sweatshirt, and sport shoes were exactly right for today's destination.

The instant he stopped, she crossed to the truck and reached for the door.

"Hang on. Let me get that for you." He set the brake as he called through the open passenger window.

"Thanks, but I can manage. I'm on the mend."

"Humor me. It's higher than you think." He slid from behind the wheel and circled the hood. "I can give you a boost up if you need it."

She offered him a flirty grin and waggled her eyebrows, juicing his testosterone. "Maybe you could do that even if I don't."

She was in a playful and amorous mood today.

Meaning he'd have to rearrange his agenda for the afternoon and eat last instead of first. Otherwise, he'd cave before she was fully informed and gave the green light.

If she gave the green light.

"Go ahead and try if you want to." He opened the passenger door and motioned to the running board.

She put one foot on it, attempted to hoist herself up . . . and dropped back to the ground with an *oomph.*

"I see what you mean." She grimaced. "I may need that hand for real."

"At your service. I'll give you an assist on the

count of three. Watch the picnic basket on the floor."

She grabbed the door again, and he boosted her up on the count of three.

Daisy stuck her head between the seats, tongue lolling out, angling for a pet.

"Ah. It's a threesome." Ashley obliged his canine friend, who lapped up the affection.

"She'll like where we're going, and there's plenty of space for her to explore. She'll be too busy to bother us. But we can drop her at my house if you'd rather leave her behind."

Daisy gave a plaintive whine.

"No way. She's a sweetie." Ashley scratched behind her ear, and Daisy reciprocated with a nuzzle.

Jon closed the door, returned to the driver's seat, and put the truck in gear. "How are you feeling?"

"Almost back to normal when I'm not climbing into trucks."

"You up for a short hike?"

"Depends on the destination."

"A secluded, private beach, lunch included." He nodded toward the picnic basket at her feet.

"I'm up for it."

"If you change your mind after we get there, I have a backup plan."

He kept the conversation general as he turned off Windswept Way onto 101, and Ashley obliged by sticking to safe topics. But based on the energy pinging around the cab of the truck, she was more than pumped for today's date.

Whether her euphoric mood lasted remained to be seen.

He continued past the road to Pelican Point lighthouse and the junction for Starfish Pier. A couple of miles north of the town limits, he hung a left onto the wooded, narrow road he'd been told to watch for.

Ashley leaned forward. "Where does this lead?"

"If my directions are correct, to Charley's house and studio."

Her head swiveled his direction. "I thought you said we were going to a beach."

"We are. His property is one of the few access points for Blackberry Beach. I've never been there, but when I stopped at his stand for tacos this week, he happened to mention how secluded it was. I told him I was looking for that sort of place for this weekend, and he invited me to park on his property and hike down."

He slowed as a modest clapboard cottage came into view in the open area past the trees, along with what appeared to be a storage shed constructed of weathered wood fifty yards behind it. But the large expanse of glass covering the top half of the north wall gave away the shed's real function.

That was where Charley painted.

"Do you think he's here?" Ashley gave the area a quick canvass but homed in on the expansive, bluff-top view of the sea the property afforded.

"I doubt it. I assume Saturdays in tourist season are prime taco-making days." He parked near the back of the drive and indicated the woods on the left. "He said the path starts over there. He assured me it wasn't strenuous. But we can go with plan B if this is too intimidating."

"Let's take a look." She opened the door and maneuvered herself out of the cab, pivoting back to him once she was on the ground. "Getting out was much easier than getting in, thanks to gravity."

He slid from behind the wheel, let Daisy out, and joined her on the other side of the truck. "You seem anxious."

"I've been waiting all week for today."

"Then let's get this date rolling." He reached in for the picnic basket, closed the door, and inspected the edge of the woods. "I think I see the path."

They walked over, and he paused at the top, assessing the difficulty. Since it crisscrossed the bluff in a series of hairpin turns as it descended, the grade wasn't too steep.

And what he could glimpse of the sheltered crescent of sand below was promising. It appeared to offer total seclusion, along with a world-class view of diamond-strewn indigo water and dramatic sea stacks. In the hazy distance, the outline of Pelican Point light was visible.

Tailor-made for a romantic picnic, if all went well.

"Are those ripe blackberries?" Ashley shaded her eyes and peered at the bushes lining the path farther down.

"I wouldn't be surprised, given the name of the beach. Do you think you're up to the walk?"

"I wouldn't miss it."

He motioned her to precede him on the single-file track. "Why don't you go first?"

She followed his suggestion, but after three steps Daisy brushed past both of them and took off at a gallop down the path.

Ashley laughed. "Apparently I'm not the only one who's anxious."

They traversed the trail at a slow pace, stopping to sample the blackberries along the way, and emerged onto the pristine beach to find Daisy already playing in the surf and chasing two seagulls that didn't seem inclined to leave. A white harbor seal occupied a rock offshore, and a dolphin arced from the water, shimmering silver in the sun.

"Is this for real?" Ashley surveyed the idyllic scene.

"Almost too good to be true. And we have it

all to ourselves." He nodded toward a large, bleached log. "You want to sit over there? We could use it for a backrest."

"Works for me."

Pulse kicking into high gear, he took her arm as they walked across the shifting sand, slowing his pace to accommodate her shorter stride—and trying with every step to psych himself up for the critical next few minutes, when his hopes would either soar like the two seagulls wheeling above them or crash with a thunderous roar like the waves smashing against the distant sea stacks.

Jon was nervous.

Really nervous.

No doubt due to the postponed relationship talk that had to be his top priority.

But he didn't have to be nervous. Shouldn't be nervous. Not after all the subtle and less-than-subtle hints she'd dropped about her interest.

Whatever his concerns, why let him fret? She ought to clear the air so they could enjoy their picnic and launch the new chapter she'd been dreaming about for the past few nights. Maybe with a kiss far less restrained than the one in the hospital.

The mere anticipation of a lip-lock goosed her respiration, and Ashley forced herself to take a slow, calming breath of the salty air.

It didn't help much.

"I've got all kinds of fancy food, courtesy of a gourmet shop in Coos Bay, but why don't we talk first?" Jon set the basket on the ground beside the log and spread out the blanket that had been tucked under the handles.

"I'm good with that plan."

"Let me give you a hand down."

She grasped the fingers he extended, grateful for the support as he lowered her to the sand. The appendicitis attack already felt like ancient history, but the twinge in her abdomen whenever she put too much strain on it was a painful reminder she was still convalescing.

When Jon remained standing, she cocked her head. "Aren't you joining me?"

"Yes, but I have something to show you first."

An odd nuance in his inflection activated her yellow alert. "Okay."

He took a few steps backward. Clenched his fists at his sides. Closed his eyes.

Yellow morphed to red, and she started to rise, alarm bells clanging. "Jon, what's wrong?"

"Stay there." He held up a hand, and she froze. "Please."

She sat back on the blanket in silence.

Waiting.

Watching.

He swallowed, and a muscle ticced in his jaw. Then he grasped the hem of his sweatshirt and pulled it over his head in one abrupt, jerky motion.

Sucking in a breath, Ashley stared at his bare chest and left arm.

Sweet mercy.

Scars covered the outside of his entire left arm and shoulder, extending partway across his upper chest.

As she tried to take in the damage, he loosened the string on his sweatpants, shoved them down his hips past a pair of gym shorts, and stepped out.

Dear God.

His left leg was as scarred as his arm.

How much pain must he have endured?

How many surgeries and months of agonizing rehab had he gone through?

How could he walk without a limp after suffering such grievous and extensive damage?

Tears welled on her lower lashes, spilling over to trail down her cheeks as she choked back a sob, fist clenched against her chest. "Oh, Jon."

He remained where he was, too far away to touch, the early afternoon sun mercilessly spotlighting all his ugly wounds. "I wanted you to see the whole package before we talk." His voice hoarsened. "All the damaged goods."

Damaged goods.

As his comment pierced her heart, she pushed herself to her feet, ignoring the sharp twinge in her abdomen. "You're not damaged goods. That term means broken or faulty or defective. You're none of those."

"Depends on your perspective, I guess. But to borrow a phrase from my sister, I'm definitely not a chick magnet anymore. I can understand why a woman would be turned off by my appearance. Why it could short-circuit electricity. The scars on my face are bad enough, but the others are worse. The doctors didn't work as hard to disguise damage that could be hidden. I understand if this is a deal breaker."

Ashley considered the stoic wounded soldier who'd lost so much, his back ramrod straight against the brilliant blue sea as he waited for her reaction—and her verdict.

Once again, her vision blurred.

No, he wasn't a perfect physical specimen anymore. No, his face would never again grace a billboard. No, most women probably wouldn't give him a second look.

But that was their loss.

Because from everything she'd learned about him, he was perfect in all the ways that mattered.

She'd demonstrate that to him in a minute. But first she had a few things to say.

Extending her hand, she closed the distance between them. "Come sit with me. Let's talk."

After a moment, he picked up his clothes and linked his fingers with hers.

She tugged him back to the log, lowering herself again with his assistance.

When he began to put his sweatpants back on, she stopped him with a touch. "Leave them off for now."

Another hesitation . . . but in the end he complied and sank down, offering her a tiny, strained smile. "I haven't had too many women want to ogle my legs in recent years."

His brave attempt to joke about his scars threatened to unleash the waterworks again, but Ashley held back her tears and got straight to the point. "The scars aren't a deal breaker, Jon."

All vestiges of humor faded from his demeanor as he searched her face. "How could you find a man who looks like me attractive?"

"Appearance isn't the only basis for attraction—or the most important one. It has even less to do with love."

He studied her, his gaze probing, as if he was trying to assess her sincerity. "I agree with you in principle, but most people would have a hard time putting that into practice."

Ashley chose her next words with care. "Let me ask you a hypothetical question. Let's say you were married to someone who was in a terrible accident that left her scarred. Would you love her any less?"

"Of course not. But this is different. We're just

getting to know each other. There's no deep-seated foundation of love to keep us together. No strings. You could walk away with no hard feelings."

"What if I don't want to?"

His expression grew skeptical. "Ashley, look at me." He swept a hand over his scars. "The doctors pulled a hundred pieces of shrapnel from my body, and there's more in here. You can feel it." He took her hand and ran her fingers over skin as bumpy as braille on his left forearm. "For the rest of my life, I'll set off metal detectors at airports. And fragments work their way out periodically, which isn't pretty." He exhaled. "After what happened with Melinda, it's hard for me to grasp how any woman would ever be able to see me in a romantic light."

"The one sitting beside you does."

At her quiet comment, his eyes began to shimmer. "Even if you could convince me of that, there are other challenges."

"Such as?"

"You got a sample of them with your former boyfriend. And when we walked through church together."

So he'd noticed the discreet glances of the congregants that day.

"Jason doesn't count—in any way. As for curious stares, I can handle those."

"But people will wonder why you settled for

someone like me. You'll end up always having to defend your choice."

There was that awful word again. The one Mom and Jason had used.

" 'Settle' implies compromise. As if I could do better. And that does you a huge disservice. From what I've seen, men don't come any finer than you, Jonathan Gray."

His throat worked. "Thank you for that. But I'm afraid you could be in for a rough ride with me. There may be more obstacles than you think."

"We'll meet them together." She angled toward him and crossed her legs lotus style. "You told me once, not long after we met, that love wasn't always enough to overcome obstacles. I think it is. True love, anyway. We're not there yet, but I know this. I'd like to start that journey and see where it leads."

A sizzle of electricity zipped toward her, the heat in Jon's eyes chasing away the slight chill in the breeze. "You make it hard to say no."

"Then let me convince you to say yes."

Scooting toward him, she rested one hand on the scars on his leg. He froze as she let the fingertips of her other hand travel from his forehead to chin, tracing every rough contour, every ridge, every smooth patch of white.

And then she leaned closer and pressed her lips to his.

For a moment, he didn't respond. But once he did, she ceded control of the kiss to him.

Because this man knew how to kiss.

He was doing a masterful job of it too, until something cool and wet intruded, pressing against her cheek.

Jon pulled back, and she turned to find Daisy's nose dominating her field of vision.

"Your timing stinks, Daisy. Go sit." Jon nudged the dog aside.

But Daisy was having none of that. She plopped down on the sand and looked between the two of them.

"Sorry about this." He scowled at the pooch. "I should have left her at home."

"No worries. Friends are always welcome." She petted the border collie as she tried to catch her breath. "What do you think about sharing your guy with me, Daisy?"

The pup gave a happy yip.

"I think I'm in." Ashley grinned.

"You're definitely in. But right now, three's a crowd." Jon dug around in the picnic basket and withdrew a doggie treat. Tossed it down the sand. "Go play, Daisy."

The dog took off after the treat, but rather than return to her game of tag with the surf after she wolfed it down, she claimed a spot on the sand.

Apparently she'd made her peace with the two seagulls she'd been chasing. They were cuddled up a few yards away, watching the human drama unfold.

"Shall we pick up where we left off before that rude interruption?" Jon refocused on her.

"By all means."

But instead of pulling her close again, he tucked her hair behind her ear, his touch as gentle and warming as the Hope Harbor sun on a spring day. "Thank you for taking a chance on me."

"I don't think it's a chance. I think you're a sure bet." Her voice scraped, and she called up a watery smile. "You better kiss me again fast or I'll get all sappy and cry on you."

"Happy to oblige."

With that, he leaned down to once again claim her lips.

And while the sounds of the surf and the caw of gulls didn't quite compare to the emotion-laden score Rose had provided the night of their almost-kiss on the porch, they were just as romantic.

For as Jon pulled her close with strong yet gentle arms . . . as his lips worked their magic on hers . . . as the world melted away . . . Ashley recognized the truth.

Music, setting, atmosphere, picnics for two, secluded beaches—all of those helped create an amorous ambiance.

But in the end, romance only required one thing.

That special person who brightened your world

and made your heart sing no matter where you were.

Finding that person wasn't always easy. But unless her instincts were failing, Ashley was pretty certain she was about to fall in love with the chain-saw-wielding landscaper who'd come to Edgecliff to repair the grounds but who'd also ended up repairing—and claiming—her heart.

Epilogue

"Where's your bride?"

At the question from behind him, Jon turned to Rose. "I wish I knew. We left the ballroom together after the ceremony but somehow got separated once we came downstairs."

"It is a bit crowded, isn't it?"

He surveyed the scene as waiters bearing trays of appetizers wove through the festive throng on Edgecliff's first floor. "It feels like all of Hope Harbor is here."

"Not quite, but a fair number." Charley materialized out of the horde, elegant in a dark suit and string tie. Quite a change from his usual jeans and Ducks cap. "I see Eleanor Cooper provided the traditional chocolate groom's cake." He motioned toward the cake table off to the side. "You're a lucky man."

"Trust me, I know." Jon met the gaze of the man who'd accepted and welcomed him from the get-go, and whose gentle encouragement had helped him find the courage to take his first steps back toward a normal social life.

Charley gave a knowing nod and spoke again to Rose. "I believe Eleanor is trying to find you. She mentioned a potluck dinner you agreed to help her plan at Grace Christian."

"I don't quite know how she talked me into serving on that committee." Rose shook her head, but her lips twitched. Apparently she wasn't too put out about being drafted. "It was probably while she plied me with her fudge cake during one of our recent get-togethers."

"I wouldn't be surprised. That cake has powerful persuasive properties. Shall we go find her?" Charley offered her his elbow.

"Yes." She slipped her hand through Charley's arm. "Jon, I'm ready whenever you are. Just give me a signal."

"I'll do that. And thank you for the very special wedding gift." He leaned closer and lowered his voice. "Ashley showed it to me last night after the rehearsal. It will always have a place of honor on a wall in our home."

"You're more than welcome. That illustration was meant for the two of you."

As Rose and Charley strolled off, Jon went in search of Ashley.

He entered the drawing room, circling it as fast as he could, but a dozen people waylaid him to offer congratulations. Kyle and Sarah. BJ and her husband, Eric. Father Murphy and Reverend Baker, both making short work of the appetizers balanced on their napkins. The police chief and her husband. Zach Garrett and his wife, whose chocolate shop had supplied the truffles guests would take home as favors. Marci from the *Herald* and her surgeon husband. Mindy Jackson, Rose's piano protégé, who now assisted Ashley part-time at Edgecliff to help with the booming business, accompanied by her minister date. Ashley's mother, chatting up the owner of Seabird Inn, where she was staying.

But where was his bride?

He slipped out the small door at the back of the drawing room and closed it behind him, muting the conversations of the guests and the music of the string quartet.

Maybe he'd stay here for a few minutes. Catch his breath before plunging back into the fray. Flawless as the wedding had been, with the sometimes-capricious April weather cooperating for all the photos they'd taken on the grounds, he was more than ready to end the group festivities and move on to a more private celebration.

Starting tonight in the master suite at Edgecliff, followed by a ten-day tropical honeymoon in Hawaii with his wife.

Wife.

His mouth flexed.

That had a nice ring.

A miraculous ring, really.

Never in his wildest dreams could he have imagined ten months ago that a woman like Ashley would enter his lonely world and fill it with light and life and grace.

It had an almost surreal—

The door bumped him in the back, and he edged aside as Laura squeezed through and shut it behind her.

"Good grief. This place is a zoo."

"I know."

She snorted. "Not from my perspective, you don't. Try keeping up with eight-year-old twins. The little hooligans have already managed to slide down the bannister twice and swipe some icing off your groom's cake." She blew a wisp of hair out of her eyes. "I may hide out here with you for the duration and let Bill deal with their shenanigans for a while."

"I'm not hiding. I'm trying to find Ashley."

"Try the terrace. I saw her disappear down the hall toward the kitchen a few minutes ago, and I doubt she's in there supervising the caterers at her own wedding."

"You never know. She's a stickler for detail, which is why all the events here run like clockwork."

"If this one is any indication, I can see why the place is a success. So long as I'm not interrupting a stolen smooch, I'll take advantage of this opportunity to give you a hug and tell you how happy I am you found a woman worthy of your love." She wrapped her arms around him and squeezed. "And to wish you a lifetime of happiness. Now I'll shut up before I get weepy and end up with raccoon eyes."

He smiled as he returned her hug. "My sister, the sentimentalist and hopeless romantic."

"I refuse to apologize for being sentimental. And I'm not a hopeless romantic. I'm a hope*ful* romantic. Life is sweeter if you focus on the positive instead of the negative." She wriggled loose and eased back. "Now go find your bride." After bestowing a final kiss on his cheek, she disappeared back through the door.

Jon didn't linger in the hall now that he had a lead on his wife's location.

Using the side exit to avoid any wayward guests, he slipped out and approached the terrace.

He spotted Ashley at once, pausing to give her a long, slow scan.

She'd been beautiful earlier as she came down the aisle, in a lace sheath that showed off her figure to perfection.

But here, standing beside the stone wall on the terrace, the ornate Victorian gazebo off to the side and the vast Pacific sparkling behind her in the distance, she was flat-out stunning.

As her wispy veil billowed behind her in the playful breeze, she lifted her bouquet to inhale the sweet fragrance of the roses, then raised her face to the heavens.

Joy radiated from her.

The same joy that had filled his heart since the day at the beach when she'd convinced him he was overly concerned about the impact his scars might have on their relationship.

And in the intervening months, she'd laid his fears to rest, handling every awkward encounter with panache, never once trying to explain how a gorgeous woman like her could fall for a guy like him.

As she always insisted when he apologized for those knotty incidents, anyone who got to know him would understand that she was the blessed one in this relationship.

That wasn't true. Or not completely true, anyway. Between the two of them, he'd been the most blessed.

And for the rest of his life, he'd give thanks every day for the gift of her sweet and loyal love that would brighten all the tomorrows they spent as man and wife.

Beginning today.

"Running away already?"

At the question from behind her, Ashley swiveled toward the man she'd just promised to love and honor all the days of her life.

An easy promise to keep.

For as friendship had grown and blossomed into deep, abiding love over the past eight months, he'd demonstrated again and again that a life shared with him would be filled with joy and laughter and caring and compassion.

Now, attired in a tux that emphasized his toned

physique, bathed in the golden light of late afternoon, her groom looked every bit as heroic as any storybook prince.

She held out her hand. "Never. You're stuck with me for life, buddy."

"No complaints." He crossed to her and folded her fingers in his work-calloused palm. "Have I told you how beautiful you are today?"

"I believe I heard a whisper to that effect in my ear after I came down the aisle."

"I'll shout it to the heavens if you like."

"No need. I've already tucked it away in my heart forever." Along with the gratitude and adoration and jubilation in his eyes that she'd basked in during her slow trek to the front of the ballroom.

He ran a finger that wasn't quite steady along the line of her jaw. "When I couldn't find you inside, I have to admit I panicked for a moment. Sometimes it's still hard for me to believe you said yes."

She took his hand and pressed her lips to his palm. Wiggled the fourth finger of her left hand, where a simple gold band had joined her diamond engagement ring. "Here's the proof. I'm yours forever, Jonathan Gray."

"Likewise." He gave her a quick kiss—too quick—and tipped his head toward the deserted terrace. "Did you come out here to escape the crush of people inside?"

"Yes. One person in particular."

"Let me guess. Your mother."

Ashley rolled her eyes. "Bingo. She keeps fussing with my hair, even though the photos are winding down. She said I should look perfect for posterity. But perfect is overrated." She squeezed his hand. At least Mom had come around and begun to recognize the fine qualities that made Jon one in a million. "Besides, the only photos left are the cake cutting and first dance."

"Speaking of that, Rose is all warmed up to play. You want to check that item off our photographer's shot list?"

"Yes. Then we can cut the cake and get this party—and the honeymoon—rolling."

"I like how you think, Mrs. Gray."

He took her hand, and together they returned to the house.

Once in the foyer, he caught Rose's attention. After lifting her hand in acknowledgment, she wove through the drawing room toward the piano while he signaled the string quartet situated on the second-floor landing above the foyer to stop playing.

He waited to speak until he had everyone's attention and the din dropped to a manageable level.

"Ashley and I want to thank all of you for sharing our special day with us. We feel privileged to call you friends and hope to be part of all your lives for many years to come here in Hope Harbor. Ashley let me pick the music for our first dance, so she'll be hearing it for the first time along with you. Since we're not flamboyant dancers, if you'll all move back to the edges of the foyer, that will give us plenty of room to maneuver."

As the crowd retreated, clearing a space for them, Jon held out his arms.

Ashley stepped in, and seconds later piano music drifted into the foyer over the slight hum of conversation from the crowd.

She recognized it at once.

He'd chosen "All I Ask of You."

One of the songs Rose had played the night he'd nearly kissed her on the porch all those months ago.

The night she'd realized they had potential, if she could get past his scars.

As they began to sway, she rested her cheek against the steady beat of his heart.

Thank heavens she'd been able to see deeper than his daunting surface and find the treasure underneath.

And thank heavens she'd taken an uncharacteristic chance last spring and written Rose with a bold proposition.

Because the adventure she'd embarked on had yielded far more than she had ever expected.

A dream-come-true job. New friends in Hope

Harbor. Success in her mission to encourage Rose to engage with the world again. And now, best of all, a man to love and cherish all the days of her life.

The song wound down, Rose playing the final notes with her usual flourish, and as the last one echoed in the foyer Ashley stopped swaying and attempted to step back.

When Jon tightened his grip, she looked up.

"There's one more song."

As the music segued into another piece, he pulled her close again to continue the dance.

But she almost stumbled once the title clicked into place.

It was the theme song from *Beauty and the Beast*.

Around them a hush fell over the crowd.

Her breath hitched, and she lifted her chin to search his face as his strong arms held her close.

"I'm not going to run away from how I look, Ashley." His steady gaze met hers, his husky words for her ears only. "Because it doesn't matter anymore. I may never become a handsome prince, like the beast in the movie did, but you transformed my life. Made it beautiful again. And I'll love you with every ounce of my being until the day I die."

Her throat constricted, rendering speech impossible. So she kissed her fingertips, pressed them against his lips, and mouthed a silent "I love you" before tucking her cheek against his heart once again.

And as the tender, sweeping music swirled around them . . . as a rainbow of colors danced over the foyer from the stained-glass window on the landing, creating a magical ambiance . . . she knew this enchanted moment would live forever in her memory.

For happy endings didn't come any better than this.

Even in fairy tales.

Author's Note

Welcome to Hope Harbor—where hearts heal . . . and love blooms.

I've always enjoyed writing books that demonstrate the power of love to transform lives, and if ever a story embodied that theme, it's *Windswept Way*. This one was a joy to write, and I hope it uplifted you as much as it did me.

As always, I want to offer special thanks to the three people who have been my loyal cheering section through the years. My husband, Tom, has been my constant ally and sounding board since the day we met, always ready with an encouraging word when I most need a boost. My parents, James and Dorothy Hannon, are gone now, but their unconditional love and unwavering support live on in my heart. For always.

My deepest thanks as well to the incredible team at Revell that brings my books to life, especially Jennifer Leep, Laura Klynstra, Kristin Kornoelje, Michele Misiak, and Karen Steele. I am blessed beyond measure to partner with such a dedicated, professional, savvy, and principled group of people.

And finally, my heartfelt thanks to all of you who have embraced Hope Harbor—a town *Publishers Weekly* calls "a place of emotional restoration that readers will yearn to visit."

I'm happy to report that there are more Hope Harbor stories coming. I'll also be launching a new suspense series called Undaunted Courage, featuring three foster siblings. Watch for *Into the Fire*.

In the meantime, happy reading!

Center Point Large Print
600 Brooks Road / PO Box 1
Thorndike, ME 04986-0001 USA

(207) 568-3717

US & Canada:
1 800 929-9108
www.centerpointlargeprint.com